GABRIEL BORN

MURIEL STOCKDALE

BALBOA.
PRESS

A DIVISION OF HAY HOUSE

Balboa Press books may be ordered through booksellers or by contacting:

Balboa Press
A Division of Hay House
1663 Liberty Drive
Bloomington, IN 47403
www.balboapress.com
1 (877) 407-4847

Because of the dynamic nature of the Internet, any web addresses or links contained in this book may have changed since publication and may no longer be valid. The views expressed in this work are solely those of the author and do not necessarily reflect the views of the publisher, and the publisher hereby disclaims any responsibility for them.

The author of this book does not dispense medical advice or prescribe the use of any technique as a form of treatment for physical, emotional, or medical problems without the advice of a physician, either directly or indirectly. The intent of the author is only to offer information of a general nature to help you in your quest for emotional and spiritual well-being. In the event you use any of the information in this book for yourself, which is your constitutional right, the author and the publisher assume no responsibility for your actions.

Any people depicted in stock imagery provided by Thinkstock are models, and such images are being used for illustrative purposes only.
Certain stock imagery © Thinkstock.

Print information available on the last page.

ISBN: 978-1-5043-7061-5 (sc)
ISBN: 978-1-5043-7063-9 (hc)
ISBN: 978-1-5043-7062-2 (e)

Library of Congress Control Number: 2016919720

Balboa Press rev. date: 12/07/2016

For my beloved husband,
Chris Grabé,
who always supports all my creative endeavors.

CONTENTS

1

HUMANIMAL

Sheila Jensen's heart jumps when the gavel is struck, and it feels as if the solid ground beneath her has suddenly fallen away. She is thirty-three and stunning in her pale-gray business suit and slick, blonde ponytail. Sitting amid an impressive rank of lawyers with equally impressive peers from her elite research unit behind her, she looks invincible. But the sink of her shoulders, like a slowly deflating balloon, indicates otherwise. The imposing female judge with a grating voice that irritates Sheila departs abruptly, and suddenly everyone around Sheila is getting up. She briskly wipes a tear from her right eye. Sheila never cries. She is a scientist who is brilliant, practical, and rational. Crying is not part of her tool kit, and the lone tear that has snuck by her emotional guard profoundly embarrasses her. One of her lawyers clumsily grabs her arm in a consoling gesture. Startled, Sheila winces and pulls away. Touching is another unnatural thing for her, and right now she feels particularly raw. She looks at the lawyer and tries to force a thin smile; then she stands up with difficulty.

Sheila can't wait to get out of this building. Even though she is tired and struggles to move gracefully with her delicate cane, she possesses a vital energy. She is swept along in a crowd of winners and losers still arguing bitterly for both sides of the issue. Her work put her here right in the center of the fray. She need say nothing. She has nothing to say. She said it all inside, and clearly the ears of the court are deaf. Sheila gasps as she squeezes through the angry press of people and out onto the sunlit platform above the steps of the federal courthouse. She stumbles at the precipice of the steeply descending stairs, and someone grabs her arm. It's Dr. Philip Ohl, her boss, who is only a few years older than her and is a great administrator as well as a scientist. He looks handsome in his steel-colored suit—much better than the lab coat and jeans she is used to seeing him in. Her heart pounds. Hurt and betrayal well up and almost swallow her whole being. She is terrified that he will see her cry. She shakes him off, determined to retain her dignity and sovereignty if she can, and tries to steady herself on her slender cane.

"That's her!" someone shouts.

A crowd rushes up the imposing steps toward her, and Sheila teeters back and falls unwillingly into Philip's arms. Police wearing imposing riot gear swarm out of the courthouse behind them. They jostle Sheila and Philip on their way past and clear a path through the riotous crowd down the steps of the court.

Sheila notices a man with absurd donkey ears brandishing a banner that reads, "HUMANIMAL." A red circle with a slash through it is superimposed over the word. He pushes against the protective police wall and screams unintelligible slurs at her. Farther down, a woman made up to look like a cat waves a sign that says, "NO GENE HUMANipulation."

The tall, official buildings surrounding the square that Sheila looks out on create an echo chamber. The noise escalates as more and more people enter from the five streets converging here and flock toward them at the main courthouse steps. Sheila's heart pounds in her chest. No one has ever seen anything like this, and she is the target of the anger.

Philip whispers in her ear, "Look forward. Don't listen to them. We know they've got it all wrong."

Sheila takes a last look out at the whole mad scene and quakes at the thought of walking down into it. So she breathes in deeply and wills herself to dispel the feeling of shock; then she steels herself and steps down the first step.

As they descend, Sheila loses sight of the TV support crews and high-tech media vans that surround the five-sided plaza. Every national channel is represented and even several foreign outlets. This is big news. The myriad of smartly dressed correspondents form a stark contrast to the unruly and angry crowd. She saw eager TV crews push toward them, grabbing startling footage and provoking protesters to further outrage. Soon enough, she will be trying to navigate through them.

"What do you think the verdict should be?" a crisp-looking reporter on the step nearby asks.

"She's a witch!" a man yells. "She should be burned like in the old days."

Sheila flinches, suddenly looking worn out. Philip is still holding her elbow. She and Philip, surrounded by their entourage of lawyers and other handlers, are swept farther down the vast, imposing stairs.

Blazing ahead of them both, wearing anger on his sleeve, is Dr. Gerald Spiner, a wiry man in his sixties. He exudes the energy of a bureaucratic boss and waves his fleet of lawyers onward. He practically spits at a grasping TV correspondent, shoving him out of the way.

Sheila looks around. "Cynthia? Where is she?"

Philip doesn't respond but forcefully guides Sheila down, clearing her path as they go. Somewhere behind them in the midst of the throng still struggling to get out of the courthouse is Sheila's younger sister, Cynthia Clark. Cynthia is a softer, rounder version of her sister. She moves with a happier bounce and a sparkle in her eye.

"Sheila, wait for me!" Cynthia yells, but her voice is lost in the tumult.

A young male reporter slips through the handlers and practically punches Philip with his mic. "Dr. Ohl, you must have known about the experiments!"

"Will you fire Ms. Jensen?" another reporter yells from farther down.

Philip scowls at the second reporter. "That's *Doctor* Jensen!"

Loraine Hampshire, PR director of the research facility, pulls Philip away and whispers in his ear. She's a smart African-American woman with a neat, retro Afro. She stands out in her bright suit with its pencil skirt. She steps efficiently between Philip and the reporter. "Dr. Ohl has no comment."

Sheila tries to keep her head high and exude confidence, but the stress she feels shows in her tight, quivering lips.

They are near the bottom of the stairs, and the police phalanx has spread thin trying to contain the raucous crowd. The crowd surges again, and Sheila, flanked by her coworkers and their vast legal team, retreats back up a couple of steps. Philip steadies her when she wavers on her cane as a woman in a furry hat spits on Sheila's lapel.

"Only God creates!"

Before Sheila can turn fully to see her attacker, the woman is gone.

A man in a devil costume steps in and pushes Sheila roughly. "Go to hell, Dr. Frankenstein!"

He viciously kicks her cane out from under her. Too late, Philip reaches for her as she trips down the last few steps and lands on her knees in the plaza.

Sheila looks up a bit stunned. The crowd backs up. Bizarre faces leer at her and shout, but she can't hear what they say. The throng shifts and spooks a flock of pigeons that flap en masse into the air, creating a murmur of wings.

From Sheila's humiliating position splayed on the plaza, it seems as if time has stopped. She spaces out. The racket whirls around her, and she just wistfully watches the birds. How great it would be to fly away.

A shaft of blinding sunshine bursts through the high buildings lining the city streets, carving deep, black shadows below. The silhouetted birds flicker light and dark, one moment sparkling and another invisible as their wings turn toward and away from the sharp light. Sheila's brain clicks into work mode, watching in an imagined construct the mysterious phenomenon of DNA clicking on and off like a binary computer code. She's so close to answers that she can taste the victory of discovery, but she can't quite see the actual shape that it takes or how to get there. But here she is, derailed from her projects, shamed, trapped, and crippled, unable even to stand up without help.

Suddenly, Cynthia is bending over her. She lifts her sister up. Philip, who has been distracted by a particularly aggressive and vociferous protestor, extricates himself and closes in on the other side, taking Sheila's elbow.

"Sheila, I'm so sorry," he says as he leans in. He feels like he's losing her. This might be his last chance to try to mitigate the damage of this groundbreaking legal ruling that affects them both but is worse for Sheila. "I had to, or we would both be out. I promise we'll get through this."

"We? *We?* You blamed me and saved your career," Sheila says through clenched teeth. It is getting harder for her to keep her cool. "*We* did this together, for good, for all kinds of good. For …" She stands up and faces him.

"To cure disease. I know," he says softly.

Tears well in her eyes. "You knew my work was my last hope."

Cynthia tugs at Sheila's other arm. "Come on. Let's get out of here. It doesn't feel safe."

Sheila turns to look at Cynthia and notices another face in the crowd—an overly made-up TV reporter framed in artificial light chattering into a camera. Cynthia ushers Sheila past the reporter and almost forces her into a nearby limousine. She slams the door and then works her way through the irate, pressing crowd to the other side of the car.

Inside the limo, Sheila fidgets behind the tinted glass. Her eyes wander to the TV monitor inside the car, and there she is, that same TV reporter already meting out her judgment. *Everyone's* judgment.

"Dr. Sheila Jensen received judgment today in the most critical trial of the millennium. The Harold Bowman Research Facility of New Empire University's La Salle Medical Center received no more than a slap on the wrist. However, they must pay fines of up to seventy million dollars for supporting Dr. Jensen's illegal genome experiments, and Dr. Jensen is no longer permitted to run any such experiments involving human DNA again."

Cynthia opens the back door on the driver's side and starts to climb in, but suddenly Philip is there. He gives her an appealing look. She backs off to give him space, and he jumps in beside Sheila. He taps on the glass divider to indicate that the driver should get going and then leans in to take Sheila's hand. She pulls away

"Don't. In fact, here." She rips his engagement ring off her finger and stuffs it into his jacket breast pocket.

"Sheila …"

His eyes beg her to listen, but she turns away. They drive off in silence.

* * *

Only a year earlier, they were excited and in love, on the verge of an amazing new discovery. Then on one romantic, candlelit night, Sheila's life went from bliss to hell.

She tries to push the memory out of her mind, but all she can do is mourn for how light, joyous, and hopeful she had been only a year earlier when Phillip had proposed. She can still see him lit by an aura of candlelight. They were in their favorite pizza parlor, and she had wondered why the place was lit like a shrine, with multiple candles on every surface, when they entered. Vinny, the owner, had mumbled something about a power outage, but the rest of the street looked fine.

When Phillip knelt down, she started laughing so hysterically that he caught the buzz too and couldn't quite find the words he wanted to say. Pretty soon the entire place was laughing and cheering him on. Other patrons started feeding him lines, like "Darling, please marry me. You know how much I love you" or "Come on, sweetie pie, let's get hitched." Finally, Vinny brought over a bottle of bubbly. It was certainly not on the menu in a place where the typical fizzy beverage is soda. Then Phillip simply pushed the ring onto her finger and kissed her.

Living and working together had never worked as well for any other couple as it had for Phillip and Sheila. She is innovative, thorough, and very, very smart. He is charming and a great salesman. He embodies confidence and a practical kind of hope that inspires investors and the research division board to trust him. It's no surprise that he emerged from this charade unscathed; it happened without his engineering it.

* * *

In the back of the limo, Sheila turns to Philip. "I'm not going home. That's why Cynthia was getting into the car."

"Oh, sorry," Philip responds. "I hope she has a way to get home."

"She'll manage," Sheila replies, refusing to look at him. "Anyway, shall I drop you at the hospital or home?"

Philip turns to her; his face is so sad and beseeching. She turns away; she can't bear to look at him. "Sheila, let's just go back to the house together. We really should talk, sort this out, and figure out how to move forward." He pauses. She's looking out the window; he's looking at the back of her head. "Please."

"No," she says without turning to look at him. "I think I'll move out. That's the only way I can move forward."

He sucks in a breath. He had been holding it, hoping she would come with him. He sits back, resolved. "Okay. You don't have to move out. It was your house anyway. I'll be gone tomorrow. You can come ... go home whenever you want."

2

UNSAFE SANCTUARY

That night at Cynthia's house, Sheila hardly says a word. She feels like she is moving through a dream. Her sense of direction has gone askew. She's cut adrift and seems to float through dinner. Cynthia's husband, big and burly Mike, who has always been a great friend to her, tries to cheer her up with a few jokes. Cynthia's kids are four and two, so the place is a bit raucous, and she can't think. Michele is the oldest. They call her Mikey, after her dad. Danny is the baby, but he's walking around now and getting into everything. Sheila grabs him and plops him on her lap in a determined effort to try to engage. It feels forced, and the child can tell and squirms away.

Dinner is a haphazard affair. Cynthia is mostly running around taking care of the kids, leaving Mike and Sheila to fend for themselves. When Cynthia finally bundles the kids off upstairs to bathe them and put them to bed, Mike gets down to the business of asking Sheila how her case went.

"I'm screwed," she says bluntly.

Mike may look like a truck driver but he is a lawyer. This isn't his area of expertise, but he is concerned for her and wants to make sure she isn't being taken advantage of in some way. He tries to tease a bit of information out of her. "Who else was involved in the project and possibly culpable?"

It's really too late, and Sheila isn't interested in talking about it at all. That's normal for Sheila, though; she's usually uncommunicative and awkward in conversation, even with family. Cynthia returns from kid duty, and she and Mike exchange concerned and helpless looks behind Sheila's back. Finally, Sheila apologizes and excuses herself, promising to wash the dishes in the morning. Right now, all she can think of is going to lie down.

Cynthia shrugs after her sister leaves. "I'll keep an eye on her. This was quite a blow."

* * *

The next day, Sheila limps through her lab, her cane almost too feeble under the immense weight she now bears. The place is a super high-tech space with all of the best equipment for the genetic-modification work they do. The surgery is enclosed in glass and surrounded by a lab with huge, interactive smart boards that link up to every piece of diagnostic equipment, everyone's computer, and the web. Attached to the lab is a room where animals are held. They call it "the sanctuary." It occurs to her for the first time to wonder if someone called it that as a joke. Most of the animals live in separate cages, but there are a couple of glass-enclosed areas where individual animals or groups of animals are allowed to run around periodically with a bit more space.

Sheila likes to enter the lab by way of the sanctuary so that she can take a quick look at all of the subjects and see how they are doing. Her office intersects with both the lab and the sanctuary. Whimpers, squawks, and the wild sounds of a farmyard contrast with the clinically bleached and fluorescent lab.

A white rat blinks askance at Sheila. His perfectly formed miniature hands, complete with opposable thumbs, peel away at the skin of a grape. Above him, a large rabbit with a set of human-shaped ears on its back chews quietly. On a tall perch to the side stands an eagle that looks perfectly normal. He stares at her with what looks like enmity. More preternatural creatures occupy the cages above and below the ones into which she has just peeked. The twenty or so cages are each inhabited by something. A monkey, a mouse, a dog, a cat, and a ferret snuggle to the backs of some upper cages. Below are pigs, dogs, goats, and even a small pony. None are normal by any means. All exhibit unusual colors and strange appendages or seem to be strange mixes of two animals, like one creature that must be part goat and part sheep. These are the cleanest pens anyone has ever seen.

Sheila fumbles with the key to her office door. The door swings open, and she stops short. Spiner is at her desk. With irritation, he summons her inside. He doesn't rise from her chair to help when he sees her struggle to manage her cane and take off her coat and bag. She hangs them on the back of the door with her lab coat. Her office is cluttered. Files heaped on the couch have displaced its cushions to the floor. The walls are covered artistically with photos of the creatures they have worked on over the last nine years. Her personal items are squashed to the edge of the desk and even stacked on top of each other or almost falling into the wastebasket. It's a busy place—a place of ideas, innovations, and many long hours. It's also Sheila's entire life. She bristles at Spiner's proprietary presence. This is her place, or at least it was.

Philip enters and hands her a stack of mail, nodding at Spiner. "It's all personal."

Spiner stands up and closes the top drawer of her desk, through which he was rifling. He wastes no time with niceties. "I'm here to collect the records of everything you've been working on."

"Now?" Sheila asks, bracing for an argument.

Spiner outlines his list on his fingers. "I need everything relative to the gene-splicing, the animal records, your hard files, your digital records, your computer files, samples, your notes, and especially any private notes you may have kept both on- and off-line."

Sheila's mind wanders. An overwhelming sense of how unfair this is washes over her. Her legs feel weak, but she stiffens, determined not to crumble. She was the one who came up with the innovative concept of looking at the regenerative capabilities of other creatures and of finding a way to incorporate or turn on that ability in creatures without it. The eagle was their best test yet. He had the gene. He had lost the use of his wings, but they had engineered a repair RNA that seemed to fix the disorder in his neural synapses. He was healed almost completely. It was a success—a huge success—but some activist had hacked her notes, which outlined her dream for the next step in the project.

For her, the next step was twofold: she wanted to create a way for humans to regenerate limbs, and she wanted to find a way to reverse the course of degenerative diseases, specifically nerve diseases. She wanted to be able to do both these things in people who had not been born with the regenerative genes. To her, these two goals were the same thing. They were a long way off, but the release of her notes on the Internet had caused a firestorm against the idea of using animal genes in human cures. A few stolen pages went viral. She became toxic; the response was unreasonable and over the top. Suddenly all her work is hopeless.

She decides to argue anyway. "But the cure is right there in that eagle. I just need more time."

Spiner graces her with a withering look. "Seventy million, Sheila. That's a lot of money, and we're still finding out how much future funding has been pulled."

Sheila feels like the planet is tipping beneath her. She's shaking and hopes it doesn't show, but she decides to keep going. "It's eight years of work. I need time to sort it out for you."

"She's right. I can't figure it out," Philip says, waving his arm toward the couch. "This couch filing system is beyond me."

Spiner is clearly irked, but he caves. "Fine, tomorrow morning then." He gives Sheila one last challenging look and then leaves.

Philip's eyes soften. He glances at Sheila, embarrassed. She looks down and shuffles her mail. She sees a medical report and catches her breath. Philip reaches for it.

"It's personal," she says pulling the envelope away from him.

Philip holds his hand out for her to give it to him. "Sheila, you can't hold anything back."

She hides the envelope behind her back. "Forget it, Philip." She relaxes a bit and gives him a pleading look. "Success is closer than you think, and you need it too."

"No," he says. "Nothing off book, okay?"

She backs away. Philip steps toward her. "Don't do it. It's too controversial, too dangerous."

With the momentum of his next step, Sheila pushes him out the door and then slams and locks it. He whirls around and peers through the glass panel.

"You'd better keep me out of it—out of everything—from now on!" Philip says from the other side of her door.

"Done!" she replies.

She watches until he is gone and then turns to look at the envelope. Her hands shake uncontrollably as she pours herself a glass of water and downs a fistful of prescription pills. She breathes. Now she can read the report: "Test results: Sheila Jensen. Degenerative myelitis … Prognosis: Terminal, 1–3 years."

The glass slips through her fingers and shatters on the tiles.

* * *

Later, Sheila is curled in a fetal position on the empty office couch watching a video.

On the screen, she moves easily without a cane through the complex lab equipment. Her onscreen self unclasps a martini-shaker-sized stainless steel tank and carefully removes a glass vial inside while she narrates for the camera.

"The theory is that this piece of starfish genetic code will promote regeneration, basically switch back on damaged neurons in the eagle's spinal column and allow it to fly again one day."

Behind her, Sheila's eagle shrugs. Its wings are limp and lifeless. Philip takes the bird's wingtips and spreads them out so that the camera can record them.

Sheila clicks the remote control, and the video goes into fast-forward mode through garbled images of Sheila performing microscopic surgeries and dashing through the lab. Philip moves about too, just as busy as she is.

The video slows to normal speed again. The eagle lies on the counter, sedated. Sheila's hands manipulate its wings as she continues talking to the camera. "The procedure was successful. Now with physical therapy, we expect to see the bird regain control of his wings and learn to fly again."

The video fast-forwards again. It stops, and the eagle flies inside the confines of the research lab's atrium. Its strong wings beat rhythmically. On the screen, Sheila laughs, her face glowing in the joy of success and hope.

Philip claps her on the back and then picks her up in a bear hug. He's the one who reads the final line summing up the eagle experiment.

"Six months after the insertion of the regeneration genetic code, we see a remarkable success story."

* * *

Early evening light streams in through the high windows. Sheila is still hunched on her couch. She sighs in defeat and rubs her ankles, grimacing in pain. A loud bang startles her, and she struggles to stand up and cross the room to peek out the industrial window in this old part of the medical complex.

In the parking lot below, violent activists shriek while they rock one of the parked ambulances. Several garbage cans are smoking. Flames spew from words as big as a car: "DEMON DOCTORS—GO TO HELL" is inscribed in smoking lines of gasoline on the asphalt. A nurse flees toward her car, clutching her sweater around her as she tries to hide her green hospital scrubs underneath.

Sheila hobbles to the sanctuary to check on the caged animals. They are restless, spooked, and squawking. Nervous, the eagle flaps his wings and stamps his feet. Sheila notices that the tether on his ankle is loose. She steps closer and reaches out to retie it.

Suddenly, a window shatters in a grand waterfall of glass. A rock trailed by a brightly colored slogan skids across the floor by Sheila's feet. A rush of cool, smoke-scented air ruffles her hair and the bird's feathers while she bends to pick up the rock. Instantly, the eagle dives for the open window, and his tether slides undone.

"No!"

The eagle slips outside and spirals upward into the purpling evening sky, screeching with joy. Sheila collapses, sobbing. The eagle was her last hope. Huddled under the animal cages, she appears as if she too were detained. Police sirens drown the noise of the rioters outside. She hears them scatter while still yelling back their protest chants.

* * *

In the park nearby, in the center of a fountain, the moon silhouettes an ornate stone statue of an angel. Three laughing and hooting rioters running from the sirens dash by.

Suddenly, wings flap. For a moment, it seems as if the statue lives, but then the eagle scampers up the stone shoulders of the angel and stands triumphant and free on the statue's head. The tether hanging from his ankle trails across the angel's forehead.

The massive, rising moon halos his strong wings, light filters through delicate feathers.

3

HAIL MARY

The pitch-dark parking lot outside is ghostly silent. Sheila is slumped on her folded arms, asleep on the lab counter. She wears a paper surgical cap, a white coat, and latex gloves. All of the lab equipment is on—spectral microscopes, computers, a huge interactive smart board, and other unrecognizable beeping, humming, and whizzing contraptions. Their flickering lights make the lab look like Times Square. The door rattles, and Philip steps inside. He scrunches his eyebrows, annoyed when he sees everything lit up. He flicks off all of the power switches. When he notices Sheila, exhausted and sleeping like a baby, he sighs.

"What are you doing?" he whispers under his breath, not intending to wake her. "You're supposed to be packing up here." He lifts her gently from the stool on which she is perched and carries her through the open office door. She mumbles and sighs but doesn't wake up while he nudges a pile of books out of the way with his foot and tucks her into the couch.

Back in the lab, he rummages through her notes. He bags discarded microscope slides, pipettes, syringes, and used cell containers—evidence that she has made several attempts at something that has failed. He opens and closes drawers, collecting flash and backup drives, notebooks, and a set of keys. He uses the keys to lock the file drawers and the sample refrigerators. He clicks on the computer and quickly reviews Sheila's last four hours of video notes.

On the screen, a huge ovum pulsates with life in vibrant color. At high speed, a needle punctures its cellophane envelope, and a red-tagged spiral of genetic material squirms out of the needle and into the cell. Suddenly, the cell devours itself from the inside out. Five more gene-splice attempts in lurid colors speed across the video screen. Each ends with the ovum turning black and shriveling up.

Sheila lifts her head and watches Philip through the office door pocketing her most recent computer backup drive. As he slips out of the lab, he grabs the master keys off the hook by the door and pockets them too.

Sheila jumps up and opens the drawer, rummaging around where her keys had been a short while before. "Damn! Okay, this is it, my last attempt. Hail Mary."

She pounds on the large, silver, walk-in refrigerator door and yanks at the handle. It's locked. She grabs a red crowbar from the emergency fire panel and pries the padlock off. A refreshing whoosh of cold air ruffles her tousled hair as she enters the refrigerator. Near the entrance, an odd mixture of lunch and snack items litter the shelves: yogurt, a bag of coffee, a plastic-wrapped sandwich, and a bowl of fruit. They seem out of place in this pristine, clinical environment of stainless steel and meticulously labeled containers. Further inside, jars of pickled creatures line the shelves. Closer examination of them reveals all kinds of strange abominations. Some have extra limbs, others missing limbs. There are odd blends that could be reptile and animal or bird and insect; it's impossible to tell. High-tech glass cases contain a myriad of numbered and color-coded glass vials. With the bright lights on and shining through them, they look like a Candy Crush video game screen.

Sheila walks all the way to the back of the refrigerator to another locked glass case labeled "Effective Controls." She pulls the key out of her pocket and opens the glass door. She runs her finger through the E line. When she doesn't see what she wants, she moves her hand to the S line.

"Ah, there it is."

She pulls out a stainless steel vial labeled "SCAS 59 REPAIR STRIP – CONTROL – TOUCHSTONE – DO NOT USE."

Back in the lab, Sheila pulls a sample out of the steel vial with a syringe. Frozen air wisps out of the open vial and pours toward the floor. Her latex-covered hands and the tiny glass tube disappear inside a state-of-the-art electronic microscope. Sheila peers over the contraption at the video screen on a massive smart board. So many technological innovations have come about since the days that the human genome was mapped. A blurry image wriggles about and then resolves into focus. Spiraling coils of live genes pulsate, magnified many thousandfold. Not only can Sheila see the

DNA clearly in its living form, but she can also see, by way of a digital identification overlay, what parts of the DNA she is looking at. She can see what the strips of life actually create, and she can snip and sew the pieces of it any way she likes. But first, within a million permutations, she has to find the exact piece that she needs.

The swirling braids resolve into a rainbow of colors representing the base components of the genes. Then the live image resolves into undulating bars of color and finally the letters *A, C, C, T, G, G, A, T, T, T, C, C,* and so on, thus breaking down the wriggling confusion of live stuff into the clear geometry of data. Each letter is associated with a specific color. It still amazes her that the machine can recognize each minute component of the genome instantly and label it in real time for her to see and track.

She types "growth/repair activating sequence," and the computer pulls up her map of the specific chromosomal strip that she wants to locate. It appears as a stripe across the top of the screen in the four vibrant colors representing each base protein. Sheila clicks Search. The computer begins processing the new material and comparing it to the map above. A progress percentage bar appears and quickly reaches 5 percent … 7 percent … Sheila sighs and lays her head on the table to watch.

The colors of the match creep across the screen directly under the map. The progress bar creeps up to 21 percent. Sheila glances at the timer—19.78 minutes to go. She stands up and paces. She grabs a yogurt and munches on it. Finally, as she sits alert, shaking her foot nervously, the match edges up—89 percent … 92 percent. Then it stops at 97 percent.

Sheila sucks in a terrified breath and holds it. She stares at the computer, fearing the worst. Nothing happens—and then the bar rushes to 100 percent.

"Yes!" Sheila leans in to peer at the live video screen. It reveals the writhing genetic material. One section is highlighted in red. Sheila's gloved hands disappear into the microscope again. She watches the screen carefully as a needle sucks out the precious red strand and sets it aside gently.

Sheila plucks out another stainless steel can from the small food refrigerator under her counter. Its label says "JENSEN/OHL 01/21." She removes another syringe and squeezes material onto a slide, which she slips into the microscope. Now a globular ovum is also quivering on the video screen.

Sheila leans over the microscope, straining with superhuman effort to steady her hand. A needle chases the wriggling ovum around the video screen, moving with uneven clumsiness. Sheila sighs. She shifts her balance and tries again. On the screen, she watches the magnified needle jab the red strand into the ovum and go right into the cell's nucleus. She sighs, relieved. The ovum is still.

"Don't die, don't die," Sheila whispers. The red genes squirm around in the ovum and then disappear. Sheila jumps up and shouts. "Live! Live! Please live! If there's any power in this universe that can make you live, please do it now." Her eyes tear up. "Please live," she whispers.

She starts punching the keyboard, adjusting the temperature, the moisture content, and the amount of light present. She breathes heavily while she makes minute adjustments. Nothing changes in the ovum on screen. Sheila hyperventilates. She reels back, feeling faint, and clamps her hands over her mouth to contain her uncontrolled breathing. She moans. Her moan turns into a prolonged forced "hummmmmmm!"

The computer resonates with her hum, louder and louder. It sounds like trumpets blaring. Her ears ring. On the screen, the ovum vibrates to the pulse of her voice. The keyboard vibrates, stuttering across the countertop. Sheila reaches out to still its movements. A blue flash of static electricity jumps from her finger to the keyboard. Electricity crackles across the keyboard, the computer, and the spectral microscope. On the video screen, huge, blue sparks circle the oscillating ovum and then blossom into a brilliant flash of white light. Sheila staggers against the equipment with a thud. Sparks fly everywhere. She dives to switch off the surge protector, but a flash knocks her out.

* * *

Viewed from above, the imposing NEU research facility and the attached medical institution are illuminated starkly. Then the entire complex goes black. High above the city, a lone eagle wings his way north. Section by section, the city lights go out in a cascading blackout. Far behind the eagle's wings, in the middle of a now very dark landscape, the distant medical institution's emergency generators kick the lights back on.

The bird soars onward.

* * *

Sheila struggles to pick herself up. White noise and scrambled pixels emanate from the video screen as the smart board lurches back to life. Finally, the ovum image reappears. It swells and shrinks like it's puffing itself up or breathing. Then it splits in two and again into four. Sheila stifles a laugh.

"Wow!"

She scrawls in a new and empty notebook. "Day 1 – Survival. It's growing. Now I need a womb."

4

PRECARIOUS ORIGIN

At the observation window in the newborn ward of the hospital, Sheila stares across rows of bassinets. Two figures in surgical robes and masks weave through them toward the door, each carrying a baby. One figure steps out of the nursery, nods to Sheila, and then offers her a baby.

"How are you holding up?"

Sheila waves her off, so the figure, Cynthia, leans over the baby to kiss Sheila on the cheek. Then she pulls back and gives Sheila the look that only a sister can give when she knows something is up. They are close, these two, both of them overachievers, but somehow Cynthia manages to wear her burdens much more lightly than Sheila. Though Sheila is older, Cynthia seems to have more worldly wisdom and certainly has better people skills than her big sister.

Sheila is almost bursting. "I need your help."

A nurse takes the baby from Cynthia, and Cynthia guides Sheila into her office to shut out the hospital drone. Sheila is flushed, almost in tears. Cynthia looks at her warily. She's not used to her sister showing much emotion. Sheila is always about business, and she is rarely unnerved.

Sheila waves her refrigerated stainless steel embryo vial. "It was successful. I'm ready."

Cynthia sits Sheila down on the couch. "I don't think it's a great time to jump into anything radical right now. You've just had a major blow, a life-changing verdict. You're not thinking clearly, and anyway, you shouldn't. Not in your condition."

"No, it's okay. The report was okay," Sheila lies.

Cynthia eyes her doubtfully. "Still, why chance it?"

"I'll do it with or without your help," Sheila says, determined, though her voice quavers.

"You sound desperate. What's really going on?"

Sheila's eyes glaze over. "I want to live."

"Sheila, this is such a long shot, and carrying a baby is a huge stress on the body."

"I can do it. I have to do it." Sheila grabs Cynthia by the shoulders and leans in, "I want my life to be normal too."

Cynthia concedes and takes the vial. "Okay, I'll have it."

"No." Sheila snatches the vial and clutches it close. "It's mine. I have to. You can't."

Cynthia takes a long look at her sister and sighs. "Okay. We'll do the insertion right away."

Sheila smiles weakly and then collapses her face into her sister's shoulder, sobbing. "Thank you, thank you."

* * *

In the following weeks, Sheila devotes her time to mopping up the wreck of her life. She spends her days answering the interminable and detailed questions of the research institution's board of governors. They are trying hard to find some way to clear NEU of wrongdoing and make her entirely responsible for the expensive judgment against them. They have agreed to pay their fine, but they want to be absolved of wrongdoing. It's the matter of future grants and credibility loss that troubles them.

In addition, Spiner is all over her, requiring that she summarize her work in intense detail "for the record." He seems to think there's more to it and that she is hiding something from him. If he knew the truth about what was growing inside her, all hell would break loose. But she has a right to have a child; it's none of their business. The child could be anyone's. It could be the product of a one-night fling that she decided to keep. They will never know. If her plan works out and the regenerative gene is present in a human baby, in her child, it will never show on the outside. So it won't be hard to keep them from finding out … will it? Still, she is nervous about it.

Finally, if these two assignments are not difficult enough, her third daily chore is arguing with Philip over what to do next with her career. It all blows up on a day when she is feeling particularly lousy and spends practically all morning in the bathroom throwing up. Sheila has an appointment with Cynthia to see the baby for the first time, but Philip is trying to get Sheila to agree to ghostwrite a grant for him. She refuses, as usual. Suddenly, with little sympathy, he lets loose.

"This is the way your career is going to be from now on. You'll never have your name on anything. No one will trust you. The only way you can ever achieve anything is by working in the background and letting others take the credit."

She walks away from him, unwilling to engage.

"Sheila, it's over for you. Don't you get it? It's over. I tell you this because I love you and I want to help you."

She realizes that she has had enough. She grabs her cane and her coat and throws her purse over her shoulder. "Thank you, Philip! You've just helped me out the door. Thank you. I quit."

Relieved that she has somewhere to go to take her mind off his outburst, she heads for the park, planning to spend the hour and a half until her appointment sitting by the angel statue and thinking about the child that she is sure will rescue her from the crippling disease that threatens her life.

* * *

Later that afternoon, Cynthia plugs Sheila into the latest ultralight/sound scope. Bluetooth suction sensors arranged strategically on her stomach supply information to a machine off to her right. A holographic ball of magnified cells that seem to be made of light projects from the machine and floats above Sheila's belly. All inner details and workings of the cells are clearly visible. A DNA strand unravels; RNA strips zipper onto it. Protein pieces scurry from all parts of the cell to attach to the newly formed DNA strand. The new strand pulls apart from the old strand. The cellophane membrane of the cell nucleus slips between them, dividing one nucleus into two. Then the cell splits to form an identical pair of cells. The embryo is growing.

Sheila watches Cynthia manipulate the light-formed image. Cynthia pinches it expertly with her fingers. The image changes perspective from the microscopic view to the macroscopic. Now they can see the entire fetus. It's about the size of a lentil.

"That's its actual size," Cynthia says.

A look of shock registers on Sheila's face. Cynthia looks at her with concern, and Sheila hurries to mask her true feelings. "Really? So tiny? Wow. But I suppose I should have realized that."

"Here, let's take a closer look."

Cynthia expands the image with a few quick and specific hand motions. The image follows her movement and swells to about eight inches in size. Sheila watches in awe. She's seen so many embryos, fetuses, infants, and births, but none were human, and none were her own.

The fetus vibrates and pulses with the beat of her own heart. She becomes acutely aware of her breath and her fast heartbeat. It has a direct effect on the image that she sees floating above her. The light-formed infant is pale pink with distinct webs of red blood vessels that create a lacy skullcap. Its almost-transparent legs and feet are nubs, and it seems to have a tail that is just as substantial as its legs. But its hands are discernible, with tiny, bulbous fingers waving right in front of two black eyes.

Sheila is worried. "Does it look human?"

"Of course. They all look like that. It's normal."

Cynthia gives Sheila another suspicious glance as she moves over to tap the machine's control panel. The 3-D image snaps back to the video screen and becomes a 2-D photo. A printer whirs behind them.

"Here's a shot for you."

Sheila takes the photo and stares at it dumbly.

* * *

Bright lights make the sterile delivery room colder. Stern, crisp nurses and doctors in white coats rush about. Sheila struggles to give birth while sinister and overwhelming machines surrounding her beep, hum, and click, making strange, animal-like noises. Sheila grunts in agony, and then a baby wails. A nurse hands Sheila a wrapped bundle.

Sheila pulls the blanket aside, revealing a baby with a rat face. Tiny human hands reach toward Sheila. She drops the bundle, terrified. The nurse looms over her and turns into a huge white bear. She tips Sheila's bed over, and Sheila spills onto the floor.

Sheila wakes up, rolling out of bed with a cry. It's late afternoon a few weeks after her first exam. She's dozing on her bed. The exam photo lies on the covers beside her. It's taped into a blank art book. Detailed notes about the image crowd the opposite page, with arrows snaking to various areas of the photo. Small sketches enhance the written material, indicating that Sheila has doubts about the proper formation of the fetus. She has been obsessing over the photo, looking at it endlessly, terrified that something might be wrong with the child. Despite Cynthia's exam and her positive conclusions about the baby's progress, Sheila is experiencing profound regrets. Breathing heavily, she grips her stomach in terror. She isn't really showing, but her face is flushed and her mind racing. A tape repeating "What have I done? What have I done?" plays in her mind on a loop, and panic rises in her gut. She retches over the toilet. Downstairs, her doorbell rings.

Philip stands outside the cut glass of Sheila's front door at 17 Maple Street. He peers in, hoping to catch a glimpse of her. An elegant bunch of hot pink roses drapes from one hand behind his back.

Sheila leans heavily on her cane and works her way down the stairs. It is clear that moving is getting more difficult for her. From the bottom steps, she sees Philip through the glass door. She stops when she steps off the last stair and into the foyer. She's trying to decide whether to waste her energy going to the door or not. It has come to that already. She's acutely aware of how much energy every exertion takes, and the six-foot walk looks daunting in her present mood.

Philip waves the flowers at her. His muffled voice carries in from outside. "Can I come in?"

She decides she can't talk to him; not now. She shakes her head.

"I want you to come back to work," he begs.

Sheila wavers, uncertain. Her hand drifts unconsciously to her stomach.

Philip notices her rub her barely rounding belly. "Are you pregnant?"

Sheila can't respond. She doesn't know how. She turns her back on him and steps out of the foyer and into the living room, out of Philip's view.

Philip stands on her doorstep, stunned. Then he slumps against the door. Suddenly, he pulls back and thrashes Sheila's front door with the flowers. "Go ahead! Tear my heart out. You obviously need it more than I do."

He storms off but then turns back a few feet away to fling the now wretched flowers at her door.

Sheila waits inside until she sees Philip drive away. After a pause, she rushes out thoughtlessly trampling over the discarded roses. On the way down the path, she leans over to retch into the bushes. Then she clambers into her car.

* * *

Soon afterwards, Sheila lies on the exam table in Cynthia's office and stares out the window at snow falling on budding tree leaves as Cynthia conducts various tests. The 3-D diagnostic machine glows and beeps as it fires up.

"You couldn't wait until morning?" Cynthia asks.

Sheila is panting. "I've made a terrible mistake! Please terminate it. It's too dangerous."

Cynthia gives her a dubious look. "Why?"

Sheila doesn't answer. She's working herself into a panic. "I'm such an idiot. Things could go really wrong …"

Cynthia puts a hand over Sheila's fluttering fingers. "Shhh! Let's just take a look."

Sheila squirms and pushes Cynthia's hand away. "I'm afraid it's going to be …" She pauses, her lips clamped shut.

"What?" Cynthia asks. A peculiar, nagging "something" has bothered her since Sheila insisted on this pregnancy.

"A monster, an abomination," Sheila says finally summoning the courage to speak.

Cynthia laughs, relieved. "Every mother goes through this stage. Did you have a dream?"

Sheila nods.

"That's perfectly normal. Look."

Another 3-D image pops into light above Sheila. The fetus is about the size of a fig now. Its hands are fully formed, and its legs are also complete. The tail is gone.

Cynthia smiles at Sheila. "That's exactly what it should look like at eleven weeks."

Sheila breaks down sobbing. She gasps, short of breath. Cynthia shakes her.

"Sheila, take a breath. It's fine. Promise me you won't go off and do something stupid."

Sheila relaxes and wipes her face. "It's normal; that's all that matters."

Cynthia continues fussing with the machine. "While we're here, let's take a closer look." She enlarges the 3-D image with a flick of her hands. The glowing fetus squirms. Cynthia twists her fingers and taps the air. The image switches to a black-and-white X-ray. She scrutinizes every part of the small body, moving around Sheila and the projection to get a good look at all sides. Then she switches to the diagnostic function again, and the image reverts to the tiny pink version of the frail and pulsating form. Cynthia adjusts the view one more time, and then they see the flow of the baby's blood. The corpuscles are overwhelming, rushing, bumping, streaming into smaller and smaller vessels. At that scale, Cynthia moves throughout the small body, examining its functions and growth. She sees the bone material stretch, brain cells multiply, and neurons build connections. The child's inner organs are well formed. Its heart beats strong and clear. All of this living stuff throbs with vigor in its thrillingly minute detail. Then Cynthia rolls back to the macroscopic view and snaps another picture of the entire baby.

"Put the other picture away now," she says, handing it to Sheila.

* * *

The next day, it hits Sheila that she is spending too much time alone. She can't do this for the next six months or she will go absolutely crazy. She has to go back to work.

That afternoon, she shows up in Philip's office, sheepish and apologetic. He's much kinder than she expected, and he invites her in, offers her coffee, and then settles in on the couch next to her.

"I'm sorry for yesterday," she says her head heavy with regret.

Philip grabs her hands. "No, Sheila, I'm sorry, so sorry, for everything that has come between us. I never meant for this to happen, never."

Sheila accepts his apology. She looks at him and smiles weakly. "Can you still use me? I'll do whatever you want. I need a job; I'm going nuts at home."

"Of course." He pauses a minute, looking at her, searching. "*Are* you pregnant?"

She nods. He fidgets, sort of excited, sort of apprehensive. He wants to ask the next question, but he's afraid of how she'll answer. "Is it mine?" he asks finally.

"It's *mine,*" she states in a way that closes the discussion.

His face darkens, but he knows Sheila too well. If she's done answering questions, that's it; she's done.

He gets up and walks over to his desk, his mind racing, trying to figure out how to pursue the question again. He decides to let it go and sits down.

"You can start whenever you want," he says coldly. He pulls a stack of paperwork out of his desk and hands it to her. "I never processed these, so you're still in the system. We'll consider the last few weeks a temporary absence for personal needs, okay?"

"Thanks," Sheila says. Then she gets up to leave. When she reaches the door, she turns back. "I really mean it, Philip. Thank you. You are very special to me, but ..."

His look warms a bit, and hope leaps in his heart. They look at each other a long moment, and then Sheila turns and walks out.

* * *

Sheila settles back into the job. It's not as painful as she feared it would be to take the role of assistant instead of lead scientist. She has her mind on her new project anyway—the child growing inside her.

5

MARKED BIRTH

At first, Sheila and Philip find themselves slipping into the old, easy, and harmonious work patterns that they had developed over the previous long years. At times, she forgets the excruciating circumstances that caused her demotion and realizes that she still enjoys the work. She's reluctant, though, to spend too much time with Philip, because he is always fishing for information about her pregnancy. He suspects something, and she doesn't want him to know that she used the eggs she had stored for their use once married. Nor does she want him to find out that she manipulated the child's genes, so she avoids him more and more.

His schedule in the lab has always been unvarying. She knows when to expect him and finds herself in her office at those times. She works in the lab when he's not there. Their offices are close, but they communicate by video chat and email pretty much exclusively. She always eats lunch at her desk. She dashes home or over to Cynthia's house after work, so they see each other in person less and less. Sheila can't remember the last time they were together in a room.

Weeks and then months pass quickly. Sheila's belly expands, and she finds it harder and harder to move around. The compounding effects of the pregnancy and her declining health exhaust her. All she can do is go to work, sit at her desk writing or in the lab experimenting all day, and then go home to eat some take-out and sleep.

* * *

It seems as though the end of her pregnancy sneaks up on her. She and Cynthia are in much the same locations in the exam room, but Sheila's stomach is much bigger now.

"How are you feeling?" Cynthia asks.

26

"I can't wait," Sheila replies. "You were right; this is the most uncomfortable I've been in my entire life."

Cynthia laughs. "Don't worry. It'll be over soon."

She shows Sheila the hologram of the baby. It's a big, healthy, and beautiful baby.

"Oh, and there it is," Cynthia exclaims. "He's a boy. Finally, he shows us."

Sheila sighs. "Really, I can't wait to see him."

That's what she says, but in reality, she is eager to start testing and find out what her gene manipulation has produced. She doesn't care if it's a boy or a girl; she only hopes that it has the regenerative repair gene. She also hopes that the gene is in perfect working order and is transferable from the child's system to hers.

Cynthia removes the diagnostic sensors from Sheila's belly. "Soon. Are you ready?"

Sheila nods. She is more than ready. She feels almost desperate.

She leaves Cynthia's exam room and heads back to her office to pick up her laptop and head home. Sheila is large and uncomfortable, and it's hard to walk with two canes through the busy halls of the bustling institution.

When she nears her area of the research facility, an orderly pushing a gurney bumps past her carelessly and knocks her off balance. Then a male nurse, his nose in a chart, dashes toward her and swerves around her at the last minute. She teeters a bit again, and Philip appears behind the nurse.

Sheila stops short. He grabs her arm to steady her. He's smiling, all friendly and concerned, but there's an edge to it—an underlying tension— and Sheila can see it.

"Look at you; it's due any day. Why are you avoiding me?"

"That's crazy, Philip," she replies. "We talk every day, and we work in the same office."

"Still, you're avoiding me, and I know something is up."

He studies her face, and she turns away.

"See? There you go, avoiding me."

He pauses for a moment, studying her. She fidgets uncomfortably and squirms out of his hold.

"It's mine, right?"

She looks at him without answering, her face a blank mask that gives him nothing.

"I'll get a paternity test! You can't shut me out."

Sheila turns and walks away. Philip presses on, following her. "Why avoid me if it's not mine? I don't get you. We could work it all out."

Sheila stops and turns to him. "Like we worked out the suit against us? I was the fall guy. It didn't work out so well for me. My career is over, like you said." She continues walking. Philip walks beside her.

"It doesn't have to be this way. I could get Spiner to reinstate you as the head of the research lab. You'd just have to stay away from genetic modifications involving humans—well, involving all animals."

Sheila can tell Philip is devastated. His look is gut wrenching, but Sheila walks off without a word.

* * *

The following evening, Sheila works late. The setting sun streams horizontally into the office bathroom, and Sheila has neglected to turn on the fluorescent lights because of the beauty of the golden, rose-tinted light filling the place. She washes up at the sink, preparing to go home. Glancing into the full-length mirror near the exit, she stops abruptly when she sees a very odd phenomenon. Her huge stomach is … glowing.

Her face wrinkles in puzzlement, and then her entire body shines gold. She sees herself radiant and transparent, like the effect of Cynthia's amazing, high-tech diagnostic equipment. Blood rushes like neon light through her system. Inside her body, she sees the fully formed baby. He is equally radiant. She smiles, ecstatic. Tears like bright stars flash on her cheeks. The baby's eyes pop open and look at her. He's alert and aware, and he smiles at her. An unconscious smile twists her mouth. Suddenly, the baby tumbles over, and Sheila squirms. Then the baby is upside down, his butt up and his back facing her. She gasps, confused and amazed.

"Something's wrong. Something must be wrong," she whispers to herself.

Sheila dials Cynthia several times, but there's no answer at her office or on her cell phone. Sheila clutches her stomach. She goes back to the mirror and stares at herself again. She looks normal now. Then she doubles over in pain.

"Ow!"

She grabs her canes and rushes out of the door toward the maternity ward in search of Cynthia. She goes as fast as she can through several wings in an effort to get there as quickly as possible. She knows the shortcuts across the institution, but today it seems as if the distance is an interminable and very difficult hike.

A patient with a walker clogs traffic as she turns a corner. He trails an attendant and a rolling IV rig. She doubles over again.

"Ow!"

She clutches her stomach, and water crashes to the floor. She tries to steady herself by grabbing a rolling medicine cart. It tips it over. Tiny, colorful pills skitter across the floor. Sheila staggers into the wall for support and leans there, breathing heavily. The nurse whose cart she just dumped grabs her.

"Are you all right?"

"Call my sister, Dr. Cynthia Clark ... maternity."

* * *

After another thorough exam, Cynthia declares that Sheila is about to deliver, and there's nothing wrong at all. "Let's get you to maternity, now."

Sheila turns to her sister, her face set and determined. "No." It's the look that Cynthia knows she should not argue against. Sheila struggles to get up. "I need to go."

Outside the exam room, Sheila limps along on her canes while Cynthia pushes an empty wheelchair. Cynthia grabs Sheila's arm. "Will you sit in the goddamned chair, please?"

"I hate it," Sheila responds. She's clinging desperately to her independence and is terrified of days to come when the wheelchair might be her only option. "I can manage," she insists.

"It's only for five minutes," Cynthia says, "not the rest of your life." She shoves Sheila into the chair. "Besides, we're almost at maternity, and the baby is coming too fast."

Cynthia steers the wheelchair toward a sign that says "Maternity Ward."

"No! No! I told you, not there. Home, now! We have to go home right now."

Cynthia opens her mouth to argue but, miraculously, decides not to. In the back of her mind, she has a peculiar worry that something is going on with this child that Sheila wants to keep secret. Also, she can see no reason not to have a home birth. She's legally obligated to comply with her patient's demand, even if it is her own sister, who is acting strangely right now. She spins the wheelchair around and heads toward the exit.

Cynthia drives too fast and cuts off an ambulance as they tear out of the hospital parking lot. "I've never heard of this before—speeding *away* from the hospital to have a baby. I don't know why I listen to you; you are absolutely crazy."

Sheila is breathing heavily and straining not to cry out. "Just drive."

* * *

Philip, taking a shortcut back to the lab from the cafeteria, overhears a nurse telling an orderly to clean up the hall where Dr. Jensen's water broke. He rushes straight to the maternity ward reception desk and interrupts the charge nurse.

"Which room is Dr. Jensen in?"

"She's not here," the nurse says.

"Where is she, then? Is she still in the hospital? Where else could she be? Give me that phone." He snatches it out of her hand.

* * *

When Cynthia and Sheila arrive at Sheila's home, Cynthia is surprised to see that Sheila's bathroom has been completely prepared for a water birth. She fills the tub and gets Sheila settled. Her contractions are coming fast. A soothing red light floods the room, and various portable, high-tech machines fill the space. Clean towels are stacked on easy-to-reach shelves. An instrument cart is nearby, should there be any need. A phone rings persistently in the other room.

Sheila's labor increases until she screams in a red rage. "How could I be so stupid?"

"Breathe, breathe. You're close," Cynthia coaches.

"Oh God. I thought it would be easier in water."

Cynthia laughs. "*Now* she gets religion. Maybe it is easier. How would you know?"

Cynthia clicks the controls on one of the machines, and the sensors on Sheila's stomach project a hologram of the child inside her. The baby's face grimaces. Through his translucent projected body, his tiny heart beats feverishly. He twists and squirms, but his movements are utterly confined, his head locked into place.

Suddenly, his head pinches, changing like a water balloon in a kid's hands. The infant's body elongates, following its head. His effort is palpable as the baby shifts slowly through the constricted space. Sheila groans and cries out, panting and breathing. With a watery slush, the baby floats free into the tub, and a momentous birth slips by, unnoticed by history.

Sweat pours into Sheila's eyes. She grabs Cynthia's arm. "I'm scared … take him away," she croaks.

Cynthia shrugs off her sister's panicked grip. "Wait a minute. I'm just checking him," she says in a deliberately calm voice.

"Why? Is he okay? Does he look okay?"

"He's beautiful," Cynthia croons to the red-faced cherub.

Cynthia hands Sheila her wriggling, wide-awake baby boy. His piercing blue gaze arrests Sheila's eyes immediately. Who is this person, this tiny, perfect, new someone that she has made, that she actually made in the lab? He stares at her, and his look is captivating.

"Please take him," Sheila says finally. "I have to get out and dry off. I'm exhausted."

Cynthia snuggles the towel-wrapped baby into the bathroom sink while she helps Sheila out of the bathtub.

Later Sheila sleeps while Cynthia examines the cooing baby. Two birthmarks on his back between his shoulder blades catch her attention. She frowns and traces the marks with the tip of her finger. Then she takes out her phone and snaps a picture of his back.

Sheila stirs and mumbles. "Is he okay?"

Cynthia plops the baby into her arms. Sheila brushes her cheek across his soft scalp. Suddenly, she stiffens and puts him down on the bed beside her.

"I've searched your entire house, and all I've found for the baby is one newborn outfit and a bag of diapers," Cynthia says. "What's going on, Sheila? You don't have a crib, baby blankets, bottles, or toys. I don't get it. You said you were ready."

She puts the baby in Sheila's lap again, but Sheila pushes him away. "I didn't have the time or the energy," is her feeble excuse.

"That's insane. You should have asked for help."

Sheila just looks at her.

"Okay," Cynthia says. "I have a closet full of stuff from the kids. I'll drop it all off tomorrow."

"Thanks," Sheila responds. She strains to get up, but Cynthia forces her back into bed.

"Oh, no you don't. You need to rest."

"I need to go to work," Sheila protests.

Cynthia is stunned by Sheila's cold response to her infant. Her brain races to try to figure it out, and then she gets it. "You did something to this child, didn't you? He's some kind of experiment." She shakes her head in disbelief. "Even if that's true, he needs clothes, bedding, and diapers. And you need to get to know each other. What's the matter with you?"

"I can't think of it all!" Sheila yells. "I'm dying, Cynthia, slowly but surely. I'm losing my grip, losing my strength, losing my balance, and my work is all I can think of. I'm a genetic engineer, and I'm running out of time. What use am I if I can't even save myself?" Sheila is hysterical, choking and sobbing. "He's my answer. I can't fall in love with him. It will be too hard for both of us. He must have the genetic code to make me well. All I need to do is check that it's there and then get a spinal sample to use as a catalyst in my own system to kick on the regenerative sequences."

"Okay, okay. Relax. You have to recover. You've just given birth. Rest, sleep, and get your strength back. Next week or the week after will be soon enough for you to go back to work."

Sheila sighs and rolls over, exhausted. She opens her mouth to argue but falls asleep instead.

* * *

The next day, Cynthia doesn't need to work hard to convince Sheila to rest for a week or two at least. Sheila is so exhausted that she can barely feed herself. What's worse is that she can't think. Cynthia notices her forgetting mid-sentence what she is trying to say. When she points it out and assures Sheila that it's normal and nothing to be concerned about, Sheila realizes that it will be difficult to wrap her brain around the intense scientific language of her trade at the moment. Ultimately, they make a deal: Cynthia will cook for her and drop off her meals daily on her way to the hospital. Sheila will get her cleaning company to come in for an hour every day to keep the place livable. All she needs to do is take care of the baby.

Cynthia assigns one of her nurses to spend a day with Sheila to make sure that she understands how to care for a newborn. Sheila sleeps when he sleeps and wakes when he wakes. She eats her meals in bits and pieces, never at one sitting and often lying down. They spend most of their time in the bed together. It is easiest for her. His crib is right next to her bed, within arm's reach. They fall into a rhythm, and desperation loosens its grip on Sheila's heart.

Weeks pass. Sheila finally regains a bit of her strength and manages to get up and about more. She spends a lot of time with her notebook, tracking the boy's progress, making notes and drawings, taking weights, and detailing his intake and sleep schedule. But this account lacks the most important aspect. She needs to get back into the lab and look inside his system, inside his cells, inside his DNA.

One day, she contacts Philip and asks if she can return to work as soon as possible, but he puts her off. Something about hospital policy and "prescribed maternity leave."

"It's a legal issue," he says.

Isn't it always? she thinks as she terminates the disappointing phone call.

More weeks pass, and Sheila is going stir crazy. She asks Cynthia to intervene for her and beg Philip to let her back to work early. Cynthia thinks that with a doctor's dispensation, he can manage it.

Later that day, Cynthia stops by on her way home from work to visit Sheila. Strolling in behind her is Philip, overloaded with brand new stuff piled high in a baby car seat. Sheila is slouched on the couch, the baby splayed across her lap sleeping while she watches a melodramatic judge show.

"Oh, thank God," she says, seeing Cynthia. "I'm so bored." Then she sees Philip and sits up, vainly brushing her hair off her face. "Oh, it's you. What are you doing here?"

He approaches her boldly and leans in to kiss her. She turns away, and he gets her cheek.

"I was so worried about you," he says, masking his frustration at this latest snub. "Anyway, I'm here to invite you back to work. Cynthia said you want to come back right away. Is that true?"

Sheila nods.

"Great, then we'll see you in two weeks."

"No, no," she protests. "I want to come back right away. Tomorrow, I have to …" She's about to say something else and then changes tack mid thought. "These judge dramas and talk shows are making me crazy. I need to get back to work."

Sheila switches the TV off and turns her attention to her guests. Cynthia plops on the couch, and then she and Philip speak simultaneously.

"I still think—"

"Great, nine o—"

"It'll be fine, Cynthia," Sheila says, interrupting them both. "And the nursery at the hospital is terrific. I can see him anytime during the day."

Philip is still standing just inside the door. Sheila points to the bureau, indicating that he can unload his burden there, but she doesn't invite him to sit. He feels uncomfortable and unwelcome, so he heads for the door.

"Congratulations," he says over his shoulder. "He's really cute. What's his name?"

Sheila shrugs. Either she hasn't thought about it or she hasn't decided. Cynthia shakes her head, perplexed by her sister's peculiar disconnect with her infant.

"Why not 'Philip'?" Philip suggests and then laughs.

Sheila doesn't find the joke funny.

He continues on his path to the door but turns at the last minute to issue a final warning. "Oh, and Sheila, the conditions are the same: no unsanctioned experiments and no risks. Don't expose the hospital to any further suits or publicity, okay?"

Sheila nods sheepishly, but Philip notices a troubling gleam of triumph in her eye. "Thanks for the baby stuff!" she calls out as the door closes behind him.

6

A FRUITLESS EXPERIMENT?

We often wonder how people can do what they do, how they justify actions that seem so obviously wrong, destructive, or cruel. Too many times one's mind overrules the heart with complex arguments, statistics, greater-good reasons, or just "it's not that big of a deal" logic. In Sheila's case, none of this is relevant. She is desperate, terrified, and determined to save herself. That's why she can't name her child, just like she could never name the animals on which she experimented. She watched herself carefully, and every time she felt a tiny bit of sympathy, empathy, or even love for any of the big, watery eyes that looked at her with a wistful sadness, she shut down her heart and bolted its door with the same metallic click of finality that every cage lock in the lab had. She wore the armor of scientist with a critical job to do as protection and justification, and actually, appeals to the greater good did factor in quite often as a defense when the armor failed.

Now her armor fails completely, and Sheila winces when she stabs her tiny son to collect blood and spinal fluids. He whimpers and then wails. She strokes his arm clumsily.

"Sorry, so sorry, but I have to do this," she whispers. Then she walks away, even though he is still whimpering. She balances her canes against a lab stool and maneuvers through the lab by leaning on the counters. She clicks a slide into the spectral microscope.

Once again, Sheila is relieved at the remarkable power of the latest technology to track DNA. The scope can see so far into the DNA that it can discern each nucleotide and its order in the sequence. On the huge video screen, immense, colored spirals of DNA writhe around. Beneath it, text reads, "5:05 P.M. – BABY JENSEN – DNA SEQUENCE STUDY." Endless letters, beginning with "ACCT," take over in rows along the bottom as a spotlight tracks along the living DNA spirals. The spotlight changes color as it tracks, matching the color of the letters below—green for *A*, yellow for *G*, red for *T,* and blue for *C.*

Under the video screen, Baby Jensen reaches up, laughing. He sees the blocks of color and dots of light flashing through the moving genetic material. It looks more like a video game than a scientific endeavor. Sheila notices his delight without any emotion. She turns her attention to the clock—5:17 p.m. She has already completed her daily duties and collected the baby from daycare so that she can begin her examination of his DNA. She has been eager for this all week, and the tedium of the day's duties, writing a new grant, were almost unbearable. Now she is doing what she has been waiting to do for too long.

She peers at the smart board screen. A percentage bar clicks toward 25 percent. It is set up to compare Baby Jensen's DNA to the genetic code outlined below and entitled "SCAS 59 REPAIR STRIP – EAGLE PROOF."

A shrill alarm sounds, and the percentage bar disappears. The phrase *incomplete match* pops up in bright red. Frustrated, Sheila rakes her hair with tense fingers.

Colors undulate on the screen. It is now 8:48 p.m. Baby Jensen sleeps. Sheila has nodded off over her computer. A friendly beep wakes her. She catches her breath. The percentage bar climbs: 87 percent, 95, 97… The match to the control escalates. This time it looks like success. Sheila holds her breath. She gasps when the number pops to 98 percent, at 99 percent, she stands up. Then the shrill alarm startles her, and the process shuts down again. *Incomplete match* flashes on the screen.

"No! No!"

Sheila pounds on the computer keyboard, and the video screen dissolves into white snow. Baby Jensen howls.

Sheila looks around for her canes, but they are beside the counter that is farthest away from her and even farther from Baby J. She stumbles toward her baby, gripping the lab counters, stools, and drawer handles. She's almost there when she encounters a six-foot expanse of open floor separating her from her baby. She decides to go for it and lurches toward the wailing child. After two steps, her legs collapse, and she plunges to the floor. Baby Jensen is hysterical. Sheila is too weak to stand, let alone lift him and comfort him. She clambers up, pushes the stroller into the hallway, and then slams the lab door to shut out his cries. But she can still hear him wailing, so she retreats even further to the inside of the refrigerator.

Inside her old sanctuary, Sheila breathes heavily. Sharp tears glittering like ice squeeze from her closed lids. Baby Jensen's wails still filter in, so she clamps her hands over her ears. Then she takes her journal out of her pocket and writes.

"Month 5: I survived. I survived. Day 1, Month 6: Still seeking the regenerative sequence in Baby J."

* * *

Sheila isn't quite as fresh as a daisy as she pushes the stroller into the hospital daycare the next morning. Frustration is wearing her down. She wobbles on her feet, her canes dangling from the stroller's handlebar.

Philip ducks into the nursery behind her. "So, how is the little guy?"

He waits. Sheila ignores him. She's beckoning a caregiver wrangling a toddler. The place is hectic with all the all the rambunctious babies. Toddlers tear around the place, and Sheila is distracted.

Philip pulls a stuffed bear from behind his back and crouches down to jiggle it in front of Baby J's face. Baby Jensen grabs the bear with determination. He locks eyes with Philip. They stare at each other, and the two of them seem to click like they are trapped in an electric current.

Sheila, who has been preoccupied with the nursery melee, notices the peculiar interaction going on right in front of her. She leans forward and tries to take Baby Jensen's hands off the bear. He fights back with surprising strength, so Sheila pries Philip's hands away from the bear instead. She wheels the stroller over to one of the caregivers and talks with her for a moment. Philip stands up, dazed. The caregiver plucks Baby J out of the stroller, and Sheila turns to leave.

Philip catches up with her in the hallway. "What's his name?"

"Jensen," she replies.

"Jensen Jensen?"

"Just Jensen for now," Sheila says, irritated. She walks past Philip toward the door.

"Who's his father?" he calls after her.

She turns and delivers the line she has been rehearsing all year. "This is a modern world, Philip. You know that better than most. We don't need fathers anymore."

She barrels through the door and leaves him standing there, stung.

In the nursery, Baby Jensen flaps his arms about, waving his new acquisition, the bear. He lies on the floor amid a bevy of bright-eyed, rosy-cheeked wrigglers. Philip meanders over. He tosses a casual smile at the nurse, who nods approvingly. Philip examines Baby Jensen's fingers. The baby turns Philip's palms up. He could equally be examining Philip's palms. Baby Jensen gurgles and drools. Philip snatches a tissue from the desk nearby and mops the baby's chin. Then he folds and pockets the tissue. Philip scoops up Baby Jensen. He peers into a mirror comparing his face to the baby's. The baby turns and looks right into Philip's eyes. Philip is transfixed once again. Baby J giggles, and Philip titters. Baby J laughs a bit more heartily, and Philip's laughter escalates as well. Soon, they are both laughing hysterically. Philip is still holding the baby, but he is bent over, compelled by laughter. A caregiver comes over and takes Baby J from Philip. He nods apologetically and then works his way out through the door still laughing.

* * *

Sheila is beginning to lose hope. Every day, through the drudgery of her work supporting other experiments, she tows the line, makes sure she is a good employee, and tries not to make any waves. Every night after hours, she sneaks back into the lab and tries to find the regenerative gene sequence that she is sure is in Baby Jensen's DNA.

On this night, she is pale and drawn. She moves with strained efficiency despite her crippled condition. She spins out a material sample, takes notes, and checks back through her notebooks. She trolls through computer data, listens to the drone of previous memos, and checks and rechecks the sequencing data on the video screen. The lab is her life. She almost forgets her troubles there and certainly feels like less of a cripple.

Suddenly, Philip slams through the door carrying her baby and pushing the stroller. "There you are," he announces accusingly.

"What are you doing with my child?" she demands.

"He stood up this afternoon," he says, a hint of pride in his manner.

"Put him down," is all she can say. She is affronted that Philip has rescued her child and peeved at herself for actually forgetting to go and get him.

"Sheila, do you realize he's too young to stand?"

"Please, put him in the stroller," she says. She doesn't even bother to look up from the computer she is scrutinizing.

"No! You'll forget all about the baby and work all night again. Don't think I don't know that you're in here at all hours, working on who knows what."

He reaches to shut off the computer, but she stops him. "Leave it. It's searching through data. Just give me my baby and go." She looks directly at him, appealing. "Please!"

Philip puts Baby Jensen into the stroller and reaches for her elbow to help her up. "I'll walk you both out."

The colorful streams of data on the video screen end suddenly. Sheila freezes. Philip looks at the blank screen. A text line pops in one letter at a time, interminably, as if time has stopped: "END SEARCH – NO MATCH EXISTS."

Sheila's journal tumbles to the floor, opening to a page scrawled with notes, information, and detailed sketches of the baby. Philip bends down to pick up the book.

"If no match is found, my life is wasted," he reads aloud. He then looks up at her. "What does that mean?"

Her legs give out, and she collapses. Philip catches her.

"I can't do this anymore. I'm done. I've failed. It's all over," she chokes out.

"I knew you were up to something," Philip says, "and I want you to tell me what."

"I'm done," she continues. "It's over, so why bother? It wouldn't be good for you to know anyway, so let's just leave it alone. I won't be coming in tomorrow."

Philip's mind races. For a brilliant man, he is struggling with two and two, emotions and actions, what and why. He thought he knew Sheila better than anyone. She had the drive and determination that he wished he could feel all the time. He respects her, and he still loves her, but he has no idea what's going on. This is a Sheila that he does not know.

Sheila sobs uncontrollably. Philip holds her, and for the first time since that terrible day in court, she releases herself into his arms.

"Don't quit," he says. "You know you'd die if you gave up."

He doesn't really know what he's asking her not to quit. He hopes she will keep working at the lab. He still feels as though his life will be over if she really leaves and he can't at least see her every day.

7

GABRIEL

The next day at the lab, it's lunchtime, but Sheila has done nothing but stare out the window at the park across from the hospital. The lab is silent—no beeps, hums, blinking lights, whirs, whistles, or thrums. Sheila's eyes are blank and unseeing when Cynthia struggles to navigate Baby Jensen's stroller in through the automatically closing lab door. Sheila turns wanly to see whose has interrupted her melancholy.

"Go away," she commands.

The baby stares at Sheila with uncanny interest for a six-month-old.

Cynthia is exasperated. "Thank God I go down to visit this child every day, because today I found out that you haven't been there all week except to pick him up and drop him off."

"I've had no time for that," Sheila responds as she turns to look out the window again.

Vexed, Cynthia looks around. "I don't see much going on here." She swipes a mess—probably a few days' worth of lunch and coffee debris—into the trashcan.

Sheila starts speaking as if to the wall. "He was supposed to be my miracle cure," she says in a way that is wrung of all hope.

Cynthia won't have it. She has no patience for this self-indulgent person who she has never seen before. "You are all wrong. He is the miracle!"

"But I made him so that he could reactivate regenerative genes, and I've failed."

Cynthia's eyes begin to water. It's too much for her to see this child starving for attention and his mother blind to his needs. "Yes you have. You've failed to love him, to see him, to acknowledge him. Open your heart, Sheila. Love him. You haven't even named him yet."

Sheila looks at her with a cold and stark frankness in her eyes. "Why bother? I lied to you. My prognosis is bad. I mean terminal. I'll be gone within months." Sheila looks at the child, and for the first time, a tear for him seeps between her lids.

Cynthia blanches. The room is ghostly silent. They have fallen into a hole in time. A crow squawks as it glides past the window outside. Cynthia's eyes follow its trajectory down and onto a path in the park. She grabs Sheila's sweater and forces her arms into it.

"Let's get some air."

She wraps up Baby Jensen, hands Sheila her canes, and pushes the stroller toward the door.

The early spring day does nothing to brighten Sheila's mood. Cynthia plunks her onto a sun-dappled park bench. She puts the brakes on Baby Jensen's stroller right in front of Sheila.

"Hot dog?" Cynthia asks turning to walk away.

"It'll kill you," Sheila responds.

Cynthia tosses back a casual, "Who cares?"

Pigeons flutter across the path. They converge around a mother and child who are sitting across from Sheila casting breadcrumbs into the hungry throng. Baby Jensen's tiny hand stretches toward a spooked pigeon that flutters up and grazes his stroller. Sheila slumps into the park bench and wraps her scarf tightly around her neck with a shiver. She watches her baby. His laughter bubbles up when the pigeon circles around once more, seemingly interested in the delighted baby. It flies so close to Baby J's head that his outstretched hand almost touches it. Suddenly, Baby J shimmers.

Sheila rubs her eyes, confused. Blinking, she looks at him again. Baby J seems to shine, and then he literally floats out of his stroller. He giggles, flaps his arms, and rolls over, flying like a light-formed cherub.

Sheila sits bolt upright, her attention riveted on her baby. Then she too begins to levitate, actually lifting seven inches above the park bench but unaware of it. Baby J giggles, and tiny, cherub-like wings made of light flutter from his shoulders. He swoops over the feeding pigeons. The mother is unaware of him, but the child is ecstatic, pointing, jumping up and down totally delighted, and trying to grab Baby J as he careens around. Sheila sways toward him in response to his movements.

A pale, stern, and oblivious young woman in a dark suit marches by, her black shoes clacking. Her somber scarf trails across Baby J's cherub butt. The woman's cheeks flush immediately and her brisk pace slows. She looks around with a kind of wonder and surprise in her eyes, but she doesn't see the baby, even though he is right in front of her.

Stan, a homeless man slouched on a bench opposite and farther down the path, stares. He tugs lanky strings of hair off his eyes and stands up. Then he slinks toward Sheila, a brown-bagged bottle dangling from his hand.

"You okay, lady?"

Sheila breaks her gaze on Baby Jensen and looks at Stan. She plops down onto her bench with a grunt, and her eyes pop wide open in surprise. Startled, she blinks at him.

"W-What?" Stan stutters, unsure and probably used to seeing or thinking he sees odd things. "I … I thought you were …" He waves his hand vaguely, lifting it up and down as if some motion will bring coherent words, then, frustrated, he offers her the grubby bag. "Hmm … have a drink."

Sheila's magical child flies right between the two of them. They both turn to watch as he swoops behind the flock of pigeons. Then he circles back through the rainbow-lit shower of water in the park fountain. The fine spray and glittering sunlight halo the event, and the imposing stone angel featured in the center of the scene seems to shimmer, soften, and move as if alive. Sheila and Stan are transfixed by the bobbing cherub baby circling around the massive statue that welcomes his antics. The statue and the flying child seem to waver in resolution, becoming clear like the fountain water. At one moment, the baby's wings are defined. The next moment they are part of the fountain's tinkling spray. Then the child's aerial form pours back into the stroller, where the solid form of Baby J lies snuggling and cooing happily. Stan and Sheila stare at the baby carriage, stunned. Finally, Stan breaks the silence.

"Hell! Doll, you don't need this, 'cause you're flying already. And I don't need it, 'cause I'm seeing things." He pitches the bottle under her park bench and stumbles off.

Sheila stands up and, with surprising ease, lifts her baby. She yanks at his clothing, pulling the onesie off his shoulders and lifting the T-shirt underneath. She pokes all over his nude back.

Cynthia drops two white lunch bags on the bench. "Here, we go," she says, and then she sees Sheila poking at the baby. "What are you doing? Here let me ..." She pulls the tiny shirt down over his bare back and tucks the sleeves of his onesie back over his shoulders. Surprised, she gives Sheila an accusing look. "Sheila, it's wet!"

Sheila is in shock, completely unable to process what she just saw, or thinks she saw. She looks around for Stan, thinking a witness might help her make sense of the event, but he is long gone.

"He ... he ... I saw ..." Sheila stares at the water fountain as if the answer might be there. Her eyes land on the statue of the grand angel at the center of the fountain. "I want to name him after that statue. Do you know who that is?"

Cynthia wanders over to look at the plaque and reads it. "It's the archangel Gabriel. That's an excellent name, Sheila. See? I knew you needed to get outside. This is a great step forward." She leans over into the stroller and strokes her hand over Gabriel's head. "Hello, Gabriel. What a huge name you have to fill."

Gabriel's infant hand bats hers playfully.

* * *

As they stroll out of the park, Gabriel's arms are still flailing, grabbing joyfully at the world around him. Sheila can't take her eyes off him. She is seeing things differently somehow. Around Gabriel, she sees a world of color, motion, connection, and vibrancy. She is unaware that for a moment she is seeing the world as her son Gabriel sees it. Swirls of energy infuse him, his mother, and his aunt. He sees a tangible life-force connection flowing between the three of them in great circles of color and light. The same rivers of energy pour between them and into the rest of their immediate world, intersecting with the pigeons, the trees, the clouds, and other people.

As they move to the edge of the park, they pass the stern young woman who has surprised herself and taken a precious moment to sit on a park bench and enjoy the bright afternoon. It isn't surprising that the colorful swirls of life swim around her as well, making her dark suit sparkle with glints of color.

Gabriel's hand brushes across a branch laden with early spring buds.

Almost as if his fingers can see inside the cells of the plant like Cynthia's remarkable 3-D sonar-laser scope or Sheila's powerful microscope, the inside of the plant is revealed. Liquids pulsate with life, following ever-shrinking versions of those mesmerizing energy patterns. Sap flows to the miniature spring buds. A vibrant cell looms large, and inside, the nucleus pulses with activity. DNA strands zipper undone, flowing beautifully in harmony with the boiling matrices of light. Cells duplicate, and flowery fabric stretches, following the inexorable influence of formerly unseen forces.

The branch goes back to normal size while the fountain angel stands in the background. The tip of the branch blossoms, and the blooms flutter away like snow. Bright-green leaves pop into being and mature against a rapidly shifting skyscape. The pitch and roll of time—of things growing, changing, and moving—reflects the secret flow of energy that only Gabriel can see. Figures of pedestrians flash past at lightning speed, blurring into sweeps and coils. Green leaves turn to red, gold, and brown, and then, like the petals, they whirl in spirals to the ground and then catch air again and write complex strokes of unfathomable words in the air. Time slows, and sparkling ice coats a bare branch, refracting sunlight. Snow melts from the Gabriel statue. Another fresh bud on the original branch bursts into spring blossom, and a small hand snatches it.

8

PLAY WITH ME

The first year and a half of Gabriel's life has flashed by, or so it seems to Sheila. In that time, she has come to terms with her failure and given up completely on the search for regenerative genomes. She has settled into the job, for that's all that it is now. She can't think of what she is doing as a career anymore. It has been difficult raising an infant in her condition, but thankfully she has not deteriorated any further, which is welcome though surprising.

Cynthia is a huge help. Sheila and Gabriel eat most evening meals with her family. Cynthia's kids love Gabriel and treat him like their little brother, and he adores them.

Philip comes by regularly, "as a friend," as he says often. Sheila wonders why he has no other friends to hang out with—friends without babies. But Philip is very sweet with Gabriel, and Gabriel seems to adore him, too, especially when they share a hot chocolate and a cookie, which has become their nighttime routine before Philip leaves. It is a peculiar dynamic, but somehow it works.

Every day, wind, rain, sun, or shine, Sheila spends a bit of time in the park with Gabriel. Sometimes it's just a walk, and sometimes they have a picnic lunch there. It has become a tradition, their special time together.

On one of their park visits, Sheila sits on her bench while eighteen-month-old Gabriel giggles and chases the pigeons. The birds circle him rather than flutter away. Gabriel toddles over to a newborn in a stroller and strokes the baby's head. The smiling mother is familiar. Sheila watches her, perplexed, as some strange memory tugs at her. Then she realizes she is the stern woman with the scarf that trailed across Gabriel's flying cherub butt. The woman is much softer now and obviously happy. Sheila turns away, she feels like an intruder and is disturbed that she has remembered that strange day. It is a day that presented data that she is still unable to process. She had the hardest time writing about it in her journal and ended up ripping pages out and starting again. The torn pages are now taped back into her notebook in the hope that the data she was unable to process then might become clear later.

Sheila turns to her journal and concentrates on the colorful data in her palm device. She jots notes in her book. It's almost full with daily data on her son's progress.

Gabriel hugs Sheila's legs, interrupting her focus. He smiles up at her and then turns and runs away. He stops at a distance and yells back. "Momma! Momma! Chase me."

Sheila can't, and he knows that. He may be a toddler, but he knows she can't run after him.

"Gabe, come back here."

"Chase me!" he yells as he circles toward her and away again.

Sheila struggles to stand up. She leans into her canes and limps toward Gabriel. "Gabriel, you know I can't run. Get over here right now."

Gabriel's eyes twinkle mischievously, and then he runs off.

Sheila panics. "Gabriel!" she cries, her voice cracking. She looks around desperately. Gabriel has disappeared behind the fountain.

On the far side, a painter is working at his easel. Chuckling, the man scoops up the boisterous child and waves to Sheila. She gulps, concerned.

Gabriel knows the painter. It's Stan, the formerly homeless man. He swings Gabriel around and grins with delight while Gabriel giggles. On Stan's easel is a rough but moving rendition of the angel statue taking flight. He points it out to Gabriel.

"That's you, isn't it, little one?"

"It's you," Gabriel responds, not missing a beat.

Sheila waves frantically at Stan, directing him to bring Gabriel back. He lifts Gabriel onto his shoulders and strolls toward her.

"Your mom worries," he mutters along the way. "Don't fly away from her like that."

Gabriel laughs and ruffles Stan's longish hair with both hands. "I was running, silly, not flying."

Sheila waits anxiously by the stroller. "Thank you. Would you mind putting him in the stroller?"

Tickling Gabriel, Stan tucks him in. Then he bounces away, making faces for Gabriel's delight.

Sheila leans in to secure the stroller straps around Gabriel. "Run away from me again, and there will be no more park! Do you understand?"

"I want you to run with me, Momma."

Sheila's face darkens. "I can't, sweetie."

Gabriel leans forward and rubs Sheila's legs. He smiles, and his tiny hands clutch his mother's knees. His hands and Sheila's legs waver like heat waves over hot asphalt as strands of energy swirl between them. Gabriel can see it clearly. Sheila frowns. A puzzled expression creases her lips, and she brushes his hands away from her knees like she has been burned. She looks at his palm. There are hot, red circles of light or heat wavering at the center of them. Sheila strokes the red part. Then she takes out her phone and snaps a shot of the abnormal phenomenon, which is fading quickly.

Gabriel peers at her with his deep eyes. "You have to run before you can fly, Momma."

Sheila looks at him, perplexed, as if he is speaking a foreign language. Then she shakes herself free of confusion.

"Time to go home."

* * *

Gabriel grows quickly, and Sheila exerts herself beyond her means to keep up with him. Even with Cynthia's daily help, she feels run ragged. She never cooks. Either they eat at Cynthia's or they have takeout or a frozen pizza. Cynthia makes sure the house is clean and the laundry done by arranging for her cleaning team to take care of Sheila's house after hers.

Gabriel loves cleaning day and is both helpful and troublesome to the team. Though the cleaning pros are determined to whiz through the house and get everything done in record time, they can't help but stop and play with him for a few minutes now and then. Gabriel also loves the weekends, when they spend most of their time with Cynthia and her family. Cynthia's children keep Gabriel occupied, and they always do something fun like go to the zoo, go to the beach, go on a picnic, or play mini golf. Gabriel is interested in everything and asks endless questions. He demands that he be shown everything so that he can examine it in detail, and he loves to interact with animals.

Philip manages to insert himself into the schedule and shows up regularly, usually unannounced, when they are out for a day trip. Sheila knows that Cynthia tells Philip where they will be, but she lets it go, because it's clear Gabriel and Philip have a natural affinity. They enjoy each other's company, so she decides it's harmless enough to let Philip join in.

After dinner one night, Sheila sits exhausted at the desk in her kitchen reviewing her records. She does the same thing every night, but usually she doesn't have energy to go through more than just logging the day's events. Though tired, she is inspired to review all of her notebooks. She ruffles through the first one, which is completely full. The first few pages are filled with multiple scientific and diagnostic notes and data. Whole pages of questions and theories are interspersed throughout the data. Occasional clinical photos of the subject, then named Baby Jensen, lack any element of warmth. In the images, he lies naked and still, obviously asleep, on a clinical-looking counter. It is actually Sheila's kitchen, which could double as a lab. Pages are dedicated to his front, back, and side views. Copious measurements surround the rare photos. The two birthmarks appear as blown-up details with a notation beside them: "Red birth marks located center back—medial to and below the scapula."

Sheila peruses the book with a frown, pondering the information. She remembers the pain of her cure eluding her. Her scientific method was not working, her actions refusing to yield results, and Gabriel was an enigma to her, as he still is. But for the first time, she is struck by the coldness of the data. The imagery is clinical in presentation, her notes detached and studious.

A tear forms in her eye and drips onto a photo of Gabriel's back. She wipes it dry and tucks a thick rubber band around the first notebook to keep the loose papers together, and then she sets it aside.

The other two books are also puffed up, every page stuffed with notes, medical reports, photos, drawings, and printouts. Test results are taped inside and spilling out. The edges of pictures stick out of the sides. These are not baby albums; they are a remarkably artistic and scientific record. It is peculiar that in this day of amazing technology, Sheila prefers to keep her documents in books. She has always made these books, but previously she backed up the information on computer. Now she only makes the books. After the cyber-hacking that exposed her dream for human gene modification and wrecked her career, she is much more careful with her notes.

She flips through the second book and stops at a particular page to review it. The page reminds her of an incident when Gabriel helped a wailing baby to stand up. The baby was only slightly younger than him and seemed frustrated, stuck on her butt. Once standing, the tiny girl stopped crying and stroked Gabriel's face. They giggled together. Sheila snapped a shot of the interaction on her phone. The printed picture is secured on the page opposite her notes. She smiles as she looks at it.

Next to a page of charts, calculations, and medical notes, Sheila had written, "He seems to have an alternate way of communicating. Despite Gabriel's size, the baby stopped crying the moment he touched her." She unfolds a bent corner of the print showing the babies together. Beneath it is a brief note: "A baby lifting up a baby." In this book, her notes are sliding into a field with which she is completely unfamiliar. Feelings, actions, and behaviors are nothing to a geneticist. She realizes that she is at sea. Her expertise is in the microscopic effects on the macroscopic form only. Behavior has never come up before. But something compels her to make these notes about his interactions, even though she is very uncomfortable with it.

Another page recounts an event Sheila witnessed in the daycare room. The place was hectic, with kids and caregivers running around, but two-and-a-half-year-old Gabriel was the calm at the center of a storm. He was intent on the cage of parakeets, hugging it. The parakeets convened right near his face and bounced around excitedly. "Birds? Birds?" she had written. "He has a strange affinity with birds. There was that incident with a pigeon when he was only months old. I still can't figure out what happened there." A close-up shot of Gabriel's wonder-filled face seen through the parakeet cage shows a yellow flutter of birds forming a halo around him.

Another page recounts an event at the mall food court. Gabriel was chasing huge bubbles that a young woman was making with a string hoop. An immense bubble landed on Gabriel's outstretched palm. Other kids were tearing across the plaza after a slew of bubbles, but he just stood stock-still, focused on the impossible prize. Sheila timed it. He stood there for a minute watching the massive bubble's swirling colors shimmy before him. A crowd gathered, with those in the front making sure that no one inadvertently walked into him and popped the bubble. When it finally popped for no apparent reason, a roar of approval rose from Gabriel's audience, and the tears that were forming because of the lost prize cleared up instantly in the huge grin he presented to his "fans." A photo of Gabriel with the bubble in his hand appeared in a local paper. Sheila's ripped-out copy is taped in the book with a huge question mark beneath it.

The next notebook makes her smile broadly. It is far from full, but at first glance it's already more colorful. To begin with, it's obvious Gabriel has gotten his hands on it. The cover is scribbled all over in multicolored swirls of crayon. Sheila turns to the first few pages, which feature more pictures of Gabriel. It looks more like a baby album than a lab journal. The clinical photos of measurements and physical changes are more playful. Gabriel is awake, grinning, his blue eyes sparkling and his arms clearly flailing even though the shot is still. Sheila's handwriting is a bit freer and often written in a colorful crayon that happened to be handy when she needed an implement. It includes notes like "I'm so proud of him. He can tie his shoes. This is a definite sign that he has advanced capabilities." Her comments show a shift in Sheila's perspective.

Nearing the last page of entries, a handwritten axiom, scribed artistically in multiple colors, reads, "PLAY WITH ME, MOMMA. I KNOW YOU." For only three years old, Gabriel is unusually competent with both writing and speaking. He says things that hint at a deep understanding, and it surprises her.

She looks over to where Gabriel sits on the kitchen floor with Philip. They are building something with Lego blocks. Behind them is the refrigerator with the same "PLAY WITH ME" aphorism laced between alphabets of colorful magnetic letters. Sheila closes her notebook, stuffs the notebooks into a drawer, and eases herself onto the floor to play with Gabriel and Philip.

Gabriel jumps up and throws his arms around her neck to kiss her. "It's a helicopter, Momma. Make it look right, please."

She digs into the box of pieces and comes up with a big flat piece.

"No, no, Momma, it has skinny wings."

"I know, Gabe. I'm making his landing pad. He has to have a safe place to land, right?"

"Oh, right, Momma. What a good idea."

Together, the three of them complete the helicopter, and when it's done, Gabriel flies it upstairs to his bedroom.

Philip follows him. "I'll do it," he says.

"No, no, that's okay. I will," she says, heading toward the stairs. "Wait for me, Gabriel."

She works her way with her two canes to the minuscule, retrofitted elevator in her hallway, but by the time she clambers out of it on the second floor and into Gabriel's room, Philip is pulling off Gabriel's shirt. Sheila practically throws herself toward them.

"Stop!" she cries a bit too loud.

Gabriel and Philip look at her in alarm.

"I'll do it," she insists.

"Okay, I'll wait downstairs then," Philip says.

"I think I'm going to lie down afterwards," Sheila says. "Thank you, Philip. You might as well go."

Philip is a bit taken aback, but he nods in agreement. "Okay. See you tomorrow then."

He clumps down the stairs, banging his way to the front door, angry at being dismissed. Then, at the bottom, he has a thought. He turns back toward the stairs. "I'll lock up on my way out."

Sheila's distracted, muffled voice wafts down the stairs. "Thanks."

Philip opens the front door and then closes it again with a loud thump and a resolute click, but he is still inside the hall. He listens as Sheila turns on the bath faucet and the sound of water gurgling through the old pipes comes through the walls. Gabriel sings a nursery rhyme, and Sheila joins in.

Philip sneaks back into the kitchen and goes straight for the drawer with Sheila's journals inside. It creaks at first tug, causing him to look up in alarm, but then he manages to open it all the way, revealing her precious records. He pulls out the pile, takes a seat on a counter stool, and rummages through the first book. He flips through the pages and inserts until he comes to a page of photos. He studies a picture of Gabriel's face and hands and then stops, perplexed, when he sees the printout of Gabriel's back and the peculiar red birthmarks. Philip takes out his phone and photographs the images.

Suddenly, he hears Sheila on the move, her canes clomping across the wooden bedroom floor.

"And can I have a cookie please, Momma?" Gabriel asks. "It helps me sleep, too."

"No, honey, too much sugar. Hot chocolate is enough."

Sheila is on her way downstairs. Philip stuffs the books back into the drawer and heads for the front hall. He ducks out of sight while Sheila works her way across the upper landing and into her elevator. Then, while she is stuck inside the cramped contraption on her way down, he sneaks out of the front door, closing it silently.

9

LUMINOUS PRODIGY

A few weeks later, Gabriel stands on the kitchen counter peering into the microwave oven. It dings. He pulls out two steaming pancakes, his hands buried in two oversized hot mitts that come all the way past his elbows.

Moments later, he bends over the coffee machine and makes an individual cup for his mom. It gurgles and spits as the cup fills to the top, and then he pours some out into the sink so it's only half full. Then he scurries across the kitchen counter until he is next to the refrigerator and tries to push the door open from the edge. It's sealed tight. He pushes again and is in danger of falling off the counter, but then the door gives and eases open. He reaches into the door pocket, grabs a butter dish, and puts it on the counter. Next he goes for the jam. He has to lean out to reach around and grab it from the middle shelf. It's a round, fat jar; yet somehow, his small hand suctions to the side of the jar, and he lifts it out. He maneuvers the jam to the counter and onto the tray with the pancakes, butter, and coffee. Finally, he reaches on tiptoe to grab a glass from a shelf over the counter. Then he manages to get the orange juice container out of the fridge door and, with two hands, pours a glass of juice.

He is so eager to grow up to be a big man and help his mom—a bit too eager. The juice spills out of the glass, pools around his feet, and then cascades to the floor. He's so tiny, but he seems to have it all together. He knows exactly what he is doing and why. He thinks it through and sees the end goal; he can't be bothered to get upset like a normal child might. He unrolls a torrent of paper towels from the dispenser next to the fridge and stomps the fluffy mass into the pool of juice until a matted carpet is stuck to the counter. It is clear that he is developing in interesting ways and has learned how to cope beyond his age. He pours half the juice off from the glass making it manageable like the coffee.

He works his way off the counter—counter to table, table to chair, chair to floor. At each step, he shifts his precious present—a breakfast tray for his mom—to a lower level until he can grab it from the chair and trot to the elevator with his burden.

* * *

Sheila snoozes in bed. Her alarm rings, and then her bedroom door opens and light streams in from the hallway. Gabriel's minute figure is silhouetted against the opening. He toddles over the fluffy carpet and, with supreme effort, slides the beautiful breakfast tray onto the bed for Sheila. The addition of a small stuffed polar bear makes the tray even more appealing.

Sheila awakens groggily and wonders at first what she is looking at. Then her face clouds with concern. She looks at Gabriel. "Did you turn the oven on?"

"I watch you, Momma," Gabriel says. "I did exactly as you do."

Sheila sits up straight. "Honey, it's hot!"

"It's okay, Momma. Look, I did it for you, just how you like them."

Sheila accepts his gift resignedly but decides to think more about the implications of this kind of behavior after breakfast. She cuts the pancake and shares it with Gabriel, who also insists on tasting her coffee. Since she knows now that he can make it himself, she lets him have a sip, which he spits out right away.

* * *

Later that week, Sheila arrives at school early to pick up Gabriel. She's just in time to watch him doing one of his favorite things: drawing. The daycare teacher, Noreen, had called her to come and see Gabriel work. Noreen is quite enchanted and can't stop raving about his talent.

Sheila leans over to look at Gabriel's drawing. He claims to be painting Noreen, and he peers at her while he splashes color on the page. The loose blobs of yellow, pink, and white, vaguely, but in a charmingly naive way, resemble a human form under a yellow waterfall. Eddies of blue, green, and red are placed strategically but don't look at all like Noreen's clothing, which is a dull sage.

Sheila bends down painfully and inserts herself in a toddler's chair next to Gabriel. He continues to look up at Noreen as he paints.

"Is that what you see, Gabe?" Sheila asks as she moves her face next to his, seeking exactly the same point of view.

"Yes, Momma," he answers, glancing at her with his piercing blue eyes.

Sheila looks at Noreen again. The plain and unremarkable woman is luminous suddenly with blue light streaming from her head and red light gushing from her hands. Great quantities of a bright yellow light fall or spew from her shoulders, and every color swirls in an aura of rainbow threads. The light seems to be moving, churning, but Sheila can't tell which way it's going or if it just moves in an oscillating loop. She's entranced. For a moment, her mind stops, and her heart flutters with a strange sense of fullness. Then her eyes drift to Gabriel's hands working diligently over the rough but accurate rendition of yellow, blue, green, and red light that she just saw. She blinks, perplexed. Then her mind clicks in, and she begins to worry about what the heck is going on. Is it him or her or Noreen?

Sheila snatches the sketch from under Gabriel's busy fingers and rolls it up. "It's lovely," she says dismissively.

"But, but …" Gabriel protests.

"It's time to go home, Gabriel." She signals to Noreen to get his coat on.

On the way out of the door, Gabriel begs Noreen to let him paint again the following day.

"Of course, Mr. Picasso," she replies.

Gabriel giggles.

10

BILL

By the time Gabriel is almost four, his interest in a nest of crows peaks almost to obsession. The nest is in the crook of a branch high up in a large oak at the bottom of the front garden, and it is clearly visible from Gabriel's bedroom window. Gabriel commandeers Sheila's binoculars, and several times a day, he waits patiently to get a peek of a tiny head or two over the edge of the nest. This gets easier as the birds grow, and soon he can see them jockeying around for space in their tight abode.

"Will they fly today, Momma?" he asks Sheila every day.

"Maybe," is her constant reply.

Then Sheila awakens one morning to a strange scrabbling noise outside the bedroom door on her tiny deck overlooking the garden. The deck is big enough for a small chair and table and enclosed in a solid wall of wood. She opens the curtain and sees an almost full-grown crow walking up and down in the small space. She steps outside, and the young, shiny, black creature looks up at her with his piercing black eyes and squawks. He walks straight up to her, chatting loudly. It is clear that he wants her to feed him. She laughs.

Just then, Gabriel runs out onto the deck. "Oh, oh, oh, look, look, Momma! It's one of them. Did he fly here?"

"He must have," she responds. "Wait!" She reaches out to grab Gabriel's arm as he slips past her toward the crow.

"Hello, hello, I'm Gabriel," he says excitedly, fully expecting the bird to understand him.

The bold, little character walks right up to Gabriel and squawks brazenly. Gabriel holds his hands out, and the crow hops into his palms, comfortable and at home. Gabriel plops down on the deck floor with the crow in his lap and talks to it in a soft, mewing voice. The crow seems surprisingly attentive.

Sheila allows Gabriel to sit with the crow for over an hour until she insists that he come in for breakfast. Gabriel begs her to give him something to feed the crow, but Sheila is concerned about the crow being abandoned by its parents. She has been surfing the Internet, trying to figure out what to do with this fledgling. She hopes its parents are watching and will come back, so she won't let Gabriel feed the noisy beggar. Gabriel protests, but they leave him on the deck and head off for the day, Sheila to work and Gabriel to school. Gabriel is furious. He begs and begs to stay home, but Sheila refuses.

"His parents will find him there. They will feed him and teach him to fly, so stop fussing."

Gabriel pouts all the way to school.

When they return home in the late afternoon, the small creature is still on the deck, shivering in the pouring rain. He looks utterly pathetic, huddled in a corner near the house with his shoulders hunched, head down, and water streaming off his back, wings, and beak. A torrent of water streams around his feet and swirls toward the drain nearby.

Sheila tries to explain that the bird is used to the rain. "The nest doesn't have a roof," she argues, but Gabriel won't have it. Soon, they are rigging up a large umbrella from the table in the backyard to give their ebony guest some relief from the downpour. Sheila picks the crow up and perches him on the back of the chair, where they have secured the umbrella. He's delighted and flutters his wings violently, sending a drenching spray of water over the two of them. Gabriel laughs with delight, and the crow, realizing he has their attention, resumes his begging yaps.

"Can we please feed him now?" Gabriel begs. "His momma hasn't been here, and he's all alone now."

Sheila glances at the nest above them. There is no sign of the parents or the other juveniles. She and Gabriel had guessed that maybe three infants had been in the nest, but now there's no sign of any. Perhaps this little one was abandoned.

The next morning, Sheila relents and agrees that the crow must be starving. After more research on the computer, they conclude that some of Gabriel's cooked oatmeal would be good for him. Sheila surmises that the mushy stuff might resemble the regurgitated food his parents would have fed him.

The crow has been squawking wildly at them and throwing his head back, mouth wide open, every time they come near him. It is obvious what he wants. Sheila marvels at the ability of one creature, a crow, so completely different from another, herself, to communicate with absolute clarity. She and Gabriel laugh hysterically when the bird swallows the oatmeal. Gabriel puts it on his finger and then stuffs his finger into the bird's mouth. The crow squawks and gurgles, eating and begging at the same time.

Their new friend, whom Gabriel has named Bill, enthralls them both. They feed him and watch him for days as he hops and gains skill with his wings.

Then one day, determined to fly, Bill gathers his courage and launches from the back of the chair into the front garden. Gabriel wields Sheila's smartphone and catches a video of the flight. Bill flaps sloppily, cries like a baby, gets some air, and bumps into things. He scrabbles up the sloped garage roof next to Gabriel's bedroom window and slides down backwards, his feet pumping to find some perch and deliver him further up the roof. It seems like he is having fun. Finally, from the peak of the roof, he launches with his wings wide and soars. He swoops out over their front yard and toward a neighbor's house. In an obvious panic, he looks for a place to perch and goes straight for a black stripe beneath the second floor window, but there's no ledge there. He bumps the wall, flips over, and tumbles down to the lawn below, yelping all the way. Gabriel cries out. Bill bounces on the lawn, rights himself, shakes his wings, and starts flapping again, this time gaining altitude gradually.

Gabriel is ecstatic. "He did it! He did it! Did you see it, Momma? He just learned how to fly. I wish I could fly, Momma."

Sheila kisses him on his forehead. "Humans don't fly, baby. I'm sorry."

For the next few weeks, the adorable Bill captures almost all of the attention of mother and son. He's funny, stealing food and looking guilty when they yell at him. He perches on Gabriel's shoulder, flapping his wings and tickling Gabriel's ears until he laughs, and then the bird takes off. Gabriel still worries about Bill's lost parents, and each day, they put different kinds of food on a tray in the backyard in the hope they will return. When Bill isn't at any of the garden feeders picking out the best pieces, a vast array of other birds stops by for the feast.

Sheila is torn. She doesn't want Bill to be a pet, and after a time, she insists that they leave him outside at night. Angry, Gabriel perches Bill on the back of the chair on his mother's bedroom deck and insists that the umbrella stay there at least to keep him dry if it rains. Every morning, Bill waits there to come in and share Gabriel's breakfast. Secretly, Sheila is relieved. She doesn't know how Gabriel will react when the bird finally does fly the Jensen coop.

Gabriel comes up with the idea that he should take Bill to school and show him to the other kids. After all, they have the yellow parakeets in a cage there. Maybe he can live with them.

"No!" Sheila says, adamant. "Bill is a wild bird. He needs to live free, to fly anywhere he wants and to go and be with other wild birds. He can't live in a cage."

"Is he going to go away?" Gabriel whimpers.

"Yes," Sheila replies firmly, knowing that this is upsetting but recognizing that it's necessary for him to understand it and move on.

"When?" Gabriel asks, tears streaming down his cheeks.

Sheila pulls him to her and squeezes him. "I don't know, love, but it will be okay. Listen, maybe your friends can meet Bill at your birthday party."

* * *

They celebrate Gabriel's fourth birthday in the park across from the hospital. Cynthia, Mike, their kids, Noreen, and a few of Gabriel's school friends are there.

Gabriel zooms through the air on a swing, lying on his tummy. Philip pushes the swing and runs up and down beneath it, spotting Gabriel. The two laugh hysterically. Sheila watches them from a nearby picnic table strewn with used paper plates, cups, half-eaten cupcakes, and pizza. The crow, now a family fixture, browses on his own cupcake on the table but isn't shy about stealing from other cupcakes too. Kids run around the table with blue cupcake icing on their lips, chins, and shirts.

Sheila feels sad that she is not the one pushing Gabriel and running up and down. For the first time, she finds herself thinking about how things might have been if she had married Philip.

Her reverie is broken by a clatter and a squeal when Mikey, chased by her brother, dashes past and knocks Sheila's two canes over. Bill takes flight, squawking hysterically. Sheila watches the canes scatter noisily across the park path like so many dashed hopes. In her suddenly indulgent mind, she ticks off her painful losses—a successful career, marriage to Philip, and her engineered miracle cure. She shakes off the unwelcome mood and thanks both kids when they return the canes to her apologetically. At least her health has been stable, she has after all shot past the three-year life expectancy her doctor predicted, and she doesn't need a wheelchair—yet.

Cynthia notices Sheila's morose expression and moves close to kiss her on the cheek. "Buck up. It's a happy day," she reminds her. Sheila forces a thin smile.

Suddenly, Gabriel is wailing. Sheila struggles to stand, fearing that he has fallen off the swing, but apparently he hasn't. She sees Philip extract Gabriel from the swing and hold him tight to his chest. Gabriel wails, struggles to get away, and waves his arms around.

"What happened?" Sheila asks.

"I don't know," Philip responds.

"Bill! Bill! Where's Bill?" Gabriel wails.

They all look around, peering into the trees. A chorus of kids voices shout, "Bill! Bill!" But the bird is gone.

Shortly afterwards, the party breaks up, and the only people remaining are Sheila, Cynthia, Philip, and Gabriel. Gabriel, red-faced and sniffling is adamant. "But he doesn't know where he is. How will he get home?"

Sheila tries to reason with him. "It had to happen, sweetie. He's a wild bird. I told you so."

"Maybe he'll come back, or maybe you'll find him at home," Cynthia suggests.

Sheila glares at her with a "that's not helpful" look in her eye.

Gabriel perks up, hopeful. "Really?"

"Come on, let's go home and see," Philip says.

Sheila grunts a stifled curse. She's certain that both of them are making it harder for Gabriel. Without another word, they pack up and go.

* * *

The next day, Gabriel is at school. It is a madhouse. The yellow parakeets fly freely all over the room. Kids chase each other, screaming and jumping and snatching at the birds. A little girl is crying. The teachers flap about trying to calm down the mayhem, but they only seem to succeed in making it worse. Gabriel is intent on disarming a chubby, snarling boy. The boy, Chuck, wields a big stick like a sword, swinging it wildly at the birds. Gabriel tackles Chuck to the floor, and they tumble and roll together in a fury.

Sheila bursts into the room and stops short, searching the room for her son. Her heart beats franticly, and then she notices Noreen untangling the scrapping boys.

"Gabe?" Sheila yells, a bit too loudly. He looks up, disembroils himself from Noreen and Chuck, and trots over to hug his mother, tears streaming down his face.

Sheila comforts him and listens attentively to his side of the story, which comes out between sobs, whines, and accusative pointing at Chuck, who growls like a dog.

Noreen drags Chuck by the arm to a time-out corner surrounded by bookshelves. When Chuck finally surrenders and slumps into a sulk, Noreen strides over to Sheila and Gabriel with stern disappointment on her face.

"Gabriel opened the parakeet cage today," she announces. "He wants to let them all go free."

"But they need to go. They can't be happy in there," he whimpers.

"Something is up with him," Noreen says. "He's irritable, combative, and generally not the cheery Gabriel we're used to. I think he can't get over Bill flying away."

"I'll take him home to rest." Sheila reaches for her son's jacket. Over his protests, she bundles Gabriel up and hurries him out the door.

* * *

Once home, Sheila prepares Gabriel a hot chocolate and some cookies. He sits sullenly at the kitchen window staring into the garden, probably looking for Bill. It is a rare mood for him, and Sheila doesn't quite know what to do about it. She tries to cheer him up by pulling out his favorite video game, but he isn't the least bit interested. They snuggle together after dinner to watch *Stuart Little*. When Gabriel starts to doze off, Sheila realizes that she had better get him to bed. She can't carry him, so he has to get himself up the stairs.

While Gabriel pulls off his clothes, Sheila rummages through his drawers to find pajamas. When she turns him around, she is surprised to see the two birthmarks on his back inflamed and red. Tickling and playing with him, she pushes him onto his tummy on top of his Spiderman sheets and rubs a salve into the red skin between his shoulders. Gabriel giggles contentedly and starts singing his favorite bedtime song from Billy Joel.

"Goodnight, my angel. Time to close your eyes and save these questions for another day."

Sheila joins in. "I think I know what you've been asking me. I think you know what I've been trying to say. I promised I would never leave you."

The song slows to a lullaby, and the two of them lie together on Gabriel's small bed, both on the edge of sleep.

Sheila's eyes glaze over, and for a moment, a rainbow-colored column seems to take form at the end of the bed. Sheila opens her eyes wide, and the form wavers and ripples, becoming clearer but still indistinct. Gabriel hums happily. He sees it too, and he reaches his hand toward the apparition and waves. Then he rolls over and grabs Sheila's phone and snaps a picture of it. The phone whirrs as it takes multiple shots, one after the other.

The light form becomes more visible and resolves into an almost human silhouette. A blinding flash fills the space, and light fans out from the brilliant form in front of them. Gabriel drops Sheila's phone and stretches his waving hand, pointing at the figure. Two shapes, possibly fingers of light, reach toward his hand, and a spark of electric blue light leaps from one to the other. A blue spark jumps from Gabriel's back to Sheila's hand, which rests over the inflamed area, and she falls backward off the bed in shock. She scrambles up from the carpet and reaches into the air where she thought she saw the apparition, but there is nothing there.

Gabriel sits up. "Did you see that Fred, Momma?" Sheila hears him ask, his face aglow with wonder.

She frowns. "I don't know, Gabriel. Who's Fred?"

His smile droops. "Not Fred, Momma. *Friend.*" Gabriel knows his mother lives in a peculiar state of practicality and struggle. He knows he has a lot to learn from her, but more than that, he knows she has a lot to learn from him. "You saw. I saw you see. You tried to touch him, didn't you?"

Sheila's face clouds with confusion as she tries to grasp what he might be saying. "It was nothing, Gabriel."

"It was. Momma, it was my friend. I know him from before I was here."

His statement hints at something out of the ordinary, and it frightens her. "That's ridiculous, Gabriel. You've never been anywhere else but here."

"I was, Momma. I remember, I was. I know him he's my best friend, and he likes you too. He told me."

Gabriel is becoming agitated. Sheila hugs him tight to her. "It's okay. Okay, I believe you."

Gabriel looks at her face and shakes his head no; he can see that she doesn't.

"Okay, Gabriel, I don't know what that was, but I'm not taking any chances," she locks her mind onto her own answer to the strange event she just witnessed. For Sheila, the magic of the moment is subsumed by her practical assumptions that flashing lights inside the house must be dangerous. She fusses around the room unplugging all the floor lamps, the baby monitor, the night-lights, and the humidifier. "We'll have an electrician come in tomorrow to check everything. Come on, you'll sleep in my bed."

Gabriel bounces out of his bed. "Yay!" He tears out of the room in front of her.

* * *

Snuggled up with Gabriel the following morning, Sheila watches the sunlight filtering through the leaves fluttering in the treetops outside her bedroom window. She cannot remember ever lazing like this before

Gabriel. She realizes that things have changed for her. She remembers how driven she was, determined to find cures, to make a difference, and to excel in her field. The pain of the two-year court case had cinched a painful rubber band around her heart, but it has loosened with time. She cares less about her work now and more about Gabriel. However, she still regrets that she can't pursue her original line of creative gene manipulation and that her intention for Gabriel has failed. He was her last chance to test her theory that a regenerative gene in one subject could be transferred to another who lacked the gene and thus reverse a life-threatening condition. She had hoped to reverse her own degenerative disorder that will surely eat away at her muscle control and leave her paralyzed and unable to breathe at some point too soon.

Rehashing old stuff doesn't make her feel any better, though. She strokes Gabriel's sleeping head. Just then, she realizes that touching Gabriel is what makes her feel better. Until that moment she didn't know or even think about the emerging fact that she really loves him. Before that moment, she knew only that she had a duty to him. Now she feels something for him, and that terrifies her.

After Gabriel was born, she was sure she would need to distance herself from him in order to complete her experimental procedures. She knew she would have to perform surgeries on him like she did on her animal subjects, and she could not feel like a mother to him and do that. It would be too hard. Also, she was so sure that she would be dead by now and that she couldn't be a mother to him and abandon him in that way. It felt too cruel. Even so, she wonders why, when it became clear that there was no chance of continuing with her program, she had forgotten to thaw her heart. She's surprised to be still alive with her health holding steady. She looks back on Gabriel's first months and years and can see that her justification for closing herself off to loving him was irrational. An overwhelming sense that she has wasted too much time washes over her.

Sheila pushes herself up onto her elbows and peers at Gabriel's sleeping face. He looks so sweet, so radiant, so perfect. Her heart swells with love, and tears well in her eyes. She kisses his forehead gently and then lies back down, sobbing quietly. She resolves to be a better mother from now on.

A tap on her bedroom window followed by an urgent squawk startles her. She looks up to see Bill standing on the window ledge. Gabriel wakes at Bill's call and leaps out of bed, delighted to see his small friend return.

"How? How did he get here, Momma?" he wonders, "We took him to the park. Does he know where he went and where he was and where we were?"

Sheila shrugs. "I suppose he must. Birds fly for thousands of miles and know where they're going and how to get back."

"Really?" Gabriel asks, awestruck. "Then I suppose he wasn't lost. He was just, maybe, exploring?" Gabriel agrees with Sheila that Bill can come and go as he pleases and promises that he won't make Bill come inside at night.

Sheila's inner shift seems to presage a coming big change. Later while making breakfast, she becomes anxious. She worries for Gabriel more than ever before. They walk from the parking lot to his preschool, hand in hand for the first time, holding on just because. Before, she was always trying to rein him in or drag him home.

At the front entrance, she clings to him extra long while he wriggles to get away and play with his friends. He's back to the cheerful, enthusiastic boy he was before. Reluctantly, she lets him go.

At the last moment, he turns back and points out over the parking lot. "Look, Momma, I think that's Bill. He's flying over the car."

Sure enough, a young crow seems overly interested in her car, and when it hears Gabriel, it swerves around and flies right for them. Gabriel ducks into school, waving goodbye. The crow swoops over the school and disappears.

11

WINGING IT

Within a week, the foreboding that Sheila felt reveals its source. Her phone rings in the middle of a busy morning in the lab. Noreen is on the line.

"It's Gabriel," she says. "He must have injured himself somehow. He has bruises and bumps on his back."

Sheila rushes to the school and, with the school nurse, examines Gabriel's back. What were previously birthmarks are now red and raw and swelling into two distinct bumps.

"Oh dear. Do you know what that is?" she asks the nurse.

The nurse shakes her head. "Never seen anything like it. Can't even guess."

Sheila takes Gabriel home, and he isn't at all pleased about it. She wracks her brain, trying to figure out what it could be. She starts to dial Philip—after all, he is a doctor, and he might have an idea—but she thinks better of it and refrains from pressing the call button. Instead, she dials Cynthia, and soon she and Gabriel are meeting in one of the examination rooms at Cynthia's office.

"I'm not sick," Gabriel protests in the back of their self-driving car on the way over there. "Don't poke me, Momma."

* * *

Cynthia palpates Gabriel's bumpy back. He giggles, ticklish. She laughs and ruffles his hair. "I have an idea," she says. "Let's use the hologram to see what's going on in there."

She fires up the equipment, and Gabriel watches, fascinated. As she attaches the Bluetooth equipment, Gabriel twists about excitedly. His bones are displayed clearly in the colored 3-D holographic image floating between him and the unit that generates the image. He's curious about everything and catches on quickly, almost as if he has some inside information on everything he encounters.

"Wow! Look, Momma, that's inside me," he babbles excitedly. He reaches up to stroke the intangible image, and his finger goes right through it. "Is that a bone?" he asks, running his finger along the edge of a projected rib.

Cynthia pushes him back onto his stomach and moves her divining scope over his back, twisting and moving it at different angles so the device can discern the macro structural conditions and micro functional activities inside. The holograph floats next to Gabriel, and he cranes his neck to look. Cynthia tugs it out of his view with a quick hand motion. She moves the wand through the 3-D landscape of his back in layers, examining his skin, muscle, and then bone. Cynthia stops, perplexed, and readjusts the wand, looking further into Gabriel's back.

Sheila leans in, too. "That's new growth. I've seen it before in my tests."

"Yes!" Cynthia replies.

The hologram shows two small, new bones adjacent to the scapula in the center of Gabriel's back. Cynthia adjusts her view, and the image expands to show the bone at the cellular level.

"And it's progressing at an astonishing speed," Cynthia adds. "It's not cancer, Sheila. It's bone. The cells are well defined and organized."

"I know," Sheila says, perplexed. As she studies the screen, her brain is calculating. She points at the swirl and flow of microscopic cells in channels of movement. "Look. Blood vessels, nerves, and muscle as well."

Cynthia looks at her. "You did do something to him, didn't you?"

Sheila gives her the "shut up in front of Gabriel" look. Cynthia starts to say something, but Gabriel beats her to it.

"That's so cool. It looks like a video game. Everything inside me is okay, Momma. I'm happy."

Sheila leans in to kiss him. "You're not supposed to be looking." She pulls on his shirt and bundles him up to go home.

"Gabe, wait inside my office. Mommy and I have to talk," Cynthia says.

Sheila shakes her head. "No, we have to go." She rushes out of the door before Cynthia can stop her.

"Wait, Sheila!" Cynthia yells after them. "Are you coming for dinner tonight?"

"I don't think so," Sheila's receding voice wafts back.

* * *

Two weeks later, Sheila's phone, discarded in the catchall basket by the kitchen side door, rings and rings. When it clicks off, a message pops up on the screen: "Missed Call: Cynthia." Above the message is a cramped stream of other calls—six from Cynthia, two from Philip, and four from Noreen.

The interior of Sheila's house is a disaster, like the cleaning crew hasn't come through for a couple of weeks and no one has left the house. Pizza and Chinese food delivery containers are stacked near the garbage, and nearly all of the kitchen dishes, glasses, pots, and pans have been used.

Unkempt and still in her pajamas, Sheila argues with Philip through the lace curtain of her front door. "I know it's been two weeks, but he needs me, Philip."

Outside on the front stoop Philip leans into the door. "Is he sick?"

"No. He's just going through an adjustment, and he needs special attention right now."

She starts picking up clothes and toys strewn in the hall. It's hard for her while leaning on her canes, but she does it.

"I don't understand," Philip continues. "Special attention? He's not sick? Bring him into the hospital. Let's do a full exam and figure out what's going on."

"No, no, he's fine," Sheila responds with mild panic. "I mean, he's not fine, but he ... he has to stay home right now. And he needs me."

In the kitchen, Gabriel jumps up and down. Tiny, bright-blue wing buds flutter on his back. His delighted whoop alerts Sheila, and she slams the kitchen door that leads to the hall, stifling his excited squeals and preventing Gabriel from coming near the front door.

"Look, I'm here. Let me in," Philip presses. "I can help."

"No, Philip, the place is a mess. I'm a mess."

He rattles the door handle and tries to open it.

"It's embarrassing," Sheila says. "Please, just go."

Philip stops and steps back. "Sheila, you know your contract is up for review, and I haven't seen you in your office for two weeks."

"I know, I know," she responds.

"You know the grant was approved, but it's contingent on your participation. If you aren't at the preliminary meeting in one hour, you'll be out of a job—again."

Sheila is torn. She looks at Gabriel through the paned glass of the kitchen door and sighs. Then she turns back to Philip. "I was planning to come in later for a little while anyway. You go ahead. I'll get dressed and see you soon."

Philip pauses for a moment and then sighs in resignation. "Okay."

Sheila watches him leave, and then she works her way into the kitchen and over to the basket with the phone. She pulls it out and switches over to the camera function. "Gabe, keep them still. I want to get a good picture today."

He bounces up and down on the edge of the counter. "I don't know how, Momma."

"Okay, stop bouncing." She holds him down. "Now, stand still and let me hold it."

She grasps the tip of one wing and stretches it open. Gabriel chortles and squirms. Sheila laughs and tickles him, and his wings stretch out beautifully.

"There, like that! Hold it."

She snaps a picture, another, a third, and then one from the side. But when she heads around him to photograph the other side, he starts fluttering his wings again and running around the kitchen counter.

Sheila catches him and holds his shoulders to keep him still for a moment. "Gabe, you're starting a new school today," she says.

Gabriel is thrilled. "Yay! I love school."

Sheila looks sternly into his bright-blue eyes. "But we need to hide your wings. No one can know. Do you understand?"

"Why? What's wrong with them?" Gabriel is clearly dismayed, his eyes welling up with tears.

"Nothing is wrong with them, honey. They're perfect. But no other kids have wings."

"I don't mind," Gabriel says.

Sheila scrabbles through the kitchen drawers in search of something while she tries to explain. "I know you don't mind, but the other children might. The teachers certainly will. I want you to keep this our secret for now."

Sheila pulls out an ACE bandage. She folds Gabriel's wings gently onto his shoulder blades and flattens them down. Then, with practiced confidence, she wraps the bandage across his chest and over his shoulders, covering the wings.

"I don't like it, Momma," Gabriel says, crying outright.

She wipes his tears and kisses his cheeks. "I know, baby. I know. Does it hurt?"

"No, Momma, it doesn't hurt, but now they can't move. I don't like it."

"I'm sorry, love, but just for now, for today, all of today. Okay?"

He nods, miserable but compliant. Sheila pulls a loose shirt and then a sweater over his head. "Now, don't take this sweater or the shirt off today. Do you understand?"

He nods again, still weeping.

* * *

Gabriel forgets about his constriction due to the excitement of a new school, new friends, new teachers, and new demands. He meets every new challenge with enthusiasm, delight, and a sense of adventure, so when Sheila drops him off and sees him run eagerly into the room seeking new escapades and new friends, she is relieved.

Her meeting with Philip and the new project team goes well, too. For the first time, she feels as though her peers have moved on from the overwhelming awareness of the destruction that sidelined her career. She's about to step back on track with her first study as lead scientist in five long years. This is huge for her, and it relieves the tightness in her heart considerably. She still has a chance to do the work she was meant to do, the work she is still determined to do. Gabriel and Sheila's first day out since the advent of his new wings goes far better than she expected. At his school, no one notices anything suspicious.

By the time she picks Gabriel up from his new class, she feels like a new woman. Gabriel is happy, too, playing with a group of three other kids and a set of colorful blocks. Things are looking up. Sheila's only concern is Gabriel's blue wings, but she hopes they won't grow any bigger and that they can keep them hidden.

* * *

On a Sunday morning soon afterwards, Gabriel lounges on the floor, brandishing the TV remote. His wings flutter freely on his back, and Bill flies around the living room ceiling. Gabriel's wings are clearly growing with exquisite blue feathers that still look at bit too fluffy to be useful. He flips through a couple of cartoon shows, sighs with boredom, and continues surfing. Suddenly, he stops and turns up the sound. It is a hosanna of Gregorian chanting.

Sheila looks up to see the shadow of a human figure encased in a field of light that sprays like wings. The video medley flips through pictures of medieval through New Age angelic art.

"Look, Momma, it's my friends."

"Your what?"

"My friends."

"What friends, Gabe?" Sheila gets up from the computer at her desk and comes over to join him on the floor.

"See? I told you, the ones I knew before I knew you. They have wings, like me. They visit here and help us, and they don't hide their wings."

"Gabe, those are angels, and they're a fantasy; they're not real."

Gabriel turns bright red. Sheila has never seen him angry or frustrated. For the most part, he is incredibly well adjusted, compliant, generous, sweet, and understanding, so this is new for her.

He jumps up and stomps his feet. "They are real! Look." He goes over to his toy box and pulls out a drawing pad. "Look, here are my friends. I made photos of them like you make of me."

He shows her one childlike drawing after another of what seem to be people with wings.

"Gabe, real people don't have wings. And those aren't photos; they're drawings. There's a big difference."

He chokes and looks at her, shocked. Then he snatches her phone and surfs through her photos. "Look, I have wings, and I've seen them," he says, pointing at an image on the phone. "You've seen them too, remember? You saw them too."

Sheila looks at the pictures as Gabriel flips through them. One after the other shows the strange wave of light in her bedroom that she forgot about completely, yet its familiarity and its strangeness washes over her in panic. She knows she has seen this before, but she grips Gabriel's shoulders so tight that he winces.

"Look, Gabriel, we have enough to deal with. I don't want people to think you're crazy. They'll lock us both up, and they'll take you away from me. Please, just don't talk about it."

Gabriel starts sobbing uncontrollably, and Sheila folds him in her arms.

"It'll be all right," she mutters, deleting the images of the angel from her phone.

* * *

As the days wear on toward Gabriel's fifth birthday, Sheila becomes more determined than ever to hide his wings and pretend that life can proceed normally. Her new project is off to a great start, she and Philip are working well together again, and Gabriel loves his new school. Thankfully, Gabriel's wings remain manageable, and though angry about it, Gabriel seems to grasp the urgency of her appeal to shut up about angels. He doesn't mention them again.

Gabriel's new campaign is to get Sheila to let his friends come over for his birthday. Sheila is also excited about his birthday, and she is determined to make sure that the day is special for him, but she still refuses his requests for a party. She worries about too much contact with his classmates. Her prime concern is that at home she won't be able to keep his wings hidden. This is his safe haven, the place he can be free and feel easy and comfortable with his new limbs. He still doesn't understand that he can't show them off, so she feels that it will be better to keep it quiet and have a birthday with just the two of them.

She decorates her place beautifully with paper lanterns and wrapped presents. She has his favorite foods and lively music. Gabriel sits at the table in a colorful T-shirt with cutouts to free his wings. The delicate blue feathers flutter behind him. His wings move in concert as he claps his hands and sings along with his favorite kid's group recording. Sheila dims the lights and music and starts singing, "Happy Birthday to you. Happy Birthday to you—"

At that moment, the front door bursts open, and Cynthia steps in.

"Surprise! We just made it. You can't keep us away!"

Gabriel laughs, and his wings bounce in accord. Cynthia's children laugh in the hall, and Mikey, dashes in behind her mom. She stops short when she sees Gabriel.

"Cool!"

Cynthia grabs Mikey and swings her back out through the dining room door. "Mike, take Mikey and Danny home please!"

"Aw, I want cake," Mikey protests on her way out.

"Is everything all right?" Mike asks.

Cynthia is flummoxed. "Uh, it looks like …"

"Chicken pox?" Sheila whispers.

"Chicken pox!" Cynthia yells back.

"Okay, let's go kids." Mike hurries them out.

Sheila hears the fading sounds of the grumbling kids and Mike saying, "I'll buy you a cake. Let's go!"

"I'll be home soon!" Cynthia yells just before the door slams.

"Chicken pox?" Gabriel looks at his mom, puzzled.

Cynthia looks at Sheila is dismay. "Chicken pox? Who gets that these days?"

"I had to think fast," Sheila retorts.

Mesmerized, Cynthia walks over to Gabriel and reaches out to stroke his wings. "Why didn't you tell me? I knew you'd been putting me off. No wonder we haven't seen you for two months. The kids miss you both."

"I know, I know. I'm sorry." Sheila says. "It's been really hard. I just lost it for a while there. I think I panicked, but we're good now. We're managing."

Cynthia looks at her with her eyes wide. "Managing? What does that mean?"

"No flying," Gabriel interjects.

Cynthia peers at him, "Can you fly?"

He nods vigorously.

"No, no, he can't fly. You can't fly, Gabe, not yet anyway," Sheila says. "I don't want you getting any ideas. Keep your feet on the ground, okay?" She bends down and studies his face. "Promise me."

Sheila is clearly on edge about this. She has worked herself up to tears, and Gabriel is starting to catch the feeling, as tears well in his eyes too.

"All right!" Cynthia says, taking charge, "Let's open your presents. It's your birthday. Let's have fun."

Cynthia collects the gifts from the credenza and places them on the coffee table in the middle of the living room.

Gabriel jumps down from the table. "I can do it," he says, grabbing armfuls too.

Suddenly, there's a knock at the door, and everyone hushes.

"Who could that be?" Cynthia whispers.

"Philip. I bet its Philip," Sheila says as she eases out of her stool and leans over to look at the security monitor screen. Sure enough, Philip stands at the front door with a huge, wrapped present. He knocks again and looks around after noticing Sheila's car in the driveway.

"Can he come in, Momma?" Gabriel says a bit too loudly.

"Shhhh. No, honey, not now. It's not a good idea," Sheila responds.

Cynthia gives her a questioning look.

"He'll go away soon," Sheila says.

Her phone rings. She grabs it. "Hi, Philip, how are you?" She pauses looking at them both with a silent warning to stay quiet. "Oh, yes, we're at Cynthia's. She picked us up." She waits again. "Oh no, don't bother. Just leave it outside the door. We're on our way home soon anyway." After another moment, she shrugs and hands the phone to Gabriel while whispering, "Say thank you."

He holds it to his ear. "Thanks, Uncle Philip."

Sheila snatches the phone away. "Thanks, Philip," she says, breathing hard. "Bye." She hangs up.

"Momma, you lied," Gabriel says.

"That's something you should never do, Gabe," Cynthia says, adding, "until you're an adult and you can figure out when it's a good idea to lie or not."

Gabriel looks at Sheila. "Is that a joke, Momma?"

She doesn't know what to say.

Soon, Gabriel is laughing and playing with his new toys. Philip has delivered a small plastic car, in which Gabriel zooms around through the kitchen, into the living room and hall, and back into the kitchen. Bill flutters along behind him, squawking away.

Cynthia watches him and then turns to Sheila. "How will you keep this a secret?"

"Not now, please," Sheila almost snarls, but Cynthia is determined.

"You'll never keep it from Philip and the hospital. What are you thinking?"

"I have to protect him," Sheila sputters. "For as long as possible. I have to."

Cynthia is dubious. "That's going to be tough, but you can count on me." She pulls her sister toward her and gives her a reassuring hug.

* * *

A few days later, Gabriel sits patiently on a kitchen stool while Sheila attempts to bind his wings with an ace bandage. They have grown quite a bit. Now the joints poke above his shoulders, and the wingtips reach his waist. The finished binding is a mess and so obvious that no sweater, hoody, or jacket will cover the bulk. Frustrated, she rips the bandage off again.

"Can I go without it today, Momma?" Gabriel begs.

Sheila shakes her head. Suddenly, she has an idea and shuffles through her tangled kitchen catchall drawer. She comes up with a pair of scissors. Then she snatches Gabriel's Red Dragon backpack off the hook by the door. The purple backpack has a cute image of a cartoon dragon on the back.

"Wait, don't hurt him! Please don't cut Red, Momma!"

"I'm not cutting him, Gabriel. I'm cutting the backpack behind him. Look."

As Gabriel watches, she hacks into the back of the backpack and cuts away a chunk of the bag. Next, she maneuvers the bag over Gabriel's head and tucks his wings inside the opening. When she's finished, she holds it out.

"Here keep this on."

He pouts. "I can't fly with them in there."

"No flying!" Sheila insists. "Don't take it off all day. I'll tell the teacher, okay?"

He continues to pout.

Sheila's face softens. "I'll take you to the park for a ride on the swings after if you're good all day and keep the backpack on. Okay?"

After a moment, Gabriel nods sheepishly.

12

PARALYZED

Sheila finds it hard to concentrate at work. She worries about receiving a disturbing call from Gabriel's school. When Philip invites her to lunch, she accepts, if only to get her mind off Gabe.

Sitting across from him in the hospital cafeteria, she remembers vaguely how nice it was to have Philip in her life. His brown eyes soften, and her heart flutters as he leans across the table to take her hand.

"Let's get back together again," he says. Sheila is surprised, but she still feels betrayed by him, so she slides her hand out of his and tries not to make it a rude rejection.

"I-I'm sorry, Philip, but I still think it's just too soon."

He sits back and gazes across the dining room and out into the park beyond, clearly hurt.

"I-I'm not saying never ... just not now," she sputters.

He looks at her for a long moment and then digs into his meal, determined to make the best of it. The conversation turns to mundane, work-related stuff.

When they're finished eating, he gets serious again and begs her to allow him to come over after work. Sheila puts him off, saying that she promised to take Gabriel to the park.

The rest of the day continues without event, and Sheila leaves the office feeling home-free and relieved. She collects Gabriel, and they head to the park together.

She struggles, clinging to the swing struts and pushing Gabriel's swing weakly. Her mind is still on Philip. It surprises her that old feelings are coming up again, but how can she forgive him? It doesn't help to think of how magical it might have been if she and Philip had gotten married.

They would be parents together now, and things would be so much easier. But they would not have Gabriel.

"Push harder, Momma!" Gabriel pleads.

Philip startles Sheila by stepping in to push Gabriel's swing. He shoves vigorously, and Gabriel squeals with glee. Sheila steps back and watches.

"This is nice, Sheila. You know, I want to help anytime."

"I know," she responds weakly.

"We can take it slow," he says, encouraged. "I know you need to trust me again."

Sheila shakes her head. "It's not that."

"What then?" He watches her, weighing his next words in his mind. When she turns away abruptly, he decides to let it go for the moment.

Sheila watches Gabriel in silence. Then she notices that, in his excitement, his wings are moving noticeably inside his backpack. She glances at Philip. He doesn't appear to have noticed anything odd yet.

Sheila steps into the path of the swing and flings her arms around Gabriel. By sheer luck, she isn't knocked over by the force of Gabriel's momentum. Gabriel and Philip are both shocked. Gabriel is ready to cry.

"I thought he was about to fall off!" Sheila claims as her excuse.

"I wasn't," Gabriel says, "I was flying!" He looks at Philip and appeals to him. "Again."

"No," Sheila insists. "It's time to go home." Philip helps her get Gabriel out of the swing, and Sheila does her best to clamp down on Gabriel's overactive backpack.

They walk off together, Sheila on her two canes and Gabriel running beside her.

Philip stands alone behind the swing, bewildered.

* * *

At the end of the following day, Philip watches from his office window as Sheila and Gabriel enter the park below. Cynthia knocks on his open door. He turns to greet her.

"There's your sister, playing in the park again," he says cynically.

Cynthia wonders if she detects jealousy, a sense of loss, or maybe a sense of hope. "That happens when you have a child," she replies.

He turns toward her and comes over to kiss her cheek. "How are you? How are the kids? Mike?"

"Good, all good," she says.

He stares out the window again. "Did we have an appointment?"

Cynthia questions her decision to come and talk to him. She doesn't want to intrude, but then again, she does. "No. I dropped by because … well … How's Sheila doing with work?"

He spins around from the window to look at her. "Frankly, Cynthia, she's slacking. Even you're not as absorbed in your children."

Cynthia nods. "It's tough for her," she says, trying to excuse Sheila.

Philip is quick to retort. "She's tough." Then he seizes the opportunity to investigate what has been vexing him in the back of his mind. "There's something wrong with him, isn't there?" Philip was already feeling that something was up, and now that Cynthia has appeared to question him, he is positive there's more than meets the eye here.

"No, no, it's just … can you go easy on her?"

Philip thinks for a moment and then nods. "Sure, but why?"

Cynthia feels like crap; she hates interfering. "Well, you know her health isn't good."

"And Gabriel? What about him?"

"He's fine."

He can tell she is holding something back.

Cynthia sees the doubt in his eyes and decides to back out before he can interrogate her. "Anyway, sorry to bother you." She turns and almost dashes out of his office.

Philip peers into the park again and then turns back to his desk. For a moment, he seems to be about to work, but then he changes his mind, grabs his jacket, and walks out.

* * *

Gabriel runs with a couple of kids in the park. Bill flutters and cackles above them. Sheila is sitting alone on the park bench when Cynthia slumps down beside her.

"I want to help," Cynthia says.

Sheila looks at her, puzzled.

81

"You can't keep this up. It's too dangerous; it's going to come out. Someone will see, and then God knows what will happen."

Behind them on the lawn, three larger boys crowd Gabriel. They poke him and tug at his backpack. Gabriel backs up. Two little kids run away. Gabriel dodges, trying to get away as well, but the big boys push him farther away from Sheila and Cynthia. The two women are oblivious.

"Cynthia, this is my choice, my success, my failure, my accomplishment, and my experiment. I'll handle it."

Behind her, the boys roll Gabriel to the ground and tumble him out of his backpack. He lies on the ground, halfway between crying and laughing, not sure how to react. Then he realizes his wings are exposed. The bullies crowd around him staring, and then one reaches for one of Gabriel's wings with his fingers, eager to snatch it.

Completely unaware of the drama behind her, Cynthia continues. "It? Sheila, you forgot to say 'my child.'"

"I don't need to say it!"

Splayed on the ground behind the two women, Gabriel dodges the grabby kid and jumps up, exuberant. His wings are finally free, and he is outside in the open air. He dashes off laughing, bouncing, and hooting. Bill swoops down from a nearby tree and flaps above him.

Cynthia and Sheila are so locked into their conversation that they fail to hear the raucous noise on the other side of the field.

"Sheila, he isn't an 'it,'" Cynthia persists. "He's a uniquely gifted child, not an experiment."

In the field, the bullies are shocked out of their fighting mood. They laugh, becoming just as ecstatic as Gabriel. They drop his backpack and tear off after him.

"Don't you think I know that?" Sheila retorts. "I'm more than his mother; I created him."

"That's what every mother does, Sheila. I'm not saying someone else should take charge of him. I'm just saying—"

"I'm not interested, and I don't have time to listen to you lecture me."

Sheila stands up to look around for Gabriel. She spots his abandoned Red Dragon backpack. "Oh my God! No! Where is he?" Sheila limps across the grass on her canes, rushing to retrieve the backpack. "Gabriel! Gabriel!"

Cynthia runs ahead of her, also calling out for Gabriel.

On the nearby playground, noisy children bound around. A tight flock of kids migrates throughout the enclosed area. Gabriel flaps in the center of the mob. His wings are exposed, but far from being shocked or frightened, the children are delighted. Squealing kids pretend to fly, pumping their arms. Gabriel hops every six or seven steps, and he is modestly airborne.

Turning off the open field and back to the path, Sheila spots Bill fluttering over a bevy of kids. Then she sees Gabriel and slams through the gate into the playground.

Gabriel jumps into the air one more time, wings fluttering. Then he dives into the sandbox, giggling. A child runs past Sheila on her way to join Gabriel's flock.

"Mommy, look! That boy can fly!" she yells back to her mother on a nearby bench.

Shocked, Sheila turns to scrutinize the girl's mother. Has she seen Gabriel yet?

Another child nearby tugs at her mother's arm and points to Gabriel. "Mommy, there's a boy with wings. I saw him flying."

"Isn't his costume wonderful, girls?" Sheila says loudly enough for the two mothers to hear. "It really makes you think he can fly."

Cynthia reaches the sandbox and envelopes Gabriel in her sweater. She picks him up and snuggles him in a vicelike grip. Gabriel is radiant, excited, and happy.

"Momma, Aunty, they loved it. They loved flying. We all flew together."

Cynthia and Sheila look around at the boisterous kids crowding the playground. Parents and nannies are all heading into the fray to retrieve their kids before trouble starts. The three bullies who started it all are the most raucous, running up the slide and then launching from the top into the sandpit and pretending to fly on the way down. The atmosphere is infectious, kids laughing and chasing each other and jumping up and down with joy.

"I saw it, Mommy. I saw him fly. I did," a little girl wails.

"What have I told you about lies, Constance?" her mother replies.

Sheila is dismayed. The girl is right, but what can she do about it? Poor child.

Suddenly, she remembers. "My bag!"

"I'll get it!" Cynthia turns and dashes off.

Sheila struggles to squeeze Gabriel's wings back inside the backpack without anyone noticing.

"I told you to keep this on," she whispers through clenched teeth.

Gabriel squirms. "I don't like it."

Sheila grips his shoulders, leaning in and pretending to kiss him. "Do as I tell you, Gabriel," she hisses.

Gabriel looks away from her.

"Do you hear me?"

Gabriel turns his head. His eyes challenge his mother. "I don't want it!"

"You must wear it," she pleads.

Gabriel has almost soared, and he doesn't want to be grounded any longer. "No! No! No!"

Sheila slaps him, and he gasps in shock. She squeezes him and kisses his reddening cheek while glancing around to see if anyone saw her thoughtlessness. She begins to sob, tears streaming down her face.

"I'm sorry, I'm sorry. I'm just so worried they could take you away from me."

Gabriel hugs Sheila. "Don't you love me, Momma?"

Sheila chokes up. "Of course I do, sweetie."

Cynthia returns with Sheila's bag and Philip in tow. "I thought you might be here," he says sarcastically. "Can you fit me into your busy schedule tomorrow morning perhaps?"

Sheila nods. "Of course, but I need to get Gabriel home now."

"Fine," he responds.

They round the bend, leaving Philip behind a line of bushes. Sheila glances back worriedly. "He didn't see anything, did he?"

"It's only a matter of time," Cynthia responds.

* * *

Back at Sheila's home, the shadows rise, swallowing the ground and then the tree trunks until bright, golden sun highlights only the leaves at the very top of the trees. Bill glitters as he careens above the treetops and then disappears into the deep, shadowy leaves below. Gabriel is too excited about his recent adventure to notice that Bill is gone.

Cynthia turns on the lights and pours three glasses of orange juice while Sheila releases Gabriel's wings. Grateful, Gabriel takes the juice from Cynthia, grabs her hand, and kisses her fingers. She laughs and kisses his forehead. Gabriel takes a sip of his orange juice and then sets it down.

"Aunty, why don't you have wings?"

"Humans don't have wings, honey."

Gabriel's brow furrows. "I'm human, aren't I, Momma?"

Cynthia and Sheila look at each other. Sheila is unable to speak, a huge lump blocking her throat.

"Of course you're human, sweetie," Cynthia says.

Gabriel takes a moment to consider his response. Cynthia is struck by the maturity he seems to possess for a five-year-old.

"I know I am, but do *you* think I am? Do you, Auntie Cynthia?" His eyes are full of hope. "I'm real, but neither of you treat me like I am." He stares at them, challenging them. Then he realizes things are not going to change. "No one knows who I am." He jumps off his stool, abandons his cookies, and runs outside into the darkening backyard.

"Gabe, stay inside the yard!" Sheila calls after him.

Cynthia resumes her campaign to talk some sense into her sister. "He's a very wise child, Sheila. Not only does he have this miraculous physical … uh …"

"Deformity?" Sheila suggests.

"No, I wasn't going to say that. I don't know what to say. Anyway, it's hard for him. He needs support, and you need support to support him. It's not going to get any easier."

"What are you suggesting?" Sheila asks, unable to conceal the vitriol rising in her gut. She's already on edge, and now she feels threatened by her own sister.

"Well, I suppose you could try to hide in some remote area, but how practical is that? I suggest that you talk to Philip and that you involve the hospital. They have resources there that could really help."

Sheila stares at her in shock. "No! They'd cage him with the animals."

"That's no excuse to cage him here," Cynthia retorts without thinking.

Sheila is livid. She turns her back on Cynthia and begins washing the dishes. "I think you should go now. Thanks for helping today."

Cynthia comes up behind her and gives her a kiss on the cheek. Sheila doesn't respond.

* * *

Outside, Birds cluster around the many feeders in Sheila's grassy yard. Gabriel flops down on his back to look up at the birds. Bill appears, squawking and fluffing his feathers.

Sheila sticks her head out the back door and is about to call out to Gabriel. Instead, she stands there watching him, trying to figure him out and wishing it could be easier.

Gabriel talks to the crow, and the little creature seems to listen. "I don't want to stay here anymore. No one listens."

"Caw, caw," Bill replies.

Gabriel imitates him. "Caw, caw."

The crow takes off and soars over the trees. Gabriel's eyes follow his path wistfully.

"When I learn to fly, the first thing I'll do is fly away and never come back," he says.

Tears well up in Sheila's eyes. She has no response to that. She has a similar wish in her own heart. At that moment, she recognizes that supporting Gabriel might mean doing something other than what she has been doing. She resolves to give him space to express himself, to learn his limits, and not to confine him to the limits she perceives. She turns back into the kitchen to prepare dinner.

* * *

Sheila is busy in the kitchen with dishes the next evening when she hears a crash from upstairs. She bursts out of the kitchen and into the hall, where she finds Gabriel perched like a sweet gargoyle on the second floor railing.

"Look, Momma!" He flaps his wings, and he lifts off the rail.

Sheila's eyes go wide with panic. "No, no, no! Get down, Gabe!"

But she is too late. Gabriel is a bit wobbly, but he sails down the stairs with his feet just inches from the steps. He swoops through the doorway and glides elegantly around the dining room table before coming back toward Sheila and tumbling into a heap on the hall rug by her feet. He's so ecstatic that he laughs hysterically. Sheila can't hold back, and she starts laughing too. This is too wonderful. He is developing fast, and she can barely keep up. Here comes her real test. How will she support him differently?

"Y-you saw me?" he asks, barely able to get the words out.

She nods and goes for it. She must be his champion and protector but not his jailer. "You did it! You flew! I am so proud of you, Gabe. Let me get the camera." Gabe runs back up the stairs to do it again.

Later, they snuggle together in front of the TV and watch the video footage of Gabriel's second flight. On screen, a purple vase with dry flowers takes a dive and shatters to the floor, but Sheila doesn't care. This development is too awesome. They watch the same parts of the video over and over, with Gabriel saying things like "Oh, look! I started to fall, but the wall pushed me up again" or "Oops, I hope I don't do that again."

Sheila entreats him to explain to her how it feels and how he knows what to do, but he can't quite grasp the answers to these questions.

"I don't know, Momma. I just did it, like when I first walked on the stairs. I still don't know how I did that."

Sheila bursts out laughing. "Of course you don't, love. I don't know either."

Soon, it's time for bed, and when Sheila tucks Gabriel in, she tells him a secret. "You know, baby, I used to fly when I was younger."

Gabriel sits up. "You did? How?"

"In my dreams. I would fly in my dreams, and it was the most wonderful feeling. It felt so real."

Gabriel nods knowingly. She leans in to kiss him goodnight, and his wings sweep up and wrap around her.

* * *

The next morning, Sheila lies asleep with a smile on her face. Her resolution seems to have shifted her entire disposition and afforded her the best sleep she has had in a long time. Her alarm beeps at 5:35 a.m. She snuffs it out, mumbles something, and snuggles back into the covers for a few more minutes.

Birdsong filters through the flapping curtains, and Gabriel's high voice mingles in. She's used to hearing him singing with the birds, but usually his voice comes from inside the house. Now it seems to be coming from outside.

Alarmed, she practically falls out of bed and limps over to the window. There is no sign of Gabriel in the front yard or on the street, so she grabs her canes and heads over to his room. The minute Sheila enters Gabriel's, bedroom, her anxiety peaks. He isn't in the rumpled bed, and the dormer window is wide open. She hears Gabriel's voice outside. By the time she reaches the window, she can barely breathe.

"Gabe, Gabriel, where are you?"

He's still trilling and tweeting like the birds when she sticks her head through the window.

"What are you doing out there?"

Gabriel looks over at her from his perch on the ledge beside the dormer. "I'm learning," he says.

In the back of her mind Sheila realizes that, like Bill, the birds may be coming around because of Gabriel and not the feeders, as she thought before. Could they possibly be his teachers? It certainly looks that way as they and Bill fly up to his face and sweep around and back again, displaying all kinds of aeronautic techniques. Gabriel clings to the roof and flourishes his blue wings while he watches the birds. He leans this way and that, flapping but also trying hard not to fall of the dormer's roof or find himself airborne. He tests the wind, his wings, and his sense of balance and strength.

Sheila isn't one bit happy about it. "What do you think you're learning out there, Gabriel?"

"Bill shows me how he flies," he responds, matter of fact.

Sheila gasps, terrified now, and glances over the garden twenty-five feet below. "Come in here right now, Gabriel."

He's perched just to the side of the window, so she reaches out to grab his arm. The startled birds swirl away, chirping their warning sounds.

Sheila is almost out the window herself when she loses her balance. She slips out and starts to slide down the roof.

Gabriel reaches to try and help her, but the wind gusts, and he soars up.

"Oh!" they shout in unison.

Sheila is lying flat on the roof, clutching the window ledge with her right hand. Gabriel tips his wings and glides up into the air in a sweeping circle. Sheila reaches up with her left hand.

"Gabriel!"

She stares up at him, and he looks back at her with a sense of shock and delight in his glittering blue eyes. She's so entranced that without noticing her own movements, she stands up and balances easily on the sloped roof to watch him fly.

"Aiiii! Ki ki! I'm a hawk, Momma!" he shouts joyfully and drifts up.

Sheila totters uneasily as an unnatural wind streams through her hair. Her arms stretch toward her son. Her eyes are riveted on him, and yet they are distant or disengaged. She, too, could be flying, or is she actually flying?

Miraculously—from her point of view—Sheila soars, whirls, and dives. She feels euphoric. She's right behind Gabriel, brushing over the treetops with leaves fluttering across her body. The rising sun halos Gabriel's flapping wings and outlines the sharp silhouette of Bill gliding beside him. As she follows, she actually feels—or imagines—her own wings flapping. She can't tell what's real and what's not; she must be dreaming.

Pink highlights from the dawn sun soften the quiet neighborhood far below. Long, black shadows etch the trees, brownstones, vehicles, and distant shops near the highway. She notices the occasional car navigating the streets on its early trip to work. She circles down at a dizzying speed. The streets whirl beneath her. She feels sick.

Still standing on the rooftop, Sheila blinks, and her vision ends. In shock, she wobbles and flops down onto her butt.

"Gabe, come back." She can barely whisper, and her voice quakes and cracks.

Gabriel is a speck in the sky, and she is terrified she will never see him again. A torrent of tears blinds her vision, but Gabriel seems to hear her whisper. As soon as the words leave her lips, he turns and makes a line for their house. Soon, she discerns his form careening toward her.

"Oh no!" She waves him off. "Slow down! Be careful! Did you learn how to land?" Her voice rises in power, as he gets closer. A cacophony of birds flocks up and out of the trees, swooping over the roof and grazing Sheila's hair.

Gabriel plunges toward his first landing. At the last moment, he spreads his wings like a parachute and stretches his tiny feet toward the roof where Sheila sits. First one foot and then the other touch the rooftop. But it's too steep, and he slips. He tries to run up the roof toward Sheila, flapping his wings to propel himself forward, but his efforts take him backward and off the front of the house instead.

Sheila shimmies down the roof on her butt and peers over the edge just as Gabriel tries to land on the porch roof below. He grabs at the vines to maintain his balance, but they come away in his hand, so he springs off the gutter and catches air. He veers sideways clumsily and then sails out over the street. Sheila crawls on her hands and knees up to the bedroom window.

Once she is safe inside, she glances down the street and sees Gabriel weaving down the street, fighting for altitude with Bill fluttering about him. A car speeds toward them. Sheila dashes awkwardly with her canes to her elevator and jabs the call button. Just then, a car horn blares outside. The elevator motor grinds, but she can hear the elevator door below isn't closing. She peers over the balcony and sees the door is stuck. The toy car from Philip is blocking it.

Sheila scrambles, almost falling, down the stairs as she heads toward the front door. She hears the terrible sound of tires screeching. Panicked, she redoubles her efforts and slips, plummeting down the last few steps and landing in a heap at the bottom.

In the street, Gabriel senses something is wrong. He looks toward the house, and his blue eyes flash. "Momma?" Then he collides with the windshield of a moving car.

The startled driver veers left and scrapes along the parked cars on the side of the road, metal grinding on metal. Gabriel tumbles over the top of the car and recovers his balance, spreading his wings as he launches off the back of the car and swoops over a fence into a garden across the street. The driver looks in his rearview mirror but sees nothing, his car still lurching down the street.

Sheila is a mess at the bottom of the stairs: crying, uncombed, in wrinkled pajamas, emotional, and very confused. Her canes have fallen out of her reach through the stair rail and landed at the end of the hall near the kitchen, so she pulls herself up on the stair railing. Then she flings her weight away from where her supports lie toward the front door.

Down the street, the surprised driver stops and gets out to examine his damaged car, shaking his head.

Elsewhere, Gabriel tries to navigate his way over the fence, over some bushes, and between trees in an effort to get back to his mother. He's on foot as much as in the air, and his wings flail. It turns out that Gabriel is across the street and only a few houses away, but he has no idea where he is. The high privet hedges confuse him, so he goes the wrong way. He's close but also very lost.

Wobbling and supported by the front door, Sheila swings it open and scans the street for Gabriel. She glances back for a moment at her canes and decides they are too far away to retrieve easily, so she plunges out of the front door without them. She teeters doubtfully for a moment, holding the rail at the top of the front stoop, and then she pitches herself down the three steps with determination and staggers across the short path to the front gate.

"Gabriel!" she yells. She can't see him anywhere on the street.

A few houses down to the right, she sees the driver climbing back into his car and pulling away. She's relieved that there's no sign of Gabriel in the street.

"Gabriel!" she yells again.

"Momma!" his voice is somewhere to the left and across the street.

"Gabe, over here!"

Suddenly, Gabriel hurdles the hedge and the parked cars from the opposite side of the street and dashes toward her. When he reaches Sheila, he clings to her.

"Momma, you walked here by yourself!"

Sheila catches her breath. She hardly realized it. "I love you Gabriel," she says. And then she collapses.

Gabriel falls on top of her and brushes her hair out of her face. "Momma, Momma, wake up! Get up! What are you doing?"

Sheila breathes with difficulty. "I'm okay, baby. Go inside, stay inside, and call Aunty Cynthia."

Gabriel rushes inside to find Sheila's phone.

* * *

Down the street from Sheila's house, Stan, the formerly homeless artist, straddles a motorcycle. This is not the first time Stan has been hanging around Sheila and Gabriel. He has harbored an obsession with Gabriel since his first encounter with him. But this may be his most thrilling encounter since that perplexing day that changed his life. He scrolls through the recent images taken on his telephoto-lens camera, perusing one blurry shot after another of Gabriel's rough and tumbling flight over the car. Finally, he settles on a reasonably clear shot of Gabriel running down the front path of his home just before he dives onto his fallen mother.

"That's the one," he says. "Too bad none of the flying ones are clear enough to see that it's really a kid and not some kind of weird bird."

* * *

Cynthia calls an ambulance and arrives at Sheila's house a minute or two after it. She's there just in time to stop the paramedics from checking the house and finding Gabriel.

Cynthia runs through the house until she finds him cowering under Sheila's bedroom window clutching Bill. He's weeping while he peeks out to watch as Sheila is strapped onto a stretcher and loaded into the ambulance.

"Oh, I did it, Aunty. I hurt her. Can you fix her, please?"

Cynthia snuggles Gabriel to her shoulder and soothes him. "It's not your fault, Gabriel. Your Momma is sick, but you didn't do it. We'll take her to the hospital and make sure she's okay, and then everything will be fine."

With tears streaming down his cheeks Gabriel puts Bill out on the balcony railing. "We'll come back; you wait here." Then he hands Cynthia his Red Dragon backpack. "Can you put this on me, please? I have to go with her."

Cynthia helps him squash his beautiful wings into the backpack. Gabriel is compliant and doesn't wince or complain at all.

13

BIG SECRETS

Things look ominous in Philip's office. He has embarked on a path that he is afraid he already regrets; he has invited his boss, Gerald Spiner, in to talk about Sheila. He and Spiner are waiting for Noreen, Gabriel's preschool teacher, to arrive. Philip suspects that she can shed some light on his questions about Gabriel, and he wants Spiner to hear it too.

Impatient, Spiner sits down and asks Philip why he is there. Philip launches into his explanation. He's a bit vague and still unsure, but he suggests that Sheila has probably used lab equipment improperly. He points out the suspicious and peculiar timing of Sheila's pregnancy, which came so soon after the notorious judgment against her. He recalls how Sheila avoided him that entire time. He insists that something about Gabriel is odd, and he is confused by the fact that Gabriel's files are missing or hidden.

While speaking, Philip is aware of how much he loves the child and would love to spend more time with him. A question though, lurks in the back of his mind and casts doubt on this choice of action: is this really the best way of making that happen? He's annoyed that Sheila is so protective, that she has shut him out repeatedly and that he has not seen the kid for weeks. Philip's resolution flips, and he is determined to ferret out Sheila's secrets; he needs Spiner's permission to access the locked files from the lawsuit five years earlier.

Spiner gets up, irritated, suggesting that if Philip and Sheila have personal problems, they should work it out between them and leave him out of it.

Philip jumps up. "No, it's not that. I think this has something to do with the hospital. I'm not sure, but I think Sheila has ..." He pauses, unsure of where to go with it.

Spiner turns back from the door and gives him a pensive look. "Listen, bring me something to go on, but until you start making sense, there's nothing I can do." He walks out, slamming the door behind him.

Noreen arrives a few minutes later. She's a bit flustered, but that's always how it is for Noreen around adults. She's much more at home with kids. Philip invites her to sit down.

She talks too much and too fast. "He's a remarkable child. He always seemed so sensitive, always caring and sharing. He walked before any other child I've ever known; always seemed full of energy and enthusiasm. Other kids love him, for the most part; troublemakers tend to harass him, but not the others. He talked before any other kid, too. He also ran, read, and drew in record time. I think he's a … a … a … What do you call it?"

"Prodigy?"

"Yes! Isn't that exciting? But he's not at all antisocial like many geniuses; he's very personable and likeable. He was always giving gifts to other kids and the teachers, like a flower he found on the way to school, a feather, an acorn, a small drawing … Oh, oh! One day he made a picture of me with wings. Isn't that strange? I was moved by it. I don't know why, but it seemed so special."

She looks at Philip nervously and launches on. "On another day, he opened the parakeet cage and let the birds out. He was very upset. I was worried about him; he seems like such a sensitive boy. He's always polite and kind to the other kids. He defers to them and lets them take toys away from him or cut in front in line, and he's never upset. But that thing with the birds, that really made him mad. He really is an unusually sweet boy. I'm sad he's left our school."

"Do you know why he left?"

Noreen shakes her head. "I can't really say, but I think he got sick or something. He got a really bad rash or bruise and some bumps on his back. I was nervous that it was contagious, but I've never seen such a thing before."

"Did the nurse get a shot of the rash?" Philip asks, intrigued.

"Umm, no. The place was a bit hectic that day, and Dr. Jensen showed up quickly and whisked him away. Now that I think about it, I think she took him to her sister."

"What day was that?"

"May 26, I believe."

Philip smiles at her. "Would you send any records you have to me?"

Noreen shakes her head slowly, unsure. "Dr. Jensen is his mother. Shouldn't she have to—"

"These are hospital records," Philip interjects. "Dr. Jensen doesn't need to know."

Noreen wrings her hands. "But Dr. Ohl, after she took him out of the preschool, she took his file. She has it."

Philip looks at her with a black scowl. Then he stands up, thanks her, and leads her to the door, closing it after her.

Back at his desk, Philip opens his computer and browses through the hospital records until he comes to Cynthia's files. With a bit of sleuthing, he comes up with Gabriel's cache and sighs with relief.

For the next hour, Philip browses through the holographic footage recorded from Gabriel's various tests. The images remain flat on his computer without the benefit of Cynthia's high-tech equipment, but the resolution is still vivid and vital. This is his field; he's always looking at animals in various stages of development, so he knows what he is looking at.

Everything looks to be normal, healthy, and growing in a timely way. None of Cynthia's notes indicate any anomalies or show that she thinks there might be anything strange about the child—until he reaches the last entry. On May 26, there's a note that Gabriel was there and that tests were taken, but there's no holographic log of the examination. Philip prints out the appointment details, complete with the lines of missing information.

A short time later in Spiner's office, Philip slaps the sheet onto his boss's desk. "This is it—proof that Sheila and her sister are covering something up."

Spiner looks at the page and then lifts his head. "It's not easy to delete the test results from the system. Do you know which one of them did it?"

"Does it matter?" Philip asks. "It certainly indicates that either one or both of them want to keep something hidden. And who would have looked? No one would bother. Ordinarily, no one would notice this particular file is missing." Philip rambles on, trying to think it all through at the same time. "They clearly have misused hospital equip—"

"Okay," Spiner says finally. "It may be minor, but wiping critical data from the system is an infraction. Get Larry Costain on it. If something is going on, I want to know about it before it blows up in my face again."

* * *

Gabriel sleeps snuggled next to his mother in her hospital bed. His Red Dragon backpack is still tightly tucked over his wings. Suddenly the door bursts open and two nurses, one male and one female, stride into the room. The female nurse nudges Gabriel and tries to roll him into her arms to take him away. He wakes up and starts flailing.

"No, no! I want to stay with my momma."

"You can't," the male nurse insists.

Both nurses have Gabriel off the bed and are about to march him out between them when Sheila stirs and grabs Gabriel's hand.

"Let him stay," she pleads.

At that moment, Cynthia enters. She flashes her hospital ID for the nurses to read. "It's okay; I'll be here," she assures them as she holds the door open, inviting them to leave.

Cynthia hugs and kisses Sheila and asks how she's feeling.

"My floppy nerves saved me from a serious break," Sheila replies. "I've decided I'm taking Gabe away somewhere." She pulls Cynthia closer to her. "But please, in the meantime, keep his secret for us both. Even from your kids. Please."

Cynthia shakes her head. "Sheila, I don't know how we can do that."

"I can. I will. I promise, Momma," Gabriel pipes up.

Cynthia and Sheila look at him. Cynthia speaks first. "Well, if you think you can, then okay."

"It's just a night or two," Sheila adds. "I'll be out hopefully tomorrow."

Cynthia and Gabriel turn and leave hand in hand.

* * *

When Cynthia takes Gabriel home to collect some clothes, Gabriel shows her how he thinks he can tuck and hold his wings inside his pajamas so they won't be noticed. Cynthia realizes then that Sheila doesn't trust Gabriel or give him the benefit of the doubt in making decisions about his life. He seems so mature and thoughtful. He's even able to apply his mind to solving a problem that he doesn't perceive as necessary. She suspects that he acts more like a baby with his mother than without her. Cynthia has seen this before and finds herself wondering for a moment just how much her own kids act more immature than they actually are when they are around her.

Mikey and Danny are thrilled to see Gabriel. It has been a long time since they last played together. The first thing Cynthia's kids try to do is initiate a wrestling match on the rug. Cynthia jumps in to stop them.

Mikey, who remembers glimpsing Gabriel's wings, can't wait to get him alone and make him take off his shirt so that she can see them, but Cynthia is watching carefully. She makes it clear that Gabriel's mom, their aunt, is sick and in the hospital. They are not to bother him or tease him. They can watch TV together, but no horseplay.

That night, Cynthia tucks Gabriel in by himself in their guest room. Usually, he would stay with the kids. They all, even he, thought it weird for him to sleep there, but Cynthia insists on the pretext that he will get a better night's sleep after his trauma.

Mike, who is usually an easygoing guy, is suspicious that something is up. The minute Cynthia climbs into bed, he challenges her.

"It's not my story to tell, Mike," she says. "I feel uncomfortable about it."

"Look, CC, this is our family too. If there's a big deal brewing like that last legal fiasco, we need to know. I'm a lawyer; it's my right to know. I don't want to end up behind the eight ball again. I couldn't help her the last time because she shut us out. Let's not let that happen again. Tell me what's going on."

Cynthia sighs. How can she? But how can she not tell him? Mike is right. "Come here," she whispers, pulling him out of bed.

Together, they tiptoe through the upstairs hall to the guest room door. Cynthia opens the door, and they both peep in. Gabriel is splayed out on the bed, exhausted, his refulgent, deep-blue wings seem to be lit with an ethereal light. They brush his back and heave rhythmically with his breathing.

Mike gasps. He pushes the door wide open and shuffles across the room to touch the blue feathers. Gabriel stirs. Cynthia pulls him away, and he follows reluctantly.

They sit up in bed for hours talking about how this could have occurred, speculating, projecting into the future, and worrying about what might happen. Cynthia is convinced that Sheila has conducted some kind of experiment, but she can't get any confirmation or information out of her. Mike is concerned about the legal ramifications and worries that Gabriel is in for a rough ride.

"What can we do?" Cynthia pleads, a helpless, hopeless note to her tone. Mike suggests that Cynthia find out everything she can, that she get all the records and comb through them to determine how a child might develop wings. If it was engineered at the Harold Bowman Research facility, that's one thing, but if it can be proven that the wings are a natural mutation, that's another thing altogether.

"Natural mutation?" Cynthia exclaims. "Oh my God! Do you think that could be possible?"

A few moments later, Cynthia, her "mom radar" always on, hears sobbing coming from the guest room. She shrugs into her robe and heads off to comfort Gabriel.

When she opens the door to Gabriel's room, she finds him huddled on the bed, crying uncontrollably. It has all been too much for him. She wraps her arms around him and lies down, snuggling him close to her. Soon, he sobs himself to sleep again, and she lies there holding him as she continues to ponder what to do next.

14

SCOOPED

After two more days trapped in bed, Sheila is released from the hospital. She and Gabriel are settled back at home. Together, they scramble to get ready for their morning. She's heading off to work, he to school. Everything is an even greater struggle for Sheila. Now she's in a wheelchair, straining to navigate the tight halls of her townhouse. She hears Gabriel tramping down the stairs and reaches for the backpack to cover his wings.

"No, Momma," he says, stopping her. "Look, I got it all figured out."

He spins around and shows her that his wings are tucked tightly inside his bulky sweatshirt. The wing tips lie against his hips and are covered by a pair of baggy pants. It just about works, but if his wings get any bigger, it won't.

"Okay, very good, Gabe. Do you think you'll be comfortable all day like that?"

"I'll go to the bathroom and flap around by myself if I need to," he says.

"Oh dear, Gabe ..."

"Don't worry, Momma. I'll be really quiet. I know this is very, very—I mean, very, very, very—important to you. I won't show them off. I promise."

Sheila looks at him intently. She can tell he is earnest and eager to please. Both of them have had a big scare, and he isn't going to do anything to risk losing his mother again. They head out the side door and down a new, hastily installed ramp to her car.

Minutes later, Sheila watches nervously as Gabriel runs up the steps to the school's entrance. He looks back and puts his finger to his lips, signaling for her to be quiet. She does the same and smiles. It is their promise to keep their secret.

A short while later, Sheila pulls up to the hospital, surprised to see a melee of press, activists, and fanatics cordoned off in the corner of the parking lot. Once again, police officers man the barricades.

Sheila sighs. "Oh no, not again. What is it this time?"

She doesn't recognize Stan as she drives right past him. He waves a newspaper. "The herald has arrived!" he yells. "Welcome the new dawn!"

Sheila looks away from the small but animated crowd quickly. She is rightfully terrified of becoming the center of another media nightmare. This can't be about her again, can it?

Inside the hospital, the guard stares at Sheila as she wheels through the lobby.

"Good morning, Bart," she says cheerfully. She doesn't want to hear any sympathy from anyone about the wheelchair, so she rushes by, not giving him a chance.

Two nurses heading toward the elevator beside her give her a peculiar look. When they step into the elevator, an older man joins them. In his hand is a tabloid newspaper. On the cover is an image of Gabriel. He's running down their garden path, clear as day, and Sheila is lying on the ground. The headline reads, "KID'S FLIGHT KNOCKS MOM OUT." Sheila snatches the man's newspaper and wheels out when the elevator door opens.

"Oh my God!"

She dashes her wheels down the hall and into her office. She slams the door and examines the photo. It is a pretty clear shot, but Gabriel's feet are on the ground—at least, he seems to be running, so almost on the ground.

Cynthia bursts through the door.

"Don't say it!" Sheila warns.

Cynthia does anyway. "You knew it had to happen."

Sheila is flummoxed and even more so when the door bursts open again.

"Now what?" she exclaims as Philip strides in.

"You've embroiled us in another media frenzy, Sheila. Tell me what's going on here."

"Philip, this is all a big mistake," she protests. "It's some kind of a joke. Look, that's a costume. He was wearing a costume when I fell. He loves birds and the idea of flying, so I made him those wings. They're blue, for God's sake. That's not a real color. He insists on wearing them all the time."

Cynthia gives Sheila a skeptical look and studies Philip's face. He is nonplussed, the fire knocked out of him.

"Of course, of course," he responds after considering her words for a moment. "How could anyone think otherwise? We'll distribute a disclaimer right away."

"Why bother?" Sheila asks. "It's so obviously nonsense; it will just blow over. There's no point in engaging with those tabloids. They're likely to put you on the cover next week and accuse you of being an alien. Just let it go."

Philip looks at them both, one and then the other, as he mulls over the situation. "You're probably right," he says, feeling a bit sheepish. He nods at Cynthia and then backs out the door.

When he is gone, Sheila turns to Cynthia. "Do you think they'll be harassing Gabe at school?"

Her sister's eyes are full of concern. "I think you should go over there and make sure he's all right."

* * *

At school, Gabriel plays in a cramped playhouse with two other children, a boy and a girl. They stare wide-eyed as he takes his shirt his off. His wings pop out and puff up to fill the tiny wooden house. The girl strokes his feathers, and the boy pokes at his wing bones.

"You can really fly?" the boy asks.

"The crow showed me how," Gabriel replies.

"Do you fly like a plane or a helicopter?"

"No, silly," the girl interjects, "he must fly like a duck or a fairy."

"Fairies aren't real," the boy hisses. "They can't fly if they aren't real, can they?"

A teacher knocks on the roof of the house. "Okay, kids, story time. Come on out now."

Gabriel folds his wings quickly and pulls his sweatshirt over his head.

"Aww …" the girl says.

"It's a secret, our secret," Gabriel says as he puts his finger over his lips the same way Sheila did that morning. The two kids make the same gesture and nod. Gabriel scrambles out of the house behind the boy. The girl is about to follow when she spots something on the floor—a bright blue feather. She sneaks it into her pocket and then clambers out on her knees as well.

* * *

Sheila bursts out of a side door at the hospital and rolls down a ramp. TV lights and camera flashes brighten the dull day. Reporters dash across the asphalt toward her.

"That's her!" a reporter yells.

A TV correspondent stuffs a mic in her face. "How did you succeed, Dr. Jensen? Can your child actually fly?"

Sheila pushes past them. "Don't be absurd. It's a costume; he's wearing a costume. Can't you see that?" She kicks her wheelchair into high gear and speeds across the parking lot toward her car.

An activist wielding a banner that reads, "Right to Life—Human Life," chases her. "You can't play God! You and your devil baby are gonna die!"

He's almost on top of her as she struggles to get into her car. The wheelchair ramp seems to take forever to deploy. Out of nowhere, Stan jumps on the activist and drags him away from the car. Sheila stows her chair, clamps her seatbelt, and instructs the car to go to Gabriel's school.

"Gabriel's school. ETA: seven minutes, fifty-six seconds," the car responds. "Avoiding Marchand Avenue due to construction and excessive traffic."

As the car pulls out of the parking lot, Sheila notices the makeup of the mob. They are riled up, with angel groupies led by Stan pushing at the genetic-purist activists on the other side. Shouting escalates, and a security detail pours out of the hospital and gets caught up in the fray. Instead of calming the pent-up anger, they seem to act as an accelerant, and the opposing crowds spill out of the barricades and run toward each other, kicking and punching.

"Gabriel!" Sheila exclaims in a worried whisper.

* * *

As Sheila's car drives around the hospital and onto the avenue, she notices the preschool, where Gabriel used to spend his days. Noreen is fending off intruders at the entrance, and several TV vans are lined up outside. Sheila sighs in relief. It's a shame for Noreen, but clearly no one has found out that Gabriel is at a different school.

"Turn right here," she commands the car, eager to avoid that turmoil lest one of the reporters recognize her. Her car, being a robot, turns obediently.

"Recalculating. Gabriel's School. ETA: eight minutes, eleven seconds."

Sheila arrives at Gabriel's school without further detour. Gabriel's teacher is shocked to see her when she bursts through the door and interrupts story time. The kids, finally calmed down after a rowdy playtime, are focused sleepily on the story. They regard Sheila with wide-eyed confusion when she struggles between them, careful not to roll on toes or fingers. A clog of seated and reclined kids near the front prevent her from moving any farther. She stops and looks around for Gabriel. She spots him in the far corner couch, snuggled with the same two kids from the playhouse.

"Gabriel, come with me now; we have to go."

He jumps up and runs toward her. His teacher, Jane, drops her book and struggles to extract her large frame from a tiny chair and stand up.

"Now wait, Dr. Jensen, this is highly irregular. You can't just bust in here and take him out anytime you want. We need proper notice, and ideally we need it at least a day beforehand."

While Jane is speaking, Sheila whispers to Gabriel to get his things. As he runs off to the coatroom to collect his new Red Dragon backpack, she notices him nod to the two kids on the couch. Both of them touch their fingers to their lips in her secret symbol. A stab of worry pierces her heart. Then she remembers that Jane is still talking to her. Jane is aggravated, her voice rising in pitch.

"I'm sorry; we have a family emergency. We have to go. So sorry."

She snatches Gabriel's hand, turns, and whisks him out the door. On the way, she glances back at the two children and sees the little girl wave goodbye to Gabriel. She's holding a blue feather.

Sheila almost stops on the way to the exit. For a moment, she thinks about going back in to demand the girl hand over the blue feather, but that would be very suspect.

Never mind, Sheila thinks. *Those kids are all going to have the shock of their lives when they watch the news tonight.*

* * *

On the ride home Gabriel grills Sheila about the family emergency, but she is unsure what to say to him. Finally, she tells him their secret may be out. Gabriel is ecstatic and rips his sweatshirt off right away. "Great, now I can fly, right?" Sheila sputters and then bursts into tears. Their life is certainly falling apart right now. For the rest of the trip, Gabriel is the grown up, gently calming and consoling his mother.

* * *

Later that night, Sheila fusses around her bedroom, emptying drawers and stuffing suitcases while Cynthia and Gabriel look on and feebly try to help. Sheila's mind is abuzz with worry, half-made plans, and anger at the loss of her career once again. Then she stops and sighs.

"Gabriel is what matters now," she announces to them both.

Frenzied, she tosses a sneaker and a paper cup into the suitcase and then lobs the other sneaker into the garbage can. Gabriel bursts out laughing. Cynthia removes the cup from the suitcase and exchanges it for the shoe.

"What will you do?" she asks.

"I don't know," Sheila replies. "We'll drive."

"Are we going on vacation?" Gabriel asks.

Sheila turns to him. "Gabriel, go and pack some clothes and toys. Not too much, though. There isn't room in the car."

Cynthia sighs in relief when Gabriel leaves the room. "Sheila, you have to face this."

Sheila is quick to disagree. "No I don't, and I need to get Gabe away."

"That's utterly irresponsible and impossible," Cynthia replies. "How and where on Earth do you think you can hide him?"

Sheila shakes her head. "What would be irresponsible is to let Spiner and Philip treat Gabriel like a lab rat, and you know they would."

"Maybe it's not in their interest to claim responsibility for such a controversial ... uh ... development."

Sheila narrows her eyes at Cynthia. "You meant to say *experiment*, didn't you?" Her eyes tear up again, and she brushes the tears away, irritated. "I didn't mean to experiment on him."

Cynthia bends down to hug her sister. "I don't want to make you feel bad. I know this is really hard for you." She pulls back. "I have an idea. Mike's family has a country house in Oklahoma that's very remote. Let's go there for a few days and think about what to do."

As Sheila looks at Cynthia, a light of hope and relief dawns in her clouded eyes. She nods, appreciative.

"First thing tomorrow then," Cynthia concludes.

"No, I need to clear out some important stuff in my office in the morning," Sheila says. "It'll only take an hour. Let's go after that."

* * *

The day Sheila's life changes forever is refreshing and bright, with the sun streaming through the windows and the sound of children playing in the park drifting in while she wheels down the hospital corridor toward her office. None of that cheeriness calms her heart or lifts her worried mood. Inside, she stuffs her notebooks and her laptop into the sack on the side of her wheelchair. She tucks a handful of zip drives and a bulky backup drive into the pocket of her jacket and then looks around to determine if she needs anything else. This is her life's work, her livelihood, but she can't leave it all behind. In the back of her mind, she is sure there is more work to be done and more discoveries she needs to make about Gabriel. She rolls around the lab slowly, taking in all its aspects. It has been home for so long, but now it's finally time to say goodbye. She deeply regrets it.

Down the hall in his office, Philip is browsing through his computer files, studying Gabriel's history, when the phone rings. He answers it and hears the brusque voice of Larry Costain, the hospital's chief of security, a bullish man with a gruff, abrupt military tone.

"You said you wanted to know when Dr. Jensen came in. She checked in five minutes ago. She's probably in her office or the lab by now."

"Great!" Philip replies. He hangs up and gets up to leave.

Sheila glides past the animal cages and says goodbye to the odd creatures, one by one. Her point of view from the wheelchair is different from before. She's closer to eye level to most of her captives. Sad eyes that seem to contain wisdom beyond their normal acumen stare at her. She has always struggled with the ethics of her work, but somehow she managed to maintain a fierce barrier of unfeeling professionalism. But things have changed since Gabriel opened her heart. Only now is she beginning to feel that openness spilling into this context.

Previously, she never noticed how deep the eyes of the rabbits were, how thoughtfully they followed her movements. Until now, she was so determined and on such a tight schedule that she didn't take time to really look at these living, feeling creatures.

She removes a rabbit with a defined patchwork of different colors and types of fur from his cage. He's a bit skittish at first, but then he settles in her lap as she pets him. She has never done this before, never actually taken time to pet any of the subjects. She luxuriates in the feel of each kind of fur in her fingers. She lifts the animal to her face and brushes her cheek with the smooth, curly, and wiry fur. Her eyes well with tears again. This kind of reaction to life's events is becoming a habit for her now. This time she gives in to it; after all, she is realizing without a doubt that her life here is over. There is no way she can continue experimenting on these poor beings. She returns the rabbit to his cage and gives him a carrot treat.

She jumps as the lab door slams open. Philip marches in and stops right in front of her.

"How are you feeling? I'm so sorry you need that now," he says nodding at the wheelchair.

Sheila lifts her head defiantly. She isn't sure why, but she feels resentful of his sympathy. "I'm fine. It's only temporary anyway."

He doesn't believe her; she doesn't believe herself. They both know her prognosis is steady decline, and it's difficult to come back from any loss of mobility due to nerve deterioration. But they feign hope for hope's sake. "Great. I'm sure you're right," he responds.

Sheila sighs with resolve and rummages in her purse, pulling out a sheet of paper. "I need some personal time. Gabriel and I are going away for a while." She hands him her resignation.

Philip works hard to keep the emotion and desperation out of his voice, to keep his voice under control. He wasn't ready to play this card yet, but it seems necessary now.

"Sheila, I know Gabriel is my son. I've started a court petition to establish that." Sheila shoots him a black and hateful look.

"You know I love him. I love you. We can be together. We should be together for you and for him."

"Look at me," she taunts, "I can barely care for him. I can't be a wife too." He bends down to massage her legs, but she pushes his hands away. "Don't … please. You can't know how I feel or what I'm dealing with."

"Sheila, we lived together for five years. I know you as well as if we were married. What is going on? I can help you."

"We aren't married," she retorts curtly.

"But we've created so much together," he replies, trying another appeal.

Sheila looks at him with a hardened gaze. "That's science, not sex, Philip."

He stands up, takes a breath, and resolves to ask the big question. "For you, it all might have been heartless, but not for me."

She looks at him coldly. He realizes she is lost to him. He swallows and then asks the question that has been burning in his mind. "Did you do some kind of experimental gene manipulation on Gabriel?"

Sheila blinks, flustered. She had no idea that he was entertaining that line of thinking. She had feared it would come, but not this soon. Now she is desperate to get away.

"I'm leaving with or without your approval." She pushes past him and wheels out of the lab.

Philip is now sure he has his answer. He steps out of the lab after her. "Okay, now I'm sure he is!" he calls. "I want you to bring him in here today. If you don't, I'll get a court order and sue for custody. What you have done is cruel, dangerous, and illegal. We need to do a full work-up and figure out what's going on here. If you're getting us into another mess, it's the least you can do. We need to protect all our work and this institution too, you know."

He yells after her, his voice escalating as she turns the corner at the end of the hall. "Sheila, you have to help us get ahead of this! No one believes that nonsense about a costume. As farfetched as wings are, you're the one to pull it off, and everyone knows that. I need to see him now."

At that moment, Larry Costain exits the elevator in front of them. Sheila tries to go around him, but Philip grabs the back of her chair.

"What are you doing?" she demands.

Philip steps in front of her. "You can make it easy, Sheila."

He nods at Larry and points to the laptop bag attached to Sheila's chair. Larry goes to snatch it, but she clutches it and stares him down. She's no match for Larry's strength though. He wrests it from her. She looks to Philip, begging for help.

"I thought you needed personal time," Philip said. "Why would you need to take this work computer with you? Or are you really going to another job and stealing intellectual property?" He knows this isn't true, but the pain in his heart makes him want to dig at her in every way that he can.

She bristles at the accusation. "You know me better than that."

He studies her face. "But you bend the rules here. You have bent the rules here, haven't you? Broken them even."

Sheila glares at him, afraid to say anything. He seems to know too much already, and she is terrified she will give him more than she should if she opens her mouth again. She checks surreptitiously to see if the backup drives are still in her pocket.

"Fine, keep it," she says bitterly, and then she turns and rolls into the elevator.

Philip and Larry head straight back to the lab and Sheila's office. Philip rambles on with his plans, more for his own benefit than for Larry's ears. "I'm calling a lawyer right now. We'll get Gabriel in here as soon as we can. I can't believe she would be so heartless." Philip fires up her computer while Larry breaks open the file cabinet and rifles through the physical records.

"What proof of paternity or tampering are we looking for?" Larry asks. "Would she file his results under Jensen, Gabriel, or some other pseudonym?"

"I don't know," Philip replies.

15

A NECESSARY EXODUS

Sheila returns to her house upset and more determined than before to get out of town. There is a flurry of activity in her driveway. Cynthia lumbers down the front steps with a large cooler. Mike and Mikey are bringing stuff out, getting ready to pack the car the minute Sheila returns. Danny and Gabriel are tearing around the yard with Bill flapping overhead. A red superhero cape shaped like batwings disguises Gabriel's own wings. He proudly thrusts out his chest, which is adorned with a picture of Red Dragon. "Look, Momma, Aunty Sheila gave me this." Sheila nods distracted and immediately begins directing Mike and Cynthia from inside the car on how to pack their stuff.

Pretty soon the car is crammed full, but quite a few bags and boxes are still strewn about the front steps of the house. Sheila shrugs and just calls Gabriel to get in the car. He trots up and climbs in with a shoebox under his arm.

"What is that, Gabe?" Sheila asks, spotting the box.

"This is gonna be a really comfy ride, for Bill," he says with quiet affection. "I made it so he can come with us." Bill is squashed into a shoebox lined with a dishtowel. Bill rolls over so that Gabriel can rub his belly.

"No, Gabe, you can't stuff him in there. That's not right. He's a wild bird, and it's time to let him go."

Gabriel tears up. "I can't, Momma. He's my best friend, and he's my only friend. He has to come."

He begins to cry outright. Sheila's heart breaks. She contemplates for a moment and then opts for peace. "Okay, Gabe, but take the lid off him. He needs air, and it's too tight for him to move in there."

Just then, a cleaning van pulls into the end of the driveway. Sheila sighs with relief. "Cynthia, please ask them to wait a moment until we pull out."

"Of course," Cynthia responds, "but what's that all about?"

Sheila shrugs, deciding to give her a soft answer. "I think I might want to rent the place out, so they're giving it the once over and putting the stuff we've left behind into storage."

"Oh!" Cynthia says, turning toward the cleaning crew.

Sheila is relieved that Cynthia doesn't press the issue. She really has asked the crew to do a complete and thorough cleanup. She's afraid Philip might still have a key to the place and will come snooping around and possibly even find something like a hair for DNA evidence of his connection to Gabriel.

"It's time to pile in!" Cynthia calls cheerfully.

Sheila turns to her and smiles. "Thank you so much. We can manage now," she says, punching in directions for the car's GPS.

"Stop," Cynthia says. "I'm coming with you. Mike you're okay with the kids for a few days, right?"

Mike nods.

"I want to see you two settled," Cynthia continues.

Sheila looks doubtful. "But—"

"No arguments. I have to know that you're going to be all right."

They climb into the back of the car. With no driver's seat, the car is roomy, with a large TV screen, a drop-down table, and a small fridge where the front passenger seat would have been. But still, the extra baggage makes the car feel cramped. Cynthia is secretly relieved that vehicle owners have the option of self-driving vehicles. It's one less hurdle that she needs to worry about Sheila managing. The car backs out of the driveway, and Sheila waves the okay to the cleaning crew. Their van swings into place after them.

* * *

They head off and pass a black sedan parked at the end of the street. Smoked glass windows hide the fact that Larry sits inside watching them as they drive past. His phone rings.

"Right, they're leaving."

He still prefers to drive, rather than let the car drive itself, and he pulls out to fall in line behind Sheila's car. They exit the neighborhood and ease onto the busy turnpike. Soon, they turn through the cloverleaf and onto the speeding city highway.

A loud motorcycle revs along behind them. The biker's jacket is emblazoned in red with the words *Angel Echo* and a set of gold wings. Stan, still in his paint-splashed jeans, glances into Larry's sedan. In front of them both, Sheila's car navigates through dense traffic and a road repair crew to cross the last bridge out. The city recedes behind them. The sedan and the motorcycle follow.

* * *

Hours later, Cynthia and Gabriel play a card game as they drive. Gabriel looks up at his mother, who has stopped playing and is staring wistfully out the window.

"Momma, where are we going?"

She turns to him and smiles with a sense of relief and freedom. "A place where nobody will see you fly."

Gabriel stops and thinks for a minute. "Ah! You mean I can fly free there?"

She nods. "I hope so."

"You can fly too," he responds.

Sheila and Cynthia look at each other perplexed. Cynthia shrugs, but Sheila shakes her head, warning off any kind of explanation or excuse. These days, she is inclined to let things go and roll with it. If Gabriel wants to think she can fly, then that's fine for now.

"Let's sing!" Gabriel shouts suddenly.

They travel down the highway joyfully. Sheila feels she can breathe for the first time in a while. Gabriel, though usually a happy child, is especially happy. They sing Gabriel's favorite songs, and they all seem to be about freedom, release, or some other soaring, hopeful state.

Even though the car is self-navigating, it still sports a set of vestigial rearview mirrors. Sheila glances in the passenger mirror and sees blue feathers sticking out the car window. Gabriel has snuck his right wingtip out of the slightly open window to feel the wind. The blue feathers ripple and roll in the rush of wind. Sheila panics.

"Gabriel! Wings! Get them inside now!"

Three cars behind them, the black sedan swerves side to side with Larry trying to get a good look. The security chief, brandishing a camera in one hand, thinks he has seen something odd, but he can't be sure, so he is trying to get a shot. Was it a scarf blowing through the window or something else?

His erratic driving attracts Sheila's attention, and she turns in her seat to look back. Larry drops his car into the left lane behind a truck. He picks up speed and drives past them, clicking the camera all the while, but he is going so fast that he sees nothing but a blur.

Miles later and further down the road, Larry's black sedan is on the shoulder, waiting. He pulls out again a few cars behind Sheila and resumes following at an easy pace.

Trees, telephone poles, farms and pockets of businesses pass, multiple cities recede into the distance and they continue to drive. Sheila, Cynthia, and Gabriel pass the time playing games, chatting, watching shows on the touch screen TV, and napping.

Everything goes well when they stop for lunch at a rest stop diner. The place is so busy and everyone so rushed that they disappear into the crowd. Gabriel's superhero cape does a super job of disguising his wings.

Later in the afternoon, Sheila is watching a movie on her palm device with headphones on when Gabriel awakens from a nap and whines about needing to go to the bathroom. She looks outside. The landscape is quite different now. Vast skies and miles of grainfields sweep toward the low horizon. The occasional forest punches through the flatness. Sheila instructs the car to navigate to the nearest gas station with a bathroom.

"Confirmed. ETA: six minutes, thirty-five seconds."

"See?" she says, turning to Gabriel. "That's really lucky; we're very close."

He squirms around. "Oh, oh, I don't know if I can wait."

"Sit tight. You can, Gabe," Cynthia encourages. "It's in your mind. You can."

He closes his eyes and appears to listen. Then he shakes his head urgently. "No, Aunty. I'm really sure it's not just in my mind, and it really wants to get out."

"Okay, look there it is!" Sheila yells pointing at a large green road sign. "Hang on, we're nearly there."

* * *

Gabriel fidgets and squirms as they loop through another cloverleaf to enter the rest stop. The second the car halts and the safety locks click open, he spills out of the car. His superhero cape is twisted like a rope and falls limply between his two wings. Sensing their freedom, Gabriel's wings flex slightly, stretching and moving after the long and scrunching ride.

Larry's black sedan is just sweeping round the cloverleaf above the gas station when he glances out and sees Gabriel out in the open racing across the parking lot, his blue wings flapping freely. *Holy cow! What was that?* Larry asks himself as he screeches to a halt and fumbles for his camera.

Sheila and Cynthia struggle to get Sheila's wheelchair out of the car. When Sheila looks up, she is shocked. "Gabe, stop!"

Gabriel is just exiting the bathroom, and his wings are still exposed. He stops, unsure of why she is yelling at him. Cynthia runs over to him.

Larry has his camera lined up and starts shooting video. Suddenly, Cynthia blocks his view, fussing with the boy's clothing.

"Damn! Get out of the way, lady!"

He continues shooting, but somehow, without being aware of it, Cynthia positions herself mostly in the way, preventing a clear shot. Then Gabriel strolls over to the car with his wings tucked back under his cape.

Larry stops recording and hits Play, hoping for at least one good view of what he thinks he saw.

"Here we go," he says. At the beginning of the recording, Gabriel steps out of the bathroom door, and there's a side view of his left wing partially open. Gabriel stretches the wing wide as he comes out the door. The other wing appears to be opening up, too. Finally, Gabriel stops short with his back to the camera and faces his mother in her wheelchair next to the car. Cynthia runs toward him. Both wings lift and flex.

"Pay dirt!" Larry exclaims. "This is big. Wow! Big! Larry, you are good. There's no way that's a costume."

He revs the car and continues down the ramp toward the gas station, where Sheila, Gabe, and Cynthia are entering the minimart with an empty tote bag. Just as they disappear inside, Larry's vehicle squeals around the bend and heads back toward home.

Sheila glances up at the noise. "Cynthia, do you remember that car?"

Cynthia searches the road, but the car is moving quickly and is now too small to identify. "I don't know. I don't think so."

They step inside and move toward the aisles, where Gabriel tosses a pile of fruit-and-nut bars into the basket, hoping that the chocolate bar mixed in will make it through the checkout.

Soon, they are off the highway and traveling on open roads through acres of farmland and forest. Low hills appear on the horizon and grow steadily as they drive toward them. The afternoon grows old, and the sky turns rich with color in the few high clouds above. A gentle breeze ruffles the trees, and Sheila breathes deeper than she has for a long time.

Gabriel sleeps soundly. Cynthia looks up from her book and interrupts Sheila as she surfs the Internet on the car's touch screen TV. "So, have you come up with a plan?"

Sheila isn't sure what Cynthia means, but the tightness returns to her chest. "A plan?"

"To keep your secret, Gabriel's secret. How do you plan to do it?"

Sheila sighs. "That's what this week is for—to figure it out, to breathe some open air, to let Gabriel test his wings, and hopefully to come up with a plan. I didn't tell you Philip is planning to sue for custody." Saying it relieves some of the tightness. All day she has wanted to share this with Cynthia, to try to work out what it might mean for them, but she couldn't say anything in front of Gabriel.

"What? Custody? Does that mean he knows?"

Sheila shakes her head, "I don't think he is sure yet, but he has put the pieces together and has a strong suspicion."

A loud flock of geese passes above close to the car, honking loudly.

Gabriel stirs. Sheila and Cynthia share the look that says, "Let's be quiet for now." Sheila brushes Gabriel's hair from his eyes.

"Did you see the geese, babe?"

"Not *babe*, Momma. I'm a boy now. You can't call me *babe*."

She laughs. "I know. I'm sorry, but look at all those geese."

"I know. They honked me awake," he says, nodding.

"According to the GPS, we're almost there," Cynthia announces. "Look out for the next sign."

"I can see it," Gabriel replies. "It says 'Willow Brook.'"

"I can't see any sign at all, let alone read it," Cynthia complains.

"Can you really see that?" Sheila asks.

Cynthia retorts, "I guess we'll know when we get close enough to see ourselves. I wonder what other talents will emerge."

Gabriel kicks his feet and fumbles with his harness, trying to unlock the clasp.

"Stop, Gabe," Sheila says. "I'll open the sunroof so you can get a sense of the outdoors, but sit still while the car is moving!"

Sheila flips the control panel open and presses a button, and the car's sunroof cranks back until the entire top of the car is open. Gabriel laughs gleefully, and Bill slips through the opening, relieved to be out in the open again.

"Oh, no!" Gabriel cries.

"It's okay," Cynthia says. "We're there. He won't be lost."

They drive between vast fields of grain with occasional trees and copses smattering the skyline. They hear a distant screech, and Cynthia looks up.

"Oh! Look! An eagle."

Gabriel cranes his neck up and peers out through the sunroof. "Aah!" he sighs.

With his superb long-distance vision, Gabriel watches the eagle. He analyzes each powerful thrust of the eagle's wings. He sees the bird's stomach feathers ruffle and blow in the rippling airstream and his yellow claws tucked back neatly to minimize drag. Not only does Gabriel see every detail of the bird and his minute adjustments, but he also sees the streams of air as they lift the bird. He sees warmer air circling within cooler air and currents of air rising while others fall. The amazing bird is surfing an invisible wave. Gabriel also sees heat waves emanating from the bird's body and, beyond that, subtle waves of energy that connect the bird to the world and even to him. They are kindred spirits.

Suddenly, the eagle turns and looks directly at him. Gabriel peers intently into the eagle's ancient eye. For a moment, he sees things from the eagle's point of view. He actually sees through the eagle's stoic hunter's stare as it appraises the peculiar boy in the car. Gabriel is aware of the bird's speed and the wind grazing its feathers. Then the eagle turns and circles away, and its mesmerizing grip on Gabriel is broken. He feels ecstatic. Flying is going to be the most amazing thing!

* * *

The sign that reads "Willow Brook," now clear to both women as well, grows larger on their right. The car swerves and enters a cut in the field; it's a dirt track through a cornfield. Spooked crows flap upwards behind them in the car's dust trail. For a worried moment, Sheila wonders if Bill will join the raucous black crowd and leave for good.

She doesn't notice a lone vehicle, a motorcycle, thundering by on the road they have just left.

Stan, the motorcycle driver, cranes to peer at the dozens of crows and the columns of dust rising from the car as it rumbles away from the road.

16

HEALING FLIGHT

Sheila's car enters a tight, dark pine forest. The track is soft and coated with layers of pine needles, and little sun comes through. Gabriel's eyes are wide; he has never seen such a place. "It feels like something out of a book," he says.

Soon enough they emerge from the dappled edge of the forest and enter a flowery meadow with occasional copses of trees. A modest, pastel house, at least one hundred years old, is nestled beneath a giant willow tree on a gentle slope. A creek burbles down the slope and beneath the house's side deck. The creek bed spreads out to flow smoothly through the meadow and enter the forest near where they left it. Gabriel whoops with joy.

As the car winds up the arbitrary curls of the ill-defined driveway, Gabriel pops his safety harness and stands up to poke his head out through the sunroof.

"Hey, sit down!" Sheila snaps.

Before she or Cynthia can grab him, he unfurls his wings and lifts out of the moving car and up into the air.

"Stop!" Cynthia yells. The car halts abruptly, but Gabriel doesn't. He glides out across the field, alternately cawing like a crow and laughing and then screeching like an eagle or honking like a goose and laughing again. Cynthia jumps out of the car and runs across the meadow after Gabriel. Sheila yanks on her wheelchair, trying frantically to get it out of the stowaway.

"Oh, Cynthia, watch him, please. I can't get out," she yells.

Gabriel plunges and climbs, dives and soars. Cynthia wanders through the dense grass that almost brushes her waist, ever closer to him, watching carefully. She can't help but smile; his enthusiasm is infectious.

Finally, Sheila gets into her chair and rolls clumsily into the rough grass, but the undergrowth is too dense for her. She gets stuck still close to the car.

Gabriel glides over the meadow, and Cynthia follows below, moving farther and farther into the colorful, gently waving flowers and grasses. Then, suddenly remembering his mother, Gabriel dives back toward her.

"Watch me, Momma. Watch me now!" he yells as he swoops closer and closer and then almost grazes her head, slapping her upraised hand in a high five. Sheila is also entranced and smiling. He locks eyes with her.

A sudden remembrance of their first flying encounter rushes into her awareness. His eyes are so clear, so compelling, so very, very blue, or possibly even a profound, otherworldly purple. She sighs deeply, filled with ease and joy, and watches as he banks around and around. He catches a thermal current that only he and perhaps the eagle can see.

"Ah," he sighs, feeling the rightness and grace of the air pushing him upward. He whirls in deliberate circles and watches with eagle vision as his mother recedes. She's etched into the landscape below, her shadow long as the sun reaches out to touch the horizon.

Sheila cranes her neck upward. She's entranced, her eyes locked onto her son, stretching to keep hold of him as he shrinks against the rich evening sky. His radiant blue wings blend with the ultramarine void so that they essentially disappear. He seems to fall gracefully into the soft, gold-tinged clouds so high above them all. Sheila stares, spellbound. Even though he is at a dizzying height and so very tiny, when he turns to look at her, their eyes lock again. His eyes are piercing sparks of light shooting toward her.

Suddenly, she stands up and steps away from her wheelchair. Her eyes are transfixed on him and following his movements, even though his face is turned away from her. She steps farther into the field, moving at first in tight, uncertain circles beneath Gabriel and then in concert with his flight path. Her body follows his movements. She's so focused on him that she is unaware of her own movement. She thinks she is still sitting in the chair. She moves in wider and wider arcs with more grace in each step. Sheila actually feels like she is flying, too. Is it her imagination, or is it real?

In a moment, the distance between them closes, and she sees Gabriel flying right in front of her. The vast landscape stretches out below her.

The house looks doll-like. Colors are brighter, the car shinier. Reality is heightened, and everything below her is inscribed with surreal clarity. A tiny image of her body moves in a wide circle on the lawn some distance from the wheelchair below. This confuses her, because she, in her more-real-than-real self, is flying with Gabriel, and this world that she sees now from so high is filled with amazing revelations.

Gabriel laughs, knowing she has accepted his silent invitation. He loops around in sync with Sheila's dance. Or does the dance follow him? Perhaps they really are one. Close behind him flies an ethereal light being that resembles Sheila. Together, they streak into the zenith.

Cynthia, still in the middle of the meadow, has been watching Gabriel diligently.

"He's gone! I can't see him, Sheila."

She looks around to find her sister. First, she sees the empty wheelchair, and then, searching the field, she spots Sheila dancing in the middle of the lawn near the house.

"Sheila!" she shrieks as she wades through the deep grasses.

Sheila laughs heartily. "I'm flying, soaring, gliding, falling," she says between gasps.

Cynthia struggles to reach her. "You're dancing, Sheila! Not just walking but dancing."

With some kind of inner *thunk*, Sheila's gaze reverts to her grounded reality, and she looks around, stunned. Then she plops onto the lawn, laughing.

Gabriel senses her shift in attention and swoops back into view, plummeting toward them. Both women watch in awe as he spirals down, closer and closer. Cynthia wades across the meadow, working her way slowly toward the lawn where Sheila lies peering up at the sky. Gabriel tumbles onto his mother. They roll across the grass together, hysterical with laughter. Cynthia breaks free of the meadow, runs across the lawn, and bends down beside them.

"Are you all right?" she asks Sheila.

Sheila stands up, steps forward and back, and then does a quick samba step and doubles over with laughter. Cynthia gasps as Sheila takes off running, hopping, and skipping. Cynthia and Gabriel chase after her, cheering. When they catch up, they all hug each other, jumping around with glee.

17

THE CHASE BEGINS

In his office, Philip mopes, unable to work. He stares out the window into the park. Someone knocks at his door.

"It's open!"

Larry rushes in, direct from his odyssey following Sheila to the countryside. "I got something," he blurts out on his way through the door. "Look." He slaps a digital tablet on the desk. They watch the brief video clip. Philip plays it again.

"Is that really what I see, not a costume but actual …" He restarts the clip and then pauses it at the best view of Gabriel's wings. "Wings?"

He sits back and takes a breath, pausing to process this amazing realization. He looks at Larry. "Do you know where they are now?"

"No," Larry says, worried suddenly. He was so excited to get the shot that he neglected to continue following them. "You said get some evidence, not find out where they're going. But we know which way they're headed, and that narrows it down."

Philip gives him a questioning look. "What about the GPS in her car? Can you track where she went?"

"Sure, we're keeping track," he says defensively. "But she has it on privacy mode, so we're waiting to give them time to settle. Then I'll go through the legal process of getting the information we need to find them. That will also give us time to get a team ready, depending on what you decide. I was—am—planning to tell you when we find out."

Philip nods, only half listening. He pounds his desk, trying to focus his mind. Then he gets up to pace the room.

"Wow, it's true. It's real. This is big. This is new territory. It's strange and a bit terrifying." He looks up at Larry. "And they're out there by themselves?"

"No, Cynthia Clark is with them. What's the next step?"

Philip pauses. His mind is racing; he's almost panicking. He takes a deep breath. "I don't really know where to go from here."

"I think Spiner will want to see this."

Philip shakes his head. "No, not yet." He isn't ready to let the situation blow up out of his control. "Let me think about it first. We don't know any of the facts, and we don't know if the hospital has any rights in this matter yet."

"Okay," Larry concedes. "Tell you what: I'll assign a team to put all of Dr. Jensen's prior work together so that you can ex—"

"No, not that either," Philip interrupts. "I'll do it. I don't want anyone else aware of this yet. It's too explosive. It would only get out somehow, and we'd have another media firestorm. Let's keep it tightly wrapped for right now. Okay?"

Philip points at the tablet as Larry reaches for it. "Send me all of your files, including all the pictures, and delete them from all of your devices. I want to keep everything as tight as possible."

"Sure," Larry says. "I understand. After that last hack, we don't need another scandal. I'll double down on cyber security as well. I suggest you store it all on an offline external drive. That's the safest way."

Philip nods in agreement. "That's exactly my plan."

18

SPOILED SANCTUARY

Sheila, Gabriel, and Cynthia have settled comfortably into the small farmhouse. The fresh air, quiet, and gentle winds have drawn them outside everyday so far. They saunter along the creek bank. To one side, the forested hill rises gently, getting tighter, denser, and darker as it reaches a crest. The forest continues on the other side of the creek, but it's open and filled with mottled sunlight. They catch glimpses of meadows and cornfields through it. Gabriel circles them only a few feet off the ground together with Bill, who seems especially excited in this new place. The winged ones buzz the two women playfully. Cynthia and Sheila duck, dodge around, and laugh. When Gabriel soars off and up through a gap in the trees, Bill follows.

Cynthia circles Sheila, scrutinizing her. "What the heck happened?"

Sheila shrugs. "Miracle?"

"Sheila, we're doctors!"

"Well, so far pills and surgeries have done nothing for me, so I'll say it again: miracle!"

Cynthia is perplexed. "I don't know. Why now? Why you? You've never been a believer. And what's a miracle anyway?"

Sheila shrugs. "Maybe it is just science we haven't quite figured out yet." She thinks for a moment and then points at Gabriel, who soars above the trees. "Look at him; he's definitely a miracle."

Cynthia stops walking. "Wait, didn't you engineer his genes somehow? I've been thinking all along that he was one of your unsanctioned experiments, but you've never explained. So tell me, what did you do exactly?"

"I'm telling you, Cynthia, I don't know. There could be some underlying reason for the wings that I haven't figured out yet."

Sheila's mind races. She has thought about and studied Gabriel for the last five years and has never been able to make sense of what happened in the lab. She has run and rerun the entire process in her mind and in her journal, but it still makes no sense. She starts chattering, a bit too fast. Cynthia stops her occasionally and asks her to repeat something or clarify, but basically Sheila tells her what she remembers of the night Gabriel was engineered.

"I took a fertilized ovum—Philip and I had them stored for future use right after we got engaged as a safety. Then I took the last of that successful genomic-zone strip that we used to repair the eagle's declining neural system. I figured if it worked once, it would work again. None of the strips I tried to generate in the same way before were viable. You have to understand, I was frantic. I'd just received a terrible prognosis for my own disease. I had no idea if I would have enough time to have a child, let alone raise him. It was a desperate play. My career seemed over, so I figured I was all in. I had nothing to lose.

"Anyway, I did the insertion, and it looked good. I'd tried it a dozen times before on nonhuman test ova, but none of them succeeded. I thought the eagle must have been some kind of aberration that shouldn't have worked. I kept trying, and then it worked—or so I thought. But suddenly, as I watched, something happened. Under the microscope, it looked as if the zygote became a supernova. It looked like it shorted the equipment, which shorted the lab, which shorted the hospital. The next thing you know, the entire city was blacked out."

Cynthia nods. "Oh, yeah, I remember that now."

"That's why I came to you right away. I was stunned when the emergency generators kicked everything back online and the zygote was still pulsing, still viable. No matter what happened, I was not going to miss the opportunity, so here we are."

Cynthia takes a deep breath. "Sheila, none of this explains wings."

Sheila nods. "Yeah, I know. I agree. I don't get it either."

They walk in silence for a long while, their minds working and reworking the problem within the framework of their understanding. They can see Gabriel gliding quietly over the treetops.

"What happened in the field back there?" Cynthia asks. "Maybe there's an answer there."

Sheila looks at her, puzzled. "You're right, this … this …" She points to her feet and hops from one foot to the other, stamping and grinning.

"This is a key somehow. I shouldn't be walking, but I am. He shouldn't be flying, but he is. I don't think it has to do with physical effects. It's not about building blocks and chemical switches. I think some greater power is at work here."

"Wait, Sheila. I'll say it again: We're doctors! Let's keep it real."

Sheila frowns. "I know, it's crazy, but … I … I have a strange feeling there's more here than meets the eye."

Gabriel zooms down to greet them, tapping Sheila on the shoulder as he lands. "You're it, Momma!"

"No fair! I can't fly!"

Cynthia runs after Gabriel. "Okay, you little troublemaker. We'll play, but no flying. Only running."

They weave around each other, dodging through the trees. Sheila laughs and stumbles.

"Come on, come on. It's been a long time since I ran. Give me a handicap!"

"Okay, Momma," Gabriel says. "I'm on your team." He tags Cynthia. "You're it!"

"Hey, wait a minute!" Cynthia yells.

They all turn and run back down the path along the creek, through the dappled forest, out across the driveway track, and onto the lawn beside the house. Once there under the open sky again, Gabriel can't help himself. He lifts into the air, swings around, and brushes past his mother and aunt, grazing them both with his feathers.

Sheila halts, catching Gabriel's overpowering look. She is transfixed. "Ah!" she sighs. "I feel so good."

Gabriel swoops around again. "Look at me! *Kee, kee!*" he shouts as he streaks past.

"Now he's imitating the hawks," Cynthia says.

Just then, she catches a glint in Gabriel's eye. Their eyes lock when he passes over her. His movements hypnotize her too. Cynthia sees his wings lift and adjust. She sees the effect of the air on them and the way they glint in the sun. Then she feels like she is flying. She sails along behind Gabriel and sees the light of the sun shining through his wings, revealing a delicate striped effect. It feels so natural, this sailing over the landscape, this lightness of being. She feels elated.

Below her, Sheila whirls like a dervish. Then Cynthia spots her body beginning to spin too. Somehow it's not strange to see herself there and to be up in the air at the same time. Only in a tiny corner of her brain do alarm bells go off; flying feels so right.

Gabriel ascends, trailed by two gleaming light-forms, one resembling his mother and the other his aunt. These sublime beings shine or glow in the late afternoon sun. They look exactly like the physical forms dancing way below on the lawn. Gossamer, silver strands attach each woman to her corresponding ethereal self, and each displays an extraordinary set of light-infused wings. Their faces all share the same euphoric and lustrous smiles.

Together, they sail through the air, swooping, plunging, climbing, ducking, and dodging. The game of tag escalates, continuing high in the air above the house. All of them move in sync like a flock of pigeons or a school of fish. They seem to ride on waves of light, twirling streams of color that lift and drop, forming passages of connectivity between them and the world around them. Bill dodges around, between, up, over, and under the three jostling flyers.

On the ground, Sheila is utterly entranced, and her physical form actually floats four feet in the air. Cynthia suddenly spots her sister floating, and her light-form springs back into her body like a rubber band snapping into a palm. Her countenance changes instantly; her face becomes somber and her eyes darker as she comes back to her "real" self. Awkwardly regaining her balance, Cynthia runs over to Sheila and yanks her down from her suspended state. Sheila's light-form spins down in a wiry coil until it recedes through the top of her physical head. The two of them plunk down onto the grass. Cynthia cradles Sheila.

"Don't fall, baby sister. I've got you," she sobs, now irrational and hysterical. Her usual calm and capable poise has cracked.

Gabriel is unaware that he has lost his followers, because a distant movement has distracted his eagle eye. He continues, slipping over the rippling airstreams and peering in the direction of some remote glint. Then he streaks toward it.

Within minutes, he careens over Stan, who is huddled behind a telephoto lens on a high hill several miles away. Gabriel rolls through the air with the athletic grace of a performer and comes up right in front of the camera, where he hovers, posing. Stan clicks multiple shots.

"Thank you! Let me help you! I'm your number one fan."

Gabriel waves to Stan and then swoops back toward the house.

* * *

Later that evening, as the shadows grow longer, Sheila sits in the classic rocking chair on the front porch of the old house scribbling in her notebook. Gabriel plays in the setting sunlight. Bill, perched on the porch rail, preens himself. Cynthia, who sits beside Sheila, stares into the darkening sky.

"I could swear I was flying."

"Me too," Sheila agrees.

Gabriel plays like a child, walking a stuffed polar bear over to a plastic superhero doll and making them fight. The unusual thing is that he has them make up, kiss each other, hug, and apologize. Then they fight again.

Sheila waves her notebook at Cynthia. "How can I ever publish any of this?"

Cynthia reflects for a moment. She's stumped, too. "Just write the facts," she says finally. "The wings, what shows, what happened, exactly what you did, and what resulted. I don't know if you can draw any conclusions yet, but for now, just document it all. After all, your proof is undeniable." She points to Gabriel.

They both think for a minute in silence.

"Philip could get it published," Cynthia finally offers.

Sheila spurts, displeased. "He would take over."

Cynthia won't let it go. She realizes what's at stake and how big this thing could get. "Sheila, you need help. I can't be here for you forever. My family is missing me at home, and besides, I'm not nearly resourceful enough to help out with what could happen here."

"What on Earth do you think could happen here, Cynthia?" Sheila snaps.

Cynthia sighs. "Sheila, how are you going to make a quality life for Gabriel? He can't go to school. You can't take him to the supermarket, the library, or the movies. You can't really leave him alone, because he's still underage, even though he seems mature beyond his years. How will you manage alone in a place like this in the middle of nowhere?"

Gabriel clambers over to Sheila, done with his games on the floor. He climbs into her lap and fidgets until he is comfy. Both women's faces crack into smiles. Sheila strokes his hair and Cynthia reaches over to smooth out a feather that has twisted over.

"Can we talk about this later?" Sheila asks.

* * *

That night, Sheila dreams a vivid, more-real-than-real dream. She runs through the city chasing Gabriel. He flies over the houses, through gardens, and down the streets, but she can't keep up with him. Eventually, she runs into a garden, and the firm lawn becomes a shallow pond that she wades through. It becomes thicker and thicker with mud until she is stuck. She cries out to Gabriel, who is silhouetted by the setting sun and receding into the distance.

* * *

The next morning, Gabriel is cranky at breakfast because Cynthia is leaving them. "This is the best time of my life," he says for the third time, spitting out cereal as he speaks. "Can you come back soon, Aunty? Please?"

There's a beep outside. Sheila peeks out of the window. "Your car is here." She's feeling sad too.

Cynthia kisses Gabriel on the forehead and wipes his mouth with a paper towel. Then she grabs Sheila, and they hug each other tighter than ever. When Cynthia breaks away and dashes out of the kitchen, both of them are teary.

Gabriel and Sheila both run after her to the porch and watch as she tosses her bag into the back of the driverless taxi. They wave as the car retreats down the winding dirt driveway. Gabriel takes a step forward and starts to extend his wings. Sheila snatches his hand and grips it tight, stalling his momentum.

"No, baby, come back. We're going out for lunch, and then we'll go shopping. But you have to behave. No showing off, okay? We need to figure out how we are going to do this."

19

DNA PROOF

Philip and Larry search through Sheila's lab for clues about Gabriel. Philip surfs through video footage of the night Gabriel was conceived. Larry rummages through the file cabinets again. Philip zooms in on the image of Sheila collecting the gene sample from the refrigerated file. He pauses the video and notes that the label says "SCAS 59 REPAIR STRIP – CONTROL – TOUCHSTONE – DO NOT USE." Next, he scrolls through the footage of her collecting the fertilized ovum. He zooms again and focuses on the image of the vial in her hand. He spots a label there, small and unclear, so he snaps a screenshot of it.

Once he has placed the video image in a photo program and enlarged it, he sighs with satisfaction. The label says "JENSEN/OHL."

"That's it," he spits, now very angry. "I couldn't use the saliva sample as proof, because I couldn't prove that it came from Gabriel, but now I have certifiable proof that he's my son."

He paces around the room, pounding the lab counter and punching the wall. Larry looks up, concerned.

"I'm done with her. Now I know and have proof that she's really gone over the top," Philip hisses through his teeth.

Larry gets a phone call, and Philip ceases his outburst. He rubs his knuckles sheepishly and waits, watching Larry with a questioning look until he hangs up.

"We caught a break. Cynthia Clark ordered a car, and we've got the location. No need to get a court order to find out where she went."

"Great," Philip replies. "I think we have enough evidence to get a court order to seize Gabriel now, but to lock it up, we really do need DNA evidence."

"We tried that," Larry counters. "She really cleaned up her place; there was nothing there."

"I know," Philip says. "Let's check it out again anyway, and this time, let's check out his school too. I'll go to the house. You check the school."

Larry stops him. "Wait, we need it to be airtight; you can't break in."

Philip reaches into his pocket and produces a key. "You forget, I lived there too. She never asked for her key back."

Larry smiles. "Great, that makes it legal entry."

Together, they head out to the parking lot.

* * *

A short time later, Larry steps out of Gabriel's school. A little girl is wailing inside.

"It's mine; I found it," she says. "Gabriel left it for me."

Larry presses his phone to his ear. "Got something. On my way."

He pauses and peers intently at something in the sunlight—a blue feather. He seals it in a plastic bag and then jumps in his sedan and makes a quick U-turn back to the hospital.

* * *

In Philip's office, Spiner paces up and down, ranting. "This is extraordinary. Are you telling me honestly that you had no idea?"

"Wait, Gerry," Philip protests. "You decided it would be best to separate the hospital from the child in case she was still experimenting with gene modifications."

"You know, I never imagined that she would have put us back in the line of fire," Spiner huffs. "I was sure it had nothing to do with us and that we could claim ignorance if anything went wrong. Now you're telling me that you have definitive proof she engineered the child in our lab?"

Before Philip can answer, Larry bursts into the room. He strides over to Philip, nodding at Spiner as he passes.

"Here's your DNA."

He hands the plastic-wrapped feather to Philip. Philip takes it gingerly and stares at it for a long moment, awestruck. Spiner, also taken aback by the evidence, reaches out and gently takes it from Philip. He peers at it closely in the bright light of one of the lab table lamps. Then he flings it back at Philip.

"Get it tested," he orders and storms out of the room.

While Sheila, Gabriel, and Cynthia wrap up their peaceful week in the open air, Philip concludes his fretful week of sleuthing with a heart-rending meeting with his new child-custody lawyer, Ben Toobin. This reed-thin and fidgety lawyer is not personable, but he knows his field and came very highly recommended. Their first court appearance that morning was frustrating for Philip. Sheila, of course, didn't even show up. They tried to get the message to her, but she seems to be off the grid. The judge was not even perturbed by it. All Philip learned was that his claim was not going to be concluded quickly. The judge appointed a guardian ad litem for Gabriel's defense and then finally scheduled a hearing for the following week, insisting that they get Sheila and Gabriel to attend. Philip enlists Larry to go searching for them.

20

ANOTHER RUN

Sheila and Gabriel pull up into the weedy parking lot of a rundown diner. Only two vehicles are parked in the lot, and one of them looks abandoned. Greasy windows and flickering lights hardly beckon anyone inside, but Sheila chose the place because of the quiet solitude. On either side are two busy fast-food places with noticeable security cameras and crowds of families piling out of SUVs to rush inside. The last thing Sheila wants is Gabriel whining about jumping with the other kids in the ball pit. She hopes the diner food is tolerable. She tugs a bulky denim jacket over Gabriel's wings.

"Let's go eat," she says.

Gabriel shifts and fidgets while she tucks him into the disguise. "Why can't I just be me?"

"Honey, you are always just you," Sheila responds, a bit taken aback. "It's just that other people wouldn't understand if they could see your wings; they would be confused."

"But why, Momma?"

"Well, you haven't seen any other people with wings, have you?"

"Yes, lots. There's Bill, the eagle, the geese …"

"Honey, those are birds. People and birds are different."

He gives her a puzzled look. "They are? Why?"

"There's lots of differences: size and shape. And birds have feathers; humans have hair."

"I have wings," he says, "and hair and feathers."

"I know you do; you are special," she responds.

Gabriel stops walking and looks at her intently. "You have wings too, Momma."

"Don't be so silly, Gabe. Obviously I don't have wings. Do you see any wings?"

"You don't understand, Momma," he continues. "You do have wings; everyone does. You just don't know it, and you don't know how to use them."

Sheila puts her finger to her lips. "Shhh … let's not talk about this in front of anyone else, okay?"

They enter the diner. To their right just past the entrance, dangling model planes fill the air over a typical diner counter. The diner's single customer is sitting at the bar. Sheila leads Gabriel across the floor and into the booth farthest from the door. A dull window gives them a clear view of their car, and there is a wall behind them. They snuggle into the deepest corner, with Sheila on the outside seat and Gabriel tucked inside next to her.

A sullen man who must be about forty-five or so delivers their menus. He appears to be the only employee in the establishment. Gabriel tries to engage with him, asking the man how he is doing, but he only gets a grunt for answer. When the man is gone, Gabriel complains to his mom about the emptiness of the place.

"Where are the other kids?" he asks the brusque waiter when he comes back to take their orders. The man plunks down a coffee for Sheila and a glass of milk for Gabriel. Then he leaves without a word. Gabriel laughs, making fun out of a dull event, and splashes his hands in the spilled milk that sloshed over the edge of his glass. Sheila snatches his hands impatiently and wipes them clean just before the waiter slaps their food onto the table in a perfunctory style that suggests he would rather be somewhere else.

This time, Gabriel mentions the weather and asks the man what he thinks. Sheila looks at Gabriel, surprised. It's like he has the playbook for initiating small conversation. But the man merely nods. When the man is out of earshot again, Sheila turns to Gabriel.

"Why do you keep talking to him? Haven't I told you not to engage with strangers?"

Gabriel looks at her with wide, questioning eyes. "But is he a stranger? He's giving us lunch."

"Yes, he's a stranger. You have to be wary of everyone you don't know."

"But I do know him," Gabriel objects. "He's not happy, and I want him to be happy. I thought if we talked, he might be happy."

Sheila's face cracks. She smiles and kisses him on the forehead. "That's so sweet, Gabe, but it's not your job to make him happy. That's his job."

The man refills their drinks with another solemn grunt. Gabriel watches him closely. For a moment, they lock eyes, and a glimmer of liveliness crosses the man's face. He wiggles his head in a habitual way, shaking off the foreign feeling, and turns to go again.

Fifteen minutes later, Gabriel nibbles at his fries and contemplates his half-eaten burger, touching it with his fingers as if he might pick it up. Sheila has finished her sandwich, and she frets while her son eats altogether too slowly. She's very uncomfortable and can't wait to get out of there.

The man stops by again with a coffee refill.

"Hurry up, Gabe," Sheila says as the man pours.

He looks at her and Gabriel suspiciously. "Do I know you?"

Sheila glances up at him, nervous. "We aren't from around here," she says quickly, and then she looks away, hoping he will go away.

Instead, the man laughs uncomfortably. "That's for sure; no one's from around here. There really is no *here* here." He laughs again, pleased at his jest. Then he looks at Gabriel. Sheila stiffens worried. "Got something for you, son," he says warmly.

Sheila finds her mind rambling again. Is this one more Gabriel marvel? The man was so shut down, unfriendly, inhospitable, and unapproachable half an hour ago, but now he seems to want to be their best friend. He hands Gabriel a cape-clad superhero toy. Gabe's eyes light up, and he looks at his mom eagerly.

"May I give this to your son, ma'am? It's part of the kid's special."

She nods, still wary. Gabriel grabs the toy, which actually looks more lost than new. Gabriel transforms it in a few clicks from cape-clad warrior to Red Dragon.

"I love Red Dragon, mister. he's my absolute favorite. I've got a backpack and a shirt with him on it. I've even got his wings, too." He turns from the man to his mother. "See, Momma?" He shows her the toy.

"Say thank you to the nice man," she replies.

"Frank, my name is Frank," the man says, but he isn't done yet. Feeling as if he has broken the ice, he continues. "Where're ya from then?"

"I'm sorry," Sheila says after a moment, "but we're in a bit of a hurry. Can we have the check please?"

"No problem. I'll hurry it up for ya." He saunters away, glancing back. Sheila watches Frank's reflection in the dark window.

Gabriel plunks his fork onto his plate. "I'm done. Fly scream?"

Sheila smiles at him. "Vanilla? We'll take it with us."

Frank returns and proffers the check to Sheila.

"Can we have a vanilla ice cream to go?" she asks.

Frank isn't really listening. He's staring at Gabriel again. "You're that little kid with wings, aren't you?"

Oh dear, Sheila thinks. Now it's clear to her that no Gabriel marvel is at work here. It looks like Frank is onto them and that exactly what she'd hoped would not happen has happened. He points to a grimy TV set hidden behind the cloud of model airplanes. Sheila is stunned. She did not notice it when they came in, and now she wishes she had.

On the screen, a male correspondent with what looks like plastic hair gives his report. Closed-captioned headlines detail Gabriel and Sheila's escape from the city. "It's assumed that the child and his surrogate mother are somewhere in Oklahoma. Evidence in this video footage points to a remote farm east of Broken Arrow." A short piece of footage displays Gabriel zooming down toward the camera. His wings flare up, and he seems to stop short. Then he poses, smiling for the camera.

Sheila wanders through the scattered tables toward the TV to get a better look. Shocked, she peers at the screen, wondering where the heck the shot was taken and how they got it. Gabriel, unconcerned and still seated in the booth, plays with his new toy.

The TV shows another correspondent in the field—literally in a field. Sheila recognizes it. Their little house is way in the background. Six large, black vans rumble down the dirt road toward the house. Dust blooms up, and crows caw and circle over them. Bill seems to be one of them, flitting about faster, more agitated, and slightly separate from the rest. He breaks away and heads off in the direction in which they drove.

Sheila gasps, her hand flying to her mouth in shock. "Turn it up, please," she begs.

The excited field correspondent details the activity on the screen. "Apparently, these vans are here to collect that mysterious child, now seen in a few short hours by over twenty million online. Our sources say that the boy is now the subject of a custody dispute between a woman who claims to be his mother, Dr. Sheila Jensen, and the father, Dr. Philip Ohl. An added complexity to the case is that it seems the boy was some kind of experiment conducted by the genome department at NEU. The doctors in charge of the experiment now say that the mother was a surrogate and that she has kidnapped the child."

The screen cuts to a press conference outside the hospital. Philip is at the mic. "We are asking the general public to keep a look out for these two and to let us know immediately if they are seen anywhere. We are very concerned about the child's safety."

Spiner pushes Philip aside and leans into the mic. "Since Gabriel Jensen is in danger and will soon be in the custody of his father, all efforts will be made to retrieve him as soon as possible to return him to this medical institution for protection."

Sheila chokes. "That's a lie. They're making this up. How did they find us?"

Frank points out to the parking lot. "Probably that fancy car you've got there. It always knows where it is, and it always broadcasts that, too. That's how it works."

Sheila is dumfounded. "No, I turned the tracking system off. They can't know."

Frank shrugs. "They have their ways. It might be off, but any hacker can get in. I ought to know. I used to do that before I got my place here in the country. Couldn't stand it. Felt like cheating, spying. Just wasn't right."

"What can we do? Can you help us?" Sheila asks, desperate.

Frank's eyes light up. "Yeah! I got an idea. They're gonna be all over this place in no time because of that car. Everyone is looking for you. You should turn your phone off right now till we can figure out how to disguise where it is. And give me your car's key fob."

Sheila is frantic, all sense of wariness frayed. She removes the fob from her bag and hands it over.

Frank turns toward the only other customer, who isn't paying attention to anything. "Hank, you still riding that bike ten miles to work every day?"

Hank looks up dully and nods.

"You want a car?" Frank asks.

Hank raises his eyebrows. He isn't used to good fortune, kind words, or helpful people, and he usually doesn't even notice if nice things happen to him, because the idea of it is so off his radar. But this feels different. Nonetheless, he is still suspicious.

"I ain't gonna get arrested for stealing or nothing?"

Sheila shakes her head. "I'll sign the registration over to you."

Frank hustles them out the door. "Okay, good then. Time to go. Hank, take a long drive, any direction you like."

"I will," he says, excited about it.

Sheila signs the car over to Hank and resets the cars computer controls, and they wave him off. Then Sheila turns to Frank. "Was that all of the idea? Do you know where we can go to hide?"

"Hell yeah. All my life I've dreamed of flying. Come with me."

Sheila looks dubious and very nervous.

"If you like," Frank adds. "I live way out, kind of private, like."

Sheila is still hesitant. "I don't know. I don't know anything about you. Can we trust you?"

Frank is really enthusiastic now. He rummages through his phone looking for pictures. "My kids and my wife will love to meet you." When he finds the album, he surfs through the photos one by one. "There's Joey, Kelly, Chuck, Trini, and Mary. She can't talk. That's my wife, Dell. She loves to cook. Not like me; I do it for a living."

When Frank talks about his family and shows her their pictures, he comes to life. Suddenly, it's obvious to Sheila why he is so unhappy in the diner. He would rather be hanging out with them all day.

"Sounds good. Can we go now?" she says.

Frank is clearly eager to take the excuse to go home. "Sure, my shift's done."

They pile into Frank's van and head down the turnpike toward the highway.

21

FRANK'S PLACE

After about twenty minutes, they leave the highway and open flat areas and travel uphill onto a forested slope. Dense trees surround them, and the road winds around steep turns for a few miles while they move further into the hills. Forty minutes after they left the diner, a final turn onto a narrow dirt road takes them between a deep cleft in the hills and through to a tight but open valley on the other side. Multihued late-afternoon light streams through the trees at the edge of a winding driveway that slopes down to Frank's house.

The house is tucked in a grassy meadow between the forested ridges. A lush garden spills out of a fenced area, proud of its fat tomatoes and waving rich, green corn fronds. Chickens forage under and around toys that are strewn about a handmade wooden jungle gym in the middle of a tidy fenced lawn.

Frank's home sparkles in sharp contrast to the griminess of the diner. Even though the house is a bit tattered and worn, it's immaculately clean and well cared for. Sheila is sure now that Frank would rather be here than at the remote, quiet, and probably boring diner all day. It seems that she and Gabriel are the most exciting thing that has ever happened to him there.

Frank's kids pour out of the house, howling, pushing each other, and yelling at the top of their lungs. Frank's ample wife waits by the door with a big, welcoming smile. She has a capable, calming look about her. Sheila's anxiety level drops down a notch. She had no idea what she was getting herself and Gabriel into by throwing away the car and driving off with a complete stranger, but seeing Dell soothes her fears.

As the van pulls up to the house, Gabriel squirms to get out of his seat. In the process, he works his way out of the denim jacket as well and scrambles out of the seat with his wings free.

"Oops," he says.

Sheila sees him looking at her a bit sheepish but with an appealing smile. She shrugs. "It's okay, Gabe. They all know now anyway. Just go, run and play."

Gabriel pops out of the van door.

"But no flying!" she adds as a firm afterthought.

He nods and tears off to join the herd of kids in the yard. The kids squeal and laugh, chasing Gabriel, who runs in front, flapping his wings.

Dell greets Sheila with tears in her eyes. "We have a miracle in our home."

Sheila shakes her head. "No, no, just a kid. I just want him to feel normal. Treat him like the other kids, please."

Dell watches Gabriel tumbling, jumping, and running and then turns to Sheila. "Oh, I would say he's a miracle. Can he fly?"

Sheila nods. "I expect you'll see him do it before long."

Dell shows Sheila a comfortable attic room two flights up with two narrow beds on either side of the dormer window. Sheila looks around, noting that there's not much room, but then she remembers that they took nothing with them.

"You'll be safe here," Dell assures her. "Anything you need, I'm sure we've got it. Just ask. There's more blankets, pajamas, socks, and stuff in those drawers there, so help yourself." She points to an old dresser tucked in a tight alcove by the door. On top of it, a medley of teddy bears, unicorns, sheep, lions, dogs, cats, and other stuffed animals practically spilling over the edges grin at her.

Dell points to the furry crowd. "If he's missing his stuffy, maybe one of those will help."

"Oh, right," Sheila says, thinking not of a stuffy but of Bill. Gabriel has not mentioned him yet. What can she do about that?

The evening goes well. Soon, Dell drags everyone in for a simple but delicious meal. Gabriel is ecstatic sitting with the kids, and they seem to love him. They all eat extremely well, and Sheila begins to feel like she can breathe and like this escape might work out after all, especially if she can find great people like this family to help her. For a moment, it occurs to her that they might be protected somehow, guided like those lines of connection she saw when she was flying with Gabriel.

* * *

The next morning, Sheila wakes up surprisingly well rested and with a new sense of hope. She stretches and looks over at Gabriel snuggled up in the other bed with all of the stuffed animals surrounding him. He did remember Bill late the previous night after they had all gone to bed. The two of them were snuggled tight in his bed and going through the events of the day when his eyes shot wide open and he remembered that Bill had been left behind.

Bill had been sunning himself on the porch rail when they left, and he had followed the car lazily down the driveway. At the cornfield, he'd veered off to join a flock of crows, and Gabriel had waved to him when they turned onto the road.

Gabriel wept at the loss of his friend. He argued that they should go back and get him, but Sheila was adamant that they could not. She suggested that maybe Gabriel would sleep better if he picked one of the stuffed animals on the top of the dresser. She helped him up onto a chair to take a closer look, but he couldn't decide. She smiles sleepily at the memory. It was just like him to be unable to choose only one. All would be his favorites.

By the time Sheila and Gabriel wash, dress, and join the family in the kitchen the next morning, the place is a madhouse. Frank sits in the dad's chair at one end of the table. The kids are squashed on one side of the table on a bench. Dell has saved the two seats on the other side for their guests. She plunks a huge plate of food down for each of them.

"Eat," she says.

"Thank you," Sheila replies, eyeing the mound of food on her plate, "but I'll never be able to finish all that."

Dell looks at her, unable to turn off her motherly tone. "Eat, dearie. You'll need your strength to keep up with that one." She waves toward Gabriel.

Sheila nods and begins to nibble obediently. Gabriel dives in, voracious.

Suddenly, Joey, whom Dell announces proudly will be nine years old soon, comes around the table to stroke Gabriel's feathers.

"Gimme one," he demands as he starts to tug.

Sheila grabs his hand to stop him. "No, no that hurts!"

Joey refuses to let go. "What do you mean it hurts?"

Sheila looks over at Frank, who is absorbed in wolfing down his breakfast, "Joey!" he reprimands with his mouth full as Sheila pushes Joey's hand off Gabriel. "How do you like it when someone pulls your hair?"

Full of bully bravery, Joey sticks his chest out. "It don't hurt that much."

"Has anyone pulled a chunk out of your head yet?" Frank continues.

Joey looks at Sheila. He gets it and drops his head, a tad shamefaced.

"You got feelings, Gabe?" Trini asks through a mouthful of food.

Gabriel gives her a mischievous look. "Tickles make me laugh."

Mary, who has been watching quietly, laughs. The other kids all look at her in surprise.

"Mom, Mary laughed!" Joey says, his eyes on his sister.

"What?" Dell asks, popping her head out of the oven.

"She never laughs," Frank mumbles, and then he swallows to clear the food from his mouth. "She never says anything."

Gabriel scarfs down his last bite and then looks at his mom for permission to leave the table. She nods.

He jumps up and runs around the table to Mary. He comes up behind her and sticks his hands under her arms. "Tickly, tickly, tickly, Mary."

She writhes and laughs, but no sound comes out.

"She'll never do it again," Joey says authoritatively from other end of the bench.

Gabriel stops short and looks at him. "Never?" He looks at Mary, who looks dismayed.

"Never has," Joey replies.

Gabriel opens Mary's mouth and pokes her tongue. She grins.

"Did she really laugh?" Dell says. "The doctors couldn't figure out why she never talked, but we manage though."

"Okay, cleanup crew," Frank pipes up. "Get to it."

Trini jumps off the bench and runs. "Gabe, tickle me!"

Gabriel growls in Red Dragon's trumpetlike voice and chases her.

Mary is right behind him. Soon, all of the kids are tumbling and giggling in a pile on the rug in front of the fireplace.

"Calm down!" Dell hollers, and the kids freeze. Dell steps into the pile and grabs Joey and Trini's arms. "You two, Dad said it already, and I won't say it again. Clean up." She drags them back in to the kitchen.

Mary pulls on Gabriel's arm. When she gets his attention, she starts flapping her arms and rolling her eyes like she is looking around.

Gabriel looks over at Kelly. "What does she want?"

"She wants to fly like you, Gabe," Kelly says.

Gabriel jumps up. "Let's go then!"

Gabriel, Kelly, and Mary jump up and head out of the living room toward the porch door.

"Wait for us!" Joey yells from the kitchen.

By the time Dell and Frank's kids trample down the steps and onto the lawn, Sheila has waylaid Gabriel and whisked him into the bathroom in the hall.

"I don't need the bathroom now, Momma," he cries as she pushes him inside.

Sheila plops him down on an old-fashioned chair piled with towels and sits opposite him on the fuzzy toilet lid. "Tell me about that thing you did with me and Aunt Cynthia," Sheila demands.

Gabriel is bewildered. "What thing?"

"You know, when you were flying and—"

"You were flying too, Momma."

She sighs. "You knew?"

He nods. "I saw you." He strokes her cheeks. "You were so beautiful, Momma."

Sheila peers into his eyes. "How did you do it, Gabe?"

"*You* did it, Momma. I can't fly you. Only you can fly you."

"But Gabe, you have wings, and I don't."

He shakes his head. "You do, Momma. You do have wings. You just don't see them yet."

Sheila's expression glosses over with confusion. She pushes this idea aside in her brain. Instead of helping, it's hurting her comprehension. She tries another question. "What will happen to little Mary? Will she fly? Can you stop those kids from flying?"

He shakes his head. Sheila's eyes fill with water. "Please try, honey. If these people fly, I have no idea what will happen. I don't know if we can handle it. Let's keep this our secret, okay?"

"But I don't know how, Momma."

"Please try," she begs.

"I will use the bathroom now," he says, giving her a look.

She laughs and gets up to give him some privacy.

Sheila waits outside the bathroom door. When Gabriel emerges, she gives him a warning look. He smiles his big, wide, sweet smile, races down the hall, and slams through the screen door. Sheila hears the kids cheer.

Outside on the lawn, Gabriel runs like a Pied Piper with his flock in tow. Dell steps into the doorway and watches them all while she wipes her hands on a dishtowel. Sheila slips past her, eager to get outside and try to manage whatever might happen.

"Everything okay?" Dell asks.

"He went," she says. Her eyes are riveted on Gabriel.

Dell is a bit puzzled. "Oh, good."

Gabriel runs across the lawn, kids fanning out behind him. Trini and Joey are there too, having rushed through the cleanup, eager not to miss a thing. Gabriel hops, and so do the kids. He hops higher, and so do they. Sheila is practically chewing her fingertips. She can see it happening; the kids are already locked in step with him. Suddenly, Gabriel's wings puff up, fill with air, and he tips forward, soaring with ease.

A chorus of oohs and ahs follow him. Dell and Frank spill out onto the lawn too, entranced by the grace of Gabriel's form arching through the air. His blue wings almost disappear in the blue sky, and he looks like an ordinary child flying.

The other children imitate his smooth, circling movements. They are playacting, but Sheila can see the phenomenon beginning to happen. Mary is the first to fly. A silvery image of her extracts gracefully from her physical form and soars into the sky after Gabriel. Sheila's jaw drops when she sees the evanescent Mary looping and wheeling right behind Gabriel. *How can she see that?* The thought rolls in the back of her mind.

In quick succession, the rest of the children's ethereal forms follow Mary's. Dell, who has more important things to deal with than watching children play, nevertheless can't tear herself away. She and Frank drift out onto the lawn where the kids move in circles below Gabriel's soaring form. At last, they also slip into the magical consciousness of flight with their children. Sheila sees seven empyreal figures circling, wheeling, swooping, and ascending joyfully behind her son. The finest gossamer thread trails from the flyers down to the dancers on the lawn. How is this possible? How can they be in two places at once? She did it, so she knows it works. She also knows that it feels as natural as eating pie, but how?

Gabriel circles around in the sky above the house, cawing, hooting, and laughing. The shimmering light forms behind him weave in and out of each other expertly, chasing, poking, ducking, and then falling back in line. Then Gabriel spots his mother standing alone on the bottom porch step. He circles back and swoops down to alight on the step beside her. The airy family plummets into the garden after him and assimilates back into their corporeal bodies. They all flop onto the grass laughing.

"Why didn't you come with us, Momma?"

"I told you not to fly, Gabe. I'm worried."

She sits down hard on the step, exhausted. The indulgence of worry has knocked her right out of her hopeful mood. Gabriel climbs into her lap and strokes her forehead.

"It'll be all right," he soothes.

* * *

That night, after the kids are tucked into bed, the adults settle down in the living room. Sheila waits nervously for the conversation she is sure will come. She has no idea how to explain what happened, but she doesn't want to run upstairs and hide, because she has an important request for Frank. She feels completely trapped and dependent on him and his generosity. She knows this situation can't last, and the last thing she wants to do is to put them all at risk.

"I need to get another car," she says. "I can't be stuck here with you all. It's not good for you, and it's not good for us. Can you help me?"

"Actually," Frank says, "I asked Hank to trade your fancy self-driving car in and get two regular cars. Your shiny wheels are worth a lot around here; we aren't so used to them yet. So Hank got a junker he's real happy with, and he got you something a bit more reliable. Come to the diner with me in the morning and get it. He left it there for you."

Sheila is effusively grateful. Relieved everything has worked out so well, she gets up to say goodnight.

Dell looks up from her knitting with a big smile on her face. "He's an absolute angel, dear, a miracle. We are so honored you're staying with us. Truly we are. You can stay as long as you like."

Sheila thanks them both and then heads upstairs.

22

REAL SANCTUARY?

The following morning, Sheila picks up her new car at the diner and heads off at Frank's direction to collect some basic supplies, such as toothbrushes, T-shirts, and extra underwear.

After she's gone, Frank is utterly fired up. He whistles as he scrubs, inspired. Cleaning materials crowd the window ledges. Unfamiliar light dapples the floor. An old man on a stool at the bar is perturbed by the changing ambiance. He glares at Frank.

"What ya doin'?"

"Place needs a good scrubbin'," Frank replies cheerily.

"Ain't never seen you clean in here before," the old man says. It sounds like a complaint.

Frank keeps scrubbing. "Never too late."

The old man grunts. "Oh! I don't know about that. Sun's a bit bright in here now."

The old-fashioned front doorbell clangs loudly. Philip and Larry stride in. Philip goes straight to the old man and shows him a picture on his phone.

"Have you seen this woman?"

It's Sheila's hospital file photo. Frank hears the question and slows down his scrubbing. He sidles over behind the counter with his back to them and leans in to get a good look at Philip's reflection in the glass pie case mirror.

"We ain't seen nobody different round here, have we, Frank?"

Irritated, Frank slaps napkins and noisy utensils in front of the two intruders. "You folks plannin' to order?" he asks in a hostile tone.

Philip nods. "Coffee, black."

"Easy eggs, bacon, juice, and coffee, light and sweet," Larry adds.

Philip pushes the phone across the counter to Frank. "How about you? Have you seen her? She's with a child, a boy, five years old."

Frank takes a quick look. Sheila's hair in the picture is smoothed back and tied up. Her shirt is neat with a smart collar, but the resemblance to the woman with wild, wavy blond locks and an artsy T-shirt that he rescued a couple of days earlier is obvious. He turns away as he answers.

"Only strangers I've seen is you two."

"Give me one of them jelly donuts, too," Larry calls after him.

Philip glowers at Larry. Larry shrugs. "Might as well eat."

"Well, hurry it up," Philip growls. "We're headed to that car dealer next."

Frank is on edge the entire time Larry gobbles his food. He tries to listen in without being too obvious as he scrubs the back counter. It's clear that Philip and Larry are on the trail of the car. When Philip brings up the subject of Sheila's phone, bank, and credit cards, Frank moves closer to wash glasses and listen more easily. All he can hear is that there have been no pings on any of those things since she left the house in Willow Brook. He breathes a sigh of relief and congratulates himself for suggesting that she take money from him to go shopping. Sheila was reluctant and only consented when Frank agreed to take a check. He suggested that he would deposit it a few days after she and Gabriel move on.

When Larry's black sedan pulls out of the driveway, Frank picks up the phone. "Hank, is Ed going to give them information on those two cars you bought?"

Hank explains to Frank that he bought his car from Ed but that he took the money and went to his cousin over in Muskogee for the other car. Frank is relieved.

"That's really smart, Hank. Just remember, when they come looking for you, you don't know nothing about who they were or where they went. Okay?"

"Course, Frank. 'S easy 'cause I don't know nothin'."

Frank laughs. "You got a free lunch coming, Hank. Soon as you want it."

Frank goes home after the lunch "rush," which is surprisingly a record six customers. He fills Sheila in on the day's special breakfast visitors. It makes her nervous. She thanks him again for arranging for the car.

146

"It's probably time to try to figure out where to go next," she says.

"No, you're fine. Stay here," Dell says. "No one expects you're here, so you'll be fine. Just relax."

"She's right," Frank agrees. "There's no sense running if you don't need to. You'll just exhaust yourselves. Relax until you have to go. Meanwhile, we can hatch a plan."

Dell hands her a hot cocoa. "Here, drink this and relax."

* * *

Sheila watches Gabriel fly low through a suburban neighborhood. He flails and strains for height while an angry mob chases him. People grab for his feet and toss things into the air to try to hit him and knock him down. Sheila squeezes through the crowd, and like the others, she also reaches for him.

"Let me help you, baby!" she shouts. "I'm here. Your momma is here!"

Her voice is swallowed in the noise of the crowd, but Gabriel still hears her. "You have to fly too to help me, Momma."

At that point, she is aware that she is trying to move through something like taffy. Her feet are caught, and she can only struggle. The mob gets wilder and more dangerous. A tall, skinny guy jumps up and grabs Gabriel's foot and tugs at it. Sheila plunges toward him, her feet freed by her raw determination. She knocks the man off balance, and Gabriel is released, bouncing up higher than anyone can reach. Sheila strains like a breaststroke swimmer floating in jelly. People push her off balance from all sides. Then she breaks free and lifts over the crowd, pulling herself up with her own arms moving like wings. People in the crowd stretch up and grab at her feet.

Gabriel floats in the air nearby, barely out of reach of the malicious throng. Sheila works her way over to him like a swimmer and pushes him up onto the peak of a house roof. They rest together on top of a dormer window. Sheila strokes Gabriel's tired face. The crowd's roar escalates angrily and then breaks into laughter and cheers.

* * *

Sheila awakens, startled. It is just beginning to get dark. She's curled around Gabriel on the comfy quilt on top of her bed. She did not mean to nap for the entire afternoon. Now she is aware of a peculiar buzz coming from somewhere. She listens for a moment. It's either laughter or humming. She can't decide, so she untangles herself and kisses Gabriel's cheek. She pulls on her jeans, washes her face, brushes her hair, and tiptoes out.

As Sheila creeps down the tiny wooden back stairs, she feels increasingly apprehensive that something really big is going on. She's terrified that Philip has arrived sooner than they imagined. Worse yet, she imagines that he has a full league of officials to back him up.

She listens from the top of the stairs, but the sound doesn't sound serious. It sounds like fun. She creeps down the stairs and squeezes through the door at the bottom of the stairs and into the kitchen. Then she stops short, shocked. It seems like a hundred strangers are crowded into the ground floor of the house, crammed into every corner.

Dell pushes her way through the friendly-looking and wide-eyed congregation. "There you are. We tried not to wake you. Are you hungry?"

Sheila is appalled, and her face shows it. "What's going on here?"

"Dinner! Potluck. You've got just about anything you might want to eat here."

Trini, overexcited, has to weigh in on the event. "They all want to fly with Gabe."

Dell puts her finger on her daughter's lips. "Hush, Trini. It's not like that," she says to Sheila.

"What is it like then?" Sheila asks. "How many people know about us?"

Frank shuffles through the crowd and fills her in. "Our family and a few friends."

"A few?" Sheila says, gesturing to the crowd. "These are a few friends?"

A guest takes her hand enthusiastically. "We just want to see your amazing son."

"Yeah! When can we see him fly?" a less considerate guest yells out.

Sheila holds her hands up defensively. "Please, everyone, I'm trying to keep this a secret."

A flurry of kids runs through the kitchen yelling, "Gabriel! Gabriel!" Mary leads, flapping her arms and pretending to fly.

Dell raises her arms. "Shhh! Everyone. Quiet all you kids. I'll get Gabe, and then we'll eat."

Sheila steps between her and the staircase that towers over the living room, blocking Dell's way. "Wait."

The crowd gasps. All eyes look past Sheila and up the stairs in wonder. Mary's face lights up like a candle. Sheila turns to look up at the landing at the top of the stairs. Gabriel stands there in a large white T-shirt that comes to below his knees with the shoulders cut out to free his wings. Behind Sheila, the space fills with oohs" and ahs as Gabriel stretches his wings, still a bit sleepy-eyed. The entire place falls dead silent.

"Gabriel, Gabriel, baby Gabriel, sings like a bird and flies like an angel," a child's voice sings. "Sings like an angel and flies like a bird."

Dell, Frank, and Mary's siblings stare at Mary.

"She said something!" Joey cries.

Dell weeps. It's unlike her, but she is speechless.

Frank bends down in front of his daughter. "Mary, honey, did you say that—"

"Shh!" Mary says sweetly, and then she stands up. She invites Gabriel to come and sit beside her.

His movements transfix the crowd. They all watch as he works his way down the stairs, stumbling a bit. They move aside when he walks through them toward Mary and squeezes onto the bench beside her.

"For bacon, eggs, and buttered toast, praise Father, Son, and Holy Ghost," Mary says before sitting down. The tension snaps, and everyone bursts into laughter.

The evening proceeds far better than Sheila expected. The crowd is respectful and undemanding. They realize they can't ask Gabriel to fly because it's already dark, although that's what they really want. They have as many questions for Sheila as they do for Gabriel. He is polite and eloquent for a five- going on six-year-old. A woman asks Gabriel if his feathers itch.

"No more than my hair."

She laughs. A man is interested in Gabriel's ability to navigate when flying.

"I kind of think I'm running," Gabriel replies. "It's just I do it and go up and down, too."

Everyone wants to touch him, to run their fingers through his curly hair and smooth their hands over the blue feathers.

Ultimately, it gets so late that Gabriel starts nodding off in Sheila's lap. When she tries to sneak him upstairs, the crowd presses in around them for one last look and touch.

Mother and son sleep very soundly that night.

23

DEVOTEE CRUSH

The next day, Sheila wakes up and is dismayed when she looks out of the window to see that the crowd has not left. In fact, the number of visitors has increased overnight. Campers and tents populate the edges of the lawn and fill the field right up to the forest surrounding the house. Campfires are set up in the trampled field with lawn chairs arranged around them in clusters. Some people seem to have been sitting out there all night. A lot of people mill about, waiting and glancing repeatedly at the door to Frank's house.

Gabriel stirs, stretches, and rolls over. Sheila looks at him tenderly. When he sees her looking out the window, he jumps up to join her.

"Oh, let's go out, Momma."

By now she knows that he is thrilled by the attention. He seems to derive nourishment from it or to be driven by some kind of noble purpose.

He grips his mother by the cheeks. "You must come too, today, Momma. You must." He looks into her face, his eyes glittering with a pressing urgency.

Sheila shakes her head. "No, honey. I need to stay on the ground and make sure you're safe." She doesn't add aloud what she is really thinking: *This isn't good. It's not good. I don't know what will happen now.* She feels as though she has utterly lost control.

"It'll be great," Gabriel assures her. "Don't worry. Say yes, Momma. Please say yes." He nods deliberately and uses his hands to make Sheila's chin go up and down as well. She laughs at his attempt to enroll her in the adventure. He's delighted and thinks he's winning,

"Yes, Momma. Together we can fly even higher. And together, all together, we will all be so good, I'm telling you."

She removes his hands and looks at him, perplexed, wondering where he gets his confidence. "Gabriel," she says firmly, "no flying, do you hear me? I mean it. I want you to promise me that you won't let your feet leave the ground."

Gabriel starts to cry, his chest heaving. The emotional shift hits him hard, and he can't breathe. "I have to, Momma."

"No you don't, sweetie. You must not."

He shudders with sobs. She hugs him, wipes his face, and makes him blow his nose.

"Let's get some breakfast. Come on."

Breakfast is uneventful. The kitchen holds only Frank and Dell's family. Dell seems to be deferring to Sheila's worries and trying to keep things calm and under control. All of the kids are well behaved, polite, and kind to Gabriel. Nonetheless, Sheila can't seem to catch her breath. Every time she is aware of it, she notices that she is half breathing, with breath only going as far as her top ribs and completely unable to penetrate deeper into her stomach. Hence, she feels tight, uncomfortable, short-tempered, and worried. The constant buzz of voices outside heightens her unease.

After breakfast, Gabriel drags her out of the kitchen and onto the porch.

"No flying," she whispers anxiously in his ear as he runs away. He looks back at her, but his expression is unreadable. She slumps down on the steps and to watch, unsure of what he might do and at a loss as to what she can do if he does fly.

Dell comes over to Sheila and rubs her hunched shoulders. "Honey, these people love him. There's no need to worry. Plus, we asked them all to stay outside the fence. See? There they are! So you can relax a bit."

Sheila does relax as she watches Gabriel play on the lawn with over a dozen kids. He dives to the ground, laughing. Big kids, little kids, and even a baby and a teenager roll around with him playing tag. They all play carefully and respectfully, helping each other and taking turns, though Gabriel is always in the center. Adults mill around nearby outside the fence. They are expectant, though no one knows what they expect. More vehicles arrive down the winding road at regular intervals, and new fans pile out to join the party. A motorcycle rumbles right up to the side of the house, and Stan climbs off it.

Sheila doesn't notice the loud, rumbling intruder, because at the moment he arrives, Gabriel trips over a toddler who has fallen in front of him. He skips a couple of times, falling forward, and then he flaps his wings and takes off. The crowd gasps and reaches their arms up after him.

"Gabe, wait, wait!" Sheila yells.

"I can't!" he yells back. "It's not me; it's them. They want it. They want to feel free, to fly and to feel it." He shrieks like a hawk. "Kee, kee, kee!"

The children imitate his sounds in a chorus. They run around in harmonious movements in concert with him as he circles above. Gabriel stays in a tight circle over the fenced lawn almost as if an invisible picket fence climbs up to touch the sky.

Then the adults join in with the dance, moving in similar circles outside the fence and in the field beyond. They move through the trailers, the campfires, and the clusters of chairs out farther into the field and congregate in a large circle in the open. The children also wend their way out of the yard to join their parents in the field. As they do this, Gabriel follows above them as if drawn by them. Sheila spots individuals one after the other as they catch a glimpse of Gabriel's magnetic gaze and his invitation to soar. At the moment their eyes lock, each person's intangible profile streams into the sky to join the gathering multitude of angelic figures surrounding Gabriel. Suddenly he breaks out of his tight circling and sweeps across the sky.

Stan gambols while snapping shots with his camera, pointing it at the crowd in the field. He grabs shots of the children streaming past him and out to the field. Then he points up at Gabriel sailing through the air with his gathering nimbus of light beings.

Sheila descends on Stan like a mother bear and snatches his camera. She gives him a fierce look when he tries to retrieve it. He gives in and then surrenders eagerly to the magical dance, the look in his eyes shifting in an instant as his ghostly form flows up through the top of his head and shoots off into the sky to join Gabriel's host.

Sheila stands in shock for a moment, utterly perplexed by the astonishing transformation she's just witnessed up so close. She'd like to punch him, but that wouldn't be fair now. Then she remembers the camera in her hand. She storms up the steps and back into the kitchen, where Frank is finishing his coffee. She hides Stan's camera under the sink.

"I told you they'd find us," she snaps. "That's the guy who put Gabriel in the newspapers before." She points vaguely in the direction of Stan's motorcycle. "He's how they found us at the last place. He's always following us. Even when I try to avoid him or get rid of him, I see him in the park and on my street. Now I know they won't be far behind him."

"Okay, okay," Frank responds, "Let me help." But she bangs open the screen door and barges outside again with a vague intention to manage the scene and keep Gabriel safe.

In the sky under a ceiling of rolling clouds and broken patches of blue, Gabriel cavorts. His entourage is massive. Faint shapes frolic behind him in the hundreds. The harmonious aeronautics resembles a murmuration of starlings as they move to and fro in circles and sweeps, changing direction en masse as one mind. The ethereal crowd flows together and apart, creating a swirl of shapes simulating a sacred text, words that can barely be caught before they change over and over again. Even Sheila, determined as she is to remain grounded and focused lest some vague worst-case scenario occurs, is moved to sigh and wish.

Before she relaxes and inadvertently joins the glorious ride, she pulls her eyes away and turns back to reality, looking at the new car and imagining their escape. Fear forces her mind to machinate overtime, and she decides to pack the car so that they can get away at a moment's notice. She looks back up the road. As far as she knows, it's the only way in and out. She peers around the property to see what alternate exits might be available. It occurs to her suddenly that it might be smart to join that exquisite flock above her and take a survey of the area.

As if hearing her thoughts, Gabriel folds his wings back and dives toward her. She doesn't notice him until he is almost on top of her. She has wandered out into the lawn and is peering around the house along the fence line and up the ridges, seeking other egresses in this tight valley. She's right near the moving mass of dancers, whose conscious attention is flying sublimely with Gabriel.

Gabriel swoops down and snatches her hand. It startles her, and she screams in shock.

"Fly with me, Momma," he begs. But her distress, worry, and agitated state merely heighten her determination.

"No, we have pack and go!" she shouts. Gipping his hand tightly, she pulls him toward the house.

At that moment, the myriad of ethereal flyers falls out of the sky. One by one, each figure reclaims its dancing form. As the people regain their physical focus, they rush toward Gabriel. The mob swells and surrounds Sheila and Gabriel. They are not malicious, just overwhelmed by their exalted experience. They are eager and emotional. Some laugh, and some weep, but all are radiant and vital like never before. They fall out of step with each other, stumbling and pushing. Harsh words burst out, and angry retorts born out of the rude awakening ignite pushing and shoving.

"Fly, Gabriel. Fly!" people yell. "Let's do it again."

Sheila panics; she can't breathe. She hyperventilates and has to bend over to try to regain her balance. In the press of the crowd, Gabriel is forced away from her, causing him to panic, too.

"Momma! Momma!" He pushes his way back to his mother and grabs her elbow to guide her out of the fray and back into the house.

They enter the house, and Frank jumps up to assist. When he sees the crowd rushing for the kitchen door, he orders five uninvited visitors to leave and posts two friends at the doors to keep everyone else out.

"Gabriel! Gabriel! Come out! Come out and fly!" the crowd yells.

Sheila shakes with emotion while Gabriel drinks a glass of juice Dell has given him. When he puts down his half-finished glass, Sheila gulps down the last of it and feels quite relieved when the sugar kicks in to sooth her nerves. Dell fusses in the kitchen, dumping cheese, fruit, and crackers onto a plate.

"What do you think, Gabe? Are you ready to go again?" Dell asks.

"No!" Sheila shouts angrily. "He's done. He isn't here for your entertainment. We came here to hide, not to gather a … a … bunch of fans." She jumps out of her chair. "You promised we would be safe," she says to Frank, pointing her finger at him. "And you"—she turns to Dell—"I bet it was your idea to invite all of these people. Who do you think you are interfering, acting like you're the great benefactors and then pulling this kind of trick on us when we're desperate and in need of help?"

She sobs and chokes, and then she is struck by another thought. "How much money are you charging those people? I can't believe you would do this; it's appalling," she accuses.

Dell is horrified. "How can you say that? We're honest, God-fearing people. We would never do something like that." Fat tears drip from Dell's eyes. She's deeply hurt.

"No one here has paid us a dime," Frank says quietly. "They all came because they feel the love. We feel Gabriel's love too, and we have to share it."

Mary sidles over to Sheila and hands her a wadded tissue. "I love my Gabe because when he flies, I feel so big, like I ate the whole sky. Please don't stop him."

Sheila looks at Mary's big, round eyes. She shudders at the sudden recognition. She could not have said it better herself. She definitely gets it. She knows what it feels like, and she would love to surrender to that feeling and not worry about anything else.

She turns to Dell. "Can you please tell them all to go home?"

Dell and Frank shake their heads. "We didn't ask them to come, but we did ask them to go. They won't," Frank responds.

"We've got no control over anyone out there, not even our friends," Dell adds. "Gabe's the only one who has any control over them. I'd say the best thing is to let them see him, let them get their fill, and then maybe they'll just leave on their own."

Gabriel gives his mother an appealing smile. Dell plants a lunch plate in front of Mary and Gabriel, and they giggle together and start eating. Sheila looks at them both, perplexed. How wonderful to be a child and not be worried or stressed, to just play and laugh.

The old-fashioned kitchen clock strikes noon. Sheila looks at it, miffed, dragged back into her troublesome and uncertain present. Then a thought strikes her. "Oh, I want to watch the news. Maybe I can see how close Philip is. Can we?"

She, Frank, and Dell move into the living room in front of the big screen. Dell sets out plates of food for everyone to snack on while Frank surfs around for the best program.

"There, there … stop!" Sheila shouts when she sees a young female reporter clad in a smart green jacket outside her old hospital. "Make it louder, please."

"Public outcry about the winged baby continues to rise," the reporter says. Behind her, fanatics wave all kinds of banners. They seem to be divided sharply into two camps: devotees and antagonists. A fanatic dressed like an ordinary churchgoer, neat and in a middle-of-the-road, sensible style, waves an angry banner that reads "SEND THE HELL BABY BACK." On the other side, a punk-styled kid with blue hair holds a sign saying "ANGELS ALL RIGHT! LET IN THE LIGHT."

Gabriel wanders in and snuggles into his mom's lap as a picture of his face is framed beside the reporter. Gabriel pops his head up excited.

"Look, look, Momma. It's me. I'm on TV!"

"NEU Research Center has offered a reward of two hundred thousand dollars for any leads as to the whereabouts of Gabriel Jensen," the vivacious reporter continues.

"Why, Momma?" Gabriel asks, looking at her.

Sheila can't speak. She sobs silently. This is exactly what she feared would happen.

Gabriel wipes her tears. "Don't cry, Momma. They only make you feel bad if you let them."

"We have to go," she manages through her tears. "We must hide somewhere else."

Gabriel is firm. Every time he flies, he gains more certainty of purpose, and today was a huge step forward for him. "No!" he exclaims. "I can't, Momma. My heart is too full up. It's too big, and it will burst if I have to squash it into a hiding place. I can't do it. It feels right to me to fly with these people. They love it; I love it. They get bigger; I get bigger. You should do it again, Momma."

Mary squashes herself into Sheila's lap as well, inserting her tiny body between them. She reaches her arms around their necks and kisses one and then the other. She hugs them tightly together.

Then Gabriel and Mary lead Sheila outside again. She submits even though her sense of distress and anxiety has become amplified by the television report. When the crowd sees Gabriel, they cheer and rush to convene on the lawn again. Gabriel launches from the porch step and soars over to the lawn, right over the heads of the amassed admirers. Mary is right behind him.

Sheila watches intently, and when Gabriel glances back at her, she is caught, too tired and weak to resist. In an ecstatic moment, she feels a wave of joy and willingness, wind and warm sun. Then, with utter delight, she sees again from her flying body.

Gabriel sails up. Euphoric dancers chant and twirl while Gabriel dips and loops overhead. Sheila feels the same sense of power and glee that all of the flyers feel as they also loop above the dancing crowd. The wind caresses her face and hair. She's not sure if she's feeling it up there or down below, but it doesn't matter; this double perspective feels so natural. She gets bumped gently and urged subtly in this direction or that direction and wonders again, *Is it up here or down there?*

For an entire exquisite hour, Gabriel wheels and swoops, floats, dives, and soars with his flock mostly behind. Sheila, Mary and all the others relish the feeling of it. It feels amazing to move in such harmony, like a choir or a dance or both blended together. They can all see the countryside for miles. The forest of the foothills they are over seems to go on forever toward the east. Off to the west, the landscape flattens out, and farms are laid out in neat, geometric patterns according to the irrigation systems. Beyond are the ragged and colorful patterns of suburbia and the nearest city, its toothy skyline hazy and muted in the distance.

The ethereal flock doesn't fly alone. Curious flocks of crows, starlings, and songbirds swoop in occasionally to explore this attractive new phenomenon. They are like moths to a flame. Gabriel laughs giddily and points at the tiny interlopers. At first, his flying students try to avoid the birds with abrupt and clumsy movements until they learn that the feathered ones are already experts that fall in sway easily with others in flight. Even a flock of geese winging west moves in close to see what's going on. For a while, the aeronautic explorers fall in sync with the flock and sail along together, looking at each other closely, with sparkling glints of amusement in the eyes of both human and goose.

Suddenly, Sheila is aware that they are quite far from Frank's house. She looks back toward the hills and thinks she can pick out the notch that leads into the valley that shelters their sanctuary. She decides to tell Gabriel that they should turn back.

At that moment, she notices several fast-moving vehicles many miles away on the highway—an ambulance, three black cars, and a police vehicle. They are racing toward the hills where she is dancing with Gabriel's devotees. Behind them are at least a dozen media vans with their TV discs and antennae waving.

With his unerring sixth sense, Gabriel hears her thoughts. She sees him looking at the vehicles and then he tips over to change course. She's relieved. She feels tired, and she notices that Gabriel is tired, too.

They all swoop back to the hills by speed of thought rather than speed of motion. Suddenly, they are back over Frank's house. Sheila suspects the wave of fear and apprehension that swept over her when she saw the oncoming adversary has drained Gabriel of his power and rippled through his assemblage.

He plunges toward the picnic table inside Dell's fenced garden. A wild cry of protest goes up from the dancers, who snap, one after another, from the flight-conscious state to the solid state of dancing on the ground. All are conscious that this is a much sadder state. Annoyance sets in for many. They sweep toward Gabriel, knocking down and trampling the fence. Sheila is caught up in the mass, and though she tries, she can't get anywhere near Gabriel. Soon, a morass of people swallows him. They lift him up and pass him around. Random hands snatch at him or stroke and pat him. Gabriel is shocked. He did not expect this kind of disordered response.

"Put me down! Put me down!" he yells as he is rolled and tumbled from person to person.

Suddenly, mama bear Dell wrests Gabriel into her arms and rages inside. Sheila sees the rescue and, with superhuman effort, changes direction. On the way through, she gathers Mary into her arms, rescuing her from the terrible squeeze of the rapacious crowd. Weak and bedraggled, the two of them struggle in through the closely guarded kitchen door.

In the kitchen, Dell washes Gabriel's face. The crowd murmurs outside, their scrambled sounds punctuated by a few good friends trying to restore order with sharp shouts and appeals.

"I tried to get to you," Sheila says as she wipes Gabriel's tears with her hands.

"Momma, why did they do that?" Gabriel asks, sobbing.

"They didn't mean to hurt you, dearie," Dell says.

Sheila reaches to take the washcloth from Dell's hands. "I'll do that."

Dell continues cleaning Gabriel's face. "No need, dear, I can do it." Well meaning, she pushes Sheila's hand aside gently. "You look really tired too. You need to rest."

Sheila snatches the washcloth from Dell. "He's my son!"

Dell backs off, realizing that she has overstepped. "Oh, of course. I have so many children that I just get carried away. You make yourself comfortable."

"Comfortable?" Sheila snaps. "We can't rest now; we need to pack up and get out of here. There's a convoy of vans on the way here right now. I saw them on the highway."

"I saw them too," Frank says. "They're less than forty-five minutes away."

"That close?" Sheila shouts as she jumps up. "How can we get out of here? Is there another road? I thought I saw an old road through the trees. Can we go that way?"

Frank shakes his head. "That's a dirt logging trail. There are too many trees down and over it. This is the only way in and out, but there's a turnoff about fifteen minutes down the hill that goes further into the hills. You should go now. You barely have time to reach it before they get into the last leg, and then you'll be trapped."

Sheila picks up Gabriel and races out to the car. Frank collects their bags from upstairs and tosses them into the trunk. While Sheila buckles Gabriel in, Dell hands him a couple of stuffed animals and dumps a bag of sandwiches and fruit on the backseat. The children and all of Gabriel's fans stand around disgruntled.

Friends appointed by Frank herd the crowd out of the way while impressing the danger and the need to rush on them.

"Please, everyone, we need to get Gabriel out of here!" Frank says. "They're coming to get him right now. Please, move back. Make room."

Only when they hear the faint sound of sirens echoing across the hills does the crowd seem to focus. Suddenly, everyone is in a flurry, throwing their goods into vehicles and rounding up errant children.

24

ESCAPE

Frank gives the go ahead, and Sheila backs up, kicking up some gravel under her tires while shifting into drive and then shooting up the driveway toward the winding canyon road. Several of the fans' campers pull in behind her.

"Crap!" Sheila exclaims when she sees them.

"Momma?" Gabriel says with a tone of disapproval.

When the remaining onlookers see Sheila's vehicle speed away with an odd assortment of vehicles trailing, the rest of them run to their vehicles to join the chase.

Frank has an epiphany and runs to get his car keys. "That's a great idea! With a crowd of RVs, we can clog Old Canyon Road, and they'll never be able to follow Gabriel. But those jokers are probably just planning to follow Sheila. They'll surely lead those vans right to her and Gabriel. Follow me!" he yells at a group still standing around.

Frank's car, crammed with Dell and the children, pulls out. Several more RVs and trucks follow.

Sheila drives too fast down the winding road. She's terrified that she is driving right into a trap, but there's no other way. Close behind her, RVs, trucks, and vans kick up dust and sway from side to side as they bank the steep curves of the bumpy dirt road a bit too fast.

As Sheila rounds the hill and bounces onto the paved road, across the much wider canyon, she glimpses the road on the other hillside. Distant flashing lights of the official escort winding its way toward the turnoff at Old Canyon Road heighten her terror. She realizes it's dangerous, but she steps on it. There's a chance she can make it to the turn first.

Both sets of vehicles are traveling the same direction toward a V where the two hills converge. Sheila sees evidence of the escape route as it emerges on the other side and winds up over where the two hills seem to cross each other. They are nearly there.

As she rounds the final bend, the road opens up for longer than usual, and on the distant side of the canyon bending toward them, she sees the first vehicle coming into view. She's closer to the turn, which she gets a quick glimpse of over the gentle slope, though she can't see where it intersects the road she is on. A flurry of thoughts fills her mind.

Will they know it's us? They don't know this car; I could be anyone on the road.

"Unbuckle your seatbelt, Gabe, and lie down on the floor!" she yells over her shoulder.

"But Momma, that's dangerous!"

"Yes, it is, but do it anyway! I want you to hide from those cars coming toward us. Hopefully they won't recognize us."

She fumbles for the hood of her sweatshirt, trying to pull it over her bright hair. Then another thought hits her: *What about this crowd of vehicles tagging along behind us? Will that give us away? Again, we could be anyone on the road, a traveling convoy.* She takes a deep breath and guns the engine, praying to reach the turnoff first.

When the intersection comes into view, she floors it and reaches the turn right before the first car in the official squadron. She's certain that Philip will be in the lead vehicle, and she hopes that they are not close enough for him to recognize her.

She puts on her left blinker. The oncoming car is too close; they have the right of way. Technically, she should stop and wait for them to pass before she turns left. But she's not risking it. After the lead car comes a long line of escort vehicles and a dozen TV trucks. Someone will spot her waiting there.

She veers left, but the first car speeds up and makes a screeching right turn just in front of her. Philip in the front seat turns around and points at her.

They are moving fast up the hill. Sheila guns the engine, and her car groans. It isn't a high-performance vehicle, and she regrets the loss of her fabulous self-driving car with all the best add-ons. She tries to get around the black sedan as they climb up the winding hill. In her rearview mirror, she sees a clog at the intersection. Philip's convoy has slowed. Some pull over, and the fans' RVs pile up, waiting or veering left between the confused vehicles. Some head up the hill behind them.

Sheila swerves left and right, still trying to get around Philip's car. Larry slows his vehicle and does everything he can to block her from passing. An ambulance follows directly behind her, sirens blaring and lights flashing. Behind the ambulance is a police vehicle. It does nothing to sooth her anxiety. She's breathing fast and talking rapidly to Gabriel, more to soothe herself than to mollify him.

"It's okay, baby. We're doing fine. I'm just going to drive around this car. Hang on. Oh, that didn't work. Don't worry. We'll be on our way soon. Ugh! That was close. Okay. This isn't dangerous."

Gabriel whimpers behind her seat.

"Oh, Gabe, I'm sorry, so sorry. Please forgive me."

"It's okay, Momma. It's okay," he responds, comforting her.

Larry speeds up, so she speeds up, too. *Great, I'll get around him now,* she thinks. Then he brakes hard and turns the wheel. His car slides along the road sideways and comes to a halt, blocking the entire road between a rock outcrop and a steep slope on the other side.

"Hang on, Gabe!" Sheila cries as she slams on the brakes.

The ambulance screeches to a halt behind them. The police cruiser and a couple of RVs from the festival of fans trail them. Philip jumps out of the sedan followed by another man. Both run over to the passenger side of Sheila's car. Sheila locks the doors.

"Open this door!" he yells. "You have to surrender Gabriel now." The other man steps forward and gently pushes Philip out of the way. "Excuse me, Dr. Jensen, my name is Joshua Tucker. I have been appointed by the court to represent your son in his custody hearing tomorrow afternoon. I recommend that you come back quietly. Your abduction of Gabriel doesn't look good to the court, and it can only go worse for you if you don't comply."

"He's my child!" she screams. "I didn't kidnap him. I'm his mother. This is insane."

A police car passes the stopped vehicles behind them and pulls up next to Sheila's car. Philip flashes a court order in front of the officers. Sheila can see him explaining, gesticulating. He is very, very angry. Joshua Tucker crouches down outside her door to be at eye level with her. He appeals to her to calm down and open the door. Think of Gabriel, he entreats; he needs to feel safe.

A police officer approaches behind Philip.

"Sorry, ma'am," the officer says. "We have a writ from the judge. If you don't open the door, we'll override the locks and open it ourselves."

She holds her hands up. "Okay, okay, wait. Let me get out first. I need to explain to Gabriel."

The officer nods. Sheila clicks the unlock button, and all of the doors unlock.

Philip opens the back door and reaches in to grab Gabriel from the floor behind the front seats. Joshua Tucker tries to intervene unsuccessfully, "Easy, Philip, let's be calm about this."

"Wait, stop!" Sheila yells.

"Momma!" Gabriel cries.

"Wait, I'm coming with him," Sheila insists, running toward the ambulance.

Philip has Gabriel in his arms. He wails, kicks, and reaches for his mother.

"You are not coming with us," Philip pronounces with his back to her as he strides toward the back of the ambulance, Gabriel clamped against him. "Wait, Philip, this is not right. You can't abduct him from his mother either. Let's be reasonable. We can all travel back together in one car." Philip is fuming, "No, I have been shut out too long, and I am not taking any chances on her worming her way out of coming back to the city."

"Momma!" Gabriel cries again.

"I'll be right behind you, baby!" Sheila assures him. Philip turns around surprised that Sheila seems to be right behind him. In his mind she was still struggling to get her wheelchair out of that car. He turns and looks at her, still holding Gabriel.

"Are you walking?"

Sheila doesn't answer she just reaches for Gabriel. Philip backs away and hands Gabriel up to the EMT reaching for him from the ambulance. Then he turns to Sheila.

"How did you do that?"

Sheila just fumes and snarls, "Give me back my son."

Philip shrugs and jumps into the ambulance. The police officer stuffs a ticket into Sheila's hand.

"What's this?" she asks.

"Speeding and driving with a child outside of the seatbelt."

"You've got to be kidding."

"It appears not," he replies.

Sheila gasps as she watches Philip struggle to strap her son into the back of the ambulance. The court-appointed lawyer tries to climb in there too, but the EMTs dissuade him.

"Sorry, buddy, we don't have room for you too back here."

"Philip, I need to go with you both," he argues.

Philip is distracted, though, by Gabriel, who tries to get free. His wings are flapping at full extension, and he tries to climb out.

"I'll go with you, Momma!"

Philip and an EMT yank him back into the ambulance and slam the door. Tucker stands in the street, stunned. The vehicle backs around in the tight road, precipitously close to the edge. The policeman offers directions and holds back the oncoming traffic. Sheila watches in dismay as the ambulance heads back down the hill. Larry swings his sedan, the car that Philip and Tucker arrived in, around in three tight turns and then follows. Tucker comes to life and dashes over to jump into the passenger seat of Sheila's car just as she is firing it up to turn and follow.

25

THERE'S NO ESCAPE

Sheila's car tires squeal, and it feels like the car is about to tip over in the tight turn she forces it to navigate. The police are left behind yelling at the assorted RVs, vans, and trucks that litter the tight route all the way from the intersection and up around the turn to the place where they caught Gabriel. She feels empty, desperate, and defeated. Tears stream down her face. Her unwelcome passenger, Joshua Tucker, apologizes for jumping in but says that he needs to get back to town and seems to have been abandoned.

"This gives us time to get to know each other and talk about your son," he offers.

Sheila snaps at him, "I can't talk and drive right now. I'm too upset. Can we just pretend we are both alone for a while?"

Tucker nods perfunctorily and turns to look out of the window.

The ambulance carrying Gabriel bumps down the country road heading back toward the clogged intersection. Larry's sedan follows. One of the police vehicles and some of Gabriel's devotees' trucks chase the ambulance. There is no way on this tight road, with a steep hill on one side and a precipitous drop on the other, that Sheila can pass any of them.

She swings from left to right, trying to find a way through. The convoy winds through the melee of tangled vehicles crowded around the intersection with the help of police, who make the fans move out of the way. Sheila struggles to keep up, afraid she will be cut off again. She gets around a smoking and lurching truck and an RV, but Larry isn't helping and won't give her any space to get around his formidable sedan. Finally, the retreating convoy makes it past the mess of vehicles and press standing on the side of the road. Cameras snatch shots or video as the ambulance passes by. When the ambulance breaks out into the open road, leaving the crowd of vehicles behind, Sheila pushes the nose of her car right up to the bumper of Larry's sedan. She's determined not to let any other vehicle get between them or any police or press to stop her. A few minutes later, they are on the highway and headed toward the city.

* * *

Gabriel and Philip are strapped into the back of the ambulance opposite each other. Each is seated next to an EMT. Philip studies Gabriel as Gabriel stares back at him.

"So, this is what you've been up to," Philip says. "I've missed you and your mom." He reaches over to touch Gabriel's feathers and runs his hand over them. "Soft."

Gabriel pulls his wing away from Philip's touch and then pushes Philip's face away with his small hand planted firmly on Philip's cheek. A blue spark of energy flashes from the angry look in Gabriel's eyes and strikes Philip's right eye. It blinds him momentarily, and he grunts and closes his eyes in shock.

Suddenly, Philip feels as if he is flying behind the ambulance. He's streaking through the air along the highway, racing between trucks and vans and over the top of cars, perilously close to the churning wheels of the tractor-trailer that rumbles along beside the ambulance.

Sheila peers ahead, shocked. She thinks she can see an ephemeral version of Philip flapping his arms wildly and ineffectually as he flies down the highway. Sheila glances at Tucker to see if he sees anything—probably not. He gazes disinterestedly in front of them with unfocused eyes.

Inside the ambulance, Philip is screaming. He rolls backwards and then leans way forward in his seat. The EMTs unbuckle themselves and rush to help him.

"He seems to be having some kind of a fit," one of them says.

Philip flails and cries out. "Stop! Whoa! Holy cow! Oh! Oh! Oh! No! Whew!"

Gabriel looks out of the ambulance's rear window and smiles when he sees Philip's ethereal form trying hard to control itself as it wings along outside.

The EMTs unbuckle Philip's shaking body and loosen his tie. He veers over to the side and steps out of his seat, stumbling around inside the speeding ambulance and waving his arms. He seems helplessly off balance and unaware of where he is.

"Watch out!" he yells, and he leaps to the side as if to avoid something and hits a wall, knocking several snap-locked safety items loose so that they scatter to the floor. The EMTs grab him, wrestle him down, and strap him to the stretcher with his arms by his sides and his head and neck positioned in a brace so that he won't choke.

Larry pulls his sedan out of the lane behind the ambulance and zooms around and ahead. He is oblivious to Philip's airy form, which rears back and tumbles over the top of his sedan and then comes upright again behind the ambulance. Philip races through the air, moving sometimes beside or behind the ambulance.

Sheila swerves onto the shoulder to avoid hitting Philip's ghostly form when it flounders through the air right in front of her. Tucker looks over at her, thinking she's fallen asleep or gone nuts. But she has no idea if someone's light form can be damaged, and she doesn't want to find out. When she noses back in line behind the ambulance, Gabriel waves at her from inside, and she waves back.

Philip sobs hysterically, muttering incoherently about crashes and flight and feeling sick. The EMTs whisper in conference about his peculiar state.

"I really think we should sedate him," one of them says. "He's going to do damage to himself if we don't do something now."

"Yeah, it seems like some kind of psychotic state," the other EMT says. "Let's do it."

Gabriel watches them intently. He knows what's going on with Philip, but he refuses to help. Right now he is very angry with Philip, and he doesn't get angry easily.

The minute the EMTs insert a needle into Philip's arm, Gabriel sees Philip's projected, filmy self spring back on its gossamer silver chord and recoil into Philip's body. Soon, he is snoring soundly. One EMT offers Gabriel some juice, which he accepts gratefully, and Gabriel makes himself comfortable for the long drive.

* * *

It takes over six long hours to drive back to the hospital. Tucker is intrigued by Gabriel's wings, and his mind is boiling with thoughts about how this might affect the case and his career. "Wow," he keeps murmuring to himself whenever the enormity of it strikes him again. He tries to engage Sheila in conversation; he wants to know how this happened.

"How did you do it?" he asks brazenly.

Sheila pointedly ignores him.

Overall they share only a few brief moments of conversation in which he fills her in on the court proceedings so far, his role in the affair, and his expectations of her for the next hearing. She doesn't ask questions or want to talk any more than necessary. He only babbles on, filling in what he thinks she should know.

The entire convoy of vehicles—the ambulance, Sheila's car, Larry's sedan, and a few fan RVs and trucks—travels together; the local police departed at the county borderline early in the trip.

Philip wakes up during the last hour and tries to convince the EMTs that he is neither crazy nor dangerous and that he is, in fact, the boss. Whether this is true or not, the EMTs insist on keeping him strapped down "for his own safety." Philip practically sends himself into an apoplectic fit, shouting at them and cursing them out, so they finally agree to telephone Spiner and get authorization for his release from the stretcher.

When Philip is free and back in his seat next to Gabriel, he sighs deeply in relief, careful to avert his eyes from Gabriel's. He has no idea what happened or why, but he is reluctant to go through that nightmare again. What bothers him most is that he can't tell anyone about it or find any way to examine the phenomenon, because undoubtedly he will be branded as crazy and stuck in a straightjacket. He breathes deeply and sits back with his eyes closed for the last hour or so of the drive.

Sheila runs the gamut of emotions throughout the duration of the trip. At first, she is despondent. Later she becomes furious, then hopeful, and finally indignant. This is the state that she concludes is the most useful to her in her efforts to get her son back. She decides to use the driving time to formulate strategies to fight Philip for her child. The distraction of Tucker sitting beside her annoys her. As soon as they are close enough to the city, she pulls over and suggests he take a cab wherever he's going. He, too, is relieved to get out of the awkward situation and jumps out.

Shortly after that, she is beside herself with anxiety and is about to slip into hysteria when Cynthia calls. She's heard on the news that Gabriel has been found.

"Sheila, where are you? Are you with him? How did it happen?"

Sheila babbles half-coherently as she recounts the events.

"Slow down. Wait, tell me that again," Cynthia says, breaking the flow of Sheila's rant.

Sheila continues after a breath, her words increasing steadily in speed and pitch as she relives the injustice of it all.

"Have they arrested you?" Cynthia asks.

Sheila is stunned. She didn't even think of that. "Oh my God. Do you think they will?"

"I don't know," Cynthia replies. "This is all very extreme. Who would have guessed they would go this far?"

When Cynthia feels she understands the situation, she suggests that Sheila let her know when she is getting close, and she and Mike will meet her and decide what kind of legal options she has.

* * *

When they get closer to the hospital, Sheila notices something perplexing: are these people collecting at intersections off the highway and along the sidewalks really here to watch Gabriel arrive? At first, it's a smattering of the curious, but as they get closer to their destination, more and more clusters gather until they form crowds along the side of the road. Yes, she concludes when she sees the banners and signs that they wave. Whether for or against the issue of human genomic interference, they are all super passionate and throw everything they can into making themselves heard. Sheila has seen all the vile accusations before but *mother of the Devil* and *Dr. Frankensheila* are new insults that actually make her laugh. What's more surprising to her is the preponderance of fans. The tide seems to have turned. People in tears wave big signs begging Gabriel to invite them to fly.

When they come around the corner in convoy, children jump up and down excitedly and shout as if the pope has arrived. It seems like they're all wearing handmade or Halloween-shop wings, and it's not just the kids. Tons of adults are wearing everything from butterfly to bat to angel wings.

Something about their enthusiasm lifts Sheila's heart. A powerful wave of recognition sweeps through her mind. She understands exactly what these onlookers hope for, and she is stunned that they understand Gabriel's gift even before seeing him fly.

Soon, she notices a news van and then two more. The vans fall in line with the hospital's official escort, creating more difficulties for her in keeping her position behind the ambulance.

By the time they arrive at the hospital, it's been mobbed. The police have cordoned off the huge crowd, which is desperate to get a good look at Sheila and her astonishing child. The hospital security staff guards all entry points. City police escort the special posse. They guide their quarry over the bridge, across the city limits, and right up to the hospital complex entrance.

Sheila waves her hospital badge, but it's clear from the gate guard's impatient gesture to move on that he already knows her and expects her. Ahead she sees the ambulance's back door open and Philip scramble out with the two EMTs. Gabriel is slung between them, his little feet struggling to reach down and get traction on the pavement.

Sheila abandons her car on the way to the emergency zone because of the horde of official and press vehicles in her way. She runs toward the entrance, where her captive child and his custodial team are entering the hospital. Gabriel looks back wistfully, searching for his mother, and at the last minute before the door closes on him, he sees her. His face brightens for just a moment, and then he disappears. Sheila chases after them inside the entrance, but they have already been devoured by the hospital, and she has no idea which direction to go.

Suddenly, Cynthia is there, throwing her arms around her sister. They hug each other tightly. Sheila is on the edge of collapsing.

"I'm so sorry," is all Cynthia can think to say.

"I know," Sheila responds. She pulls herself up, drawing on reserves of strength in order to keep going. "You said it. You thought something like this would happen. You warned me."

They separate, and Mike steps in to grab Sheila. She collapses again, relieved to have strong family members around her. When he pulls back, he looks into her eyes.

"Okay, Sheila, we have some work to do. We need to sit down and hear the whole story. I want to help, but we have to strategize. The first step is the facts. Let's head back to my office."

Cynthia steps forward and puts her arm around Sheila. "Maybe she needs a rest, a meal, and a chance to clean up first, Mike. There's time to plan the next step. Let's just get you home right now, Sheila."

Sheila shakes her head. "No, no, I can't do either. I have to follow Gabe and make sure he's all right." Then she looks at Mike. "Do you think I have a chance to get him back?"

"I don't know," Mike admits. "We're going to find you the best person in the field. First, though, we have to find out what your rights are and what they're claiming, and then we'll know how to proceed. I do think that if you barge in there and try to take Gabriel now, you will damage your case."

Sheila's face darkens as dismay washes through her, adding to her exhaustion. She starts to sob. Cynthia puts her arms around Sheila's waist and leads her back toward her car, which is still running.

"We'll find a way to get Gabriel released. Right now you need to rest."

Sheila weakly protests, but she is too tired to fight. Cynthia ushers Sheila into her car and drives to her warm and friendly kid-filled house.

That night, Sheila can't sleep. She paces around, playing scenarios out in her head. She hardly eats anything. Cynthia's kids tiptoe around her, afraid to upset their aunt any further. Mike admits that he is worried about her. She has never been so low or so quiet before. The kids are curious about Gabriel and don't understand why they can't see him.

Right after dinner, Sheila climbs up the stairs to the guest bedroom intending to try to sleep, but she can't. After the house is quiet, she pulls out some old running clothes from the days when the sisters ran together, gets dressed in them, and ducks out of the front door. Sheila is too upset to sleep, think, meditate, or even talk. She remembers how in the old days running calmed her, so she pounds the pavement. Before long, she is standing in front of her house again. *We'll move back there,* she decides. *I'll get him back,* she hopes. Then she notices a blue envelope stuffed between her screen and the glass front doors. It is addressed to her and dated for the previous week; it's her notice for the first court date that she has missed. She crumples the document and stuffs it and the resentful anger it fosters into her neighbor's garbage bin standing at the curb. She continues to run, not thinking where to go but just feeling the rhythm of her feet and breath.

Sometime later, she is pounding the streets past the hospital. It's worse there now than it was five years before; more crowds are camped around the protected parking lot in the parkland on one side and the shopping center lot on the other. Police range around, intending to keep order, and since it's late, things are mostly quiet. Sheila is aware that, unlike the crowds of that earlier event five years ago, these crowds have a real, unique being to focus on. This time it's her son.

26

BEREFT

The next morning, after her fretful night of wandering, Sheila sits dazed on a stool at Cynthia's kitchen counter. Her sister, who is preparing breakfast, turns to fill a coffee cup for Sheila. She's still rolling her disturbed waking dreams of the night before through her mind and trying to dispel them. Fragments of terrifying thoughts make her shiver. The total loss of her son felt so imminent when she found the blue summons tucked in her front door. It seems likely that more uncontrolled crowds like the one at Frank and Dell's house are in Gabriel's future, considering the gatherings at the hospital. She cannot see where she can turn for help or how to get out of this torture. *What to do, what to do?* is like an earworm in her head. It's the closest she can get to a coherent thought that might lead to a rational plan. Rarely has she felt this helpless and defeated.

Mike strides into the kitchen, dressed, shaved, and ready to go. He grabs a bite of toast and points to the silent, clear-glass kitchen television that looks more like a window than a piece of technology. "You should watch that. They're at the university right now."

Sheila slides off the stool, but Cynthia gets there first and turns on the unit, which immediately clouds up to obscure the view through to the garden and then presents a crystal clear TV image. The first footage they see is a wide aerial pan of city streets, parks, and parking lots around the hospital. Masses of people have crowded into the area. It is far more crowded than it was just a couple of hours earlier when Sheila ran by. People are encamped in the park, tents are strewn throughout, and the paved area surrounding the angel statue seems to be a gathering place where musicians and artists display their skills. The police have failed at keeping the crowds out of the facility's parking lot. Barricades have been toppled and crowds press in toward the hospital.

Sheila's mouth drops open. "Wow! How does the staff get into work?"

Mike leans in and kisses Cynthia on the mouth and then turns to head off to work. "Sheila, come by today, and we'll go over your case. I'll find out who's the best lawyer to get as lead for you. You'll want to do this quickly."

Sheila nods, unable to wrench her eyes from the television. A reporter babbles inanely, clearly having nothing new to say, no updates from the hospital, and no idea where Gabriel is exactly inside that indomitable institution. Thankfully, they haven't found her yet. Sheila glances out the window. The street outside Cynthia's house is still free of interlopers. The reporters do love conjecture, though, and so with supporting imagery from the university's genome department website, they speculate wildly as to how Gabriel came about who will be in charge of this remarkable new "phenomenon."

Just like reporters to depersonalize, Sheila thinks with a twinge remembering her own former disconnect.

"Dr. Philip Ohl seems to be assembling a research team to study this new phenomenon of a flying child," the dark-haired, crisply enunciating young reporter continues. Sheila watches, appalled, when her own picture from the website fills the screen. "One person who we know will *not* be on the research team is Dr. Sheila Jensen, the child's surrogate mother."

"And why should that be?" Sheila practically shouts at the TV. "They need me. I'm the one who did this. I'm the only one with all of the information. And I'm his mother, not a surrogate, for God's sake."

"We can only guess what they might need to do to him at this point," the reporter concludes. "We know another custody hearing is imminent, but it doesn't look good for the woman who kidnapped him."

The broadcast cuts to a female studio anchor. "Is it best for him to stay there at the research institute, do you think, Joel?"

"Well, Maureen, it's hard to know at this point. This is totally new ethical territory. No one knows what his rights are at this point. There have been questions raised about whether Dr. Jensen is really his mother, but once they determine the facts, the decisions will be easier for the judge."

"Thank you, Joel," Maureen replies. "That is a perfect segue to our next guest. Amelie Johnson is a human rights lawyer, foremost in her field and recipient of the International Critics Prize for her gripping nonfiction book that reads like a novel, *The Line Crossed: Humanity Enhanced.*"

The camera turns to Amelie. She is a fresh-looking, neatly coifed woman with serious eyes. "The first thing I need to say on the issue of rights here is that no child should be ripped away from his mother in such a disturbing way. No matter what the legal ramifications of his genesis might be currently, Dr. Jensen is the boy's mother, and separating a mother and child in such an aggressive and destructive way is only going to cause harm. We are on the precipice of great change, whether it means genetically enhanced newborns or technological or even genetic enhancement of adults, and we can't forget our inalienable rights as human beings. This is what's at stake here."

Sheila sighs. "I want her."

"I think that's a good idea," Cynthia says. "I'll call Mike and get him to find her."

Sheila has another idea. "I'm going to get on that research team. I don't care what they say. I'm really the only expert so far. They need me."

Cynthia thinks that's a great idea too. After all, there's no one better in the field than Sheila. It would be foolish of them to pass her up, despite the emotional minefield she will have to navigate, but Cynthia is still dubious that Sheila will be welcomed with open arms.

"You're right, Sheila. You should be on the team. See what the lawyer says first, though, and make sure you get to that hearing next week."

Sheila is already on her phone, though, and waving Cynthia to wait a moment. Philip surprises her by answering right away.

Cynthia sits across the counter from her sister. "Sheila hang up."

"Philip, I want to be on the team," Sheila pleads.

"Don't beg," Cynthia whispers. "You have a right. He's your son!"

"Please, Philip." Sheila cannot control the desperate edge to her voice.

Philip pauses. He has her exactly where he wants her. Now they can get some answers. "Okay, listen, I want you to write up a report detailing everything relative to Gabriel's inception, development, growth, and acuity. There are a quite few questions we need to answer. There are some anomalies in the findings and in the process records we have that only you can clear up. Please get it to me before the hearing."

Cynthia waits anxiously, wondering what he can be saying to her for so long.

"Fine, but I need to see my son right away," Sheila responds finally.

"Let's see what happens at court. The best thing you can do now is write that report," Philip says.

Sheila is devastated that she must wait. She tries to think of other ways to get Philip to let her in to see Gabriel right away.

"You have all of my files; you need me to work with them."

"If you are missing something, send a request by email."

She sighs, deflated, and then her anger rises. "He's my son. He's not a petri dish! You have to let me see him."

Cynthia comes around the counter and puts her arm around Sheila, trying to calm her. Sheila gruffly shakes her off.

Philip takes a cool, calm breath before replying. "We'll talk when you're finished." With that, he hangs up.

"Did you get that?" Sheila asks Cynthia, "I have to write a paper like a grade school student before I can see my son."

Cynthia ignores her sister's rebuff and pulls her into her arms, hugging her tight; she too has tears in her eyes. Sheila breaks down sobbing.

"I think I've cried more in the last twenty-four hours than I have in my entire life, even as a kid. This is just awful."

Cynthia nods. She knows very well how tough her sister is.

* * *

The next day, at Sheila's request, Cynthia manages to get into the lab portion of the facility with her hospital pass. She's surprised at how easy it is. She strides into the lab and sees Gabriel through an observation window into the sanctuary. He is strapped to a chair on a table. She surreptitiously takes a couple of shots with her phone of him tied up there. Several doctors and technicians bustle about the place. Along one wall are the animal cages still housing many of the strange creatures that were part of Philip and Sheila's ongoing research. They produce a cacophony of noises: bird shrieks, animal grunts, and monkey hoots.

Gabriel points to the cages along the wall. "Do they ever go out?" he asks one of the lab workers. They all ignore him and continue their tasks.

Gabriel winces, prodded at the origin of one wing by an instrument held by an unsympathetic technician. Cynthia pushes into the room and shoulders the young woman aside.

"What do you think he is, a mineral?" She hugs Gabriel.

"Aunty!" he yells excitedly.

"Mommy sends her love," she says, smiling at him. Then she whirls on the gray-haired woman who is charging indignantly toward her. "Why is he in here? Where is his father?"

"Dr. Spiner is concerned about security, and you are not supposed to be in here," the wiry woman with steel-gray eyes, Leticia Newman, replies officiously.

Cynthia refuses to back down. "This is completely inappropriate. You can't treat him like these animals, and he should never be placed in this particular lab. He's a human being and should be at home with his mother."

"I like the animals, Aunty," Gabriel interjects. "And they like me. Can you let them out?"

Cynthia leans in and takes his hands. "I'm afraid not, love. Do you want something nice? Some homemade cookies?"

Dr. Newman steps in to seize the plastic tub of cookies that Cynthia produces from her bag. "Sorry, but he's on a strict intake regimen. Hospital services are providing all of his nourishment."

"What?" Cynthia exclaims as she dodges Newman's grasping fingers, pops the container lid, and hands a cookie to Gabriel. "He's a kid. What are you talking about? He needs more than calories and vitamins; he needs love."

Gabriel grabs the cookie and takes a bite. "Thank you, Aunty C," he says, his mouth full.

"I'll bring you some toys and goodies tomorrow," she says and then kisses him on the forehead.

Dr. Newman picks up the telephone. "I'm calling security. If you don't leave right now, you will be escorted out."

"Fine," Cynthia retorts. "I'm going. But you are not having my cookies, and I am going straight to Sheila's lawyer about your treatment of my nephew. This is just not right."

She hands another cookie to Gabriel, clamps the tub shut, and stuffs it into her bag.

* * *

Ten minutes later, Cynthia is back at her office and on the phone ranting to Mike. "Did you find that lawyer?" she asks.

He says that he has and that Amelie Johnson is delighted to step in as lead council on the case.

"Thank God. When is she meeting Sheila?"

"She's just reviewing what she can right now, and we'll get her together with Sheila tomorrow," Mike replies.

"I don't think Sheila's going to be sitting around waiting, especially when she sees what I saw today. Check your inbox and send those shots to Ms. Johnson please. Gabriel should not be kept in the lab like a test animal," Cynthia asserts.

* * *

By the time Sheila meets Amelie, she has compiled a comprehensive account of Gabriel's creation process, as she understands it. Her low-tech notebooks are all she needed. She still has all of them, and she is determined not to hand them over to anyone. She extracts the material to present to Philip in her own way on a few descriptive pages. She is determined not to share any of her photos, drawings, or diagrams.

Each of her notebooks is more like a work of art than a scientific record and is mostly inscrutable to other eyes. They include detailed drawings, graphic printouts, photos, color charts, and written notes in different colors and shapes according to Sheila's own method of organization. To the unfamiliar eye, the notebooks might look a bit chaotic, but to Sheila, they are crystal clear. She has no problem referring back and forth to corroborate her thoughts as she compiles her summary. Her proprietary color and shape code throughout the texts helps her to find everything she is looking for. Everything relative to nutrition, whether it's on the scale of cellular nutrition or nutrition of the whole child, is marked in green. Anything that relates to behavior on all scales is noted in yellow. Incidents that refer to the micro scale are enclosed in boxes with rounded edges. Incidents about the macroorganism, Gabriel himself, are enclosed in sharp-cornered rectangular boxes. The books are written in real time with a date in each upper right corner, and hours, where relevant, run in military time down the right side of the page. The bottom sixth of each page is reserved for notes that refer backward or forward relating the current information of that page to something earlier or later. She can flip through all of the books and zero in on specific information she needs easily to compile her report. Her complex organizational method was devised over many years, beginning in high school. It is peculiar, but it works for her.

As she proceeds through her document for Philip, she stops periodically to muse on the strange events. Random red squiggly lines that suddenly catch her eye mark these unexplainable incidences. First is the electrical anomaly, the spark that caused the blackout that occurred at Gabriel's inception. She finds herself flipping back to the pages that account for the events of that first night often. Deep inside, she harbors some hope that if she looks at it again, all will become clear and she will understand the reasons for Gabriel's mutation. She stops also to muse at the frank and practical language that she used when Gabriel was so tiny. "The subject sleeps well and soundly; he seems well-adjusted," for example. She remembers a bit painfully how much she resisted falling in love with him, how much she convinced herself that it was important to remain objective. Sheila sighs so loudly that she almost moans. How hopeless she feels, utterly in love with her son and completely bereft. Sheila sobs herself into a fitful sleep again only to awaken in the middle of the night and find herself at first pacing her room in a tormented state and then once more running absentmindedly toward the hospital.

* * *

At the same time, Gabriel sits on the window ledge of his hospital room and peers outside. That day, after receiving a complaint from Sheila's lawyer, Amelie Johnson, about mistreatment of Gabriel, Philip decided to move him. He is now in another wing of the institution on the opposite side as the lab, but the park is still visible over the parking lot. He sees the angel fountain, his namesake, not too far in the distance. He stares wistfully at it, remembering the many times he has run playfully around it. The early-morning light is evidence of predawn, and the birds begin to sing; a cacophony of shrills, trills, chips, and squawks fill the air.

A crow sails by, and Gabriel grapples with the window, trying to open it. "Maybe that's Bill," he says hopefully. He pushes the window hard, but it opens only about four inches and then stops. Gabriel puts his face to the opening and caws like a crow, wishing the bird would turn and be Bill, but that bird doesn't come back to him.

Gabriel lies down on the window ledge and drapes his hand out of the window, moving it gently through the light wisps of morning wind. He's always one to make the best of any situation, but this trap is tough for him. He needs the open air. He needs freedom, clouds, and his mother.

* * *

The meeting Mike arranged for Sheila with Amelie Johnson finally happens. Sheila has finished the account for Philip and is about to launch into the unknown and terrifying territory of having nothing to do. Without work and without Gabriel, she has only time on her hands, and the state of her mind is already driving her crazy. She needs to step forward to make new plans and take on new challenges, and Gabriel's retrieval is first on her list.

Sheila and Mike arrive at Amelie's prestigious office. That morning, Sheila wrapped and labeled a hard copy of her file for Philip, but she refuses to send him a digital copy. As far as she can see right now, this file is her only ticket inside to see her son. She has emailed a copy to Amelie, though, thinking that she might need it. Sheila hopes it doesn't contain anything incriminating. If the regenerative gene splice she attempted to install had shown up in Gabriel, it would have been definite proof of her disobeying the lab's policy, but it's not there. However, if the gene splice had worked and a regenerative gene had shown up and been a success, then everyone, including the university, would have done everything they could to claim ownership of it—especially if that were the reason she could walk now. As it stood, though, the causes of Gabriel's mutation and of her surprising recovery are utterly confusing. Both events are absent from her account for Philip. Both are still untraceable and unexplainable, so what can she possibly say about either. She has been through every micron of Gabriel's DNA several times, examining it for patterns that might answer these questions, but has found nothing.

The meeting with Amelie goes well. The bright-eyed lawyer is definitely on Sheila's side. Her viewpoint on the issue of mutations, gene manipulation, and technological augmentations is that all who benefit from such leading-edge technology should be afforded complete, unqualified human rights and be subject to the laws that any ordinary person might be. A principle concern of her book *The Line Crossed* is that nefarious influences within corporate conglomerates will seize the chance to create a race of mutated or technically enhanced subhumans to use as slaves or, worse, as military agents. Many think Amelie is a bit of a nut, but for her, Gabriel's situation is a perfect case and an exact representation of her fears. This is why she is eager to take it on.

After two hours with Amelie and Mike, Sheila comes away hopeful. Amelie assures her that her rights supersede Philip's, especially since he has placed Gabriel in the institution and not at home with him. "A research hospital is no place for a child, and this is a precedent I would be loath to permit."

* * *

Finally, Sheila's day in court arrives. She is fidgeting, eager, and terrified. Thankfully, this proceeding is taking place in one of the newer court buildings outside the five-sided plaza where her former court nightmare occurred. It's a low-slung building that is more modern inside, with lighter wood finishes, lower ceilings, and warmer-colored corridors. It's a family court, and it feels altogether friendlier than the intimidating, massive stone-and-marble monument further down the block.

The crowd outside, however, is very reminiscent of her case five years before. All eyes and cameras are again focused on her, but this time she has Gabriel to worry about. Also this time she is flanked only by her sister, Mike, and Amelie as they work their way through the strident and opinionated mob.

According to Philip's lawyer, Mort Stein, his case rests on the fact that Philip has established that he is Gabriel's father and that Sheila kept that from him. In addition, Sheila's absconding with Gabriel and avoiding the first court date sets her in a very bad light. Her irresponsible actions—taking her son to strange places, moving in with strangers, and leaving home without notice, plans, or proper supplies—puts her qualifications as mother into question. On the other hand, Philip has placed his son in the safest place that he can in light of the throngs that follow Gabriel everywhere. The lawyer insists that in the research institution, "Philip has a top-notch team treating Gabriel well. He has everything he wants or needs and the best protection he can get."

Amelie counters forcefully, and Cynthia acts as witness to the cruel and unjust treatment of Gabriel, presenting her photos. A complaint is registered that Philip has moved Gabriel to an unknown location in the institution and that he has kept Gabriel from his mother. Sheila appeals to the court as Gabriel's mother and the only one he has spent all of his first five years with, as well as the only one who understands the complexities of his unusual life. The last to present a case is Joshua Tucker, who speaks for Gabriel. He surprises Sheila by agreeing with her. Apparently Tucker has spent quite a bit of time with Gabriel over the last week interviewing him about his life, and he has concluded that life in an institution can't compete with life at home with his mother.

Finally, the judge deliberates and concludes that Philip had no right to remove Gabriel from his mother in the way that he did and that he has no right to keep Gabriel from Sheila either. He asks if the parents would be willing to be amicable and share custody. Sheila is infuriated at the proposal, and an argument breaks out. Neither parent is willing to give up their son. So the judge who is by now tired, irritated, and hungry appoints a child psychologist to examine Gabriel and get back to him in some vague future. Geraldine Archer, the psychologist who has been standing by expecting this, nods to the judge. "Meanwhile, Gabriel will go home with his mother," is the judge's final directive.

27

REUNITED

Plans to get Gabriel out of the research facility and home with Sheila quickly become very complicated. Sheila and Philip leave the court together and go directly to the institution to gather Gabriel. Sheila is determined to take him home immediately. The psychologist, who is eager to begin her interviews with Gabriel and her evaluations of his parent's homes, will be meeting Sheila and Gabriel the following morning.

Gabriel is thrilled to see his mom. They rush to each other, and she squeezes him tight. Gabriel gently strokes his mother's cheek and whispers how much he loves and missed her. Both are teary-eyed. When Leticia, the officious, rail-thin lab technician that Sheila has never liked, steps in to try to separate them, Philip waves her off. Then an argument breaks out among the staff about removing Gabriel from the safety of the hospital.

"How will you get him out of here and past that crowd?" Leticia demands. Spiner shows up also to weigh in and appeals to Sheila. "You know how dangerous it is out there, Sheila. Think of your son. Think of his safety."

Ultimately, Sheila loses patience with the arguments and with all their efforts to deter her. She storms off with Gabriel in tow. Her march through the hospital corridors to Cynthia's domain becomes a bit of a parade. Gabriel's wings flutter free and waft behind them. Orderlies, nurses, patients, and even doctors, join the line and jockey for position to stroke Gabriel, to clasp Sheila's hand in some form of comfort, or to ask random questions of either of them. Philip tries to stay with them but keeps getting jostled and shouldered out. Finally, Sheila and Gabriel escape into Cynthia's office and lock the door. Sheila instructs Gabriel to sit tight while she exits through the door on the other side of the office into the exam rooms to go and find Cynthia. By the time his mother and aunt return,

Gabriel has eaten through a bowl of fruit on Cynthia's desk, leaving only remnants of orange peel and apple cores, and Sheila has a plan for how to get Gabriel home.

* * *

An hour later, Cynthia pulls into Sheila's driveway as close to the side of the house as she can manage. No one is there—no press, no protestors, no devotees. The place has been quiet for a couple of weeks now, and clearly it seems to be off the public's radar. Sheila is immensely relieved. She and Gabriel pile out of the back of Cynthia's car and toss the blankets they used to hide under back onto the seat. They wave Cynthia off, and then Sheila grabs Gabriel and runs for cover into the house through the garage side door. It's a comfort to be home again, at least for now.

28

ANGER FLARES UP

It takes only a day for Sheila's delusion of safety and freedom to utterly unravel. That morning, Geraldine Archer arrives bright and earlier than expected at 9:00 a.m. sharp, ready to interview Gabriel and check out conditions in her home. Sheila has barely moved back in. She is dismayed that her kitchen is bare of provisions and her car is abandoned in the hospital parking lot. Meanwhile, Gabriel scrambles around in the attic hoping to find an old toy or two to play with. So without breakfast or entertainment, Sheila and Gabriel are summoned to the living room to answer Geraldine's questions.

It soon becomes apparent that Sheila has no plan for how to proceed, no idea how Gabriel will go to school or where, no thought of how to deal with his special talent, and no means to protect him from the public. "We'll just stay home," is her only idea. "I'll homeschool him. We'll build a wall around the front yard, too, and just stay in here."

Geraldine looks at her dubiously, thinking, *Perhaps this woman is losing it. Stress has clearly taken its toll on her.* "What about you, Gabriel? What do you want to do?" she asks.

Gabriel launches into a litany of plans; he wants to learn everything, see everything, meet lots of people, and teach people how to fly and how to be creative and have fun. "I know I can do all that. I can." Geraldine writes copious notes, seeming more preoccupied with her notebook than her subjects.

The two-hour visit wears Sheila down. Gabriel is hungry but unfazed and remains bubbly throughout. When Geraldine finally leaves, Sheila gets on the computer and starts ordering supplies. Within another hour, stuff starts arriving. First the supermarket delivers a dozen bags of groceries, and then a local toyshop drops off a box of Red Dragon paraphernalia. Gabriel

186

is delighted. But the activity at 17 Maple Street has caught the eye of their first and biggest fan, Stan. He cannot help himself and tweets "He's home again. My angel is back. 17 Maple."

Within two hours, the hordes begin to gather. Maple Street is soon impassable, and the police find it difficult to cordon off the boisterous masses. People naturally congregate, just as they did in the park by New Empire University, into groups of fans and devotees and of protestors and haters of change. These last are the ones to fear, although both groups terrify Sheila. Everything has changed in the course of one morning. The house is no longer safe and will probably never be safe again.

As the day progresses, things get worse. The rabble outside is louder—chanting, shouting and demanding that Gabriel come out and show them his wings. Finally, toward the end of the day just as the sun wanes and shadows gather deeper, several teams of riot police swarm the street and break up the crowd sending groups and individuals scattering in all directions. Though he's had firm instructions to stay safe in the guest room at the back of the house, Gabriel has snuck into Sheila's bedroom at the front and is outside on the tiny deck over the front porch watching the police activity in the street below. Sheila watches from the living room window through a chink in the tightly closed curtains until ultimately the area appears to be cleared.

Sheila is still uneasy and continues watching Maple Street for a couple of hours after the melee has been chased away. Finally, she climbs the stairs and, fully dressed, quietly squeezes into Gabriel's bed next to him. He only stirs a moment and then settles, comfortably snuggled beside her. She sinks instantly into a profound and much-needed sleep.

The peace is fleeting, though. Suddenly, when the night reaches its darkest moment, a malicious faction of activists manages to cut the power to the lights on Maple Street and sneak up toward number 17 by traveling between gardens on the opposite side of the street. Most of the few remaining officers on watch are distracted by the blackout and wander further away, looking for the source. The band finally strikes, leaping over the hedge of Sheila's front garden and running right up to her living room window. One troublemaker smashes the window, the two behind him toss Molotov cocktails inside the room, and two more on the street spray paint the sidewalk with the words *DIE, EVIL DEVIL, DIE.*

Upstairs, Sheila stirs and turns over. The shattering glass is loud but not loud enough to wake her from her dead sleep at the back of the house. The miscreants are gone in a moment, the street quiet again. Inside Sheila's living room, spilled fluid licks across the floor, and fire spreads from the carpet to the couch. Soon the room is engulfed. Flames fed by the breeze from the broken window streak through the partially open hall door into the foyer and toward the stairs. The open elevator door functions like a chimney, sucking more heat toward it and up through the shaft. Suddenly the upstairs glass exit of the elevator shatters with an earsplitting clatter. Flames spew from the opening of the elevator at one end of the upstairs landing. More flames whip up the stairs on the other side of the landing and across the carpeted floor toward the hall outside the room where mother and child sleep.

Sheila awakens, startled, jumps out of bed, and dashes toward the door to the hall. She stops short when she smells smoke and sees flickering light peeking through the cracks at the edges of the door. She turns and bundles Gabriel out of bed while also shaking him to wake him. He sleeps soundly and takes a while to wake up completely. Together they scramble out of the back dormer window and onto the roof of the house. From there they can already see flames thrashing the front, street-side corner of the roof above her bedroom. Sheila gasps and clutches Gabriel close to her.

The police can barely be heard shouting in the street. "Don't go in there, Joe. It's too hot."

Another yells, "The fire truck is on the way; wait for it."

Meanwhile, Sheila and Gabriel huddle on the roof in the back of the house with no way to climb down. Sheila makes a decision and turns Gabriel's worried face toward her. "I want you to fly Gabriel. You must get away right now."

"No, Momma, what about you? How will you get away?"

"I will, Gabe. Don't worry about me," she assures him. She turns him around to face out toward the back garden. "Now, Gabe, now. Fly away. Go high so you don't hit any power lines or trees in the dark. Do you think you can find your way to Aunty Cynthia?"

Tears stream down his face as he nods yes. "But Momma, what about you, the fire?"

"The firemen are coming. Go, Gabe, go. Go now." She gives him a gentle push, and he sails quietly off the roof, looking back at her and weeping. "Go, Gabriel. Go to Aunty Cynthia now. I'll come after."

Gabriel turns reluctantly and glides into the darkness outside the glow of his blazing home. The moment he is gone, a ladder smacks into the edge of the roof to her far left in the corner of the house farthest from the fire. She can only just hear sirens in the distance, so where did this ladder come from? She scrambles over to it and peers over the edge. Half way up the ladder, she can see Stan, his features flushed and rippling in the flickering light of the fire blazing inside her kitchen.

"Hurry," he yells. "Where's Gabriel?"

"Gone," she replies.

"Gone? Where?"

"He's flown away."

"I guess that's good. Let's get you gone too, then."

By this time, he is at the top of the ladder. He helps her carefully place her foot on the first rung and then guides her all the way down.

When they reach the grassy garden, Sheila turns to go out to the front and greet the police and the fire engine, but Stan stops her. "No, don't go there. The guys who lit your house up are still lurking about. Let's get you somewhere safe. Where do you want to go?"

"My sister," she says.

Stan retrieves his motorcycle at the side of the house. In no time, Sheila is gripping the back of his angel-wing-adorned jacket while they speed down the street away from number 17.

* * *

Gabriel swoops away from the house in the direction he thinks his aunt's house is, but the dark confuses him. After a few blocks, he feels disoriented, so he turns back. Attracted like a moth to a flame, he veers toward the light. He navigates through trees and over power lines, eager to see his mother again and to do whatever he can to help her, to save her. He banks sideways and wings close to the blazing house, circling it in the dark sky above and seeking his mother.

The roof where they stood just a short moment ago is now engulfed in flames. Fire trucks surround the house, and firemen are on full alert. But his momma is nowhere to be seen.

Life is knocked out of Gabriel's chest. He feels deflated, like he has in a moment become incongruously heavy. He loses altitude and feels like the wild air currents around the fire are sucking him nearer to the conflagration. It is so very hot. He panics, flaps wildly, and seems to fan the fire even more toward himself. Gabriel pushes against the rip tide of air that holds him fast, and then all of a sudden, a super-hot blast seems to propel him like a spark into the heights. Soon he is hanging high in the sky, almost touching the stars. Gabriel rests on the updraft of the fire, well out of danger. Thankfully he is also well above the helicopter that swoops over the house. A newsman hangs out of the side with his camera dangling. Gabriel seeks out another updraft and retreats further away from the activity. His heart beats too fast, and his mind is ablaze with terror, could his mother be gone forever?

* * *

Stan drops Sheila at Cynthia's shortly after her timely rescue. He refuses to come inside and be thanked properly. Sheila is not sure what to make of him. This man keeps cropping up. She can't tell if he's a complete pain-in-the-neck or her guardian angel. If she had known about his earlier tweet, she would certainly have been less grateful to him than she is right now. Still, the man has saved her life.

Stan zooms away, and Sheila fretfully knocks on Cynthia's door. Gabriel has to be here by now; it's a short distance as the crow flies. Cynthia opens the door and pulls Sheila inside. Sheila demands to see her son right away, but Cynthia doesn't know what she is talking about. Still in a panic, Sheila mutters incoherently about fire, roof, man with a ladder, loud noises, still sleeping, "I pushed Gabriel off the roof," she blurts. Cynthia can't follow her and only gets the gist of what happened. She tries to help Sheila make sense while she pours water over a chamomile teabag from the hot drinking faucet. Both women are distraught when it becomes clear that Gabriel clearly has not found his way here yet. Sheila shuns the tea and darts toward the door.

Mike, roused by the noise, follows her. "Cynthia, you stay here and see if he comes. We'll go out and look for him."

Cynthia nods. "Just what I was thinking."

* * *

Gabriel does not know what to do with himself. He is completely bereft and lost. He hovers way up in the sky above the burning house and the buzzing copter. The warm currents that lift from the fire keep him aloft without too much effort. His eyes are blurry from crying and smoke, and he can't make out any landscape features through the haze to help him get his bearings. So he just hangs.

The night wears thin, and light tinges the east. If Gabriel had had just a bit more education, he might have learned how to orient himself by the rising sun, but this idea still eludes him, even though he is a genius in so many other ways. All he can think about is that soon other people might see him floating over the city, and this frightens him right now. He drifts over sideways and glides toward the darker horizon, away from the fire, the helicopter, and the frenzy of activity below. He doesn't know that this direction takes him away from Cynthia's home.

* * *

All day Sheila and Mike search for Gabriel. News of the fire on the TV prompts Philip to appear on Cynthia's doorstep. She invites him in and fills him in. He is relieved that neither Sheila nor Gabriel was trapped in the fire, but he is furious too.

"How could she just push him off the roof like that? Maybe he can fly, but it was reckless. And now he's missing."

"I am sure he's just lost," Cynthia insists.

"You don't know," Philip argues while he dials his phone. "I'm calling the police. We need an alert; we need to find him immediately."

Cynthia reaches out to stay his hands. "Philip, don't. You know how many nut cases there are out there. What if one of them finds him?"

"That's why we need the authorities searching. We'll be more likely to find him then." He's already speaking into the phone and reporting that Gabriel is missing.

Cynthia shrugs and turns on the television. Sheila's house is the main subject of the local news, with many shots over the roof of the house from the helicopter. Suddenly the camera turns and pans across the gradually lightening sky. It locks on the fleeting image of a vast pair of wings in the distance just catching the first light. The reporter says, "We caught this shot just about twenty minutes ago as the sun was rising. It appears to be Gabriel heading toward the river."

Cynthia interrupts Philip, who is in the hall absorbed in imparting the required information to the police. She drags him back into the kitchen and points to the screen just as it replays the footage of the quick flutter and dive of Gabriel's wings disappearing into a stand of trees.

Philip hangs up in a fluster and heads to the door. "I'm on it."

* * *

By the time Philip, Sheila, and Mike converge on Corley River Park, all entrances are swarmed with people trying to find and get a look at Gabriel. A crowd amasses at one corner of a field near the path at the water's edge and under a copse of trees. Philip charges off through the field toward this suspicious-looking gathering with Sheila and Mike following. Disregarding all park rules, Stan arrives and zooms across the field on his motorcycle.

When they finally reach the gathering, Sheila can just barely pick out the shadow of Gabriel perched in the high branches of one of the trees. Police have arrived and urge the crowd to move back. A small ladder truck trundles down the mulched horse path next to the river walk and comes nearer at a slow pace.

Sheila pushes through the crowd and is stopped by an officer when she tries to break through to get to the base of Gabriel's tree. She calls out to him. "Gabriel, baby, come here to me." Gabriel turns and sees her. He sobs and shudders at the top of the tree, clinging tightly to its wide trunk.

The fire truck pushes on through the crowd and settles just under the tree. Philip argues with the police and finally convinces them to permit Sheila through the barricade with him. They meet the firemen unfurling the truck ladder. Philip convinces the chief to allow Sheila to climb the ladder with a fireman to be the first to greet Gabriel. Gabe is obviously upset, cowering in the top of the tree. Philip and Sheila are afraid he will fly off again if a stranger tries to grab him.

Soon Sheila is gingerly climbing the precarious contraption toward her weeping child. A burly, uniformed fireman follows close behind and makes sure that her footing is secure and that she holds tight to the rail. All the way, Sheila coos to Gabriel, soothing him and assuring him that everything will be all right. Finally, tucked within the crowded leaves and branches of the tree, Sheila and Gabriel are reunited. Below, Cynthia can barely see what is going on, but soon enough, Gabriel is carefully brought to the ground, clinging to his mother. Everyone is shocked to see that his wing tips are singed charcoal black.

* * *

Gabriel is once again brought by ambulance to the hospital. This time Sheila doesn't mind. She approves and wants to make sure her son has no other injuries. She travels in the back with Gabriel, and Philip joins them too. The ER doctor admits Gabriel to a private room and announces that they will keep him overnight for a full checkup. Sheila insists on staying with him and curls up on a chair in the corner of the room. Philip posts an orderly at the door to keep an eye on them.

29

SHUT OUT AGAIN

A day later, Sheila stands in front of a mirror in Cynthia's guest bedroom. She wears only a bra and a gray skirt. Cynthia is considering a smart royal-blue jacket over a bright-blue blouse she holds in one hand and a creamy-yellow blouse under an off-white jacket she holds in the other. She tosses the white-and-cream combo on the bed and returns the other to the closet.

"White seems innocent. You should wear that," Cynthia says.

"Innocent?" Sheila snaps. "I didn't burn my house down."

"I know. But you need to keep the judge on your side, and the house is a big problem now. Where will you live?"

* * *

Later that day, Sheila is back in the courtroom before the judge with Amelie beside her and Cynthia behind her. A fleet of high-powered lawyers at the other table flanks Philip. Spiner sits in the first row behind them. The courtroom is abuzz, jammed with onlookers—interested public and press. That sickening sense of déjà vu washes over Sheila yet again. She's terrified that the fire will affect the judge's final decision and that she'll lose Gabriel again.

It's been a long day, and Sheila is unable to tell which way the decision will go. Amelie is sharp and on the ball, but a massive corporate legal team paid for by Spiner backs up Philip's claim. Sheila looks around and feels vastly outnumbered. The child psychologist, Ms. Archer, presents a damning summation of her visit to Sheila's house shortly before the fire. It seems Sheila's explanation that they had only just returned to the house didn't register. In Archer's opinion, Sheila had no idea what kind of environment, nourishment, and comforts the child needs. In addition,

Philip's legal team frames the house fire followed by Gabriel's free flight as her mistake, her ill-conceived error.

"She should have known better. She should have protected him. His wings were scorched, for heaven's sake," the lawyer brazenly accuses.

Desperate, Sheila finds herself shrinking in her seat and praying that the judge has kids, that he understands, and that a mother's love—her love—will prevail. She tosses anything and everything that she thinks might help into her ragged prayer. She's out of practice at this and wishes she could get a handle on the process. She especially wishes that she could believe in it.

Glancing across the crowded audience, she is surprised when she spots Frank and Dell clutching each other as if their own child is on trial. Dell nods to her and grabs the cross at her neck in a manner that shows she is praying for Sheila and Gabriel. Sheila sighs, and an odd sense of support and relief hits her.

Wow, they know how to pray, she thinks. A tear licks out of the corner of her eye. She acknowledges Dell's gesture with a nod and then turns back to the ominous proceedings, feeling a bit calmer.

All arguments have concluded, and the judge explains his decision. "Unfortunately, in light of the imminent danger and distress to which the child is subjected, I feel it is necessary to fast-track my decision here. Dr. Jensen, you have shown gross negligence in protecting the … uh … subject, Gabriel Jensen. I am sorry to inform you that your son will from now on be in the custody of his father, Dr. Ohl."

Sheila stands up. "I didn't burn the house down. I've raised him safely for five years."

"Even so, you have no home to take him to now, do you?" the judge replies.

"My sister, she'll take us in until we can get a new place," Sheila protests.

"Dr. Jensen you cannot subject your sister's family to the onslaught of press and protestors that gather wherever your son goes. We have to think of the larger picture here," the judge continues. "Look around you; you've caused a firestorm of political, social, and ethical upheaval. The courts, the medical community, our legislature, law enforcement, and the general public have been blindsided by an issue that most of us can't even begin to understand. It is a hostile environment out there for this unique child that you have put in direct danger several times already. I have to think first and foremost of what's best for him. His father and this institution"—he points to Ohl, Spiner, and the hospital's team—"have the resources to control this volatile situation and to protect the child. Gabriel Jensen will remain in custody of his father, Dr. Ohl, I regret to say that I can think of no place better suited for the child than the institution. An ordinary home is no longer an option."

"Can I see him at least?" Sheila begs.

"I leave that decision up to those in charge of Gabriel Jensen's well-being. If Dr. Ohl deems it suitable for you to see him, then that's up to him. Thank you. That concludes this case." The judge gets up and walks out through a back door.

Philip's team shakes each other's hands triumphantly. Philip looks on stunned.

Amelie drops a consoling arm around Sheila's shoulder. "I'll start prepping an appeal right away."

Sheila slumps in dejection, not sure what to do with herself. Cynthia comes around from the spectators' gallery and hugs her. Together with Amelie and Cynthia, Sheila exits the courtroom.

Outside in the corridor, reporters and fanatics assail her.

"What's your next step?" a reporter asks, jabbing a microphone into Sheila's face.

"Please, no questions," Amelie replies on Sheila's behalf.

"How do you feel about the judge's verdict?" another reporter asks.

"How do you think a mother feels when her son is taken away from her?" Cynthia asks, irritated.

An activist steps in front of Sheila with a sign that reads "No GMH" and features a cartoon image of a human with leaves for hair struck through with a red line in a red circle. "I am not a lab rat!" the wielder of the sign spurts venomously.

Sheila snatches the sign and tramples it. "Leave me alone!" she yells, and then she sobers up when she spots Philip glaring at her.

* * *

The next morning, Sheila weaves her car through the phalanx of press outside Cynthia's house. She arrives at the hospital at seven thirty. She knows that Philip always starts at eight, so she wants to be there when he gets in. Before that, she wants to get in and prowl around. Maybe she can find Gabriel.

The parking lot is still occupied by what seems to be a permanent crowd of protestors. The fans and detractors are sparring off against each other with words, signs, and even painted faces and costumes. Other than that, it is relatively quiet this early in the morning, but from the trash, burned garbage cans, and police stationed all around, it's clear that things were rowdy during the night.

Once through the new and hastily erected guard station at the entrance to the parking lot, Sheila discovers that parking is tricky. The lot has been shrunk due to the occupiers who have set themselves up around the edges and spilled into the streets and into the park adjacent to the hospital. Sheila is aware of another case in the courts right now. The institution is attempting to end this illegal squatting in the hospital and the park, but it has been a slow process. Life for everyone who visits or works in the hospital is miserable right now.

Sheila is directed to the underground lot and has to park on one of the lowest levels that are usually avoided. When she emerges above ground, she ducks her head and marches briskly toward the hospital entrance.

"Don't recognize me. Please don't recognize me," she repeats under her breath, her eyes scanning the quietly stirring protestors. Determined to avoid any trouble, she skirts around a knot of suspicious-looking people crossing the lot in front of her. They appear to be taking a shortcut back to the occupied zone from the business district on the other side of the hospital. Considering that they are carrying armfuls of bags from a local fast-food joint, Sheila suspects they are heading for a breakfast party. Pretty soon, the crowd will be up and chanting, yelling at each other and tossing slurs at the hospital again. She shudders, feeling slightly guilty.

Relieved to be inside the front door, she flashes her card at the familiar front-desk guard, Bart, assuming that she can walk right through. Instead, he blocks her.

"Sorry, Sheila, honey. I can't let you just go up. I was told if you came in to let them know, and they'll send someone to get you.

"Okay, Bart," she says. "Will you see if Philip can see me?"

Bart nods. "Sure. Can you wait over there, please?" He points to the array of couches next to the gift shop in the lobby. She nods dutifully and then heads over to sit down, cursing under her breath.

Over the next hour, she sits there looking around and trying to come up with a plan for how to sneak in, but Bart has his eye on her. Clearly, his instructions were quite explicit. Occasionally, one of her old coworkers comes through the lobby. Most of them take one look at her and then scurry past, afraid to engage her. As a result of a couple of these uncomfortable and mutually embarrassing encounters, Sheila decides to plant her face in her phone. With her focus locked on an inane newsfeed that can't hold her attention, she sighs, relieved for the protection of the invisible tech shield. Even so, one of Cynthia's nurses, Jilly Sheridan, sees Sheila just as she scurries past on the way to her shift. She stops short in front of Sheila. When Sheila looks up, Jilly smiles and then walks over and sits down next to her.

Jilly takes Sheila's hand and holds it. Tears form in Jilly's eyes, and she squeezes Sheila's hand. Neither of them can think of anything to say. Jilly is a pediatric nurse. She has deep wells of compassion for babies and mothers. She has seen much joy and much suffering, so she knows very well that sometimes her presence is all that's needed. Jilly's hands are warm and comforting, and her face is radiant and full of nourishing hope. Sheila feels her heart lift a bit, and hope takes root and blooms a bit stronger there.

What is it about some people that touches us? Sheila wonders after Jilly gives her a quick hug and then gets up to go to work. Not a word was spoken, but somehow a deep, encouraging exchange took place. *Sometimes it's someone you hardly know who says or does the right thing,* she thinks gratefully.

Sheila's escort, Lucy, finally arrives. Lucy is an ever-so-trendy young woman who is obviously a new intern, eager to impress. The girl is polite and attentive.

"I'd like to see my son, Gabriel, first," Sheila announces, stressing the words *my son.*

Lucy balks. "Oh, I don't think I can do that. They said to bring you straight upstairs."

"Where are they holding Gabriel?" Sheila asks.

Lucy frowns. Her instructions were explicit but not clear enough that she is sure what she can and can't say. She shrugs. "He's in the third-floor amphitheater right now. They've closed it off. It's the only place with a bit of height and room so they can let him fly."

Sheila's face brightens. "Well, since we're going up to seven, we can go through the mezzanine and see what's going on there on the way up then."

"But they expressly told me to bring you straight up," Lucy protests.

"You are, aren't you? We are just going to walk by, that's all."

Lucy gives her a sympathetic look. "Oh, I suppose there's no harm in that."

As they approach the mezzanine, Sheila gets more and more fidgety, afraid of what she will do. She has never been out of control in her life except where Gabriel is concerned. If she sees something she doesn't like, she's afraid she might lose it.

Sheila is relieved when they step off the elevator and see the glass wall overlooking the wide amphitheater. She strides over to the window and looks down. It is a wide space typically used for seminars, teaching surgeries, and other public and private events. Most of the entrances are cordoned off so that the space is only accessible on one side. It's bright and airy, thanks to the wide, domed glass roof. The usual configurations of seats and tables have been cleared, and a temporary lab has been set up on one side. Throughout the space are exercise machines and examination tables. Cameras are everywhere, and huge video screens show in real time the footage being captured. A team of about fifteen people mills about below. Four videographers wield cameras and point them up into the air. Sheila directs her attention to their focus.

Gabriel flaps through the space about twenty feet off the floor of the atrium and somewhat above her level on the mezzanine. Live-action details of his moving wings are duplicated on the massive video screens. Some members of the team below take notes, and others shout instructions.

"Turn left! Tip right!"

Gabriel laughs and swoops up and down. He dive-bombs one distracted doctor, Leticia Newman, who is rummaging absently through a stack of papers. Gabriel bounces a foot off her head and then tips and glides up again, laughing hysterically.

"Hey!" Leticia yells as her papers fly all around her, caught in Gabriel's updraft.

Gabriel continues to swoop about, bumping instruments over and "accidentally" knocking books or implements out of the researchers' hands. Some laugh, and some get testy.

Philip yells at Gabriel and the amused crew. "Calm down, everyone. Come down here, Gabe." He is barely able to restrain his laughter.

"It's not funny," Spiner says under his breath.

"He's just a kid," Philip retorts.

"He's making a fool of your team," Spiner hisses.

"We are in complete control," Philip assures him.

On the mezzanine above, Sheila snickers under her breath. "That's it, babe. Show 'em what you've got."

When she says it, it occurs to her that no one on the team is entranced in the way the fans at Frank's house were. The people on this team are in control of their faculties—cool and trying to proceed with a professional mien, as much as Gabriel will let them. He seems determined to have some fun and to force them all to join in. Sheila looks carefully at each person down below and then at Gabriel to see what could be different now.

Gabriel lands, as ordered by Philip, and trots over to him. Sheila has a pang in her heart when she sees the warm and welcoming way that Philip squats down to envelop Gabriel in his arms and swishes him into the air like any proud father. He spins Gabriel around, and Gabriel laughs in delight like any other kid. Sheila snorts in annoyance.

Once Gabriel is installed on a stool with his back to her and a cup of orange juice in his hand, she returns to her examination of why there seems to be no special connection between this team and Gabriel. She can see nothing in his face or theirs to account for it. Her mind turns while she examines the space below and then the glass roof above, and all she can think is that perhaps he is reluctant to pull them into the adventure because they are stuck inside. Then another thought hits her: this also indicates that Gabriel has more control over the phenomenon of sharing flight than he told her previously.

Philip glances up and spots Sheila staring down with Lucy at her side. He signals Lucy with an annoyed flick of his hand to take Sheila up to his office immediately.

Lucy tugs at Sheila's arm. "Excuse me, Dr. Jensen, Dr. Ohl … um, we have to go."

Sheila shakes herself out of her reverie and leads the way. Lucy trots behind in her absurdly high and inappropriate heels. Sheila reaches Philip's office before him. At first, she thinks this is a great opportunity for her to prowl around, but Lucy invites her to sit on the couch and then waits just inside the door. Sheila suggests that Lucy can go, but Lucy shakes her head and adds that she was instructed to wait with her. Sheila is still upset from seeing Gabriel essentially captive, and she can't wait to rip into Philip, to take him down a peg or two. It infuriates her that he is inserting himself between her and Gabriel and that Gabriel seems to be taking to him and enjoying his company.

The minute Philip arrives, Sheila goes on the offensive. "The way you're treating him is inhumane! I am going to tell the judge at the appeal."

Philip flinches as if cut. He holds the door open for Lucy to slip outside before responding. "The way I'm treating him? You cut me out completely. You didn't tell me he was my son. You and I were planning to have children together, but you went ahead without me. Not only that, but you took our proprietary gene modification procedures designed only for animals and crossed the line. You experimented on our child. *That's* inhumane!"

She tosses her report on his desk and ramps up her argument. "Here. Here's what you asked for weeks ago. All the details are in there. As for proprietary procedures, you and Spiner cooked up your scheme to blame it all on me, remember? I was the fall guy that saved you from the bad press and the sanctions that threatened your funding and your license to practice and continue your research. So whose proprietary procedures are we talking about? Are they registered to you or to me? I would say that, considering the damnation and blackballing that I've endured, they are mine, not yours. Now, if we don't want to rake all that over the coals again, I urge you to let me visit him every day at the very least."

Philip considers her report for a moment. "Let me look this over and get back to you tomorrow. Come back in the morning."

She sighs. "No, Philip. I want to see him right now."

"Look," he sighs, attempting an appealing tone, "I'm trying to do the best for our son now, Sheila. Spiner is concerned about security. I'm concerned about it too. We are trying to calm things down and divert interest away from here. If you are coming and going all the time, we'll never get rid of the rabble outside."

"You are coming and going," she retorts.

"I work here still," he responds. "For Gabriel's protection, we need to keep him in this institution. Spiner is losing patience with the crowd, so we can't provoke them. You know that you or I could never control them; this is the only place we can keep our son safe."

"We? Does that mean you plan to include me?"

"I can't right now," he replies, slumping his shoulders. "Give me time to work on Spiner. I think I can bring him around and get you in soon. I really am sorry."

He opens the door to his office and pokes his head out. "Larry, can you show Dr. Jensen to the lobby, please?"

Sheila looks at Philip, stunned. "How can you be so cold? I can't believe I almost married you. I can't believe we almost became friends again."

"And I can't believe we share a child, but we do," he replies.

"You call this sharing?" she says, fuming.

She storms out of his office and tromps down the hall to the elevator.

30

A PUBLIC FIASCO

Sheila spends the next week waiting, checking in every day with Philip. He doesn't return her messages. Amelie makes only a snail's progress with her appeal. Nothing is moving; there's no word from anyone. The only person who gives her any sliver of information is Cynthia, and that's only rumors that float around the hospital, like "He's a real handful" and "Four people from the team have been replaced and no one knows why."

"Gabriel refused to eat today," Cynthia's contact in the cafeteria reported, "something about wanting to see his mother." Upon hearing this from Cynthia, Sheila sighs, heartbroken.

Every night, she can be found slumped in front of a television. Gabriel is still a big story in the news cycle. The mobs still surround the hospital, and reporters still camp outside Cynthia's house trying to get something out of Sheila or Cynthia. The entire family is exhausted by it.

The only nourishing thing for Sheila is the nightly report on the possible status of the magical child. Gabriel took the world by storm and then disappeared inside the glittering fortress of New Empire University's research center. Everyone wants as much information about him as they can get. Each day, a new piece of video surfaces from the time before Philip took Gabriel. Many of the dancers or fliers who came to Frank's house shot some footage and photos on phones or cameras during the events there. They are all over the web, and the best copies go out into the mainstream media each day.

Frank and Dell travel through the news media circuit telling the tale of their encounters with Gabriel. One day they are announced as guests on six different New York-based shows—three on television, two on the Internet, and one on the radio. Even the children are involved. Mary has become quite a little spokesperson, praising Gabriel and expounding ever so eloquently on her experience of flying.

"He shows me how to be my real self, my free self, my self that can do anything, and my self that can always be happy. I know he's not with us anymore, but I am so happy that he was. I say a prayer for him every day, because he showed me how to fly and now I'll never forget."

Stan, the first person to recognize something special in Gabriel, has become a famous and highly sought-after artist. His photos and paintings of Gabriel fetch a fortune. He can't paint them fast enough. His distinct personal style is little different than it was in his homeless days, even though he now sports an expensive artist look that really suits him. His motorcycle wears its own set of soft, sculpted wings that flare out behind him and flutter in the breeze as he zooms down the highway. *Sunday Morning* on CBS airs a special on him in which he speaks of Gabriel with such reverence that the interviewer, Mo Rocca, is struck speechless for a moment. Stan's eyes water when he recounts the first time he saw Gabriel and how he was sure the child was floating out of the carriage. He stutters when he remembers that he also saw Sheila floating.

"I-I thought I was mad, that it was the drink or something, so I threw away my last bottle right then and there. I was done. I didn't care for it anymore. That baby saved me; he gave me my life. He opened my eyes and made me see the world in full color and all the magic in it. He made me what I am today, and I will always be grateful."

* * *

One night, Sheila receives a video call from Cynthia. Something is cooking at the hospital. The inner courtyard that faces the park and is flanked on three sides by the major wings of the hospital has been closed off. Major construction is in the works, and no one seems to know what's going on. Cynthia thinks that they have repurposed the playground for some kind of show, and she suspects that Gabriel might be at the center of it. All anyone talks about at the hospital, no matter which department they are in, is Gabriel. Instead of interest in the mysterious boy calming, it is forever escalating.

Cynthia asks Sheila how she's feeling. Sheila has become increasingly reclusive.

"Oh, I'm okay. They're out here now," she says referring to the news corps on the street. She felt so guilty about the ongoing harassment of Mike and the kids by the reporters encamped outside their house that she has moved to a local hotel.

"Sheila, we have to talk about something," Cynthia insists. They rarely had time to talk at Cynthia's house, and Sheila couldn't bring herself to talk about any of it anyway. Everything was too confusing. It was like having the rug pulled out from under her and then having it pulled out again. She's still processing her thoughts and feelings and is still very confused. She spends each day reviewing her notes and revisiting every study and record of Gabriel's history, hoping to get a better understanding of his wings as well as her sudden and peculiar healing. Ultimately, she must also find something that will give her an edge over Philip and that meddling and controlling Spiner.

"Have you watched the interviews and the videos?" Cynthia asks.

"Yes," Sheila responds warily.

Cynthia leans in closer to the computer camera. "We both did it," Cynthia says with caution, hoping that Sheila won't shut her down and end the call.

"What?" Sheila asks.

Cynthia takes a breath, afraid to mention it, afraid that maybe it was different for Sheila and that her sister will think that she is crazy. "Flew. We both flew, right?"

Sheila sighs. "Yes we did."

"How?" Cynthia asks.

Sheila shakes her head. The one thing that perplexes her the most is her experience of flight. She has not talked about it with anyone, not even Cynthia, and she experiences a weird sense of violation when she hears others on the television describing their experience. It was almost too sacred, too special, and too mystical to smash it up and tear into little pieces of language in order to describe it. She has no idea what happened or how it happened, and every time she tries to work it out in her mind, she gets a fierce headache and has to lie down and sleep for a while. Yet, when the subject comes up and she just listens to the ecstatic accounts or remembers her own experience, her heart becomes euphoric. She remembers the elated feeling and offers lighter, gentler words to Cynthia.

"Yes, it's true. We flew. I flew several times. But how—why—I have no idea." She pauses a moment to reflect. "I wish I did. It was … um … it was …"

"Glorious!" Cynthia interjects.

Sheila savors the word. "Glorious, yes."

That seems to satisfy them both. They are silent for a long time.

"Yes, I know," Cynthia says finally. Then, at a loss for further language, they each put a hand toward the camera as if to touch each other and then terminate the connection.

* * *

With time away from Gabriel, Sheila has found the best way to process this confusing development in her life is to meditate a lot. She's aware that this is some kind of open and more whole-body thinking, and she finds herself questioning her shifting sense of reality. What is this new experience of thinking with her heart? It is definitely something that came with Gabriel, something she never knew before him, and yet it's so clear now. She can actually taste the difference in her modes of thinking. One tastes tinny, constricted, apprehensive, and fraught with problems. The other tastes sweet, as if her entire body is made of chocolate. It feels expansive, full of potential and possibility, and, if she really embraces the feeling, euphoric.

She turns on the news, and everything is about Gabriel. Every channel weighs in. They parse the pros and cons of genetic manipulation and argue about what to do with this rare mutant child. They try to determine what rights a child like this would or should have and what role his parents or guardians should play. Everyone has an opinion, and they are all "experts." The most important question everyone wants answered is, "When will we all get to see him fly?"

Both Sheila and Cynthia have been glued to the news, Sheila always with the hope that she might get a glimpse of her son. But there have been no recent sightings, other than Stan's and other stolen clips. Gabriel is under a tight lockdown.

Everyone has heard that watching Gabriel fly is a magnificent experience, that something mystical or magical happens. Word has spread quickly, and rumors of the momentousness of the experience have taken all kinds of forms. "Life-changing," is one description. "Heavenly," is another. Many insist they actually flew, but those who were not there find it hard to believe. Stan, Frank, and Dell have become media stars, and Sheila derives some sort of comfort from watching them in various interviews. They bring back the memory of momentary freedom, a brief time of hope and joy, although she has to admit they were never truly safe there.

Eventually, Sheila falls asleep in front of the TV. She awakens the next morning to the shocking announcement that Gabriel is likely to fly today.

"People are gathering at NEU Research Hospital after hearing a rumor that there will be a demonstration of the flying boy this morning," the unfamiliar blonde talking head announces.

Sheila pops off the couch and immediately calls Amelie to insist that she find out what is going on and try to get an injunction to stop it. Then she races upstairs to clean up and dress.

* * *

When Sheila arrives at the hospital just before seven that morning, crowds are already gathering. News media vans are setting up throughout the parking lot. Extra security has cordoned off all access routes. They herd newcomers away and restrict entry to all but a few. It seems that the institution and the police have had some success disbanding the occupiers, because most of them have moved into the park across the street, but the crowd of interested onlookers has swelled immensely and filled their place. Doctors and nurses arriving for or leaving work look pissed as they wrangle their way through the mess. The only untrammeled route is the emergency entrance. Several guards are posted there to ensure that the area stays clear.

Sheila works her way toward the courtyard sheltered in the U-shape created by three wings of the hospital complex. She flashes her ID card several times to get closer to the area. Her attention is drawn to a fuss on the edge of the space near her. Larry is ejecting Stan from the inner circle. Sheila makes a mental note to avoid both of them.

The first thing she notices is that a large net encloses the courtyard and reaches twelve floors up to the top of the building. It covers the top area between the rooftops from one wing to the next and is secured at the back to the hospital's central wing. At the open side of the courtyard, it drapes right down to the ground. It's apparent that they want to give Gabriel some room to fly but not the opportunity to get away. Her stomach lurches, nauseated.

As she gets closer, she sees a flurry of activity in what used to be the playground. Workers are still removing the cafe tables and chairs that usually crowd half of the space. A construction crew finishes up a jungle-gym-like launch/landing pad. Painted in the center of the structure is a large yellow bull's-eye that suggests some kind of futuristic sport.

Doctors scurry around with notebooks and instruments. She sees Philip enter the zone and makes a beeline for him.

"Philip! Philip!" she yells.

A security guard runs over to ward her off, but Philip waves him away. "It's okay," Philip says.

Sheila is shaking. "What's going on here? This looks like exactly what I didn't want for him. He's not a spectacle or sideshow."

Philip takes her arm gently. "Look, Sheila, we are trying to get on top of this. People want to see Gabriel fly. The speculations, rumors, and crowds outside have become unmanageable. Spiner thinks this is the best way to satisfy them and get them to clear out. Hell, I want to see him fly."

"But this is insane," Sheila says. "What if he gets caught in that net?"

"He can see it," Philip says. "He's been tested for control, vision, and maneuverability, and he seems to have it all under control."

"I think I should be here," Sheila says. "He will want me near him."

Philip shakes his head. "No. That's impossible. You would throw him off. We're just getting to the stage where he trusts me and seems willing to work with my team. So, no, you'll have to leave now." Philip leads her gently toward the exit.

"This is payback, isn't it? You're still mad at me, and you'll do anything to punish me."

Philip stares at her. She might be right, but he refuses to believe it. "No, I have a job to do now. I suggest you go home and watch it on TV."

Sheila feels like crying, but she steels herself. "You have no idea how cruel you are, do you? My lawyer is going to stop this." Then she turns and marches off into the crowd.

Once she is out of sight, Sheila doubles around the building and enters through the employees' side door. She's surprised at how easy it is to duck past the guard, who is absorbed in watching the craziness on the other side of the hospital on the video monitors. Inside she goes straight to Cynthia's office, where she finds her sister on the phone.

"Yes, watch the TV right now. It looks like he's going to be on soon."

* * *

Cynthia hangs up and looks up when Sheila enters. "Oh, thank God you're here. Did you see that setup out there?"

Sheila nods as she rushes over to Cynthia's window to look out over the courtyard below. They are five floors up and thus not too high to see what's going on. Cynthia sets up a television stream on her computer for the local KPY TV channel. They can see the media van right outside, so they know there'll be coverage on that channel. Cynthia plants the computer on the top shelf of a cabinet so that they can both see it from the window.

Together, they watch the team down in the courtyard adjusting and readjusting equipment. The TV coverage is a blow-by-blow of nothing. There is no sign of Gabriel, no press release from the hospital, and no program of events so that everyone can know what's going on. There is only endless nattering of correspondents, audiences waiting with bated breath, and peering eyes all eager to catch a glimpse of Gabriel. Periodically, Sheila checks in with Amelie, who is having difficulty getting hold of a judge who will put a stop to this fiasco.

The morning blossoms bright and sunny and then withers into a dull gray sky by lunchtime. Still nothing has happened. A few people show up to watch the show in Cynthia's office, but when they see Sheila there, they look embarrassed, apologize to Cynthia, and leave to find another vantage point. Only after Jilly Sheridan shows up and stays are other people less wary of entering the space and potentially intruding on a private family event. Jilly has not seen Sheila since their encounter in the hospital lobby. She's thrilled to see her again and gives Sheila another huge, warm hug.

They drag several chairs down the hall and arrange them next to

Cynthia's large window like a viewing gallery. Sheila is given the prime spot at the center. She keeps mostly silent and to herself, forgoing any conversation and not even responding when spoken to. No one knows how to relate to her; they don't know what to say or how to act. This is such strange and new territory. What can she say to a comment like "You must be so proud" or "How did you do it?" The whole situation is bizarre.

Amelie shows up with news that she has made no progress with any judge since she has no actual proof that Philip and Spiner intend to create a public display of Gabriel. Without written statements, they have nothing.

Cynthia hears Sheila's stomach growl and orders food from the cafeteria. No one is willing to leave his or her prime viewing spot, and Cynthia's office has become a party. At least fifteen people share a couple of pizzas. The excitement is palpable. It is likely that no one in any department of the research facility, the university, or the hospital is working now unless it's an emergency. Most of the people who are not currently on their shifts have shown up too. No one wants to miss this amazing opportunity to see Gabriel fly. If this building were a cruise ship, it would surely tip over. They can see the windows across the courtyard in the opposite wing jammed full with onlookers.

Shortly after lunch, Mike and the kids pile in.

"We just had to come," Mike says. "I figured it was worth the risk of missing it if we could get here in time. Far better to see it real in real time, right kids?"

The excited children nod. Sheila is thrilled to see them and hugs each child long and hard before she sets them up on stools in the front near her.

The afternoon ticks by, second after endless second. The crowd outside is restless, jostling and pushing. Angry words are exchanged. A couple of people are trussed up by the police and hauled away. The throng has grown, and the local traffic cops have given up trying to keep people out of the street between the park and the hospital parking lot. Hordes spill clear across the lot, through the four-lane avenue across the median strip, and straight into the park's grassy hills.

"Boy, if they don't finish up and start this soon, it's going to get dark," Mike says at about four o'clock.

Sheila doesn't comment, although she was thinking the same thing. Danny groans, and his big sister, Mikey, punches him swiftly in the arm.

"Shhh!" she hisses.

"Mikey!" Mike reprimands her.

Suddenly, down below it looks as if the preparations might be complete. The construction and technical teams have cleared out. Loraine Hampshire, the hospital PR director, walks through the space with a clipboard and what looks like the stage manager and all the department heads—lighting, video, installation—research team supervisors, and a few others that are harder for Sheila to identify. Then Loraine leads Spiner and Philip through the space with the stage manager, checking everything again. Philip tugs on the net in answer to a question from Spiner and points up to where it's secured at the roof. They ask a videographer to pan through the space, and then they watch the video screen to see how much area each camera covers.

On the open side of the courtyard where the net falls down to the ground, news teams forming a solid wall jockey for position. The survey team breaks up, and Spiner and Philip head back toward the hospital entrance. Loraine walks down to the line of press to talk to them. Correspondents and camera people lean in and yell at Philip and Spiner, trying to get them to look their way. Snippets of the action appear on Cynthia's computer behind Sheila.

On the television stream that has droned away in the background all day, they have heard assorted speculations about what's going on. Now they hear the news anchors introducing Dr. Philip Ohl, head of the genetics research department of the Harold Bowman Research Facility of NEU, and Dr. Gerald Spiner, chair of the facility. Key elements of both men's careers are tossed out like the batting records of favorite baseball players. Experts have come and gone all day, speculating, postulating, and trying but failing to educate the public about the complexities of genetic modification and natural versus augmented mutation. Now they are called back in to guess what Gabriel might do. The anchor announces that it's likely that over 1.5 billion people are watching the live event.

Sheila moans. "This is exactly what I didn't want to happen. They've made him a spectacle."

Amelie looks up from the phone call she's on. "Now that they've announced it, we might be able to get some action from the court, though I doubt it will be in time."

Cynthia tries to console Sheila. "Spiner thinks it will bring the public around. Everyone wants a piece of him. He's a medical coup, a religious cause, a new age cure, an emissary of hope, a sign from hell, and a publicity phenomenon. You can see how much he divides the crowd. He's dividing the country, Sheila, even the entire world. Emotions are very high on this issue."

"But isn't there a law against this? Doesn't anyone see that he's just a child?" Sheila asks.

"No one sees him, Sheila," Cynthia says quietly, trying to get her to see what she sees out there. "They see a freak, a misbegotten experiment, and an abomination. Some see an angel, and others see the devil incarnate. No one sees Gabriel, your child, Sheila. I say this to try to put it into their perspective for you, not to hurt you."

Sheila looks at Cynthia, shocked and ready to retort in anger, but in her heart, she knows Cynthia is right. Her face is red and hot, and her eyes smart, but she concedes Cynthia's point.

"I have to get him out of here," she announces, "any way that I can."

Cynthia puts her hand on Sheila's arm. "What's worse, in here or out there? The hospital is a shield at least."

"But the mob," Sheila says, staring at the TV coverage on Cynthia's computer. "Look at them; they're dangerous."

Cynthia nods. "Yes, very dangerous."

Just then, Spiner steps in front of a microphone. A hush washes across the jostling press and the impatient crowd. Philip and Loraine stand behind him. Larry, several other members of the security team, and board members of the institution who demanded front-row seats, as well as the mayor and even the governor, surround them. Sheila spots the judge that ruled against her cozying up with the bigwigs in the front. She points him out to Amelie.

"No wonder I can't reach him," Amelie says.

"This is appalling," Cynthia moans.

"Good evening. I'm Dr. Gerald Spiner, director of the Harold Bowman Research Facility at New Empire University Hospital. We are proud to welcome you all today. Thank you, Mayor Grantham, for all your assistance in managing the crowds who have come to our fair city for this event. Governor Chester, thank you for augmenting the city's security resources so that we can share our great accomplishment in a peaceful environment. Thank you to everyone out there watching. We urge you to keep the peace, try not to push, and stay in your zones, and everything will be all right. If you can't see, just look over at one of the large screens we have installed near you or log on to the university website, where you can watch a live feed." The university website URL scrolls across the large video screens.

Spiner pauses for a moment to let the instructions sink in and then waves at Philip before turning back to the microphone. "Let me introduce Dr. Philip Ohl, head of the genetic modification research department and father of Gabriel as well as head of Gabriel Jensen's research team. Dr. Ohl has spent over twenty-five years working to develop genetic mutations that will augment, repair, or improve various conditions of diseased or injured animals. He has had success regenerating lost, broken, and diseased limbs and nerves, extending life expectancy, and enhancing cognitive function in primates and other species. He has won—"

Sheila huffs in disgust, "—yes, won because of my work." She clicks the sound off for the time being. She can't stand to hear Spiner describe the rewards of Philip's career. When Philip steps in front of the microphone, Sheila turns the sound back up.

"Thank you, Director Spiner," Philip says. "We are so proud to be able to share this miracle with you today. Yes, I do use the word 'miracle.' I know it's a surprise, but in spite of the hours of painstaking and detailed work we do with the smallest components of the living organic form, it's never anything less than a miracle when we see some kind of successful result."

"What is he talking about?" Sheila blurts. "He doesn't have any idea how *I* got to this." The entire room looks at her sympathetically. Jilly pats her on the back. Sheila sags a bit, apologizes, and clamps her mouth shut as Philip continues.

"I have to add one thing. We could not have managed this without the assistance of Gabriel's *surrogate* mother, Sheila Jensen." He seems uncomfortable with the word, and yet he said it.

"What?" Sheila stands up, livid now. "How dare he? Now everyone thinks I was just some paid incubator."

Fuming, she tries to pace, but the space is too crowded. She bumps past the kids, gets stuck, and doubles back to her chair. No one knows what to say. They murmur in disapproval. Everyone there knows plenty about the constant maneuvering that goes on to secure one's proper acknowledgement for work well done.

"Now, for the first time, you will see the scientific miracle that is Gabriel Jensen," Philip says, raising his voice. He waves at someone behind the door and leans in closer to the microphone so that he can emphasize his words. "Please welcome Gabriel Jensen, the first gene-spliced child. A miracle of modern science, Gabriel is the first human successfully crossed with nonhuman genetic material."

Lucy, in an inappropriately tight dress, steps out of the main glass doors with Gabriel in tow. The audience gasps. Gabriel looks around and smiles in delight. For him, this is an adventure. He rushes past Lucy and into the middle of the courtyard. He stops, gazes around, and then stretches and ripples his wings. Cameras flash, and video lights blaze hot and white, making the place unnaturally bright and the surreal vision of a child with wings even more fantastic. The phalanx of press correspondents chatters on. They are far from tongue-tied in amazement like the onlookers in the hospital windows and out in the parking lot. Huge close-up images of Gabriel in crystalline digital color fill the massive screens arranged around the place. The crowd stares up at him, utterly transfixed.

The KPY TV correspondent on Cynthia's computer babbles on about Gabriel's wings, his hair, his features, his form-fitting sweat suit, his countenance, and the way he laughs. "Gabriel seems very eager to show off. It looks like he is delighted with all the attention he is getting," she says.

Cynthia suggests that they flip through the TV channels and listen to a snippet from all of the main channels. The reporters use words like *adorable, miraculous, angelic, lively*, and *poised* to describe him. They anticipate his movements, saying things like "It seems like he's about to stretch that right wing. Yes, there it goes, and now, yes, the left one is stretching too" or "He's sure of his feet. Let's see if he's got the same kind of confidence in the air." The commentary is utterly inane, but it could be about a game and the well-known star athletes participating.

After a boringly detailed preamble about the need for safety and the precautions they have taken for this first flight, Philip practically begs the audience to stay calm, be quiet, and remain respectful. "After all, Gabriel is only five years old. The last thing we want to do is scare him,"

Gabriel spins around like a miniature fashion model or a rock star; he doesn't seem a bit scared. The audience roars, drowning out Philip's voice as he describes the scope of the first flight planned. White-clad doctors collect Gabriel and escort him to the yellow bull's-eye in the center of the courtyard.

With his unerring eagle eyes, Gabriel spots his mother at the fifth floor window above him. He waves, and she smiles and waves back.

Philip looks up, curious to see at whom Gabriel is waving. He can't see anything as clearly as Gabriel can and fortunately, due to the reconfiguration of the courtyard, he has forgotten that Cynthia's office is up there. The noise of the crowd dies down, and Philip can be heard again.

"First, we will see a short flight."

He nods at Gabriel's escort. The doctors release Gabriel and step back. Everyone waits.

Gabriel looks around, perplexed. The audience still waits. The news people are also transfixed, expecting something to happen. Then music is piped in, the Rolling Stones singing "Jumping Jack Flash." Gabriel grins broadly and starts strutting, pointing, and jumping. He darts back and forth, doing his best Mick Jagger impression. The crowd stares, astonished, and then they are overcome by his enthusiasm and his adorable sense of fun. They cheer boisterously.

Spiner yells at Philip, who is open-mouthed in surprise. "He's doing it again! I told you he would make a fool of you and your team!"

Philip covers the microphone with his hand, creating an ugly, grating sound. He hopes that no one else heard Spiner's angry outburst. There is no way they could, though, because the crowd has joined in with the music and sings along with the perennially and hugely popular Stones tune.

Sheila laughs and flings open the window to listen. Gabriel prances about on his ministage painted with a massive yellow bull's-eye and entertains his audience, mouthing the words, waving his arms, and twirling about.

Philip shoves Spiner out of his way and marches over to the main AV control unit. He yanks the plug out; sparks fly and the music stops. Gabriel ceases mid cavort, one arm in the air and one foot poised floating mid strut. He turns elegantly to his audience and takes a deep bow. The audience goes wild with applause. They are having so much fun, and he hasn't even flown yet.

Furious, Philip marches toward Gabriel. The boy sees him coming and dodges playfully. Philip is not amused. Suddenly, Gabriel opens his wings, catches some air, and leap frogs up and over Philip, kicking one foot off Philip's shoulder and the other off his head. The crowd gasps.

The correspondent on Cynthia's screen shouts gleefully like an enraptured sports reporter. "And he's off! There he goes, soaring into the sky with such grace, such skill. It's a miracle!"

Sheila leans out the window. Gabriel slaps her hand as he streaks by.

"I love you, baby!" she yells.

"I love you too, Momma!"

He banks around away from the wall of the building and glides down through the enclosed courtyard toward the crowd. People are awestruck as they watch him live through the barely visible, massive net. Enclosed in the arms of the institution, he circles gracefully in the open space. He sweeps down until he is about ten feet off the ground and then swoops up again to the top of the space. The crowd gasps and cries out. He swings down again in the widest circle he can make until it looks as if he will land, and then he swoops up once more.

Sheila watches, ever fearful that the strange phenomenon of shared flight will happen again, but perhaps because of the net or maybe because Gabriel can control it, she sees no other people getting caught up in his tail stream.

He continues his upswing once more. Philip is gesticulating wildly now, demanding that Gabriel land already, but no one can hear him. The air is filled with sighs and cries. People sway with the up swings and down swings of Gabriel's path. Finally, he descends gently as if to land near the television teams. Suddenly Gabriel disappears from view behind the first line of press teams lined up just outside the net. A collective sigh wells up from the crowd, who can no longer see him. The sigh swells and wafts through the entire crowd, rippling back through the parking lot and across the street into the park. The collective sigh then sweeps back toward the hospital again, across and through the multitude, and like a tidal wave, it generates a real wind in its wake.

Suddenly, a fierce gust of wind swirls into the courtyard. It eddies from the crowd, whips up the bottom edge of the net, and then whirls up into the enclosed area. The net swells up like a balloon. "The crowd gasps as they watch in surprise and trepidation. Then the net reaches its limit and rips straight across the top. The wind gusts out. A huge flap whisks up and blows back in the force of this unified breath. No one imagines that the crowd below might have generated this wind except for Gabriel, who knows that his audience wants him to fly. It takes a moment for anyone to notice that he has also been caught in the updraft. His wings are like a parachute as he seems to fall upward and out through the hole in the top, twelve floors above his massive audience.

Gabriel laughs with joy and cries out gleefully, "Kee, kee, aieeya!"

Philip and his team of doctors look up, stunned. The press loses sight of Gabriel and rushes out into the parking lot, pushing the crowd violently in an effort to locate Gabriel over the top of the building.

Philip is furious. He glances nervously at Spiner, whose mood shows in the livid skin of his face and his flailing hands. Spiner points to the sky, to Philip, and then to the security team and his team of doctors.

"Get him back here, now!"

He turns to bully Loraine, who stands there utterly shocked with a glazed look in her eyes like she has checked out mentally.

From Cynthia's window, Sheila watches the wind blow Gabriel up, up, and away. "Fly, baby, fly away!" she whispers.

The moment she can't see him anymore, she and Cynthia dash out of the office. Sheila dodges into the nearest stairwell.

"Wait, let's take the elevator," Cynthia says.

"Too slow," Sheila objects. "You know how long you have to wait there." She barges through the stairwell door and takes two steps at a time. A thought flashes through her mind, and she glances back at Cynthia a few steps behind her to share it. "Pretty different from the last time I was in this hospital in that horrible wheelchair! I was so sure I would never get out of that thing."

Cynthia huffs to keep up with her. "Yes, and you've wasted no time getting back in shape."

"Chasing Gabe!" Sheila retorts. She's short of breath too, though.

Seven floors later, Sheila bursts out onto the roof, gasping for breath.

Her lungs burn, and her legs ache, but her heart is exhilarated. She races to look over the side and sees Gabriel swoop past the edge and back down toward the audience below. He's coming back around the hospital from the other side. She and Cynthia watch as he glides over the people and captures their attention with his magical, piercing stare.

This is what he lives for, giving his audience the ride of their lives. The rhythmic breath of his wings sucks away all vocalization as he slides over their heads. Everyone—the crowd, the press, the doctors, the stage crew, the police, and the guards—freeze in awed silence. Cameras, notebooks, and microphones are all poised but forgotten.

Gabriel completes his sweep over the crowd like the pied piper collecting his band and then launches off toward the heavens with a mass of disembodied, glimmering figures in a lyrical tow that wafts and waves behind him. Not everyone has joined in; not everyone can see the ephemeral phenomenon.

When Gabriel disappears again into the high reaches of the sky, pandemonium ensues below. Some people are dancing ecstatically while some other part of their being flies through the air with him. Others are dashing about in confusion, trying to figure out what's going on.

Philip is in the latter group. "Find out where he went!" he barks to Larry and his security team.

Spiner is so furious that he is unable to summon a word. He grabs Loraine by the arm and drags her with him to follow Philip. She shakes herself, a bit stunned, like she is just waking up. Once alert she looks around, and like the professional she is, she kicks into management gear.

"I'll calm the press," she says as she marches off.

Sheila and Cynthia watch Gabriel's ascent and then glimpse his vivid blue eyes when he floats past them. Suddenly, they are aloft and soaring with him and his huge congregation. They all sweep across the sky in harmony, a confluence of motion, dancing in multiple dimensions, multiple ethereal bodies together.

Sheila is aware of the incredible diversity among the assemblage, which includes older folks, young people, and even tiny children and babies. There are multiple ethnicities and various types of affiliations, from punks, to bikers, to laborers, business people, and more. There are folks who have nothing and might even be homeless and others with expensive habiliments, all described in their glimmering light, ephemeral forms. No matter his or her background, everyone moves through space, sky, cloud, and air with equal grace and respect, giving way to each other and moving in an amazing synchrony like a school of fish or a flock of pigeons. It is like they are of one mind, knowing where to go next, when to turn, when to go up, and when to dive down. They laugh and roll like children, whether they are old or young, lithe and fit or out of shape.

Leading them all is Gabriel, deliriously happy with his eager playmates and their obvious enthusiasm.

31

FALLOUT

Back at the hospital, Spiner and Philip are in a frenzy shouting at each other. Spiner blames Philip; his voice is broken and hoarse.

"You guaranteed that this would work. What happened with that net?"

"You were the one who insisted we use Marco Construction!" Philip retorts. "I didn't think they knew what they were doing, but I didn't have a say in that, remember?"

Loraine strides into their sphere, returning from damage control duties, and grabs their arms. She drags them both inside the hospital, reprimanding them both on the way. "Not out here, gentlemen. This is *not* the kind of press we need. If we want to mitigate the repercussions, you two need to calm down, sit down, and start strategizing."

Larry dispatches his security detail to search for Gabriel and then pauses to look around. He notices that a number of audience members have organized themselves in a strange way. They seem to be arranged in a large, circular mass and are moving together in harmony, waving their arms and weaving in and out of each other without crashing or bumping into each other. He watches for a moment, baffled.

An agitated young woman bumps through the swirling crowd at the north end near the park, possibly looking for a lost child. She's clearly upset and pushes people aside carelessly while saying something that Larry can't hear. What is oddest about this is that none of the dancing mass of people seems the least bit upset by her rude and disruptive behavior. They just slide around her or glance off her gracefully. Larry watches her, perplexed, until he sees the woman sigh in relief and clutch a young girl into her arms, picking her up off her dancing feet. The girl was twirling in the labyrinth of bodies. At first, she tries to get down and rejoin the crowd, but caught in her mother's grip, she collapses and starts sobbing.

He looks over at the TV crews, who seem stalled. They wander around looking muddled. Some in the audience stand around befuddled as they watch friends, coworkers, or family members in the strange dance of Gabriel's fans. Other people seem dizzy or giddy. Perhaps they almost went for the ride but pulled back at the last minute. Here and there, people sit on benches with their heads in their hands as if recovering from some shock or airsickness. A few vomit.

Larry has no idea what's happening or what has affected so many people so strangely. He can see nothing of the unexplainable out-of-body flying phenomena. He decides to walk out to the edge of the parking lot with a pair of binoculars and comb the sky for Gabriel.

When he finally works his way through the ragged tangle of people, he realizes that the roof would be a far better vantage for his search. He turns and jogs back toward the hospital.

* * *

Sheila's light body sails over the city. She feels an extraordinary sense of freedom, a kind of ease, and joy that she has never felt before. She's completely fulfilled and comfortable in this ride, cushioned in the air. When she flies with Gabriel, it's like she has never been anywhere else. It is as if this is the only place to be, as if there are no other concerns, no other obligations, and nothing else that needs to be done. Each flight has been different. The first was a bit terrifying, and the second was a surprise and was worrisome. But now she lets go and surrenders to the experience. At the peak of her bliss, she feels a jolt and is ripped away from her exalted state.

On the roof, Larry grabs Sheila's arm in a vicelike grip. He speaks into his phone with his other hand. "Yeah, she's up here. I suggest you get up here right now."

Sheila's awareness recoils into her body with an abruptness that shocks her. Suddenly, she is standing on the roof again, reeling and dizzy with starry points of light whirling before her eyes and the wind whipping her hair. Larry has her arm twisted behind her back and pinched to the point of numbness. Her knees are weak, and she crumples to the floor, her arm wrenched even further behind her. Not far away, Cynthia still moves in graceful arcs, completely unaware of the intrusion.

High in the sky, Gabriel feels his mother's ethereal form plunge away from the flock and recoil back toward the hospital. He watches a moment and then banks to the left and dives toward the hospital roof. The aerial throng follows close behind him.

The sky darkens. Black clouds roll in, and distant thunder threatens. The weather seems to join into the quickly changing mood. As Gabriel races back to the hospital, he senses something is wrong. While he sweeps over the crowd outside the hospital, one by one, his aeronautical students fall out of formation and rejoin their dancing forms below. Almost alone now, Gabriel surges up again to crest over the edge and land on the roof. Cynthia is only just coming back to herself. She drifts across the roof in a dazed state.

Once on the roof, Gabriel runs toward his mother. "Momma, Momma, are you okay?"

A light rain begins to fall. Still on her knees, Sheila pushes against Larry so that she can turn and see Gabriel. He rushes toward her and throws his arms around her. She has only one arm to hug him. Larry still has her other arm twisted behind her. With his phone in his other hand, he is at a loss as to whether he should try to grab Gabriel and let go of Sheila or drop his phone and hold onto both of them.

"Gabriel, my baby, why did you come back?" Sheila asks.

"Because you need me, Momma."

"I do, my sweet," she replies. "I do."

A door behind them creaks open, and Philip and his hospital troops explode onto the rooftop. Two orderlies sprint across the tar surface and seize Gabriel, pinning his wings to his sides and lifting him up so that his feet are in the air. They withdraw, hustling him inside the stairwell, his little feet pumping.

"Momma, Momma!"

"I love you, Gabe! Don't forget your Momma loves you."

Just then, it starts to pour. Lightning flashes nearby, followed almost immediately by thunder. Larry drops Sheila, and she collapses, completely spent. Then Larry dashes behind Philip and the rest of the team back to the stairwell.

Cynthia jolts when she hears the stairwell door slam shut. She jogs over to help Sheila up and coax her inside, too.

* * *

At Philip's command, the orderlies drag Gabriel down and into the hallway toward the lab. Spiner marches toward them. Once more, Stan is in the thick of it, now wearing a press badge. He would be the only one to get into the hallway, shooting video of them all. He captures footage of Gabriel struggling.

Spiner is so furious and red-faced that he almost spits when he says, pointing at Gabriel, "Get that troublemaker inside and locked down."

Larry points behind Spiner, who turns to see Stan. Loraine makes a beeline for Stan.

"Get rid of him!" Spiner yells, exploding with fury.

Larry and two of his security guys hustle Stan into the elevator, ripping the memory card out of his camera on the way.

"Wait, wait!" Loraine yells. "That's the kind of treatment of the press that will make it much worse for us."

Spiner whirls on her. "Worse? Worse! I don't think it can get any worse. This has been a disaster, and it's as much your fault as it is anyone else's. Get out there and do your damage control, and get rid of those fanatics and the press outside while you're at it. I'm sick of them all."

Just as Loraine disappears into the elevator and the victors turn back toward the lab with their blue-winged captive, Sheila bursts from the stairwell.

"Let him go!"

Cynthia is right behind her filming with her phone.

Spiner points at Sheila. "Get rid of her, too."

Two security guards grab Sheila and drag her away.

Gabriel starts sobbing and yelling. "No, no, no!"

Cynthia backs away from Larry. He moves toward her, reaching for her phone.

Philip puts his hand on Spiner's arm. "Wait, Gerry, we need her."

Spiner snorts. "You've got her notes. That's enough."

Gabriel gets loose and runs to Sheila. They cling to each other. Larry turns away from Cynthia and moves to grab Gabriel again.

"Please!" Sheila begs Philip.

Spiner steps in, grabs Gabriel, and drags him into the lab.

"I got that on video, Gerry!" Cynthia yells.

The lab door slams. Before Cynthia can react, Larry snatches her phone tosses it on the floor, and stomps on it. Then he follows Spiner into the lab.

Philip turns to Cynthia and Sheila. "Let me see what I can do," he says apologetically, and then he disappears into the lab.

Two guards escort Sheila and Cynthia to the elevator. Cynthia is permitted to go back to her office, but Sheila is escorted right to the lobby door and practically shoved outside. The minute the guards turn their back on her, Sheila runs around to the emergency entrance. She has no idea what she is going to do once she gets back inside, but she will figure something out.

With her head down, she tries to dodge past the check-in desk, but when the nurse challenges her, she has to look up.

"Oh, Dr. Jensen," the young woman says.

"Hi, Margie," Sheila responds, glancing at the nametag dangling from the nurse's pocket. "Do I know you?"

"No," Margie responds. "I saw your face on TV today. That must have been so hard for you."

Sheila leans in, desperate and conspiratorial. "Listen," she rasps, "I have to get back into the research center. I need to see my son."

Margie steps back, a bit shocked. "They don't let you see him?"

"Can you let me in?" Sheila asks.

"I can't," Margie says regretfully.

Sheila slumps, crestfallen.

"Look, I can't while I'm on duty," Margie says, "but I'll tell you what, take this." She pulls a plastic-wrapped set of scrubs from under the counter and pushes it across to Sheila. "Come back any time after seven tomorrow morning. I don't want you sneaking through here on my shift, okay?"

Sheila nods eagerly.

"I can't help you with the badge," Margie says. "You'll have to figure that out yourself."

Sheila thanks her effusively. Waiting patients start to look over at them, suspicious. Margie pushes Sheila's hands away gently.

"Please stop. You're attracting attention."

Sheila glances around. A man eyes her quizzically. She turns away from him and mouths a final thank you to Margie.

"Good luck," Margie says, and then she turns away to respond to a beeping phone.

32

CLIPPED

Gabriel is sequestered in his room, which is more like a cell. It is on the same mezzanine that overlooks the third-floor atrium but on the opposite side from the hall where Sheila witnessed Gabriel teasing the doctors. The room is small, but despite the efforts of Philip's team to make it feel like a kid's room, it's not cozy. A few toys are scattered around, and bright stickers adorn the walls. Still, they are unable to warm up the clinically white walls, sanitary floor, and standard cold, bright overhead lighting. The room has minimal, colorless furnishings. There is a small hospital-style bed and a chest of drawers, and a tall wardrobe next to the drawers for hanging things. There is also a small, red plastic table with a set of multicolored children's chairs that refuse to add cheer to the room. It was not intended as a bedroom and is barely retrofitted for that purpose.

Gabriel is terrified. Things have gone terribly wrong, and he is extra sensitive to the feelings around him. To him, Spiner feels like an ugly, dark pool. The man wears his anger fervently all the time. Gabriel would love never to see him again, or better yet, he would love to get that man to fly. However, he doubts it will ever happen.

Philip is a mire of diverse and confusing feelings. He holds a lot of anger, too, and Gabriel can feel it. He feels a clear, dark-green band of sticky, unpleasant feelings that Philip holds with regard to Gabriel's mother. Gabriel knows that if Philip would fly just once, willingly, then that sticky resentment might start to clear up. He regrets now that he foisted that ride of terror on Philip in the highway traffic when Philip came up to get him in the mountains. At the time, Gabriel was just feeling out his talents. He had no idea how each person would respond. Philip's reaction was a shock to Gabriel. He really thought Philip would relax into it, but that didn't happen. Because of that, Philip is very guarded around Gabriel now. Gabriel doesn't blame himself, but he does feel a bit responsible, especially now that he has a much better ability to see the waves and patterns of emotions that swirl around and through people and also to see how those energies interact and affect each other.

Gabriel is cowering on top of the wardrobe when Philip enters. Philip ushers another man in behind him. The man is wearing a safari outfit with a theme park logo over his right breast pocket.

"Do you think you can clip them?" Philip asks.

The man, an ornithologist named Gary Maxwell, wears his picture, title, and name on a colored badge hanging from a lanyard around his neck. "A wing is a wing," he replies.

He looks around the room and then notices Gabriel crouching on top of the wardrobe. Gabriel's wings are folded and tucked up behind him, but their magnificence is undiminished. They are a rich blue with multicolored sparks strewn throughout. The feathers are delicate, gently curved, and layered perfectly.

"Wow!" Maxwell exclaims. "Are you sure you want to do this?"

Philip is about to take drastic measures; he excuses his radical decision, even though he feels terrible about it. "Yes, we can't control him."

Philip is afraid that if he doesn't act directly, he will lose his nerve, his job, probably his career, and certainly control over Gabriel. He's convinced that it's far better for Gabriel if he as his father remains in charge and here in the hospital, so he needs to regain control. He looks up to Gabriel and orders him down.

Gabriel, saucer-eyed, snuggles farther back on the wardrobe and begins to hum. "Mmm ooommm, oooom, mmmmooommma."

Philip drags Gabriel's bed across the floor without releasing the brakes, it screeches painfully. The noise makes Gabriel whimper. Philip shoves the bed right up to the chest of drawers. Then he tramples onto Gabriel's Red Dragon superhero sheets. One shoe squishes a stuffed teddy. He clambers onto the chest of drawers shoving stuffed animals and toys out of the way with his foot. A tangle of colored plastic and fake fur tumbles to the floor. Philip grabs Gabriel, who can't quite cringe far enough out of the reach of Philip's fierce grasp.

Philip yanks Gabriel off the wardrobe. Gabriel's wings flail, reaching out six or more feet across. Maxwell gasps and backs up to get out of the way of the wildly thrashing wings. Gabriel flaps them with enough power to make it difficult for Philip to hold onto him. They struggle against each other, and it almost seems as if Gabriel might lift Philip off the bed with him. But the ceiling is only four or so feet above Gabriel's head, and he is unable to escape Philip's grip.

Maxwell steps into the fray and reaches a gentle hand up to grasp Gabriel's outstretched hand. He pulls down, and Gabriel, holding the practiced hand of a man who has soothed eagles, folds his wings and settles.

Philip puts Gabriel down on the bed so that Gabriel and Maxwell are standing eye to eye. A look of wonder shines on Maxwell's face.

"May I?" he asks, indicating that he would like to touch Gabriel's wings.

Gabriel nods, no longer wary. He knows he has won the heart of this man. Maxwell strokes the glorious blue feathers, admiring the luster and the glint of other colors.

"Well, well, I really didn't think this story was for real. I thought it was some kind of stunt, so I haven't paid a lot of attention. But here you are in the flesh and with feathers."

He turns to Philip, flushed and moved by this encounter. "It's a shame, you know? Is it really necessary?"

"Uncle Philip, I didn't fly away," Gabriel protests. He still can't get used to calling Philip *Dad*. It pains Philip every time. Gabriel continues defending himself. "I came back. I wasn't going anywhere; I was just giving your people what they wanted, what they all came here to see."

Philip looks at Gabriel, puzzled momentarily. Then his face goes stern. "You don't pay attention, and you don't do what you are instructed to do. You think all this is playtime and fun. Yes, we need to do this, and we need to do it right now." He turns to Maxwell. "Did you bring your tools?"

Maxwell starts to answer and then stops, his mind weighing the options. He makes a decision. "You know, I didn't really know what you hired me for here. I didn't know this was a kid, and I'm not sure what's legal here. I could lose my license, you know. So I think if you want me to do this, you probably need to get some kind of court order or something first." As he turns to leave, he grabs his phone and opens it. "Can I take a photo?" he asks Gabriel.

"No," Philip pushes the phone down and forces Maxwell through the door.

Maxwell shrugs and on the way out says, "I'll send you a bill for the consultation. You can let me know when you get that approval."

Philip goes pale. This tussle has knocked the supercilious wind out of him and kicked his good senses back to life. He collapses on the bed and pulls Gabriel into his lap. He hugs his son tightly and sobs. Despite his tears, Philip is immensely relieved. This was an awful day and an all-around a disaster. But Gabriel is still here, and he still has his job—for the moment.

Philip puts his hand on the back of Gabriel's head and bends his face to kiss the child's forehead. "I'm sorry, so sorry. Please forgive me. I didn't want to."

Gabriel pats Philip's shoulder and hugs his neck sympathetically. "It's okay," Gabriel says. "Tell you what, let's have some cookies and hot chocolate, and then we can go to the park and play like we used to."

Philip chokes. "Yes, we can have the cookies and hot chocolate, but I'm afraid we can't go to the park right now, buddy."

At that moment, Spiner bursts in. "Is it done? Did you clip his wings?"

Philip wipes his face and sets Gabriel down on the floor. "Everything is under control," he replies, jumping up to almost salute Spiner. He isn't going to talk about whether or not Gabriel's wings were clipped until he can figure out the next step. "We're good. We're good, and Gabriel can't fly off now."

He winks at Gabriel, who nods in agreement.

"Good, good," Spiner says approvingly. "I think we've had enough excitement for one day. Lock this door and gather the team. I want a full debriefing from this wreck of a day by noon tomorrow. I don't want the team to lose a minute more of our time on this issue. Hand your debriefing files off to the legal and PR departments. Loraine can manage the fallout."

33

SECRET VISITS

Early the next morning, about thirty or so members of the Gabriel Jensen team gathers around a large oval table in the conference room that abuts Gabriel's room. Larry and his security team crowd together in one corner. Other support staff, including Lucy and the other interns, stands along the sides. A flank of doctors and technicians are seated around the middle of the table. The crew from yesterday's fiasco, including lighting, scenery, video, stage management, online media, and other folks, are tucked tightly together at the far end of the table. They all look dour, as if they expect a good reaming. The one guy who should be there and is not is Joe Marco. It was his net that failed. The administrative team, including Loraine, sits at the head of the table near the entrance beside Philip. Spiner leans nonchalantly against the wall just inside the door. A massive one-way mirror spans the wall that this room shares with Gabriel's. On the other side of the glass, Gabriel plays listlessly on the floor with a bunch of stuffed animals.

Philip and Loraine kick things off. Philip starts by outlining the points, format, and timeline for the information he requires to conclude the previous day's business. Loraine requires notification of anything and everything that might get out to the public in any way. She admonishes everyone about leaks and sloppiness and informs them that a new program has been installed to track the source of all information leaving the institution, so if they leak, they'll be caught. She's angry, but she keeps it cool and professional. Her job of trying to paint a pretty picture of the torn net, escaped boy, chaotic crowds, and aborted press conference is tough, and she has been up all night working on it.

After forty-five minutes of listening to arguments, criticisms, and admonishments flung from department to department, Philip glances through the window into Gabriel's room. He's disturbed to see that Gabriel is huddled on the corner of his bed with his wings wrapped around him. It causes him physical pain to see the child so unhappy. He looks around the table and decides it's time to break it up.

"Okay, I want you all to go back to your offices and recount every minute of yesterday's activities from your own points of view. Each team needs to come up with a clear picture of what happened. Please get it to Loraine by noon. Thanks."

* * *

Philip is the first to step out of the room. He heads straight for the cafeteria on the second floor. As he works his way through the line, Sheila, wearing scrubs and a paper cap, falls in beside him unnoticed.

"Philip," she says.

He turns toward her, and his eyes widen with surprise. "What are you doing here?" he whispers, glancing around nervously.

"You know what I want," she replies. "I have to see Gabe. I have to know that he is all right."

"Okay," Philip says. "Get some breakfast and come with me."

"I'm not hungry," Sheila replies.

"You may not be, but I'm pretty sure Gabe is," Philip says.

"Oh, of course. Okay."

Sheila starts collecting Gabriel's favorite foods. She buys entirely too much, giving him the choice of a breakfast burrito, a croissant, fried eggs with home fries, cereal and milk, an apple, and both orange and apple juice. Philip buys cookies and hot chocolate. For themselves, Philip grabs two pre-packaged sandwiches and some water bottles. He doesn't even look to see what kind of sandwiches they are.

"Keep your head down," Philip says as they walk down the hall. "I don't want Spiner to find out that you're here."

"Let's take the stairs," she says. "It's easier to avoid looking in the cameras there than in the elevator."

Philip looks at her, surprised at her deduction but also alarmed that she needs to think that way.

They reach Gabriel's room, and Philip stops her outside the door.

"Wait, I don't want you to rush in there until I make sure no one is in the conference room watching. I'll be right back."

Philip walks past Gabriel's door to the entrance of the next room. He pokes his head in and then shuts the door and locks it.

"All clear, but keep it down," he says as he returns to her. "We're videotaping everything in there, and if they see you jump on him, crying and hugging like his mom, you'll give yourself away. Try to be cool. I'll go in and warn him first. We'll say you're Cynthia; she's still works here and is likely to visit."

Sheila nods, and then he steps inside. Sheila fidgets nervously while she waits to be invited into Gabriel's room. When Philip opens the door, she can hardly contain herself. She wants to be effusive and to smother her son in hugs and kisses, but she is aware of the danger. So she gives him a warm and cozy hug and several kisses on the face just as Cynthia would.

"Mmm … Aunty C, you're here," Gabe says, throwing his arms around her, just as he would if it really were Cynthia.

Philip pulls up the child-sized table from the corner of the room and three of the four small plastic chairs for them each to sit on. He arranges Sheila's chair to face her away from the mirror and the cameras that he knows are in the room. Even though the conference room is locked, a few others have keys—Spiner for one—so he is still concerned that she will be exposed.

"How are you, baby?" Sheila asks Gabriel.

"I want to go home," he whines.

"I know," she agrees. "I do, too."

They both look at Philip.

"Listen," he says, "this is not how I wanted things to work out either. You should have come to me in the beginning, Sh—" He stops himself before he says her name. "Surely there's some way we can work this out."

Sheila gives Philip a cold stare. "I'll free him; that's my only goal now, my mission," she whispers. "You can't lock him up like this; it's just not right."

"Don't do anything radical," he replies just as quietly. "If I'm fired, we'll lose the protection of this institution and be out there fighting the mobs alone. Let's just forget about this right now and enjoy breakfast, okay?"

"Okay," Gabriel agrees joyfully.

They rip into the bags and the ecological food containers, making a big mess of the tiny plastic table. For a while, they almost forget the circumstance and enjoy a fun breakfast together. Gabriel surprises them both by remembering things that happened when he was a tiny baby.

"Remember that pigeon?" he asks Sheila. "Remember him that flew me out of the stroller?"

"I do remember that, Gabe," Sheila replies, "but how can you remember it? You were just a baby."

"Oh, I remember everything," he continues. "I remember you pushed me real hard on the swing, Uncle Philip, and Momma almost fell over. So we all went and got hot chocolate and cookies afterwards. I think that was the first time I found out it's my favorite thing."

They laugh together and eat almost happily. Even before he finishes his meal, Gabriel climbs into Sheila's lap on the tiny chair and falls asleep. He sighs contentedly, able to truly relax for the first time since he was captured and interred in this cold, unfriendly place.

"He's exhausted," Sheila says.

"It's no wonder," Philip adds. "He's been very active all morning."

"Is he sleeping well here?" She looks over at the hospital bed, evaluating it. Then she looks up at the ceiling and notices the lighting. "Do you keep those lights on all the time? It's such a … sterile place. It's not at all comfortable for a child."

Philip looks up at the lights. "They dim, but they're always on. We are grabbing twenty-four-hour video of Gabriel."

Gabriel stirs in her arms and twists a bit. She looks fondly at the sleeping child in her arms. "We should let him sleep." Sheila stands up awkwardly and carries him to the bed, depositing him there under the covers. She bends over and kisses Gabriel on his forehead. Tears wet her cheeks and smear onto his head. She wipes it gently with her hand. Then she and Philip tiptoe out of the room.

They head into the conference room, and Philip locks the door behind them. They circle around the table and stand at the one-way mirror, peering in at Gabriel.

"I'm taking my child out of here," Sheila announces. "I don't know how, but I'll get him out."

"Sheila, it's not a good idea," Philip replies. "All of this is to protect him."

He pulls her to a window that looks out over the courtyard and the parking lot. "Look out there. How will you be able to protect him from that? You know what the press is like; they'll hound you wherever you go. You'll never be free. No one can tell what the fans and the wackos will do. They could kidnap him and tear him apart. They have already burned your house down. There's no way you'll be free of them. They'll always find you, and you can see some of them are not too happy about genetic modification. They're nuts and out of control."

Sheila peers out at the crowd below. A glaze of worry crosses her eyes and ripples her forehead, but she shrugs, summoning courage. "I can't worry about all of that. All I know is that this isn't right. I should be with him, and you and Gerald won't let me. So he's coming with me."

Philip sighs and changes his tactics. "Sheila, I loved you. I still love you, but you are the one who shut me out. This is the only way to protect him—and you. You know that."

"You mean this is the only way to protect *your* job, *your* career, and *your* reputation," Sheila replies, cold and unmoved. "How can I trust you after you abandoned me?"

"I never wanted to hurt you," Philip replies, a soft note of appeal in his voice.

At that moment, the door swings open, and Spiner strides in. It is clear that he knew she was there. Either he was tipped off or the video gave her up.

"What's she doing here?" he demands, but he's not really interested in an answer. "Dr. Jensen, Gabriel isn't going anywhere. He's not flying anymore either. We've clipped his wings. If you don't leave right now, I'll call security, and they will drag you out."

Sheila gasps and doubles over as if punched. She recovers and lunges for Spiner. "How could you? Philip, how could you?"

Philip shakes his head in a perplexing way, but Sheila is too angry to comprehend. He grabs Sheila before she can do any harm to Spiner. Spiner backs up to the other side of the table.

"You need to leave right now. It won't look good on your appeal if the judge discovers that you came here uninvited and that you attacked me," Spiner warns.

Sheila struggles out of Philip's grasp. "Oh, but I was invited."

"By who?"

Spiner looks at Philip. Philip stiffens and straightens his back. He's still holding Sheila's arm. He considers how to respond and then chooses not to confirm her statement. He gives Spiner a slight shrug and shakes his head. Sheila is appalled and utterly furious. She gives Philip a fierce look and storms out.

"You will be hearing from my lawyer today," she threatens. "We have another judge, one who's not in your pocket." She marches out.

Once Sheila is gone, Spiner turns to Philip. "I was coming here to confer with you on a thought I had, but when Larry called to say she was in Gabriel's room, I made my decision. Apparently, it's too easy for her to sneak in any time she likes. Her sister works here, she knows the place inside and out, and she has too many friends here. The mob out there is getting worse, too, so we have to move him to a more secure facility."

"Where?" Philip asks, startled.

"You'll find out tomorrow."

"We're leaving tomorrow?"

Outside the conference room, Sheila presses her ear against the door. She hears Spiner continue.

"Yes. It's impossible to do anything here now with this kind of public scrutiny. In addition, because Sheila sneaks in every second, I want him moved up to the twelfth-floor wing immediately. And keep his relocation absolutely quiet."

Sheila hears Spiner stomp toward the door, so she sprints to the nearest stairwell and slips inside. She eases the door closed quietly. The conference room door opens abruptly, and Spiner's shrill and bossy voice is muffled through the stairwell door.

"Be ready to head out tomorrow morning at seven. No one sleeps or leaves the building tonight until we get Gabriel safely out of here."

His footsteps thump down the hallway. It sounds like he's coming straight for the stairwell door. She looks around, terrified, and then darts silently down a half-flight of stairs. She holds her breath. Sure enough, the door bursts open, and Spiner's trim figure pops through. Sheila jumps, swinging on the handrails while holding her breath. Without making a sound, she jumps three stairs at a time to get to the door below. Her hand rests on the handle. She knows if she opens it, he will hear her. Only if he comes this way will she need to open it, though, so she waits. Spiner's shoes click on the concrete floor directly over her, and then she hears the rhythmic tempo as he trots up the stairs. She sighs in relief at the last echo of his ascending footsteps and the final click of a door on the tenth floor slamming closed. *That's how he stays thin and hungry*, she thinks. The silence settles over her, and she opens the door and leaves.

34

DESPERATE DECISIONS

Sheila drives directly to her lawyer's office. Amelie is expecting her. The reconnaissance was planned to try to strategize her winning defense, but now Sheila feels the urgency of it. Amelie invites Sheila inside, and Sheila paces while she tells Amelie about her encounter with Philip and Gabriel. She's particularly upset that they have clipped his wings.

"We must be able to use that to get him out," she says hopefully. "Also, Spiner plans to move Gabriel somewhere completely unknown first thing tomorrow morning, so we have to act fast."

Amelie gets Sheila a hot tea and encourages her to sit down and relax. "Did you see anything else that would threaten Gabriel's wellbeing, either mental or physical?"

Sheila babbles about the lunch, the room, and Philip's handling of the child. Nothing else seems to be a glaring breach of appropriate treatment.

"Look, it's tough to get a case moved to another judge," Amelie says. "I'll look into the possibility that wing clipping is an offence, but it's a completely new area. I don't know what we'll find, and I know it will take time."

Sheila sighs. "But they have him locked up. That's got to be illegal."

"I'm afraid it's going to take longer than we thought, even if we can prove mistreatment," Amelie says. "They'll argue that it's for his safety, and recent events seem to back up that conclusion."

Sheila loses her cool, her voice escalating hysterically. "Isn't it enough that they snatched him away from his own mother and are experimenting on him like a lab rat?"

"Sheila, the state has already found you guilty of a worse mistreatment. They see his wings, and they think they are evidence that you engineered his DNA. That's illegal. You broke the law first."

Sheila stands up so fast that she knocks over her chair. "Well, if you won't help me—"

"I am helping you," Amelie interjects. "These things take time; there are few precedents here."

"Okay, I'll help speed it up, I'll get him out."

"Sheila you need to be patient."

"I'm done with patience!" Sheila shouts. She pounds out the door, determined to take things into her own hands from now on.

Amelie leans back in her chair and sighs.

* * *

It's dark when Sheila loads her car, preparing to flee once again. She doesn't have much to pack this time. She's already been on the run and left things behind here and there in various quick escapes, so now she knows that she really doesn't need much of anything. Having cleared out her bank accounts, she stuffs a wad of cash into the bottom of the center console and locks it. Then she shoves her last couple of items into the trunk and speaks into her phone.

"I have to do this, Cynthia. Just get me inside, and I'll take it from there."

Cynthia protests, but her main points are all the same as Philip's rationalization for why the institution should continue to shelter Gabriel.

"They're moving him to a secret location, and I will never see him again," Sheila says.

Cynthia gasps. She gets it. "Okay, okay."

* * *

Sheila stows her car as close as she can to one of the hospital's side exits below her lab. At that late hour, the parking lot is sparsely filled. Office hours, classes, and visiting hours are over. No one wants to be there at night unless they have to. The place is still surrounded by frightening and angry crowds who have a beef with doctors who think they are gods, at least as they see it.

Cynthia meets her at the emergency room entrance to escort her into the heart of the institution. As they hurry past the distracted desk attendant, Sheila informs Cynthia that she heard Spiner tell Philip to move Gabriel to the twelfth floor, but she doesn't know where exactly. Cynthia is sure it must be the southeast corner. It has just been renovated and is barely reoccupied by the pediatric cancer ward, which is sparsely filled at this time. Also, she heard Lucy directing assistants to move boxes into the La Salle wing.

After a quick and tearful hug, Cynthia and Sheila separate.

"If you need anything, let us know," Cynthia says. "We'll try to help. We'll do whatever we can, okay?"

Cynthia nods at Sheila, trying to impress upon her that she is not alone. Neither of them really believes it though. Sheila doesn't know how Cynthia can help, as she has no idea where she is going yet, other than to a border as quickly as possible.

Cynthia feels like a huge hole is opening up and might swallow her. She was always sure that her sister would be nearby. She knew they could always count on each other. But now Cynthia feels like she is failing Sheila, and she has to watch her dearest, closest friend disappear from her life. Cynthia chokes and weeps profusely when Sheila darts off down the corridor toward the other side of the complex.

It is after midnight, and the halls are empty. The lights are on the nighttime energy-saving setting. Sheila steels herself when she takes the elevator to the eleventh floor of the La Salle wing. The elevator stops with a friendly chime. Thankfully this is a floor with exam suites used only during the day. The reception desk is dark and empty. Sheila waits a moment, her hand on the door to keep it open, and listens for any sounds of life. When she is certain the coast is clear, she dodges out and over to the nearest stairwell that leads up to the twelfth floor. Her sneakers don't make a sound as she tiptoes up the stairs.

She opens the door to the twelfth floor and peeks into the hallway. The nurse's station in front of her and opposite the elevator is quite for the moment. She has no idea what to expect or where Gabriel, Philip, or even Larry might be. The La Salle wing is huge.

A few doors down the hall, Sheila sees a guard standing in front of a room. Just then, Philip approaches. She ducks out of sight, keeping her stair door open only a smidgeon so that she can see what's going on.

Philip stands in front of the closed door, staring through its window for a moment. Then he turns to the guard. "Are you on all night, Harry?"

Harry nods.

"Okay. Don't let anyone in, and let me know if anyone tries to see him. Tell me if you see anyone in the hall other than the night nurse. There is no other business going on up here at night, so there shouldn't be anyone around."

Philip concludes his list of instructions and then turns his back on Sheila and the guard. Sheila watches him walk down the hallway to the far end and then turn left. Then she takes a moment to consider her next move.

Prior to dashing off to this corner of the hospital complex, Sheila and Cynthia tried to recall the basic layout of the La Salle wing. The building is a large T shape. Cynthia recalled that there are six stairwells, one at the end of each wing and one near the center of each of the three long hallways. Sheila can see now that she can't get near Gabriel from this stairwell. She's at the base of the T. The other stairwell is in the center of the hall across from Gabriel's room, but it is too close to where the guard is sitting. Though these stairs are closest to Gabriel's room, the guard is right there, and the minute she steps through either door, he will turn and see her. Sheila backs quietly down the stairs.

Back on the eleventh floor, she follows the hall beneath her destination, counting doors until she estimates she must be right under Gabriel's door. A little farther down, she finds the other stairwell off to the right and sneaks upstairs to double check her location. Too afraid to open the door in case it creaks, she crams her face against the window and tries to see as far down the hall as possible. She can just see the guard settling down into a stiff chair next to Gabriel's door. She backtracks down the stairs and heads off to the other end of the hall. Just around the far corner on the left side is the next closest stairwell.

This is the way Philip turned, so she is afraid she will have to pass his office. He always keeps his door open, especially at night when the place quiets down. If she takes one of the other stairwells all the way at the end or the center of the right wing, she will have to cross the end of the hall and risk the guard seeing her. She hopes that Philip's office is further toward the other end of the left hall and decides to take the stairwell to her left.

She inches up the steps and opens the door cautiously. A quick glance in both directions reveals that the hall is empty. She can see the right turn to the hallway that is her goal just past a couple of offices. She exits the stairwell and closes the door carefully so that it makes no noise. Determined to get to Gabriel, an insane plan takes shape in her mind.

Between her and the direction she needs to go, one office door is open with a light on inside. Just as she expected, it's Philip's office, and she has to get past it.

She skulks up to the door and peeps in. Philip is sitting at his desk with his head down. A brief pang of fondness for him grips her heart, melting a tiny bit of her resolve. She didn't realize that her determination was so fragile, and she begins racking her brain for alternative courses of action. She briefly entertains the possibility of enrolling Philip in her plan and of all three of them running away together. But after a long pause, with her heart beating so loud she is afraid he will hear it, she concludes that she must do this alone, he has shown where his loyalty lies.

She turns her head slightly and glances into the room again. Philip's head is still down, so she slides down the wall and onto the floor. Flat on her stomach, she slides past his door, her eyes fixated on the top of his head, hoping that he won't look up. Once past, she stands and then trots silently to the next and last office on the same side of the hall before the turn toward Gabriel's room. She ducks inside. Thankfully the door is unlocked, and no one is inside. She's sweating, but so far so good.

This is the oldest part of the hospital. It is a graceful building with tall, narrow windows that swing out, unlike the windows in her office in the new part of the complex that slide open. Sheila cranks the window open and then realizes it has been rigged to gape no more than four inches. She studies the opening contraption and sees there's a window-washing function that, once unlocked, permits the window to swing open fully. All she needs to do is close it again and disengage the safety lock. She pulls a dime out of her pocket to unscrew the safety lock, and it comes free. The hinge releases, and there it is, a fully-opened window.

Outside the window is a one-foot ledge that traverses the length of the outer wall about two inches below the window line. To the right, the wall turns perpendicular to the window wall, and right there Philip's office window faces straight down the edge of the wing and past Gabriel's window. Sheila can see Philip inside with his side to her, seated at his desk, head down. All he needs to do is look out, and he will see her on the wall at his level. She sinks to the floor, stymied. She can't come this far and get caught; this has to work.

She decides to wait. It's late already, well past midnight. Philip is bound to finish up and go home soon. Sheila settles onto a couch in the room to wait. From her position on the couch, she can see the light of Philip's office. Her only hope is that she won't fall asleep. She sets her phone alarm to vibrate every fifteen minutes.

Time goes by, and Philip's light is still on. She gets up regularly and looks over to see if he is still there. To her chagrin, he still sits hunched over his desk. By three o'clock, she is wondering if he will ever leave, and she is beginning to feel panicked. Then, shortly after four, she looks over to his office, and though the light is still on and he is still there, it looks safe; Philip's head is down and turned away from the window. He's fast asleep at his desk.

Relieved and determined, Sheila pokes her head out the window. Wind snatches at her hair and clothing. She's nervous. It's a long way down, and she isn't going to be aloft in any ethereal form but rather in physical peril, clinging to the side of the building twelve floors up in her weighty and fragile body.

She steps out boldly onto the ledge. She stands for a moment, breathing heavily, panic rising from her gut. She controls her breath, covering her mouth with her sleeve and breathing into it so that she doesn't hyperventilate. Her back is glued to the window behind her. She is terrified to move, but she must. Inspired by the thought of Gabriel being lost to her forever, she shuffles her left foot out along the ledge toward her son's room.

"I'm coming, my baby," she whispers.

Pasted to the wall, she sidles along a dozen feet and then twenty feet. She doesn't see a small gap where a piece of the stone ledge has fallen away. Sheila's foot is inches out over the foot-wide space. She fumbles around trying to find a solid surface and loses her balance. She swings out and hangs, suspended in midair, for a long and peculiar moment. Though her life hangs in the balance, she is calm. Time seems to stop. She feels an inner quiet that she has never known before but that is reminiscent of her flights with Gabriel. It's as if she is unable to tell if she is in her physical form or in her evanescent form that she has grown to know so well and to love so much. Then a strong and sudden wind blows her back and presses her against the wall, securing her once more on the ledge.

This strange, abrupt wind seems to congeal into a light form resembling Gabriel, but not as she knows him. The form suggests Gabriel as full grown. His ephemeral but strong arms pin her to the wall. Sheila is certain she feels them. Then, without warning, he disappears, but not before she recognizes his crystal-clear blue eyes that shine like lights. Sheila clings to the wall, breathing hard. Her mind is utterly baffled. She's unable to fathom what just happened.

It takes a few minutes for Sheila's courage to return. A slight breeze ruffles the absolute quiet. Lights flicker below. The waning moon reveals a ragged edge through a cloud and then disappears again. Aircraft flash above. The darkness of night creeps toward dawn. She has waited too long. A ripple of panic returns. She clings to the wall in a cold sweat. Her resolve to get moving again finally settles in. She inches her feet along, making sure she has something to stand on before she leans her weight over. She senses and steps over two other gaps in the ledge before she reaches Gabriel's window. Once there, she pauses a moment to catch her breath.

A small voice startles her. "Come inside, Momma."

She leans out ever so slightly to look into the room and sees Gabriel standing on the inside window ledge looking out at her. He clambers down and tries to open the window.

"No, no wait, Gabe." She points to the catch on the window crank. Fumbling through her pocket, she produces the dime and slips it through the partially opened window toward Gabriel. "Do you know how a screwdriver works?"

"Yes, yes!" he exclaims excitedly. "Uncle Philip showed me once."

"Good," she says, struck by the irony of it. "Use the dime like a screwdriver and unscrew that knob off there first. Then you can open the window enough."

Gabriel fiddles with the coin, trying to fit it properly. He flounders about trying to turn it and slipping frequently. His hands are not dexterous enough yet. After all, he isn't even six, she reminds herself. Finally, he removes the locking device and cranks the window wide open. Sheila spills off the ledge and into the room with an immense sigh of relief. Mother and son fall into each other's arms. Gabriel looks up at her and opens his mouth to speak.

"Shh …" she says, putting her finger on his lips. "There's a man outside who will hear you. Whisper."

"I'm so glad you found me, Momma."

Sheila sobs and clasps him close to her.

"Are we going out of here?" Gabriel asks.

"I think so, baby," she replies.

"Oh good, because I don't like it here. It's no fun. They're so serious, and no one will fly with me. I like it when all the people come with me and when you come too. That's the way it's supposed to be."

Sheila chokes. Gabriel has said something that resonates deeply—something important, something profound about what's going on with him and his flying expeditions. But whatever it is, she can't make sense of it. All she knows is that he is right, and it feels good.

"But baby, can you still fly? Didn't they cut your feathers?"

"Oh no, Momma, look," he replies, spreading his wings and pumping them to show her their complete span. The whoosh and sweep of air alarms her, and she grabs his hands hushing him.

"Shhh, shhh. The guard outside will hear you."

Gabriel climbs onto the windowsill. "Fly with me, Momma!" he begs.

"Gabe, I … I can't fly," she replies.

"You already have," he responds.

"No, Gabe. That was some … some kind of out-of-body experience. I would fall if I tried it for real."

Gabriel eyes her seriously. "No you wouldn't."

She shakes her head in denial. Gabriel can see in her face that she is still far from trusting, despite all of her extraordinary experiences, including the most recent one on the ledge.

"Okay," he says, "I'll fly home and meet you there."

"No," Sheila protests. "It's too dark and too dangerous. You got lost before, so no. Come with me. I'm going to walk back to that window down there that's open. You can meet me there, okay? Don't fly too far way; there are wires all around this hospital."

She holds his face and looks deep into his eyes. Her own eyes are pooled with emotion. She wills him to accept her conditions, wills him to behave and do as she asks, wills him with all of her authority as a mother and as someone who loves him deeply. He sees this and then nods slightly and kisses her on the lips.

Gabriel swoops out the window and circles around close to the building. Above them, the nighthawks screech. Gabriel screeches in reply. Sheila clambers out the window and hisses for him to be quiet.

"Shhh! You'll wake Philip."

She scurries sideways, back flat against the wall, and inches her way toward the open window. Gabriel circles above her. She can sense his ecstasy, his elated sense of freedom. As she gets closer, she sees Philip still slumped and snoring over his desk. She can only imagine the weight he must feel right now, the work he must complete this night, considering the important move they are planning for the following day. She chuckles inside at the thought of how much time he has wasted and how, by the coming morning, she will have relieved him of it all.

Finally, she climbs inside the room again and waves to Gabriel, who swooshes onto the ledge and hops inside. Just as Sheila closes the window, she spots Philip stirring. How will they get past his office now? Sheila instructs Gabriel to wait quietly until she can figure out how they are going to escape unnoticed.

She sneaks out of the room and dashes on tiptoe to Philip's door. Once there, she can hear him moving about, but she doesn't dare to peek inside in case he sees her. She cooks up a plan to get past, but in order to implement it, she has to cross over the end of the long hallway that leads to Gabriel's room and still contains a guard on watch. It might work. He's a long way down the hall and unlikely to be looking her way.

Sheila pauses at the corner and then peers around it. Half way down the hall, the guard is slumped in his chair, snoring. Sheila sighs with relief and then slips across the hall and into a supply room a short way down. Inside, she scuffles into a set of coveralls and covers her hair with a paper cap. Then she rolls a large hamper out of the closet and down the hall, trying to be as silent as possible.

Safe across the end of the hall again, she opens the door to the room where Gabriel is waiting and rolls the hamper inside. Sheila helps Gabriel clamber inside the bin. Then she plops a heap of blankets, sheets, and towels on top of him.

245

As they pass Philip's office, Sheila feels a sense of relief to see Philip hunched over his desk, absorbed in his work. He seems unaware of their passing. Just past his door, despite her precautions, the hamper hits a wobbly tile, causing it to rattle and squeak. Sheila hears Philip's footsteps approaching the office door. She parks the hamper outside another room and ducks inside. Lucky for her, it is a recovery room, and there is plenty of bedding within easy reach. She grabs a blanket and tosses it into the open laundry hamper outside the room.

Outside his office, Philip stops and looks around, he sees a blanket or something sail through the air and land in the hamper. "Housekeeping. I forgot," he mutters. Then his footsteps recede, and he closes his office door behind him.

Sheila dashes out of the room, prevents the door from slamming, and then whizzes the laundry bin down the hall toward the elevator. Gabriel jumps up and throws his arms in the air,

"Whee!" he whispers.

"Shhh!" Sheila says, barely suppressing a snicker.

They crowd into the elevator with the laundry bin. Sheila tucks Gabriel into hiding again so that the elevator's security camera won't see him.

* * *

Philip is just sitting back down at his computer when it occurs to him to check on Gabriel. He opens the computer to a surveillance program and navigates to reveal Gabriel's room. He looks at one image and doesn't see Gabriel. He clicks to another view, still no Gabriel. He moves to the bathroom, and he's not in there either. In the final view, he notices that the window is wide open. He rewinds the captured footage and watches in reverse the unfolding events of Gabriel's escape. Then he leaps up from his desk.

"He's out!" Philip yells into his cell phone as he runs toward Gabriel's room. "It was less than ten minutes ago. Seal the exits. Yes, look for Dr. Jensen; she's got him. Get a searchlight; it looks like he flew out, but she certainly didn't."

35

TRUTH-TELLER

Cynthia drives too fast through the suburb this early morning. She is leaving a message via her Bluetooth phone.

"Sheila, I figured it out. Sorry, I know you told me not to look through your Gabriel books but I had to. I need to tell you something. Where are you? You're not home. God, I hope you're not doing something really stupid. I'm driving to the hospital right now."

She hangs up. The car turns the corner, and the hospital looms into view. Suddenly lights flash and sirens blare, something has happened. Cynthia pulls the car right up to the front entrance and races inside, following two security guards.

36

HUMANGEL

The hall emergency lights blast on. Sheila yanks Gabriel out of the rolling basket, and they run down the hall and dodge into a stairwell. They hear doors opening and closing below them and heavy boots tramping up the stairs. Sheila grabs Gabriel, and they dash out of the stairwell again.

She reaches out to jab the elevator button, but Gabriel stops her. He leans in to listen and hears muffled, militant voices in the shaft. The light dings. Sheila seizes Gabriel's hand and drags him through a set of double doors that lead into the research wing.

They burst into the animal lab. The place is a cacophony. With emergency lights on full at this early hour and the racket of sirens, all of the animals are upset. They encounter screeching, hooting, cawing, yapping, and a general babble of angry creature noises. Gabriel is moved. He has seen all of these creatures before, but it has been a while. Now he makes a decision and starts throwing cage doors open.

"They want out, Momma!"

"Oh no, Gabe, they'll never survive!"

"Maybe they will," he says. "They need to try. They want to try."

He releases rabbits with human ears on their backs, a blue monkey with extra fingers, dogs with silky human hair, and more strange creatures that should not exist. The creatures flee in all directions. Some dogs go right for the food bin and tip it over. They scrabble around in the spilled kibble, enjoying their early-morning feast. Sheila can't help but laugh. It is both tragic and humorous at the same time. Gabriel props open the lab doors, and the sounds of security shouting in the distance filters toward them.

"Let's go," Sheila says.

They dodge into a remote stairwell on the other side of the lab. Philip's team spills into the lab right after Sheila and Gabriel leave. Philip stops and stares in shock. Animals chatter and howl and bounce all over the place, fighting, eating, chasing, and hiding. Some still cower inside their opened cages.

Sheila ushers Gabriel down the stairs. A door below them thumps open. Larry can be heard yelling into his two-way radio. Sheila quickly spins Gabriel around, and they dash up the stairs again. The clatter of their footsteps ricochets off the walls and down the stairs, giving them away.

"Dr. Ohl, got 'em. Southwest stairs, headed for the roof."

Sheila bursts through a door and out onto the roof. Gabriel follows, clearly relieved to be in the open air again. Outside, the world is just beginning to brighten. At the edge of the roof, Sheila and Gabriel pant and gasp for breath after having raced up six flights of stairs. Below, a sleepy picket line of protestors determined to remain on duty at all hours scatters when a nurse runs from the hospital screaming. Several odd creatures pursue her across the parking lot and into the park. A woman in the picket line faints. The caterwauling noise of animals, sirens, and screaming people tarnishes the enchantment of the half-light and blends acrimoniously with the dawn chorus.

A flock of starlings that was spooked a moment ago and scattered upward now swoops back down to greet Gabriel like one of their own. They swing around his head, chattering and chirping in circles. Gabriel imitates their noises gleefully.

Philip and his team blast through a different door a couple of dozen yards away. The birds flee. Sheila and Gabriel retreat to the edge of the roof.

Cynthia pops through another door nearer than Philip. "Philip, stop!"

Sheila puts her hand up. "Quiet, Cynthia! Please don't interfere! Take care of yourself. It's too late."

"He must know, Sheila," Cynthia presses on. "I've found something that changes everything."

"I know it all," Philip admits. "I know that she manipulated Gabriel's genes."

"You don't know it all," Cynthia replies. "Sheila didn't splice any specific physical attributes. She changed nothing that is; she only changed what could be."

Philip looks at her, perplexed.

Sheila gives Cynthia a look, indicating that she should shut up. "No!

Cynthia. Gabriel has to be a natural mutation. I combed over my work. I examined every step of the process, and nothing that I did accounts for the result. It has to be a natural mutation."

Cynthia won't accept it. She's on a mission. "That's wrong. *You* did it. You did something totally new. It's not DNA manipulation; it was the RNA. You switched on an instructor gene. You enlivened an inherent dormant wing gene with the RNA instructor gene. It cleaned up or activated what we regretfully refer to as 'junk DNA,' all that extra DNA that seems to do nothing. Well, it turns out that 'junk' is full of potential. Who knows what other possibilities exist. Wings are probably just one miraculous option."

"That doesn't help me now," Sheila says. "They'll still take Gabriel away from me." She jumps on the wall of the roof. "None of that matters now! I'm beyond caring about slicing and dicing and alternate possibilities. Look at me!"

She prances on the wall, confident, easy, and graceful. Cynthia and Philip both lurch forward, but Sheila puts up both hands to stop them.

"Look at me! I'm proof that something bigger is going on here. How is it that I'm walking and running and jumping and"—she gulps emotionally—"flying? This isn't due to some gene manipulation or some chemical or surgical fix that I endured. It's life, and life is unpredictable. I performed that procedure, but I have no idea what I did, because some greater power of action got involved. The result has blossomed and affected me in ways I could never have guessed. It has affected so many others, too. Just look over this wall into the parking lot below if you don't believe me. Those people are not here because of augmented ears or skin repair. They're here for something more, for some miracle that affects the heart and makes it soar."

They all pause, contemplating her outburst. Sheila feels like she is making sense for the first time in her life. Then Philip scowls. He's done trying to figure out what the heck they are talking about. He strides forward, reaching for Gabriel.

"I'm taking my son back to safety."

Gabriel backs away from him.

"You are not!" Sheila yells.

"Oh, come on, Sheila," Philip responds. "I have rights too. I have the evidence to back up my claim as his father. Come here, Gabriel, your mother is certifiably crazy."

Sheila steps between them. "Philip, you can't lock him up. He needs to fly, and he needs to fly freely so that he can be what he's meant to be and show us what we are meant to be."

Philip is stung and furious. "I also want my son to be everything he can be. But this is not the way. This wild, out-of-control, free-for-all attitude puts him in danger. You put yourself in danger. I know what's best for my son."

At that moment, Spiner slams the nearby door open and pops onto the roof and into the argument. He turns to Larry, who is off to the side listening to the discussion. "Grab that kid and get her out of here!"

Philip ignores Spiner and keeps his attention on Gabriel, who is close to the edge and could fly off at any moment. Philip holds his arms back, waving everyone else off. "Gabriel, get down!"

Spiner turns to Larry and points at Gabriel. "I said grab him!"

"Shut up, Gerry!" Philip snaps. "I've got this." He moves toward Sheila and Gabriel.

Sheila chokes and sobs. "How can I ever trust you again?" she asks through her tears. "Don't come any closer."

Philip is seething. "Please get down, Sheila," he begs through his teeth. He can barely control his voice as he says it.

"Stop it! Stop it! Shut up! All of you!" Gabriel yells.

Everyone freezes, stunned. No one has ever seen him so annoyed before.

"Wake up and stop arguing," Gabriel continues. "Will you fly with me, Momma? Or is it more important to argue?"

Sheila looks at Gabriel and then at Philip. Her body ripples with conviction. She quivers a moment. Then, gradually, she takes on a golden hue, and light blossoms from her shoulders. Choking back her emotions, she blows a kiss to Philip, turns, and dives off the parapet. Spiner chokes and collapses to his knees. The security detail gasps. Philip leaps forward. "No!"

Gabriel dives after Sheila. Philip hangs over the wall and watches her tumble down. Gabriel plunges after her. Police vehicles with sirens blaring screech into the parking lot below and swirl to a stop. The people are just beginning to wake, they look up, startled.

Gabriel snatches Sheila's hand. Wind whistles past their ears. An awesome hum vibrates louder and louder like a church pipe organ, and Sheila looks up. Millions of lights fill the sky. Once again, time stands still. Sheila and Gabriel float in the air. The dome of the sky blossoms into a radiant host of light forms like Dante-style angels hovering above.

Below in the parking lot, some people stampede away and into the park while others freeze and look up in awe. Still others cower and hide. Police stumble out of their vehicles and flounder about in a daze, trying to figure out what to do while people stumble past them.

On the roof, Philip and Cynthia stare, transfixed by the astonishingly bright sky. The security team halts midstride, frozen and poised. Spiner crouches and whimpers under his clenched elbows. In front of him, Philip and Cynthia glow with a light that seems to come from within. Above them, a radiant host hovers.

Spiner summons his courage and peeks out. To him, Philip and Cynthia look stupefied. He sees no mystical sky event at all. His courage floods back on a wave of fury when he sees that Sheila and Gabriel are gone. "She's done for," he says. "Get Gabriel back now!"

Spiner then dashes to the exit stair. Philip wrenches his eyes away from the sky and bolts after him.

Angels hum over the parking lot. Sheila loses grip of Gabriel's hand and resumes her fall. She panics. Gabriel grabs her hand again, and nearly solid wings of light unfurl from her back. Sheila loosens her grip on Gabriel's hand and soars up, Gabriel trails behind her. She laughs with joy. Gabriel points to the statue in the park nearby. Sheila gasps and nods. She's ready. They glide toward the sculpture together. Sheila flinches one last time, and then—*whoosh*—they land. Sheila tumbles and rolls over in the grass and then jumps to her feet.

"Ha! I did it. Wow! Wow!"

Swarms of angels shower out of the sky, alighting, or perhaps congealing, next to various individuals. Only some people are aware of it.

Weeping openly, Stan strokes the cheek of his own angel. He can see her and even touch her.

An especially bright angel glides down in a column of light and merges with young Gabriel. Gabriel blossoms into an effulgent, radiant splendor. He becomes full-grown, his form described entirely in light. He turns to Sheila.

"You can do anything," he says in a voice that blends that of a child and the tenor of an older, more mature version of himself.

Spiner charges out of the hospital. The world is grayer for him, devoid of the light. He sees a nurse sobbing and an activist hugging thin air. Frantic, he looks out over the crowd, which is behaving strangely. Spiner sees no angels. Philip stumbles up behind him. His face is radiant. From Philip's point of view, the same crowd reveals people and angels intermingled, communicating and embracing each other.

Spiner spots Gabriel in the park across the street, but only the physical child form. He dashes toward him. "Get that child!"

Then he stops short. He sees Sheila standing there whole, easy, and laughing. He hesitates, astonished. Then he yells at the security team, which is finally emerging from the hospital. In a daze, Cynthia follows them.

"There, over by the statue, get him!" Spiner yells.

Sheila and Gabriel look over at him. The security team and some police officers jump into action and run toward Sheila and Gabriel, who are still holding hands.

"We are the creators, who are also you. We always create new ways to experience life. This is the new adventure for humans, but it's really an old adventure, too, because this is where we come from," Gabriel says.

Philip catches up to them and then puts his hands up to stop the oncoming security onslaught. "Wait!" he yells, and then he looks directly at Larry. Larry halts the team and hangs back. Philip turns to Gabriel. "Gabriel, I … I … what … can …" He's completely tongue-tied and has no idea how to ask the huge questions rolling around in his head.

Gabriel knows exactly what he needs right now. "You can't stop this, but you can't make it happen either. Some will know how and fly, and some won't. The power of the human spirit is extraordinary. You are light. You are light, and the sky is no limit."

The resonance of pipe organs swells, and voices join in song until the overwhelming sound reaches a crescendo. Gabriel pounces into the air and soars up. Swarms of angels leap up after him. The crowd sways and hums. Frank and Dell, who are among them, reach their arms into the air and sway. Dell bursts into song. Others join her.

The angels fill the sky, arcing overhead in a dome of light. Sparks shower from their outstretched hands. The angels pulsate and become too bright to see anymore. They blend together and disappear until all that remains is a cloudy sky.

Gabriel circles quietly overhead. He's alone now.

Philip throws his arms around Sheila. "You're okay! Thank God you're okay."

Sheila melts, sparkling with tears of joy. "Oh! I flew! Philip, I literally flew!"

Cynthia plows through the ecstatic, dancing crowd and throws her arms around Sheila. All three stare up at Gabriel.

"Get him down from there!" Spiner shrieks.

The security detail surrounds them in force.

Sheila steps right up to Spiner. "You can't contain him."

Gabriel whooshes low over the crowd. The fans respond joyfully, shouting, jumping, and waving. He streaks up high again. He pulsates and becomes his full-grown, huge, bright, light-being self. Then he becomes the laughing child, bright, easier to see, and "real" again. Once more, he expands and brightens and then settles back into the familiar form of Gabriel, the mischievous child.

"Get back down here!" Spiner yells again.

Philip turns on Spiner. "Will you shut up! This is extraordinary and not yours to control."

Spiner's jaw drops, and he looks up. Gabriel giggles and waves.

Sheila looks up at her son, her face brightening with understanding, and then she floats gently up off the ground. The crowd gasps and steps back. Some people faint; others fall to their knees. Philip reaches above his head to grab her hand and pull her down.

She smiles. "He showed us that the sky is no limit."

Gabriel swoops out of the sky, provoking a roar from the crowd. He descends on his parents and throws his arms around both of their necks, drawing them together. Then he whispers in his mother's ear, "I need you, Momma. We will grow up together."

THE END

ABOUT THE AUTHOR

Muriel Stockdale's creative compulsion has manifested itself in numerous disciplines. This is her first novel. Her career started in rural Vermont where she secured a federal grant to form a company presenting theater to schoolchildren who had no opportunity to see a play.

She went on to direct several shows in New York City and in New England, to perform onstage, crew backstage, design costumes and scenery, and manage costume shops. Soon Disney, NBC, ABC, PBS, and more began turning to Muriel for costume design. So did dozens of US and European regional theaters. She has worked with world-renowned, award winning performers, directors, writers, and composers such as Edward Albee, Adriana Trigiani, Richard Adler, Hayden Panettiere, Colleen Dewhurst, Tony Roberts, Lonette McKee and Kermit the Frog.

Wanting to "pay forward" the rich lessons of her career, Muriel taught at NYU's Tisch School of the Arts, Graduate Design Department for fourteen years.

In 2003 Muriel produced and directed a short film entitled, *New York City Spirit*, celebrating diverse ways New Yorkers connect to their divine impulses.

As an artist her US art flag series, *E PLURIBUS*, celebrating the diverse cultures of the US has been shown in multiple venues during the last 15 years including the Martha Stewart American Made Summit in 2015, The New Britain Museum of American Art in 2009 and two New York Libraries in 2008.

In 2005 she returned to costume design for the feature film, *Conversations with God* produced and directed by Stephen Simon and in 2013 for the Opera Omnia production of *The Return of Ulysses*.

Currently her focus is on production of her art flag series and various writings including a new opera version of *The Ramayana*. Her secret passion has always been spirituality, science and the mysterious, she has read countless science fiction and fantasy books and many of the world's scriptural texts but she also devours books that explain the latest scientific knowledge. With a Bachelor of Science and Phi Beta Kappa key from the University of Vermont and a Master of Fine Arts from New York University, it is clear from the beginning that Muriel is not only well rounded in her interests and pursuits but also well rounded in her accomplishments.

ACKNOWLEDGEMENTS

Special thanks to my brilliant, best friend, and husband, Chris Grabé, for coming up with an awesome idea for the cover and for so much more.

Heartfelt thanks to my readers: David E. Baugnon, Skip Hunt, Vickie Ramirez, Kathleen M. Robbins, Paul Shavelson, Sharon Stockdale, Ed Strosser, Laura Sweeney, Alyssa Vitrano, and Donna Siciliani for their fabulous feedback.

Thanks to Viki King for her guidance and encouragement.

Thanks to Kevin Miller for completing the initial edit.

Thanks to Balboa Press for the great support provided to new writers.

Thank you to you, reader, for taking a chance on a first time novelist and for reading this book. I sincerely hope that you enjoyed it.